HER
Forgotten
SHADOW

BOOKS BY PAMELA FAGAN HUTCHINS

Detective Delaney Pace series

Her Silent Bones

Her Hidden Grave

Her Last Cry

Patrick Flint series

Switchback

Snake Oil

Sawbones

Scapegoat

Snaggle Tooth

Stag Party

Sitting Duck

Jenn Herrington series

Big Horn

Maggie Killian series

Live Wire

Sick Puppy

Dead Pile

Katie Connell series

Saving Grace

Leaving Annalise

Finding Harmony

Seeking Felicity

Emily Bernal series

Heaven to Betsy

Earth to Emily

Hell to Pay

Michele Lopez Hanson series

Going for Kona

Fighting for Anna

Searching for Dime Box

Ava Butler series

Bombshell

Stunner

Knockout

HER Forgotten SHADOW

PAMELA FAGAN HUTCHINS

bookouture

Published by Bookouture in 2024

An imprint of Storyfire Ltd.
Carmelite House
50 Victoria Embankment
London EC4Y 0DZ

www.bookouture.com

ISBN: 978-1-83525-895-8
eBook ISBN: 978-1-83525-894-1

First and foremost, this book is for my stepdaughters. When I write Kat and Carrie and think about Delaney's love for them and her worry about keeping them safe, I relate so hard because of how I feel about the two of you.

As always, though—thirty-six books and counting later—there would be no stories without the best partner. Thank you, Eric Hutchins, for believing and encouraging and supporting. The world would be a better place if everyone had an Eric.

PROLOGUE

Lightning ripped across the night sky as hail pelted a sopping wet Delaney. She pictured the killer she was chasing. She hadn't seen a weapon. She prayed there wasn't one. *Who am I kidding*—the mountain provided all the weapons anyone could need. Rocks to bludgeon. Branches as clubs. Plus, Delaney was outweighed by a good seventy-five pounds. She'd be facing a body that was a literal battering ram.

Worse, she was on their home turf. Dark and claustrophobic in the best of weather and broad daylight, the forest was rife with hiding places. The killer could wait her out until she ran out of steam or off a cliff. They could be watching her now. Lying in wait. Ready to ambush her. Between the muddy snow, icy water, vegetation, and rocky obstacles on the ground, she was navigating a minefield. She'd be lucky if she didn't break her ankle or her neck. She'd be a sitting duck, lost and alone, with a limited supply of ammunition. The killer had already shown complete depravity, kidnapping young girl after young girl, raping them, driving them to their deaths, and God knew what else.

She came to a meadow and stopped on its edge to catch her

breath. How long had she been running? Was she chasing a human or her own tail? For all she knew, she could have been running in a circle. Her head whipped around as she used the lightning to search the area. No one. But what she saw stopped her cold. Around her was a field of bright flowers of every color, all in bloom. *Impossible. It's too early in the season.*

The flash of light had passed, but the afterimage of the flowers burned in her mind. She examined it and realized many of them didn't even grow in the mountains. *Plastic. They're plastic flowers.* She was standing in a dark meadow of plastic flowers high in the mountains chasing a maniac as rain and hail beat down on her.

It was completely macabre.

And then she noticed something else in the afterimage. Little wooden crosses. Four of them. A graveyard. *Girls? Pets?*

But Dr. Watson had said their first victim carried at least one pregnancy to a fairly late term. What if she'd had the baby? Or babies? What if they'd died? Or been killed? She spun, looking again for her quarry as she fought an urge to throw herself on the ground in front of the little markers and weep.

A blur streaked across her peripheral vision. Movement? *It could have been an owl. A bat. A trick of light. Or...* She eased toward it, peering into the darkness. There was nothing moving now. *Still,* she had to check it out. She took cautious steps toward the trees, where she'd seen it, whatever it was.

A heavy weight hit her body from behind, knocking her to the ground, landing on her, exploding the air from her lungs.

Delaney tried reaching for her gun. Her pepper spray. Her multi-tool with its knife. Anything. But her arms were pinned. She was immobilized. Unable to draw a breath. She saw spots in front of her eyes.

I should have waited for Leo. Now she might never see him again.

ONE

Marilyn Littlewolf ducked from the thundering flap of owl wings. She wrapped her arms around her head as she raced breakneck over the rocky forest floor. Air whooshed across her face. She screamed at the beast. So many times her mother had warned her about the spirit animals. So many times Marilyn had dismissed them as the rantings of someone lost in a past that was out of time and place, if it had ever even existed. She wished she had paid more attention. Maybe then she would know what to do now that the nightmare visions were coming for her.

"Mama," she whispered into the darkness. Into the alone.

Her bare toe stubbed into something hard. As she tumbled face first, she braced herself not for impact but for sharp talons digging into her neck. A curved beak gouging out her eyes.

Neither came.

She curled into a ball to protect her soft places. The thundering noise continued, but without the rush of air. Was this owl real? *Maybe the sound is only blood pulsing in my ears.* It was growing harder to tell the difference between the horror of her life and the dark imaginings of her mind. At first she'd kept track of the days she'd been imprisoned mentally, marking them as if with charcoal on a clean white page. There were no clean white pages, of course. There had been no charcoal. There had been nothing but the terror, pain, and hunger of captivity, and the hulking presence that she tried to block out.

She became aware of the cold against her cheek. The wetness of the snow. The dank scent of the earth. The throbbing in her ankle. The stirring in her belly that had driven her to escape with the promise of something dear. The numbness of the feet bare because she was never allowed shoes, to keep her from running. To keep this from happening.

Must keep going.

She pushed herself up, half expecting the owl to attack, but nothing happened. She turned and retched, spilling out precious morsels of food. Careful to avoid the sick, she climbed to her feet. The dizziness made her sway, but she ignored it.

That's when she heard another sound. Footsteps. Coming in fast. For a horrible second, she imagined the smell surrounding her. The smell of the cabin where her childhood had been stolen. The stink of unwashed body. The endless, gritty ash of fire as the only thing warding off the bone-deep cold. Of gamey meat left out for days in a cast-iron skillet.

"I forgive you, Marilyn. God forgives you. I love you like He loves you." The voice. The voice of everything bad in the world. The voice of lies. The voice of years spent locked away and abused. Made to feel inhuman. She could never go back. Never.

How had they figured out so quickly that she was gone? Where she had gone? It didn't seem possible.

She whimpered and started running again, terror pushing her past what seemed possible. If only it were daylight, and she could be sure of where she was. But it had been years since she'd known that. When she had escaped after dinner by pretending she needed to use the outhouse—pushing out the boards she had loosened in the back of the tiny building so carefully over weeks and weeks—she'd known she would have to navigate by the stars. Her home, if it could still be called that after years spent up in the mountains, was east. Orion's Belt pointed to the northeast, so she'd marked it and turned slightly to the right of it. Now, hours later, the tops of tall, bushy evergreens blocked her view of the sky, Orion, and his belt.

A wrong turn in the mountains could be fatal. *Getting caught could be worse.* That heavy body crushing her. The attacks—sudden and inexplicable. The months nursing cuts and broken bones, constantly expecting any time would be the next time. The one that might finally kill her if grief didn't first. The fear drove her onward again, faster now. If it came to a choice between capture and death, she would die trying to get away, with a prayer of thanksgiving on her lips.

The trees thinned, exposing her under glaring moonlight. She had to find cover. Her pursuer was so close. If she was spotted, it would all be over. She pushed herself, her breaths coming so fast that it didn't feel like the oxygen reached her burning lungs. But she wouldn't let that stop her.

She saw a stand of rocks ahead. If she could reach it, if she could get past it, it would block any view of her. She couldn't remember the last time she'd had exercise, though. Lately she was forced to be indoors. Restrained, penned, imprisoned. She was running on pure adrenaline now. The snow grew deeper in the center of the meadow, weighing down her aching thighs. But what had looked like flat ground had been deceptive. She struggled through a thicket of willows that whipped her face. Her footing turned treacherous. Her ankle-length skirt caught on a branch.

Finally, she broke free of the willows near the rocks. She ducked behind them, not daring to stop for breath. Was her captor closing in on her? She ran onward but noticed that the terrain had shifted. To her right was a bare hillside, sloping upwards. To her left, the same but downward, only so steep that she gasped. Not a cliff, but an incline worthy of a mountain goat. The section ahead of her veered downhill across the face of the slope. Gravity pulled at her injured, weakened body. Wobbling close to the drop-off, she overcorrected and threw herself down, landing on her hands and knees. But that was fine. Solid ground meant she wasn't freefalling through the air.

Before she could push off her hands to stand, she felt a vibration. It grew in intensity so rapidly that she stayed frozen on the ground, confused. The vibration had a sound. A grumble that became a loud rumbling and then a locomotive bearing down on her. A gust of cold air blasted the top of her head. She looked up to see an angry wave of snow crashing and exploding against the rocks above her. *No, not snow. Mud.*

But what it was didn't matter. What mattered was getting up and getting out of the way. She jumped to her feet, but it was already too late. *So loud. So, so loud.* The mudslide hit her, knocking the wind out of her and muffling its own sound. It flung her backwards into the air. Cold enveloped her.

I'm free. I made it.

Then her head crashed into something unforgiving. Her last thought before blackness was *I'm coming soon, my angels.*

TWO

Deputy Investigator Delaney Pace tramped into the pasture that doubled as the Pace homestead front yard. Arrow-shaped balsamroot leaves waved up at her. Lupine stalks near to blooming held their shoulders high and proud. She tried not to crush them under her boots as she made her way to private investigator and part-time nanny Skeeter Rawlins, who was on grill duty. If the adage to never trust a skinny chef was true, she and her guests would be safe in Skeeter's hands. She set a tray of hamburger patties, hot dogs, and Portabella mushrooms on the folding table beside the grill.

Skeeter pushed salt-and-pepper hair off his sweaty forehead. "Still don't know why you stuck the grill all the way out here. Makes for a lot of hauling."

She grinned. "Because the snow and ice and mud are gone. The grass is green and tall. I want to enjoy every second of it."

"It's you running back and forth anyway, not me. But you should make the girls help you."

The girls in question—tween Kat, Delaney's niece, and high school junior Carrie, who Delaney had met and taken in after her mother's murder—were making themselves scarce. Delaney guessed Carrie and her friends were clustered in front of the TV screen in the living room, gaming. Delaney *hated* the gaming. Not only because she thought it was too sedentary and a waste of brain cells but because as a detective she'd concluded that online gaming was a cesspool of sexual deviants on the prowl. It worried her.

Only four months into her official adoptive parenting gig, Delaney was wondering if there would ever come a time when she wouldn't worry. Here she was on a beautiful spring day with friends gathered, worried there wouldn't be enough food. The girls had basically invited everyone they knew, because, in Carrie's words *hello, winter is over*. Delaney was worried the food would suck, since she'd had a hand in preparing it and grillmaster Skeeter had been topping off his Solo cup from a flask in his back pocket. That she needed to do something about the giant money pit in storage—her tractor Gabrielle from the ice-road trucking days Delaney would never return to now that she had daughters. That she hadn't had any luck finding the mother who'd abandoned her when she was younger than Kat. The same went for her missing-and-presumed-dead brother Liam, aka Jefe, aka number five on America's most wanted list, who'd disappeared in an avalanche in January, just after admitting he had murdered their father and hinting that their long-gone mom was still around. That her phone would buzz with a callout for her or Sheriff Leo Palmer in the middle of her party.

Speaking of Leo, he and his crew hadn't arrived yet.

"I think I'm doing mothering wrong, because I can't get the girls to do squat," she said.

"They know you love 'em enough that they can get away with all kinds of stuff now."

"When'd you get so smart?" She punched his upper arm and regretted it. His arms were shockingly hard and muscular. She felt a rush of bemused affection. What would she do without him? He was a great protector for the girls, and they loved him.

Kat bounded toward Delaney from a group of her friends, curls bouncing. Coltish legs ate up the pasture. Her black and white French bulldog, Dudley, ran beside her, going airborne in gazelle-like leaps with front and back legs fully extended. Delaney knew he was trying to stay out of the grass, which made his belly itchy. Only his love for Kat and the possibility of snacks had him out here at all.

"Aunt Delaney, Freddy texted. They're almost here." Kat's eyes were sparkling in a way that screamed trouble. Freddy was Leo's nephew and the source of Kat's sparkle.

"It's about time. I was thinking we'd have to eat without them."

A sheriff's department truck was at that very moment parking in the grass by the long driveway to the old, white farmhouse. Spaces between the house and outbuildings had long since been taken.

Leo climbed out. Even from a hundred feet away, Delaney was able to appreciate some of his God-given attributes. A muscled but lean body. A height perfect for reaching glasses in the top shelf of a kitchen cupboard. The things she couldn't see yet she knew by heart. Dark, wavy hair. Electric blue eyes. A chiseled face that could have been on movie screens but instead had found its way from southern California to north central Wyoming, where it was a source of constant torment to her. After a year in Kearny, he barely even looked out of place. His cowboy boots and hat were starting to wear in, and he'd ditched his designer jeans for Clinch and Wrangler. Just in time, too, with the primary only a few months away for the sheriff election. Leo was interim in the role now. He had a lot of rubber chicken dinners to eat and babies to kiss before the voting if he was going to keep it.

Freddy unfolded himself from the back seat. If anything, he

was going to be taller than his uncle. The kid had inherited the family looks but still carried a little city polish with his floppy bangs and Air Jordans.

Kat sighed. "There he is."

A second later, two females exited the vehicle. Delaney had been expecting to see Leo's petite sister, Adriana, who was Freddy's mom. But instead, the passenger side front seat spit out a curvy redhead. Delaney felt her forehead bunch into wrinkles. She willed it to relax.

The sharp intake of breath from Kat wasn't about the redhead, though. A tall, pretty girl was standing beside Freddy, holding his elbow while she fixed her sandal. Her smile was brilliant and her dark eyes sparkly under a high forehead with a heart-shaped hairline. Delaney was pretty sure it was Ashley Klinkosh, whose father was an Episcopal priest and whose mother took a personal role in making sure the less privileged in their community had food and shelter options.

"Are they... together?" Kat's face was stricken.

Delaney put her hand on Kat's shoulder. "I'm not sure. Is that Ashley from your school?"

"Yes. She's in my grade. I'd seen them talking, but I didn't know they were hanging out."

Delaney's eyes were glued on Leo and the redhead. He put his hand in the small of her back, guiding her toward Delaney. Had he brought a date to her party? He hadn't told her he was going to. Not that he had to ask permission, as she'd written "bring a friend, the more the merrier" on the invitation. Only she hadn't intended that to apply to him. Or Freddy. Not that Delaney would date Leo. She'd told him repeatedly that he was her boss, they were co-workers, and it was impossible. She just hadn't expected him to start dating someone else. Or that it would sting so much if he did.

The Palmer posse drew closer, laughing and chatting. *No. No. No.* She and Kat needed a minute.

They didn't get one.

"Hey, Delaney, Kat. Nice party. Thanks for having us." Leo smiled, and Delaney could swear the sun glinted off his teeth like some kind of cheesy toothpaste commercial. "This is Liesel Tate. Liesel, this is our host, Delaney Pace. And this is her niece, Kateena."

"I'm so pleased to meet you, Delaney." Liesel shifted closer to Leo.

Delaney thrust a hand at the smaller woman. "Welcome."

Liesel shook, looking almost startled. Delaney did pride herself on a firm grip.

Kat's voice was soft and thready. "Hey, you guys. Hi Freddy. Hi Ashley."

"Yo, Kat, I've been telling Ash about your place." Freddy turned to Ashley. "Clock this, Ash. They have a vintage race car in that barn. Wanna peep with me?"

Delaney wondered if she'd sounded as goofy to adults when she was their age.

"Can you take us, Kat?" Ashley said. Her eyes were warm and friendly.

She doesn't have a clue that Kat is in love with her boyfriend.

Kat shrugged. "Sure. Freddy knows the way." Gone was the bounding and the bouncing. She fell in behind her crush and his new girl and the three of them walked toward the barn.

"So, um, Delaney, Leo said you work with him, right?" Liesel asked.

Delaney felt a surge of hope. The woman didn't sound like she'd reached girlfriend status. "Yes." Delaney stopped there, taking pleasure in the awkward silence.

Leo said, "I'll go grab us some drinks."

"White wine for me," Liesel said.

Delaney knew she didn't have any, but she didn't mention it. "There's a keg by the front door. The hard stuff and mixers are on a table beside it."

"And by front you mean the one no one ever uses?"

"Correct."

He saluted and started to walk off.

She called after him. "If you see Carrie, tell her I said to get her butt outside."

Leo walked backwards, laughing. "Not on your life. Teenage girls aren't in my skill set."

Then he was gone, leaving Delaney to babysit his date. Normally, she would have balked at the job, but today she was Liesel-curious and feeling truculent. "Have you and Leo been dating long?"

Liesel giggled and tugged at her top. The stretchy fabric accentuated breasts two cup sizes larger than Delaney wore. "Oh, no. We're brand new."

"So—how did you meet?"

"Match dot com, I think. But I'm on eharmony, Bumble, Tinder, Christian Mingle, and FarmersD. So... one of those for sure, at least."

Delaney couldn't believe Leo was on a dating site. Why hadn't he told her? "Oh. My."

"Are you on any of them?"

"No." Hell would freeze over before she'd sign up for one.

"Are you dating anyone?"

Personal, much? But she had started Liesel down this road. "No."

Liesel's green eyes widened. Her lashes batted. "I get it. Female cop. You just didn't look that butch to me."

Delaney snorted. "Thanks, I guess. But I'm not gay."

Leo reappeared, holding three beers. "Sorry. No wine."

Liesel took the sole beer from his left hand. Delaney took one that his finger had been in when he'd clutched it with his right. Whatever germs he had, she was already exposed to on a daily basis.

Her phone buzzed.

Leo's eyebrows rose and he slapped his back pocket. "Mine, too."

Delaney shook her head. "Every time I make any plans, this happens."

"Maybe it's nothing," Leo said.

She read her phone. A text from dispatch.

Mudslide. Injuries. Vehicles involved. Request aid from all law enforcement and rescue personnel.

She closed her eyes and shook her head. A mudslide was going to wipe out her spring party.

Leo looked up from his phone. "It's not too far away."

"Why don't you ride with me? That way we can be there and back before Kat is out of high school."

"She doesn't look old enough to be in high school," Liesel said.

Leo turned to his date. "I hate to ask this, but would you mind going solo for a while here? We should be right back. Maybe an hour, tops."

Liesel glanced around at the growing crowd. "I see a few people I know. No problem."

Leo gave her his best smile. "Thanks. See you soon."

Delaney flashed a facsimile that probably seemed corpse-like in comparison. Then she strode toward the house. "Time to eject some kids from Shotgun Shelly," she said, referring to the vintage Chevelle that had belonged to her dad before her.

Leo hurried after her, dumping his beer in the grass. "Are you sure you want her up there where there's been a slide?"

Delaney only had to think about it for a second. Mud and bad traction? She'd have to be careful, and Shelly would need a bath afterwards, but *Hell, yeah.* "I think it will be all right. I have to grab my purse and throw away this cup first, though."

Leo followed her inside. As expected, Carrie and her

friends were gaming and shouting at the top of their lungs. Leo's and Delaney's phones buzzed again as Delaney slung her purse strap over her shoulder and picked a light sheriff's department jacket off a coat tree.

Leo read the message aloud. "'Officer on scene reports a body trapped in the slide. Teenage girl, deceased. Suspicious circumstances. No ID.'" His face contorted. "Oh, no."

A thump and a wail sounded from the living room.

Carrie had dropped the gaming controls and jumped to her feet. Her eyes were wide and stricken. "Who is it? What happened?" She'd barely escaped with her life a few months before when a kidnapper buried her alive.

"We don't know anything else yet. I'm so sorry, Carrie." She stepped toward the girl with open arms.

Carrie collapsed into them, her slim body trembling. "She died under the dirt, alone?"

It was a gruesome thought, and one Delaney knew Carrie relived in nightmares, often. Delaney would rub her back and stay with her after her bad dreams until she fell back into fitful sleep. This poor girl's death wasn't going to help Carrie's trauma recovery.

"Don't worry. Leo and I will find out what happened to her, I promise you."

THREE

Leo refused to grip the edges of his seat as Delaney fishtailed her vintage Chevelle up the muddy road. Her driving seemed more sadistic than usual. He snuck a glance at her profile. Her cat-green eyes were electric as she handled the jerking steering wheel with strength and grace, seemingly in time to the classic rock she insisted on blasting from an eight-track player.

He'd never found her more attractive, and he hated himself for it.

His phone chimed. Thinking it might be about the slide victim, he glanced at it. It was a notification of a new match on his dating app.

"Between your phone and your tablet, I've decided that if you die you're going to be reincarnated as a microchip." There was laughter in Delaney's voice. A by-product of driving her beloved car. "Is it about the girl?" She glanced over.

He tried to dismiss the notification. "Uh, no."

Her eyes cut back to the road. She swung Shelly into a snowmobile parking lot and around to face outward in a relatively dry spot. She cut the engine and turned the glowing slits of her eyes on him. "You didn't tell me you were fishing."

"Fishing?"

"For women."

Emotion flared in him. "You want me to be alone?" There had been a moment a few months before when he thought he wouldn't be. That he and Delaney would cure that condition together. But as quickly as she'd opened the door she had shut it in his face.

She got out, shaking her head. "A dating app. Bringing strangers to my party and setting up new dates as you drive away. It's just not like you."

Leo gritted his teeth. Now was not the time or place to have this conversation. Who was he kidding? There was no time or place. He was the sheriff. She was one of his deputies. His most important deputy. He had to protect the partnership. The friendship. He couldn't tell her he wouldn't be on a dating app if she hadn't pushed him away. That he'd resorted to meeting strangers online hoping he'd feel a flicker of interest in someone besides her. Maybe he should have moved back to California instead of staying here and running for sheriff. If it wasn't for the tenterhooks the DEA still had in him, how well his nephew was doing here, and his fear of the Bajeños cartel back in San Diego—the Bajeños he'd infiltrated undercover for the San Diego PD and who he suspected were on to him—he might have.

Oh, who was he kidding? He'd stayed because of Delaney, dammit.

He imagined drinking a tall glass of ice water, cooling his heated emotions. It worked, mostly.

Outside the car, he immediately reached back in for the jacket he'd brought from his own truck. Three thousand feet above Kearny, the wind was biting, the sun behind a cloud, and the temperature at least ten degrees colder than in the valley. He set out toward a cluster of officers and emergency personnel up the road a few hundred steep yards. Delaney climbed silently beside him. A wall of forest rose in front of them, giving off the fresh scent of pine. Seasonal runoff rushed noisily past the road. His boots slid every other step in the slick, gravelly mud. By the time they reached the others, he was puffing like a bellows and his shirt was sticking to the sweat on his back. So much for needing the jacket.

Deputy Joe Tarver raised a hand in greeting. He'd been on-duty today, so it made sense that he'd arrived first and in uniform. The older deputy looked noticeably less grandfatherly. Since he'd announced he was running against Leo for sheriff, he'd been working on his appearance. Hair dye. What appeared to be large quantities of moisturizer. Plucked brows. Cool sunglasses and a new off-work wardrobe. Leo had even overheard Joe on the phone talking about the weight-loss drug he was taking. Ozempic. If it helped his health, that was good for Joe and good for their department.

"Leo. Delaney." Joe had quit addressing Leo as Sheriff when he'd started his own campaign.

Delaney waved and motioned that she was out of breath.

"Hey, Joe. You know enough yet to give us a rundown?" Leo said, barely able to gasp the words out. He'd heard of people who bicycled, walked, ran, and cross-country skied up this road. He didn't know whether to feel respect or fear.

"A few residents in the area heard a rumbling noise late last night, but most everybody slept through it. We've gotten word that people trying to come off the mountain this morning had to turn back. You know, campers in Jeeps, off-road vehicles, dirt bikes."

Leo's breathing was returning to normal. "Was the road even clear of snow?"

"For a few miles. Muddy as all get out, of course. Lotta snow this winter plus an early spring so it's a crazy melt. Anyway, the ones on the mountain were stranded and couldn't get phone signal to call it in. Something was going on with the towers. It wasn't until people started trying to go *up* the road that we found out about the slide. And now the ones on the mountain are in touch by phone as well." He took a deep breath as if to suck in his stomach, standing taller and putting his hands on his hips. "I'm told the road won't be open for days. It has to dry out and settle before it's even safe to work on it. Search and Rescue is going to bring the people stranded on the mountain out in tracked vehicles in the other direction. Snowmobiles, Snow Cats and the like."

Delaney was staring up the hillside as if reading it for answers. "I'll bet this thing started as an avalanche."

"That's what Search and Rescue think. They said they've been on high alert, what with the rapid thaws and refreezing of the snowpack and then the spring snows on top of that. Lots of layers. Conditions were ripe."

"Any injuries or vehicles involved?"

"A few people got stuck."

Delaney snorted. "This time of year, the mudders are frenzied. I'll bet they accelerated when they saw it." The line of Jeeps and off-road vehicles heading up the mountain the last few weekends for playing in the mud had been unprecedented. All the extra snow that winter meant more runoff and thus more mud.

Joe nodded. "I wouldn't doubt it, based on how embedded one guy's Jeep was. No injuries, though. I think the vehicles on this end are mostly out now. It was when a crew was up working on one of them that they found the girl."

The girl. Now they were getting to the crux of it. "Can you take us to see her?" Leo said.

"You're gonna get muddy."

Leo and Delaney were already walking past Joe. He hurried to catch up.

"Has she been moved?" Leo asked.

"My understanding is they dug her out and moved her out

of the way, but they marked exactly where they found her. There's concern about stability. A secondary slide."

Delaney said, "Do they have the engineers here to evaluate the road?"

"Our local guy is on a family trip. A woman is on her way up from Casper."

Leo withheld comment. He was feeling the altitude again.

The sound of a motor grew louder as they turned the corner. A bulldozer was pulling a RZR off-road vehicle out of the edge of the slide.

And what a slide it was. Mud subsumed the road that man in his hubris had blasted out of the smooth slope of the mountain. In the path of the disaster, trees lay flattened and upended. Rocks had been thrown down the hill. Big rocks. Bigger rocks.

"Mother Nature was pissed at something." Delaney had stopped and was taking it in, jaw slack.

"It missed the highest house on the mountain face by no more than a hundred and fifty feet," Joe said.

A surveyor flag tied to the end of a broken tree was sticking out the ground. Leo pointed. "That's where they found her?"

Joe nodded. "Come on. She's off to the side over here."

The three of them walked off the road a few steps. Leo saw the corner of a ratty blanket, then the broken body of a young woman encased in mud atop it. The girl's long hair was so caked it was impossible to tell the color. The mud was drying to an ashy gray.

Delaney stopped and pressed a fist to her mouth. "It's almost like mummification."

Leo on one side of the girl, Delaney on the other. A bone protruded from one thigh. Her arm was turned the wrong way at the elbow.

"Is she nude?" he said.

Delaney pointed at fabric around the girl's chest. "I think

she had on a bra or undershirt. I wonder if the slide ripped her clothing away?"

The bulldozer engine rumbled to a stop.

Leo nodded, then looked away. The power of the mud and the hazards it had swept with it had been too much for fragile skin and bones. "The chances this isn't accidental are slim, but we still need to determine the cause of death and follow wherever it leads us." *Please Lord, let it be accidental.* It had been months since they'd had a suspicious death in Kearny County, much less a murder. Leo was eager to continue that streak, both for the safety of the community and for his campaign. Between dirty cop Tommy Miller who was awaiting trial and the very large number of murders since Leo had arrived in Kearny a year before, his opponents had plenty of cannon fodder.

Delaney said, "We have to figure out who she is and find her family. Let them know. I assume there was no ID?" Delaney asked Joe.

Joe nodded. "Everything they found is with her. Which is to say, nothing. No ID. No shoes. No other clothing."

"Help me turn her on her side," Leo said.

Delaney joined him on his side of the girl's body, and they tilted her up. Mud oozed off her backside where her body was slowing the drying process.

"I don't see anything suspicious," Delaney said. "No bullet holes, anyway."

"Me neither."

They eased her back to the ground.

Leo stood and wiped his hands on his pants. "I think we're going to have to send her to Dr. Watson." Thank goodness there had been no unusual deaths in the last few months. He still had plenty of budget to send the girl to the forensic pathologist instead of the elected coroner's funeral home.

Leo heard footsteps, then a cleared throat. He turned.

A man with long, stringy black hair and mud-splattered

coveralls over a pumpkin-shaped belly was standing behind them. He removed his KING ROPES ball cap and pressed it against his heart. "That looks like Marilyn Littlewolf. I wonder where she's been these last few years?"

Leo stepped toward him. "You know her?"

"Nah. I remember from the news her going missing. There was a big hunt for her. She was so young. Only about fourteen then, I think."

Delaney reached for the man's elbow. "She was never found? What happened?" Then she dropped his arm and gestured between herself and Leo. "Neither of us lived here then."

"Yeah, she was reported missing. People thought maybe she was taken."

"Anything else you remember?" Leo asked.

"I heard she got in touch and told her family to quit looking for her. That she was never coming back. But I guess she did. Looks like maybe she should've stayed gone. It didn't turn out so good for her here in the end."

Leo sucked in a breath. The poor girl. He took the man's information in case of need for follow-up. "Thank you for the information."

"Hey, you the one who's running for sheriff?"

It was Leo the man was talking to. "Yes. I'm the sheriff. Running to keep the job."

Joe flinched.

"You gonna give a damn about our girls? Or are you gonna be like all the rest of them?"

Leo turned back to the mud-covered corpse. The mud-covered *young woman.*

As Leo gave a strong nod, Delaney said, "He's gonna give a damn—he already does. And I'll be here to make sure of it."

FOUR

FIVE YEARS EARLIER

Standing sideways in front of the mirror in a tiny bathroom, Skeeter Rawlins curled his right bicep. He'd just gone up in weight. A lot of guys let themselves go after an injury like he'd had, but he wasn't going to be one of them. Especially at his age. Forty. Now was the time to double down on fitness. His only concession to being out of the oil fields was his mustache and the length of his hair. His employer had a bullshit rule about no facial hair. He pumped his arm again, letting out a half-groan, half-shout of pain and effort.

He lowered the weight and backed out of the bathroom, setting the barbell on the floor. The oil fields had been good for him. Out of high school, he hadn't had the grades for college or the money for technical school. He'd applied for some blue-collar jobs and even been hired for one, then failed the drug test. Uncle Sam had come calling and he'd answered. For ten years, he kept answering, working all kinds of jobs until one day he'd just had enough. He'd come home and gone straight to the oil fields. Then he got hurt and they offered him a big, fat check not to come back. He was figuring on investing it in real estate or something. But a military buddy who'd become a financial planner had pitched him on cryptocurrency. He promised to make Skeeter a wealthy man. Skeeter was mulling it over.

Take that, Pops. And you said I wouldn't amount to nothing.

Skeeter had seen the ads for jobs in law enforcement in Kearny. He'd researched the area, deciding it was the ideal spot. A low cost of living, great hunting and fishing, and they were paying signing bonuses. Plus, he'd always had a thing for Native American girls, and the Crow reservation was just up the road. The only drawback was more of the harsh winters he'd sworn he'd never return to after growing up on the shores of Lake Michigan. But he could make it work, because job prospects were bleak and housing expensive in Florida, which is where he'd really wanted to go. Maybe he still would someday.

His doorbell rang. He looked out the peephole. It was his neighbor, a woman half his height with frizzy gray hair who brought him cookies once a week. The poor old girl was just lonely. She wouldn't mind the damp chest hair sticking out the top of his tank top. He opened the door with a grin.

"Hi, Gladys."

She wasn't holding a plate of cookies. Her nose wrinkled. "Oh, my. That smell." Then she thrust an envelope at him. "This was in the wrong mailbox. It's for you, hon."

"Thanks. You all right?"

"Good enough. But my show is about to start. I'm making shortbread later. Should I bring you some?"

It wasn't his favorite, but he wasn't turning down free food. "I'd love it."

She shuffled away, waving goodbye.

He glanced at the envelope in his hand. The return address was Kearny Police Department. *This is it!* "Bye, Gladys."

Kicking the door closed behind him with one foot, he ripped the envelope open. He unfolded it on the kitchen countertop and switched on the lights. He read the words once, then a second time, disbelieving what he was seeing.

Dear Mr. Rawlins:

Thank you for your recent application. We are unable to offer you a position at this time.

Best regards,

Shelby Morehouse

Chief of Police

Skeeter walked to the couch and sank into it. Like the rest of the furniture, it had come with the furnished apartment and was cheap but serviceable. He put his elbows on his knees and lowered his head into his hands. Why hadn't they wanted him? They'd advertised for candidates. It made no sense. *Maybe they've staffed up*. He could apply again later. But the process to get to this rejection had taken a month longer than he'd thought it would. He was burning through money. His apartment was paid up for another month, though. He'd just have to look for another job.

He'd always wanted to be a cop. So, if he couldn't work for the city police, he could apply at the sheriff's department. Nodding, he stood. He'd hit the shower and go fill out an application today.

He thought about the self-help guru he'd been following online—something he never would have admitted to the roughnecks or soldiers he used to work with—but this was part of the person he wanted to be for the rest of his life. The lifestyle started with positive affirmations he was supposed to recite to himself. He'd settled on one that seemed to fit all the challenges he'd overcome. From the learning disability that made it so hard for him to read and wasn't diagnosed until he was twelve. To the time he'd busted his head in middle school on the monkey bars and doctors had said it would hold him back the rest of his life. To the worthless dad and the mom he'd never known. To the girl who'd broken his heart and then ruined his good name in his hometown by telling everyone he was a stalker. It included the injury to his back that meant he'd never work on a drilling rig again. Even to the years in the military when he'd been forced to work in kitchen and janitorial services instead of getting out in the action like he'd wanted to. Everyone underestimated him. Everyone except himself.

You are a winner. You are a winner. You are a winner.

He just had to block out all the voices he remembered from his entire life telling him the opposite.

FIVE

Delaney rocked in her desk chair with her beautiful color maps of the area on either side of her, alternately tapping a pen on her department electronic tablet and the blank notepad that she hoped to fill up with information about Marilyn Littlewolf. Her maps were no help to her today, even though she loved to use them on her cases. Had to use them. Felt they were critical. To the extent that her co-workers thought she was a little nutso in her zeal for studying topography, geography, geology, and other things relating to location that ended in -y and sounded sciencey.

Her phone buzzed in her pocket. The kind of buzz that meant she had a call. "Delaney Pace."

"Ms. Pace, this is Clark Applewood. I'm a special agent with the ATF. The Bureau of Alcohol, Tobacco, Firearms, and Explosives." His diction was crisp and his speech rapid.

She pressed a hand to her forehead. She wasn't a law enforcement rube. She knew what the ATF was. "How did you get this number? Why are you calling?"

"Didn't Sheriff Palmer tell you to expect my call?"

Had he? A few months before, Leo had tried to convince

Delaney to talk to someone with the feds, citing their interest in developing her as an outside consultant, which she'd thought was a terrible idea. She didn't want them in her business. She couldn't believe after Leo's involuntary servitude for the Drug Enforcement Agency he would have recommended it to her. But had he mentioned the ATF? She didn't think so. She for sure didn't remember the name Clark Applewood or any recent discussion. *Leo gave him my number, though.* "Why are you calling me?"

"You do like to get right to the point—I'd heard that about you. I like it."

"Mr. Apple-pie—"

"Applewood."

She was not interrupting her research into Marilyn's plight for the feds. There was absolutely no way. "Now is not a good time. Please call me back some other time. Or not at all."

"It's not an emergency. I'll call you later this week."

She ended the call, irritated. She'd talk to Leo about it later. She set the phone down and accessed the record management system through her laptop, then navigated to the old missing person case from Marilyn's disappearance. The Kearny Police Department had handled it, but under the police and the sheriff's department shared records system, she was able to access all police cases except the most sensitive ones—mostly homicides.

She'd been unable to banish thoughts of the girl in the slide the night before. What she went through. What her last thoughts had been. What had led to her being there? How easily Delaney could have ended up missing or dead during her own troubled teenage years, and no one would have cared. But mostly the devastation Delaney would feel if it were one of her own daughters meeting that fate. All that life and promise and spark, snuffed out like a candle flame. If Marilyn had ended up there because of something someone had done to her, well—Delaney would be coming for them.

She snuck a look at Leo's office, then tore her eyes away and leaned forward to force herself to review the information on her screen. Leo had used the recent departure of former deputy Tommy Miller as an opportunity to rearrange the bullpen, theorizing they would notice Tommy's absence less—and thus focus on their work, instead of how Tommy had disgraced them all—if he moved everyone's cheese, er, seats. A game of law enforcement musical chairs, of sorts. Delaney had gone to Leo to claim the cubicle closest to the door, the bathroom, and the breakroom before the music stopped, at least in Joe's opinion. She told herself it was coincidence that it was also the cubby with line of sight to Leo if she leaned back. It was the best kind of torture to position herself close enough to Leo that she was almost never out of the tractor beam that seemed to radiate from him to her. That it riled Joe as the most senior deputy was a bonus. The prime cubicle was actually the one farthest from the sheriff, with the mountain view through the back window, which Joe took and pretended to be put out about.

Delaney found herself reading the same words over and over and shook her head to make herself more alert. The previous night had been brutal, creating the Mondayest of Mondays for her now. Her eyes felt gravelly. She was—per usual—worried about one of her girls. Carrie had been waiting when Delaney had arrived home from the mudslide. It had taken longer on scene than she and Leo had planned. They'd stayed to oversee removal of the girl they believed to be Marilyn to the morgue, then to work to secure the scene until the techs arrived. Delaney had attempted to track down Marilyn's mother while still at the scene, only to learn that Peg Littlewolf had taken her own life four years earlier. Marilyn had no siblings, no father on record, and no living grandparents. No one to identify her. *No one to grieve for her.*

Carrie had fired off a volley of questions when Delaney got home, but she had nothing but unsatisfactory half answers to give her. The sheriff's department couldn't disclose identity until they confirmed it.

"How can you not know who she is?" Carrie had said, eyes red, voice shaking. "Someone has to know. She isn't no one."

She isn't no one. The words were still haunting Delaney this morning. As were the last known pictures of Marilyn that Delaney had pulled from online news articles and blogs late into the night in between her back and forths to comfort Carrie through her triggered nightmares. Marilyn had disappeared when she was only fourteen. Two years older than Kat. Three younger than Carrie. A single mother's only child. No wonder Peg Littlewolf hadn't survived the loss.

"Delaney." It was Leo's voice, Leo's presence—a rearranging of the molecules in space with his bumping into hers as if by some alchemy so that she knew he was there before he spoke.

"Sheriff." She'd taken to calling him that. It helped her feel like she was maintaining her distance, even if her heart hadn't gotten on board with the plan of action yet. The traitorous thing seemed to be headed in the opposite direction in fact.

"Have you been able to track down anyone who can confirm our mudslide victim is Marilyn Littlewolf?"

She rotated her chair to face him. "I'm striking out so far on next of kin. I'm sure we could find old school friends, but I'd like to save that as our last resort. I mean, she was hardly recognizable last night. It would stir up gossip and trauma and wouldn't be definitive. And it's not like we're pressed for time."

"True. What do you have in mind?"

"I was thinking I'd start calling dentists this morning."

"A dental match would be good."

"And once Dr. Watson has her cleaned up, we can compare her to photographs."

"Faces can change a lot between the ages of fourteen and nineteen."

"Yes." She gestured at the screen. "I was just starting to

review the old file. Maybe I'll find something identifying from when they originally looked for her. Birthmarks. Scars. Abnormalities."

"Maybe she was fingerprinted for some reason. Schools offer it."

Delaney snorted. "I'd be shocked. Most of the Crow families around here aren't big fans of opting in to big brother programs." She snapped her fingers. "I'll ask Clint Rock-Below for ideas. The community is close-knit, and he's really cultivated his relationships within it."

Clint, a state cop, was a member of the Crow Nation. She'd gone on a few dates with him when she first moved back to Kearny, but there hadn't been any spark. At least not for her.

The scowl on Leo's face told her he remembered the dates. "Keep me posted. I'll let you know when I hear from Dr. Watson."

"Yes, Sheriff."

"I hate it when you call me that."

She smiled sweetly up at him. "Then heaven knows why you're campaigning to keep the job."

She glanced at the screen pointedly. When he didn't leave, she raised her brows until he took the hint, giving her a quick view of his second-best side on his way to his office.

Scrolling through the documents in the records system, she kept her pen at hand, ready to jot down identifying features or leads on next of kin. She doubted she'd find anything, but the name of Marilyn's doctor or her dentist would work just as well. As expected, she came away with nothing new. Quickly, she checked the Automated Fingerprint Identification System for a record connected to Marilyn. Leo's idea had been a good one, but, again, nothing.

Time to dial for dentists. She pulled up all the dentists Google could find for her within a hundred-mile radius. To people living in metropolitan areas, her search radius would have seemed ludicrous. However, in northern Wyoming it was common to travel significant distances for medical and dental care. Not that there weren't local providers—there were. But often people didn't like sharing their personal business with neighbors. Or they believed they could get better care in larger communities. Or they paired the trips with shopping or visiting family. The list of reasons was long.

Despite that, she prioritized her calls by geographic proximity to Kearny. Over and over, she repeated the same words. "This is Deputy Investigator Delaney Pace of the Kearny County Sheriff's Department. We are trying to verify the possible identity of a Jane Doe. We may have to do that with dental records, but first we need to see if we can find her dentist. May I speak to whoever is in charge of your records, in the strictest confidence, please?"

Over and over, no one had a patient named Marilyn Littlewolf, even when narrowed down by her birthday—which Delaney had found in the record system—and a range of possible treatment dates.

It made for a frustrating few hours. The whole time, Delaney fought against the soul-sucking possibility that Peg had not sought dental care for her daughter. Dental treatment wasn't a given.

Halfway through her list, Delaney plated her picnic leftovers, which she ate at her desk. Skeeter had done a good job on the burgers, and her own potato salad was downright edible. She wished she hadn't missed her own party. Skeeter said people stayed for hours. It had been a lovely day in a pretty place with lots of food, drinks, and games. Cornhole. Horseshoes. Darts. The triple crown of country drinking games.

She sighed and took her plate to the dishwasher. A Honeycrisp apple was sitting out on the counter. It jogged her memory. The phone call she'd received from the ATF agent. Clark Applewood. She'd forgotten to ask Leo about it.

She marched to his office. The walk wasn't long enough to rebuild her indignation to a fever pitch, but she dug deep and found a kernel. His office was empty—a letdown.

Sighing, she returned to her desk and continued making calls to dentists. She was nearing the end of her original list when she had an epiphany. What if Marilyn and her mother hadn't lived in Kearny long enough to establish with a dentist here? That would mean calling dentists near wherever they'd lived before.

Delaney dug back through the case records. Sure enough, she found reference to a previous address in Lodge Grass, Montana. Groaning aloud, she googled again. Her search results overlapped, but there was no denying the task had just become more daunting, as this opened up Billings, Montana, which, at a population of one hundred and fifteen thousand was by far the largest town for hundreds of miles. With one hundred and sixty-one dentists, it had three times more than her original list.

However, there was a clear starting point for her search now. The Indian Health Services Clinic in Crow Agency, Montana had a pediatric dentist, which would be free or close to it for tribe members. A single mom would access free health care first, she suspected, so she dialed, biting her lip.

"Dentist office." The voice that answered clearly belonged to the most bored man in the world.

Delaney repeated her mantra, asking if he was the one she should talk to.

"Yes."

"And your name is?"

"Bill."

"Okay, Bill. I'd like to give you a name, but I want to stress that our deceased person may not be her. I don't want to unnecessarily upset any loved ones."

"Okay."

"Did your office treat Marilyn Littlewolf? She was born—"

"Yes."

"You did?"

"Yes."

"You're sure, without looking her up."

"I said yes. I worked here then. Knew her mama. Peg and I went to school together."

Delaney raised a triumphant first in the air. "Thank you. Can you send her dental records to me so our forensic pathologist can see if they're a match?" She gave him her email.

"Okay. What happened to her?"

"I'm sorry. I can't tell you before we identify her and notify any next of kin. It may not be her."

"Okay."

"Thank you. Thank you so much."

"You're welcome."

Delaney hung up the phone, smiling. They had a lead, even if it was a tiny one. And Bill might have been bored, but he'd been very helpful.

Her cell phone rang. She pulled it from her pocket. Kat. It was already four o'clock. Where had the day gone? "Hey. What's up?"

"Can you hear me?" Kat was whispering.

"Yes," Delaney fake whispered back. "What is it?"

"I'm in my closet."

Delaney sat bolt upright. "Are you okay? Is someone trying to hurt you?"

"What? No! I just don't want Skeeter to hear me."

Delaney exhaled forcefully. *Relax, mama bear.* "You scared me."

"Sorry. It's just, well, Skeeter is acting funny. He's sitting outside and he's... he's *crying*."

Delaney blanched. Skeeter, crying? "Did he just chop an onion?"

"No. And he wasn't watching an old Green Bay Packers game either."

Skeeter did have a peculiar, self-flagellating habit of watching replays of the Broncos beating the Packers in the Super Bowl. In *1998*. He'd probably watched the game a hundred times, and he still shed tears every time quarterback Brett Favre turned the ball over. Even Delaney had the one fumble and one interception memorized now.

"Did you ask him what's wrong?"

"I did. He said he made a mistake."

"What kind of mistake?"

"That's all he said."

"Okay. I'll give him a call and check on him."

Delaney frowned. She really knew so little about Skeeter's life outside his work for her, other than he'd been in the Army then worked as a roughneck. That he'd grown up as a lake rat in Green Bay. And of course, his deep, fanatical love for the Packers.

"Thanks."

"Anything else?"

"Nope. Dudley is snoring. Carrie is playing games, again. And I finished my homework at school."

"Why don't you make some chocolate chip cookies? We can have them after dinner."

Kat sighed. "Maybe."

Delaney laughed. "I love you. Bye, Kat."

"I love you, too. Bye, Aunt Delaney."

As she ended the call, Delaney thought about the hours she'd put in the day before. The compassionate thing to do would be to give Skeeter a break when she could. She gathered up her notes and grabbed her purse.

She poked her head in Leo's office.

His jerked up. "What's up?"

"I found Marilyn's dentist."

"Good. No word from Dr. Watson yet."

"I'm heading home. We're all exhausted after last night. You know—Carrie. Flashbacks." It wasn't the real reason, but something made her hold back out of a protective instinct. Skeeter was part of her brood now, too.

"I'm really sorry. I can imagine the impact this has on her." His phone chimed. His eyes cut to it, then he jerked them back to Delaney. *It's another dating app notification. It's written all over his face.* "I'll, um, see you tomorrow."

"Mhmm." She backed out and left, driving home in a daze, her thoughts on Leo's love life, the unexpected pain of it, and the lack of her own. Whether she should join a dating app. How much she hated the idea. Whether she'd ever date again. Deciding probably not. Two daughters and her job were all she could handle. *If I can't have Leo.*

* * *

She parked her department truck outside the back door to her house—she only drove Shelly to work once or twice a week and had parked and covered her the night before, after stopping at a drive-through car washing station on the way home from the slide site—and went inside.

"Surprise. I'm home early. How are my favorite people?"

Skeeter and Kat were in the kitchen. Carrie was punching controls from her perch on the couch.

"Hi! I'm making cookies!" Kat said.

"Hi, Delaney." Carrie didn't look away from the screen.

"And I'm making lasagna." Skeeter waved a wooden spoon, splattering red sauce across the kitchen. He didn't seem to notice. He was an excellent cook and terrible cleaner upper.

Delaney was his inverse, so she didn't mind. "Great. How can I help?"

"You worked all weekend. We're treating you to a family feast."

Whatever had been wrong with Skeeter before, it wasn't showing now. Delaney was bone weary. A bath sounded so good to her. She would talk to him later. "If you're sure..."

"Yes!" Kat said.

"But when I come back, no more games. I'm talking to *you*, Carrie."

Carrie waved Delaney off. "Go. I'm about to outscore my highest ever."

Delaney laughed and headed to the bathroom. Once inside, she filled the tub with water as hot as she could stand it and dumped in a cup of lavender Epsom salt. Just before she stepped into the water, she saw Skeeter's phone on the counter. She picked it up. Should she put on a robe and take it to him? As she wavered, a text notification popped up. It was from someone named *Sam*. She wondered if this text would reveal what had made Kat so worried about Skeeter. Whatever it was, she reasoned, if it affected his care of the girls, she needed to know about it. *Or is that just the detective in me overstepping?* She did know his passcode. He didn't keep it a secret. Both the girls knew it, too. He regularly would ask one of them to check his messages when his hands were busy, calling out the digits.

I don't know a Sam. But that didn't give her the right to snoop without his permission. She was sure whatever it was that had been bothering him earlier, he'd tell her if it was serious. She set the phone back down on the counter.

She picked it up again.

She typed in the code, then she flipped it face down and slammed it on the counter.

What is wrong with you? Have a little faith. Sometimes she wondered if being a detective was making her a terrible person.

She slipped into the bath up to her nose and tried to push

the whole world away just long enough to soak all the heat out of the water.

SIX

The Mountain Man strolled Kearny's Main Street sidewalk, watching people in plate glass window reflections. Avoiding eye contact kept gazes off him. He didn't want to be looked at. Examined. Judged. He was taking a few days to mourn. After Marilyn's death, he'd howled and questioned God's will. He'd torn out tufts of his hair. He'd split a cord of wood and left the logs scattered in the yard. Then he'd calmed himself.

But even in a state of calm, his pain was unfathomable. Losing his bride of five beautiful years—the longest relationship he'd ever had—hurt worse than anything he could imagine. She'd been soft and lovely. Sweet. A wonderful mother to their children. He'd turned his energy into honoring her memory and chiseled a stone marker. He erected a simple wooden cross by the others and dug a shallow base for the stone. It read:

MARILYN, BELOVED BRIDE, ANGELIC MOTHER, GONE TOO SOON

Pressing the stems of plastic flowers into the dirt around it, he'd come to a realization. Her death was no accident. There was someone to blame. Someone who'd driven her out into the night and into the path of nature's fury. That person had killed her, as surely as God reigned.

THOU SHALT NOT KILL.

He was not one to strike in anger, so he'd prayed for guidance. Prayed and prayed and prayed, until he received it, clear as if God was standing before him, staring into his eyes with his hand on the Mountain Man's shoulder, speaking directly to him. What a blessing! He'd walked back into the house and doled out the punishment. His knuckles were bloody pulp when he was done, but it was that one act that had released his pain and opened his eyes to the truth.

Man without woman was incomplete. He was an abomination in the eyes of the Lord without a bride. He had to prove his devotion. God demanded no less of him. He'd taken his side-by-side off-road vehicle the long way down the mountain and into town.

Now, a group of teenagers was walking toward him, five abreast. They were taking up the whole sidewalk. One of the boys, a pimply, pale-skinned brute, barreled into a woman leading a toddler by the hand. The mother's body bounced into the wall. The tiny girl fell backward on her bottom and started bawling.

The boy shot them a look. "Watch where you're going." He added an ugly expletive.

The group was almost upon the Mountain Man. He stepped to the side, flattening his body against a brick building. There were three girls and two boys. They were laughing and gesticulating with bold tosses of arms and heads, wild shoves, rough nudges, and look-at-me smirks. The pimply white kid threw his arm around the shoulders of a very tall, brown-skinned girl. She walked in the middle, lithe and athletic, pale eyes arresting, and the Mountain Man immediately saw she was trapped in the eye of the storm. Motionless as the other kids raged around her. A Madonna among heathens. The boy jerked her to a stop and the Mountain Man averted his eyes as the kid pushed her head back and attacked her mouth. Savaged it. Invaded it.

Rage built inside him.

The assault ended. The boy laughed. The girl glanced around as if to see if anyone had witnessed her degradation. She offered the boy a tentative smile and they began walking again, behind the other three now.

They passed the Mountain Man. Close-up, he could see that the girl was Native American. Probably Crow. Subjugated to the white man even after all these years. He caught a whiff of her. Fear, budding womanhood, and a cheap perfume with an astringent undercurrent.

He remained stock-still for a few seconds more, watching flower baskets twist and sway on hooks, listening to a honking horn, feeling the prickles of knowing on his skin.

Then he turned and followed. She was the one. The next one. The one meant for him. He mouthed a prayer of fervent thanksgiving as he maintained fifty feet between him and the glorious creature he would rescue and protect from evil.

SEVEN

Standing outside the hospital, Delaney handed Leo Vaseline and Vicks VapoRub, one by one. He smeared the petroleum jelly below his nose and the mentholatum on his chest. He was already chomping Juicy Fruit gum.

"You ready for this?" she asked.

He sucked in a long breath then blew it out forcefully in three puffs. Repeated the exercise. *It's like he's about to deadlift a house, not walk into a hospital.* And for some reason, it was utterly endearing to her. He shook his fingers and rolled his head. "Let's do this."

They entered and walked the long hall to the morgue. Inside the oversized stainless steel and concrete room, they found tiny Dr. Watson pulling an occupied stretcher from a cooler. She gave them a crisp nod and a smile. "You're here quicker than I expected."

"You caught us on a slow news day." Leo's breath came out in a Juicy Fruit-scented cloud.

She locked the wheels on the gurney. "It's a shame I'll have to ruin it for you."

"Oh, no. What's the matter?" Delaney cocked her head.

Dr. Watson folded back the drape, revealing a face that resembled the pictures Delaney had seen of Marilyn Littlewolf at the age of fourteen.

"I'll start with the executive summary. This young woman has been subjected to long-term trauma and abuse. I believe her cause of death was asphyxiation, from being buried in mud. If she hadn't died from that, her broken neck or head injuries would have killed her. I'm not certain she could have survived the crushing of her chest. Time of death is less than forty-eight hours ago, which is consistent with the mudslide."

"Accidental, then?" Leo's voice was hopeful.

"Given the abuse, I can't rule out whether she was forced into the path of the slide or pushed or dumped off the mountain or accidentally fell. Let's call it troubling. The rest is your job."

Leo's head had dropped forward. The facepalming emoji come to life. "You believe it could be murder."

"I'm a scientist, Sheriff. I deal in facts—you decide what they mean. Let's review what I found before you connect the dots." Dr. Watson lifted the drape from the girl's left ankle. There was a groove around the front of it. "See the deep indentation here? Something actually cut through her skin."

"Did she catch her foot in something?"

"While that's possible, the mark isn't across the back." She lifted the ankle gently. "See? No damage."

"Could she have been pulling against something?"

"Again, possible, but I would expect to see evidence that she'd twisted her leg if she was trying to free herself. Imagine causing yourself that kind of pain, too. It seems less likely than what I envision, which is that this ankle was held down by some kind of smooth cable—I didn't find any fibers in the wound. Nothing from rope, cloth, or metal. I'd guess it was coated." She lowered the ankle. "And see these scars?" She traced her finger in the air above white lines in the brown skin. "It happened repeatedly. With the other foot, too." She re-draped Marilyn and exposed the other ankle. Delaney and Leo followed her to have a look.

Delaney shook her head. "I'm having trouble envisioning it."

"My theory is that the cord or cable was attached to a board or flat surface, because the marks end abruptly and uniformly on either side of the wounds."

Delaney sank down on her heels and held her head. Someone tortured this child over and over. *Kat... Carrie...*

"Are you okay?" Leo put his fingertips on her shoulder.

She took a few steadying breaths. "Just lightheaded. Sorry. This is just so..."

"Disturbing," Dr. Watson said.

"Times infinity."

"Is there more evidence of abuse?" Leo said.

Dr. Watson reached over and touched Marilyn's hand, which was covered by the sheet. "Every finger on both hands has been broken. I think at different times based on how completely they have healed—or not. I doubt she received medical attention for any of them."

"This... this is evil."

Delaney stood and gripped the edge of the table. "And whoever did this is somewhere out there and will do it again."

Dr. Watson covered the girl's foot. "There's more. I believe she's had at least one pregnancy."

Delaney felt woozy again. "A baby? There could be a baby out there somewhere with a monster?"

Dr. Watson held up her hand. "I don't know if she delivered a live child. I can only tell you that she has stretch marks on her abdomen and hips that in a girl her age point pretty strongly to an advanced pregnancy. She wasn't lactating at the time of her death. But—" She closed her eyes and swallowed, then paused for a moment. "She was pregnant when she died. Eight or nine weeks, I'd say."

Leo started pacing the room. *He's handling the death dungeon better than usual.* "Playing devil's advocate for a moment, is it possible these were desired pregnancies in a long-term relationship?"

Delaney shuddered. "In a young girl suffering this kind of abuse?"

"I don't disagree. I'm just trying to think through all the possibilities."

Delaney's phone buzzed. An incoming call. She declined it. Moments later, the phone buzzed again.

"Do you need to get that?" Dr. Watson asked.

Delaney fished the phone from her back pocket and read the caller ID. It looked familiar. She quickly reviewed her Recents. Midday. Son of a... She declined it again. Putting it back in her pocket, she glared at Leo, then remembered she'd forgotten to tell him about the call from Clark Applewood with the ATF.

To Dr. Watson she said, "Sorry about that. Please go on."

"Can you tell us anything that would lead us to this bastard?" Leo asked.

"I don't have much. Her stomach contents reveal her last meal as rabbit and onions."

Delaney tried to remember the last time she'd eaten rabbit. "Not a common meal these days."

"Rabbits are usually game animals. She was living somewhere that hunted meat was part of her diet," Leo said.

"You mean Wyoming?" Delaney rolled her eyes at him.

Dr. Watson slid the girl's arm out from under the drape and rotated it. "She also had a tattoo. A rather shoddy home job."

Delaney leaned down to see the marks on the inside of the forearm. "Is that EP522?"

"That would be my guess."

"A license plate number?" Leo guessed.

"Someone's initials and the date May 22nd?" Delaney countered.

"An EP is an extended play musical release. You know, like artists do before they release full albums. Maybe it's related to music?"

"You lost me there, partner." Delaney shrugged. "Whatever it is, maybe she got it before she disappeared from home."

"The kids she ran around with might be able to help us with that."

Dr. Watson turned the girl's arm back over and patted it, like she was soothing her. "That's the only other remarkable thing I noted. You'll have my full report tomorrow."

"We need to confirm her identity. I'll send you over the report from a dentist I located once I get it." Delaney said.

"Sounds good."

"Thank you," Leo said. "You've ruined my day, but, as always, you did it with the utmost of professionalism and the highest quality work."

Dr. Watson laughed. "Get out of my morgue, ingrate. You, too, my sweet Delaney."

Three steps out of the morgue, Delaney's phone rang again.

Leo grinned. "You're popular this morning. Kat, Carrie, Skeeter, or Mary?" Mary Galvez managed the Loafing Shed, a bar that had been in Delaney's family now for three generations, counting Kat, since she owned it in trust after the death of her father. A death that was legal but not factual. Liam Pace had faked it to cover up his real identity as a jack-of-all-crimes.

"Funny you should ask since I wanted to talk to you about it. The calls I am repeatedly declining are from Clark Applewood. Does that name ring a bell?"

"No, should it?" Leo pushed open the door and held it for her.

"He said you were supposed to give me a heads-up he'd be calling."

Leo scraped his bottom lip with his teeth as he shook his head. "Sorry. No bells."

"He's a special agent with the ATF."

Leo's mouth opened. "Ohhhhh. Well. I told you they wanted to pitch you a consulting role."

"And I said I wasn't interested."

"I guess they wanted to try anyway."

"Which you made easy by giving them my cell number." Delaney unlocked the doors to Leo's truck with his fob and got in, then dropped the fob in one of the cup holders.

Leo climbed in the other side. "Wait, what? No. I didn't."

"Then who did?"

"I don't know. But I wouldn't jump to any conclusions. He's with the federal government. If they want your private number, they have their ways."

Delaney harrumphed and turned on the radio. Pop music blasted the interior. It was a song she liked. Ava Russo duetting with someone whose high twangy voice made the song less aggressively hip hop than Russo's last few singles. She decided to leave the station alone.

She pulled the truck out onto the road and pointed it toward the joint station for the police and sheriff's departments. Sharing space facilitated collaboration under Wyoming's mutual aid statute. Cops normally handled issues within city limits and the sheriff's department issues outside city limits, but within Kearny County, each had explicit encouragement and permission to work outside those bounds to assist each other. Hence their shared records system.

Beside her, Leo's phone started chiming. Then chiming again. And again.

"What's going on with your phone?"

He turned off the ringer and flipped it face down. "Just notifications."

"Oh, my god. Dating app notifications?"

A blush crept from his neck up to his cheeks.

"They are! I thought you were dating Liesel."

"I just brought her to one party. We're not *dating*."

"Are you going out with all the women lighting up your phone?"

"I don't know. Maybe. Some of them."

"I didn't know there were that many single women in Kearny!"

"There aren't. They're from all over." The blush deepened.

Delaney felt a wave of nausea. She covered it with bravado. "You're reenacting a Wyoming version of *The Bachelor* before my eyes."

"It's not like that."

"I don't see how you're going to have time for your job, the campaign, and your dating career." He started to speak, and she held up her hand. "Change of subject, please. Marilyn Littlewolf."

"Or whoever she is."

"I'm thinking we should pursue it as a murder case. We can always walk it back if we need to."

His head shake was immediate and vehement. "Walking it back never works. If word gets out that we think this is a murder and we don't find a murderer—even if we decide it was not murder—then we have a failure."

Delaney's passion for finding out what happened to Marilyn overwhelmed her senses and turned to anger. "Failure? You're worried about public image?"

"I'm worried about public fear and confidence."

"And its impact on your campaign?"

He threw his hands up. "Delaney, you know me. Yes, I want

to win the election. But that's because I think I can do this job well. I believe I'm the best candidate. Would you rather Joe or Chief Yellowtail or someone outside law enforcement takes my chair?" Recently, Kearny Police Chief Mara Yellowtail had declared to run against Leo for sheriff as a Democrat. It was audacious, since Wyoming wasn't known for electing Dems. And it was a slap in Leo's face. Mara wasn't a bad cop. She was just a recent promotion to her position, and she wasn't Leo. No one was. "Definitely, a loss of public confidence could turn the tide against me. But even worse, it could make it harder for all of us to do our jobs. It could create unsafe interactions. It could stymie people from reaching out to us when they need us. Come on."

Leo's words stung Delaney because he was right. Maybe, just maybe, part of her anger right now was about other things, too. Like the ATF. And those damn dating apps. But she wasn't wrong about treating Marilyn's case seriously. To investigate it like it might have been murder. "You make valid points. I'm... I'm—uh..."

"You can't say it, can you?"

She shouted it. "I'm sorry!"

He grinned. "Apology accepted."

"But I know you don't disagree that there is a possibility Marilyn was murdered, and that there is a certainty she suffered horrible long-term abuse. Permission to pursue *that* case."

"Why don't you just quietly reopen the missing persons case and see where that leads you? Do the investigation that needs doing but do it quietly."

"It's my middle name."

Just then, she saw a late model Mustang rocket out of a parking lot on one side of the four-lane street toward the opposite sidewalk where an elderly man was walking a small dog. She punched the accelerator to the floor and aimed to intercept it.

The impact rattled her teeth and sent shockwaves up her arms, but she accelerated for follow-through, pushing the front end of the runaway car to point in the direction of the traffic flow and somehow keeping Leo's truck in front of it. The Mustang's engine revved. Delaney gritted her teeth and kept dancing the truck to stay in front of the Mustang. She couldn't see anyone in the driver's seat.

"What the hell just happened?" Leo shouted.

"I think the accelerator is stuck. Or something is wrong with the driver. Someone needs to turn off that car."

Leo leapt out and ran to the Mustang. Delaney glanced up the street to see the man and the dog half a block away, looking peacefully oblivious to their near-death moment. She returned her attention to Leo, who had opened the driver's door. From her angle, it seemed like he threw the car into park and turned it off. The engine quieted.

Immediately, the pressure on her truck from the Mustang stopped. She lowered the window. A woman ran across the road, screaming. Leo stepped away from the car with a young child in his arms. Suddenly, the whole situation made a lot more sense. The woman held out her arms for the child as people gathered and took pictures of Leo.

Delaney whispered a quick prayer of thanks. God had been looking out for the little children this time, for real.

Leo returned to his truck as Delaney was radioing in the incident.

"I think you totaled my truck," he said.

"I think I just won you the primary." Then she climbed out and accepted hugs from the tearful mother.

* * *

Hours flew by. Delaney lost track of them. She did a presentation at a tiny elementary school serving three of the smallest towns in the county. Stranger danger, when to call 911, and why officers are your friends—the kids loved it and she did, too. But the drive there and back—in her own truck—took two hours alone, plus the hour she spent at the school. When she returned, there were a flurry of crises to deal with that tied her up until it was nearly time to leave for the day. At least she'd been able to check in with the new Missing and Murdered Unit agent in Billings. They'd had no information on Marilyn Littlewolf, but they were opening a file, and the agent gave her a mobile number to keep them updated. She'd also called out the crime scene unit about feasibility of a search of the slide area. The supervisor gave her an earful about the size of the slide area and instability of the dangerous, devastated terrain, but in the end they'd agreed to work with Search and Rescue and the engineer to see what could be done. Likely, her wait would be lengthy for information, if any, but she had needed to try.

Now, the Marilyn Littlewolf disappearance records loomed on her screen, accusatory and unread.

Another hour, she told herself. The Indian Health Services dentist had sent Marilyn's records. She forwarded them with a request for comparison via email to Dr. Watson. Then she drafted a request for cooperation and coordination in reopening Marilyn Littlewolf's case and forwarded it to Leo with a note.

Can you deliver this to the chief with a heads-up?

Finally, she scanned Marilyn's records. Missing person. Juvenile female. Single parent household. Crow heritage. The words mocked her. She reread the final note in the case file.

Mother reports that her daughter sent word that she left home voluntarily to live with her father and will not be returning.

It was initialed CP. Caitlin Porter? If so, she was still working for the police, just on the other side of the same building Delaney was sitting in.

Why didn't the police track her down anyway to confirm she was with the father? The girl was barely fourteen. She might have still been out on the streets. Just because she'd run away didn't mean she hadn't run into trouble, before or after she left. Maybe trouble with someone older who was manipulating her, taking advantage of her, or forcing her to lie to her mother.

Or maybe she just went to live with her dad. Delaney had lived with her dad. Although her mother had left her. Which parent would Delaney have picked if she'd had the choice? If her mom had stayed and her dad hadn't been murdered? Probably her dad.

But now that Delaney had daughters of her own, she questioned Peg, too. Why hadn't she insisted the police remain involved? Why had she simply let the girl go? Had she been relieved to unload a difficult teenage girl? Then she remembered the woman's suicide. Mental illness might have played a role in Marilyn's departure and in Peg's death. Substance abuse? Poverty? Hopelessness? With each thought, her spirits sank further.

No matter what the answers were to these questions, someone owed Marilyn more than she'd gotten from the police department five years ago. The someone who would give it to her would be Delaney. She began jotting notes for next steps, considering and dismissing pulling up one of Leo's investigation templates on her tablet and instead using her tried and true method of chicken scratch on a blank sheet of paper.

Her phone buzzed with a text just as her stomach growled.

Carrie: *where r u —u promised pizza*

Delaney leapt to her feet. She spoke voice-to-text: "Sorry! On my way. Are you at Say Cheese?"

Carrie: *yeah —Skeeter crying & texting, hry*

Skeeter acting weird again? Delaney bolted out the door, regretting now that she hadn't read Skeeter's text last night.

EIGHT

Leo grasped the sides of the podium and leaned his weight into his hands. "I believe in the law, I believe in enforcing it for order, and I am committed to doing that safely and with respect for every nickel of our tax dollars."

One hundred and fifty eyes—give or take, because he was sure he saw a glass eye or two and one fellow with a patch—stared back at him, judging him and deciding whether to give him their votes. But was that even true? Half of them might be there to see their buddies and of the remaining half; maybe another thirty percent just wanted lunch cooked by someone else. Leo was going to pass on eating it himself. Based on the smell, the broccoli was soggy and overcooked. A few of the rest of the group seemed engaged with his comments, though, so he tried to focus his energy on them.

"I'm Sheriff Leo Palmer, your law-and-order candidate, and I'm asking for your vote in the primaries. Thank you for having me out to your Rotary Club luncheon today." He gave a smile meant to convey confidence, strength, and trustworthiness. He'd practiced it in the mirror that morning. It felt wrong on his face now.

A few people began to applaud. Leo wished he had been able to convince Delaney to come. She'd begged off, citing a severe allergy to public events. He would have had a lot more confidence with her by his side, other than the possibility that half the audience would have preferred that she run instead of him. His phone chimed. He slapped his pocket. Too late to silence it now.

"Any questions for me?" he asked. *Hopefully not about murder, Tommy Miller, or whether the department is adequately staffed.* His new hire to replace Tommy was at training in Douglas and hadn't even started yet.

His phone chimed again. Notification sounds of all types started to sound in the room. Then he noticed heads ducking as people read their phones.

A man in a boxy brown suit and plaid bow tie struggled to a stand.

"Yes, sir, do you have a question?"

The voice that answered was thin and wobbly. "No. I was going to the can then getting my dessert. Carry on, young fellow."

Titters rippled through the audience.

A voice shouted, "I've got a question!"

Leo searched for the speaker. No one was standing. The edges of the room were darker, making it hard for him to see bodies and faces there. "Fire away."

"Is it true Sue Wiley has gone missing?"

Leo squinted. Now he *really* wanted to see who he was answering. He'd never heard the name Sue Wiley. He started to say that when his phone chimed again. And suddenly, he felt very sure the texts he was receiving at that moment would confirm that yes, in fact, someone named Sue Wiley was missing.

Another voice shouted, "She's only fourteen years old!"

And then another. "What are you going to do about it, Sheriff?"

Half an hour later, Leo hung up his hat and sank into his chair. He shouted, "Delaney, you out there?"

"I am, your royal highness. Which you'd know if you called or came out here."

He'd been about to ask her to come into his office to talk about the missing girl, but he thought better of it, smiling. Her sense of humor could be prickly, but she amused him. He stuck his head out the door. "Meet me in the conference room? I'm grabbing a coffee if you'd like one."

Delaney beamed rays of fake sunshine at him. "Why, thank you. Yes, please. I'd like a shot of sugar-free hazelnut sweetener and some of that almond milk creamer."

"Of course. Oh, and bring everything you have on Marilyn Littlewolf."

When he arrived—laptop under one arm, coffee in each hand—she was already seated at the head of the table, waiting. He struggled in the door and then moved to close it with his foot. She watched without offering help. She'd already put a coaster by her spot, so he set her coffee on it.

"I hope it's to your liking, oh-queen-of-crime-solving." He sat catty-corner from her.

"I prefer mistress of murder. It's a little edgier." She lifted her mug to her lips and sipped. "Nice job on the coffee. What's up?"

"You've heard Sue Wiley is missing?"

Delaney's knit brow said no. "Sue Wiley is in middle school with Kateena, although I think she's in Freddy's year. What happened?"

"Where have you been? Everyone in my Rotary Club luncheon knew about it before me."

She waved her hand. "I had to requalify at the range today. I went early to warm up and forgot my phone under a pile of papers on my desk. I literally had just sat down when you bellowed for me. Now answer my question. What's going on?"

"Clara got a call from Sue Wiley's mother about forty-five minutes ago. Sue didn't show up at school today. The mom called all Sue's friends and drove all over town looking for her. She can't find her." Clara was their department administrative guru. The one without whom the whole house of cards would fall in an instant.

"Does she have a boyfriend?"

"A high school senior named Elijah Campbell. Do you know the name?"

"No, but Carrie will."

"The mom thinks he's a good boy but admits they haven't found him yet either. He's not at school." If Vegas was offering bets on the outcome of this disappearance, he'd bet it all on the girl and the boyfriend holed up somewhere.

"Has anyone gone out to talk to her yet?"

"City cops. They got out in front on this."

"The Wiley family lives in town?"

"Yes. Just inside the city limits."

"She's Crow, Leo."

"But her last name is Wiley."

Delaney shrugged. "What's in a last name these days? The girl is Crow. Could you give the chief a heads-up we'll be working the case, too?"

"Things aren't great between Yellowtail and me right now."

"And they really won't be when she sees you on the news saving a little boy and an old man and a dog. But another young teen Crow girl has gone missing from our town, and I'm working on the first one."

"That was five years ago."

"You don't think it's incredibly suspicious that Sue disappeared at the same time Marilyn showed back up?"

"Potentially suspicious."

Delaney looked unhappy.

Leo held firm. Theirs was just a difference of opinion on a case that had barely gotten off the ground yet. Correction: a case that wasn't even clearly a case yet, and, even if it was, the police were competent.

She said, "You can grovel later when I'm right. These are connected. I don't want them to be, but they are."

"Obviously, a live girl missing takes precedence over an old missing person case with the subject deceased."

"Obviously." Delaney took a snippy tone. "But mark my words. You'll be coming back to tell me I'm right. Did you send the chief my message about working on Marilyn Littlewolf?"

"Not yet." It was going to be agency soup. The police, the sheriff's department, and the Wyoming Division of Criminal Investigations, who would definitely be showing up for this one. And the Division of Criminal Investigations would probably take a role with Marilyn Littlewolf, too, if that headed the direction he feared it would. He opened his laptop just as his phone chimed. It was from his sister Adriana. She'd heard about Sue Wiley and was panicked. All the parents of middle schoolers were panicked.

"Oh. My. God."

Leo looked up. Delaney had pulled his laptop over to herself and was reading, jaw hanging open. Heat flooded into his face. He knew what was on his screen. He reached for the laptop, but she pulled it away from him.

"Leo, you're tracking the women in your dating apps in a spreadsheet."

"I'm a data guy. I'm just trying to keep things straight. I don't want to offend someone by forgetting a name or mixing them up." He tried to grab it again.

"This one has a dog named Louie. Oh, and this one likes cats and roses."

"That's private. Give it back to me."

And then she went quiet, and he knew why. He only thought he'd been embarrassed before. Because the last column of the spreadsheet was for his comments. So far, for every single one of them, he'd typed the same thing. *Not Delaney.* She pushed the laptop back to him.

He avoided her eyes and sent her email for Yellowtail to the printer. When he looked up at her, she was almost smiling.

"I'll pretend I didn't see that if you'll go tell Mara we want in on Sue Wiley."

"Fine. I'll hand-walk your email over to her and do it now. Give me fifteen minutes. Be ready—after that, you and I are going to meet Sue's parents."

"There's the Sheriff Palmer I'm voting for. A bit of a ladies' man but a whiz with Excel."

He shot her the bird without turning back as he left the room.

* * *

Leo refused the chair in Mara Yellowtail's office and watched her read the message he'd printed and handed to her. It wasn't a power move. The police chief had recently redecorated, and her metal-framed sling chairs were uncomfortable. The decor was a blend of contemporary with traditional Native American. Besides not liking the chairs, Leo thought it looked pretty cool. Mara had married Eugene Yellowtail around the time Leo had moved to Kearny but had only taken Eugene's last name a few months before. He had no idea of her heritage, but she had a New England accent and her name had been Gipson when he met her. It was also on the diplomas she'd removed from her walls in the remodel. He tried to think charitably—that she'd changed her name because of love or family. The cynic in him believed it was an attempt to win the Native American vote, given the timing.

Mara dropped the paper on her desk. She vacated her chair and stood, looking as powerful as a draft horse. Her fingernail-length hair was no-nonsense, as was her direct manner. "You're reopening Marilyn Littlewolf? You can do what you want, obviously, but Caitlin Porter is a damn fine officer. I won't put up with any politically motivated smear tactics."

Leo's cheeks hurt from smiling. He'd butted heads with Mara over how she handled a case the previous January, one where false allegations had been lodged against Delaney. Mara had cut him out of the loop and pursued Delaney aggressively. The fact that she'd been proven wrong had mollified Leo somewhat, but it had soured their relationship. With the upcoming battle for sheriff, he didn't anticipate things between them improving any time soon.

He said, "All we want is to figure out what happened to Marilyn. How she ended up dead in the Bighorns, pregnant and suffering from long-term physical abuse."

She didn't react to the information from the autopsy, and he wondered if she'd talked to Dr. Watson. "Suddenly you care about the plight of Crow girls. Grab the spotlight anyway you can, I suppose."

He gripped his duty belt so he wouldn't ball his fists. "What in the world are you getting at?"

"I'm anticipating your press release." She made air quotes. "Hero sheriff, champion of the downtrodden. I won't let you co-opt our community for your PR."

"Mara, I'm offering coordination between us on Marilyn and on Sue Wiley. Extra hands and brains. Bringing Sue home safely and eliminating any threat to the youth of our community is my only agenda."

"I'll want to know what you're doing before you're doing it."

"To the best of our ability. I'd appreciate the same from you."

She didn't answer, which he took as a polite no thank you.

"Right now, I'm heading to Sue Wiley's home with Deputy Investigator Pace to interview Sue's parents."

"We've already done that."

"Great. Can I see a copy of the evidence you collected, any statements you took, and the officer notes from the interviews?"

"You can when they're entered into the records system."

Leo turned his smile up a notch. He appreciated knowing where he stood with the chief, and that was on polar opposite sides of any issue as long as they were running against each other. "Good talk." He nodded at her and left.

His smile disappeared like it had never been there as soon as his back was turned.

NINE

Leo shifted forward in the Adirondack chair. Jayla Russo—Sue Wiley's mother—was rocking furiously beside him in a porch swing. Delaney was leaning against the deck railing, facing them, blocking his view of Interstate 90 running past the backyard.

"I appreciate that this is difficult for you, Mrs. Russo. And I know you've already spoken with some officers who came by earlier," he said.

"I just want to find my daughter."

"We're going to help you do that."

The back door burst open. A man limped onto the deck. Leo noticed the thick sole of his left shoe. The man's wild eyes darted from Jayla to Leo and Delaney. "Jayla. I just got your messages. I came as fast as I could get off work."

Delaney met Leo's eyes. She nodded for him to take the lead.

Leo stood, offering his hand. "I'm Sheriff Leo Palmer."

The man shook his head and didn't take Leo's hand. He backed away. "No. No. This can't be happening."

Delaney slipped off the rail. "Are you Mr. Russo?"

The man pulled at brown-going-gray hair that was already standing out in every direction. "Ugh. I am. Yes, yes. Samuel Russo."

"I'm Deputy Investigator Delaney Pace, Mr. Russo. Sheriff Palmer and I were just about to talk to your wife about Sue. Mrs. Russo, would you like your husband to join us?"

Leo watched Delaney with deep admiration. She had a deft touch that put witnesses at ease. *The whole package.* Now, if only she wasn't impetuous, reckless, and refused to listen to input from sheriffs past or present, she'd be the perfect partner.

Jayla was nodding. "Yes. Samuel should be here. He's her stepfather."

"All right, then. If that's good with you, Mr. Russo, let's all sit down and work through this."

Samuel was worrying his thumbs, but he sat in the swing with Jayla. "I don't know nothing, though."

"Right now, we're just taking a step back to learn about Sue and what she's been up to. When was the last time each of you saw her?"

"Last night," Samuel blurted. "She missed her curfew. Out with that boy again. Jayla had to be at work early this morning, so I waited up for her. I reason it was about midnight when she came in. I told her she'd have to deal with her mama today, then I went to bed."

"Was Sue upset?"

He snorted. "She was drunk, was what she was. Laughed in my face."

"Mrs. Russo?"

"Yesterday, at breakfast. I made her waffles." A single tear wet her dry cheeks. "I was gone before time for her to be up this morning."

"Did either of you see her between when she arrived home last night and now?"

They both shook their heads.

Leo said, "Do you know when she left the house again?"

Again, they both shook their heads.

Jayla said, "I thought she went to school."

Samuel said, "I didn't have to go in to work until nine, so I slept in past when Sue normally left for school. I thought she'd gone there, too."

"Can we get a list of her friends and their phone numbers? And her boyfriend's name and number, too."

"I already gave that to the other cops," Jayla said.

Leo smiled and didn't let Jayla wiggle out of eye contact.

Finally, she said, "Samuel, will you get me a pen and paper?"

"If it's easier, you can share the contacts with me from your phone," Leo said.

"Yeah, I can do that."

He gave her his number and she started texting him contacts.

"I think that's all of them."

"Okay. Can you tell us about her friends?"

"She's known most of them since kindergarten. I know their parents. They're nice girls."

Samuel snorted.

"What's that about, Samuel?" Leo asked.

"They used to be nice girls. Now they're hormonal and bratty. Disrespectful. Sneaky."

"What do you mean?"

"Like last night with Sue? She didn't used to be like that. And that's how her friends act, too. And now they're dating older boys."

"You're not being fair. She made good grades. She played volleyball. She was beating the odds," Jayla said.

"She's quitting volleyball for the relays. And now she's a statistic."

"No! This is a misunderstanding. We'll find her!"

"Is there anyone you can think of who would want to hurt her?" Leo asked, keeping his voice gentle.

"No. No one. She is a nice girl," Jayla insisted.

"Had she talked about leaving? Running away, I mean. About being unhappy?"

Jayla crossed her arms. "Never."

Samuel laughed. "You're kidding yourself. She talked about getting out of here all the time."

Jayla shook her head, her mouth a grim line.

Delaney smiled at her. "I have a niece a year behind her in school. Middle school is a tough time. My other daughter is a junior. She's gotten into gaming. What was Sue into?"

Jayla's eyes lit up. "Oh, the gaming, yeah, all of her friends were playing these games. Samuel, what was the one?"

He rolled his eyes and shook his head. "Something loud with a lot of magical beasts."

Jayla gave a sharp nod. "*Phantaztik Beaztz*. But spelled funny. Ph instead of F. Zs instead of Ss. Maybe a K at the end of Phantaztik."

Delaney said, "Did they have regular friends they played with? Not kids at their school, but online friends?"

"I think so. Maybe."

Leo liked where Delaney had taken this. "Would you mind giving me her login? I'd like to see who she was interacting with. Just in case. Sometimes predators hide behind fake identities online."

Jayla's eyes widened. Her voice was a whimper. "You think someone like that took her?"

"Not necessarily, but we need to be thorough."

"Okay. She logged in through our TV. Can you get it from there?"

"I can. And you know what would really help is any laptops or tablets or phones or computers she used. Did she leave any of them here?"

"Not her phone. But she doesn't usually take her laptop to school. It should be here."

"Did she take anything with her besides her phone?"

"I-I'm not sure. If she went to school she'd take her back-pack. And she had a little crossbody bag like all the girls want. She bought it with money she saved up from her allowance." She said the last with pride. "If she didn't take the backpack and the purse, they'd be in her room. With her laptop."

"I can make a copy of the hard drive on her laptop real quick before I go. It will help if you know her passwords or at least how to login."

Jayla straightened. "I made her give me all her passwords. It was a rule. I have a list."

"Great. Do you have a locator on her phone, like Find a Friend?"

"Yeah. I tried it. I got nothing. Like she turned it off on purpose, you know?"

Or like someone had destroyed it. But Leo didn't say that. "Last thing. Would you let us look around in her room?"

Samuel was shaking his head. "Jayla, they're acting like she's a criminal. We shouldn't be opening everything up to the cops."

"She's my daughter! They can look at anything they want if it will bring her back."

"She's not going to like it."

Leo said, "She's not your daughter, Mr. Russo?"

Samuel shot him a disgusted look and went back in the house.

Jayla said, "Samuel and I got married two years ago. He's her stepfather."

"Do the two of them get along?"

She shrugged. "Good enough."

"How did she feel about you getting married?"

"I don't think she liked it too much, but she mostly cares

about her friends. And I told her how much it was going to help us. You know. Having a man around. Samuel takes good care of us."

Alarm bells were ringing in Leo's head. Was Samuel in Sue's room tampering with evidence? He jerked his head at Delaney. That was all it took for her to move out quick and stealthy, like a panther. If Jayla had even noticed, she gave no sign.

"Let's go get that list of passwords. All right?"

"All right."

Leo followed her in the house, praying Delaney had made it to Sue's room in time to find whatever it was Samuel Russo didn't want them to see.

Leo pulled the flash drive from Sue's laptop just as he heard the shouting from the back of the house. Delaney's voice. Samuel Russo's. He shoved the copy of the hard drive in his pocket.

"You got no right to be digging through her drawers!" the man shouted.

"Her mother gave me permission. Please move out of my way." Delaney sounded firm and unruffled.

Leo knew how quickly a worm could turn. He ran toward the voices. At the door to a room decorated in gray and shocking pink, he stopped. Delaney was rifling through a drawer, not even looking at Samuel.

"Is there a problem?" Leo asked.

Behind him he heard Jayla's sharp intake of breath. "Samuel, what is wrong with you?"

"They need a search warrant. They ain't got one."

"No, they don't. I told her to do it."

Leo eased between Samuel and Delaney as she moved on to another drawer. "What is it you're afraid we're going to find, Mr. Russo?"

The man's eyes darted from Delaney to Leo to Jayla and

back in rotation. He threw his hands in the air. "This is bullshit. I'm the only one who cares about Sue, and I'm not even related to her. I'm outta here."

Leo didn't have cause to stop him. "Where are you headed, Mr. Russo?"

Samuel pushed past his wife, knocking her into the wall.

"Samuel! Wait! Stop!"

But Samuel waited for no one. Leo heard an engine rev to life, and then Samuel was gone.

TEN

Delaney savored a bite of the Cowpoke Cafe's homemade corned beef hash, upgraded with a liberal splashing of Cholula Hot Sauce. Salty, greasy, and spicy, with a black coffee chaser. The only thing that would have improved upon her breakfast was if it hadn't been served up with a side of Leo on a date at the same restaurant. An ear-piercing laugh from the woman of the moment made it hard to concentrate. As did her age. She was easily a decade older than Leo. There was nothing wrong with that, of course, but it was surprising and no less painful than when he'd brought a younger date to Delaney's party.

She'd thought this would be a working meal. In fact, she'd planned to invite Leo to join her so they could talk through her search of Sue's room the day before. She'd collected a few odds and ends from the room, like birth control pills and unsigned, overwrought love notes—nothing threatening or pointing to a location. And she'd found a postcard begging Sue to visit. It was from Patricia Cox, Sue's best friend. Patricia had mailed it while traveling to move out of state with her mom, after her dad had gone to prison for multiple counts of identity theft the year before. The new hometown hadn't been named. Jayla didn't know where the pair had moved to, and the phone number she had was out of date. To top it off, the mom—the one whose name would presumably be on leases and utility contracts—had a different last name than her daughter. Tracking Patricia down would be difficult.

Delaney slowly ate her breakfast while she poked around on social media, searching for Patricia, and keeping her eyes averted from the live action episode of *Date My Mom* playing out twenty feet away. Her phone buzzed. Caller ID said it was Mary from the bar. Delaney glanced around. The restaurant was half full—not too many people to bother by taking a call—and Mary only called when it was important or sensitive.

She kept her voice low. "This is Delaney. Hi, Mary. What's up?"

"Oh, you know. It's Michelada o'clock at the Loafing Shed. I swear, breakfast rivals happy hour as our busiest time. But that's not why I'm calling." Her voice dropped. "I wanted to check if something is up with Skeeter."

Delaney pushed her hash away. "I'm not sure. Why?"

"He's been spending a lot of time here the last few nights. I'd seen less of him since he'd started working for you."

"Is there a problem?"

"He's getting hammered. Sloppy, crying in his beer hammered. Closing the place down hammered. And he's here now, with the hardcore crowd. He looks like shit."

"Has he said anything? About there being anything wrong, I mean."

"Woe is me kind of stuff. I've never done anything right. I hurt everyone in my life. Everyone is going to find out what I did. When I ask him what's wrong, it's never anything specific."

"He hasn't said anything to me, but both the girls have noticed he's been emotional."

"Maybe he had a death in the family? Lost an old friend?"

"Maybe. He never talks about family or his life before."

"Yeah. Come to think of it, he talks a lot, but it's about nothing, you know?"

"Right. Well, keep me posted if you learn anything. Or if it seems like he's day drinking."

"I'll lean on him hard if he tries to. And for sure, I'll call if he spills his guts. I care about him. He's a good guy. I hate seeing him like this."

"Me, too. He's family to the girls and me. Thanks, Mary." Delaney's first priority had to be the wellbeing of her girls, but she cared about Skeeter. Cared about him like the goofy old uncle who shows up for dinner every Sunday and takes home a doggy bag.

Leo slid into the booth across from her. "Am I interrupting?"

She put her phone down and reached for her coffee. "No. Your date over?"

"It was just breakfast. I have to eat. And yes." He reached for one of her toast squares.

She slapped his hand, but she let him take it. "Did she say anything interesting enough to add to your spreadsheet?"

Leo pointed to his full mouth and didn't answer.

Delaney let him off the hook. "I checked in with police this morning. They're talking to the kids in town, teachers, coaches, and trying to get Sue's phone records. I'm going to focus on the boyfriend Elijah and the best friend Patricia today. I'm hoping Patricia will know whether Sue would have run off and where she'd go. Or maybe that Sue has gone to see her."

"Would Sue leave the boyfriend?"

"If those mushy love notes are any indication, probably not. But that's assuming Sue and the boy aren't together."

"True. I'll have time to comb through her *Phantaztik Beaztz* connections and dig around in her laptop. But I went ahead and contacted the FBI today. You know, their Child Abduction

Rapid Response Deployment Team. We're going to be crawling with help soon."

Delaney waved for her check. "How is it going with the chief?"

He pointed at her plate. "You done with the hash?"

"I was going to take it to go."

"I was going to drive my truck to work, but it's in the shop."

"For good reason. And at least you weren't the one to mess it up this time." Leo had made a name for himself quickly damaging county vehicles because of his underestimation of Wyoming conditions. "But fine. It's yours."

He waggled his eyebrows and dug in, using her fork.

"The chief?" she repeated. "How is it going with you two?"

"She's torn between thinking I'm out to make them look bad and believing I'm going to use the epidemic of Native American girls who disappear without a trace as campaign PR."

She handed the waiter a twenty with a smile and a thank-you as the woman passed by.

The waiter paused to say, "Nice picture online, Sheriff."

Leo smiled. "Thanks."

As Delaney had predicted would happen, the picture of Leo carrying the little boy to safety from a runaway car in a busy street was getting a lot of social media shares.

The waiter walked away, whistling.

Delaney stood and grabbed her pocketbook. Leo shoveled in a huge bite, then chased it with the last of her water.

She said, "For everything about the chief that rubs me the wrong way, she's not wrong about the epidemic. I've always known about it at some level, but I didn't know about the ones missing from Kearny. And it hits differently with me as the mother of teenage girls. It shouldn't, but it does."

* * *

That afternoon, Delaney and Leo attended a community search for Sue. Really, though, the event was about using volunteer manpower to cover ground, and after helping kick it off, they returned to the department to better use their time on investigating—the part only they could do. It wasn't long before Delaney felt like she was spinning her wheels. Social media wasn't yielding any clues on the whereabouts of Sue, Elijah, or Patricia. She decided to give her brain recharge time while she tackled a problem with a concrete solution: Writing and posting an ad on Facebook Marketplace to sell Gabrielle, her tractor. She'd been dreading parting with her and kept putting off the task. It got her deep in her feels. Sometimes setting aside a pressing work problem allowed her brain to background process, so that when she came back to it, she had a solution. Conversely, tackling a dreaded personal issue with the ticking clock of that work issue forced her to face her emotional block head-on and vanquish it so she could give work its due.

Think logically. Think college education for two girls.

She frowned and typed, fighting back tears. After several rounds of revisions, she said, "Enough," so loudly that she looked around to see if anyone had noticed. Joe shot her a funny look. She added a price to the ad plus pictures she'd taken weeks before for this purpose. She clicked to post. "There." A wave of vertigo tilted the room. Why was this so hard? It was just a machine. With wheels. A comfy little cabin. Her custom-built supply and equipment boxes. A sweet paint job. And it was a twenty-four/seven escape hatch, from her memories and her fears. For years, the road had been her meditation, her therapy. To her, Gabrielle wasn't an albatross or a lead weight. She was a decade of wide-open spaces and road anesthesia.

That's what she was giving up, but somehow it was all tangled in Leo and his dates. She grabbed her phone and hotfooted down the hallway. A walk would help. She did her least feeling and best thinking when she was moving.

Clara was walking back to her desk and waved as Delaney blew through the lobby. The older woman looked like she'd blow away in the Wyoming wind, but in truth she was as steady as a fence post. A retired rodeo star and part-time horse trainer, she and her husband lived on his family's ranch.

Delaney lifted a hand in return. "I'm going to make some calls in the sunshine. Back soon."

"Sounds good."

Delaney rammed the exterior door like a prisoner on the run punching through the last barbed wire fence before freedom. Bright sun hit her eyes and she shut them, walking blind for a few steps. Her sunglasses were in her pocketbook on her desk. Well, she wasn't going back. She headed across Main Street toward the walking path along the banks of the Cheyenne River a few blocks away. The northern end of Main was light industrial and noisy. Her brain emitted nothing but static until she was within earshot of rushing water. Spring thaw was in full force and the river was overflowing its banks, pushing at the trunks of trees, pooling up in the grass and in some places even spilling over the walkway. Across the river, cattle grazed. A pair of trumpeter swans were gliding over the treetops.

Delaney moved off the path away from the water. Her breaths started coming easier and her thrumming pulse slowed. The heat of her anguish cooled. Her mind unlocked and thoughts of Sue returned. Who could Delaney turn to for help finding the girl's friends?

The answer was suddenly clear. Clint Rock-Below, who she'd planned to consult anyway. Somehow he'd fallen off her radar. *Thank you, Mother Nature and Cheyenne River.* She accessed Clint's contact record and called him.

"What did I do to deserve a call from Delaney Pace?" His tone, ever sardonic, always sounded like he was speaking through a wide smile under eyes with a mischievous glint to them. "Let me guess. You miss me. You're rethinking our entire relationship. You're calling to beg me for another chance." She heard road noise in the background. As a state cop, Clint burned a lot of highway miles.

"You're the cockiest guy I've ever met. And while you are a catch and will make some lucky woman very happy, I'm calling about a case. Or cases."

"You'll come around. How can I help?"

Delaney stooped to admire the purple bud of a prairie crocus. "Teenage girls. Crow heritage. One disappeared five years ago."

He cut in. "Marilyn Littlewolf. Word was she ran away."

"And one yesterday."

"Sue Wiley. You think the cases are related somehow?"

"Maybe." She detailed the horror of Marilyn's abuse. The unsatisfactory conclusion of the case.

"Have you talked to the cop who handled her case?"

Delaney winced. "Caitlin Porter. No, I haven't. I don't want to make her feel like I'm gunning for her. I was wanting to give it a cold eyes review instead. And she's busy, because of Sue."

"I think she's going to feel worse if you do it behind her back."

"That's fair. Anyway, something bad happened to Marilyn, some of it recently. We found her dead, now Sue's gone. That bothers me."

"It bothers me, too."

"First and foremost, I want to find Sue. To follow the evidence and bring her home. The piece I'm working on is trying to find her best friend and her boyfriend. I'm striking out."

"They're both gone?"

"The best friend moved away last year. With her mother. A girl named Patricia Cox. Have you heard the name?"

"No. Should I have?"

"Her father went to jail for identity theft."

"Malcolm Cox. Yep, I've heard of him."

"The mom is Linda Castle."

"Can't say I know her."

"What about Elijah Campbell?"

"That punk I know. I pulled him over for driving under the influence. He lost his license. He's a mouthy little weasel."

"It doesn't sound like any of these people are Crow, except Marilyn and Sue. Am I missing something?"

"Definitely not Malcom or Elijah. I'd think I would have some familiarity with Linda or Patricia if they were. It's not that big of a community. You probably remember the recent sad events that led to disbanding the Crow tribal police five months after it was established."

"I do. The teenage boy who died in a car chase."

"But I can still call some friends—an elder and a few of the elected officials—and see if there's anything happening on the reservation that would shed light on this. If I get anything useful, I'll let you know."

"You're helpful even when you're not helpful."

He laughed. "If I were you, I'd ask your girls how to get in touch with the friend and the boyfriend. Kids know everything. They don't like to tell cops, though."

"I'm a cop."

"Yeah, but you're their cop."

"That just makes it worse. Mom plus cop."

"Maybe. But the things they've been through... other kids might not understand the gravity of the situation. Your girls will. Just one Indian's opinion."

"I'll take it."

"You'll take me to dinner? I accept. When and where?"

Delaney laughed again. "Bye, Clint. Thank you."

She ended the call and jogged back to the station. It was four in the afternoon. The girls would be home from school.

And Clint was right. They might have a handle on where to look for Patricia and Elijah.

* * *

Kat and Carrie sat at the kitchen table, Delaney opposite them. Dudley, surprisingly, was sleeping in Kat's lap. *That little demon never sleeps.* He was probably just staying in optimal snack range. Skeeter had taken off when Delaney had gotten home. He had been withdrawn, like he'd been with her at pizza, too. Whatever was wrong, he wasn't opening up about it.

"I want to talk to you about something hard," Delaney said.

"Okaaaay," Kat replied, eyes slitted.

"You guys know Sue Wiley is missing, right?"

"The whole state of Wyoming knows that," Carrie said.

"It's all my friends are talking about," Kat added.

Delaney watched them carefully. "I just wanted to check on you. I love you, and you've both been through some bad things. Maybe this makes you think about them again."

Carrie's eyes were dark hollows. "It doesn't make me feel great. And that other girl, the one that got buried alive, yeah. This week pretty much sucks."

"I don't think people get it. That them talking about it all the time is different for me. And for Carrie," Kat said.

"You're right. Most of them don't. It's okay to tell them that. Or to walk away." Two pairs of somber eyes regarded her. Two heads nodded. "I'm working with a lot of people to help find Sue. Right now, I really need to talk to a girl named Patricia Cox who used to live here."

"I know her," Kat said.

Dudley let out a loud snore. His eyes were open.

"Do either of you know where she lives now?"

Two head shakes.

"Is there anyone you think would know how to get in touch with her?"

Kat said, "Sue."

"Yeah, I figured. But we don't have her phone. And if Patricia is on social media and interacted with Sue there, I haven't been able to identify her."

Carrie shrugged. "I only know her because of gaming. I see her online."

Delaney felt like the world's biggest idiot. Gaming. Carrie and Sue both gamed. She should have asked about that already. "What game?"

"It's that new one. *Phantaztik Beaztz*. I'm not that into it, but some of my friends are."

"And Patricia played with you guys?"

"I'm pretty sure it was her."

"Can you contact her through the game?"

"Yeah, but I never have. She's in a Discord group I'm in though."

"Discord. That's the chat app you use?"

"Yeah."

"Have people been talking about Sue on it?"

She nodded. "She hasn't logged on since... you know."

Delaney was thrumming with excitement. "Show me." She stood up, hands on hips.

Dudley rose in Kat's lap, but when Delaney didn't go for a bag of chips, he sighed and resettled.

Carrie logged into Discord on her phone. "It's like so totally bogus to have a parent on here. They'd toss me if they knew."

"Do you have to tell them?"

Carrie shrugged. "Nah. What do you want me to say?"

"We don't want to scare her off, but I really want her phone number. Or for her to call me."

"I can try, but that's kind of pushy."

"How about you tell her the truth? The Mom Cop wants to

talk to her about Sue. I want to bring Sue home safely. That Sue is not in trouble, no matter what."

"Should I give her your number?"

"That would be great."

"I'm sending her a private message." Carrie's fingers flew. "Done."

"Okay, now, I need her usernames. On the game and on Discord."

"Ugh. You don't want me to have any friends."

Delaney sat back down and lifted Carrie's chin with a finger. "I want you to have friends who don't disappear. Who come home and sleep in their own beds."

Carrie nodded slowly, eyes suddenly wet. "Fine." She took a screenshot on her phone, then opened a gaming app, scrolled around, and took another screenshot. She texted both to Delaney. "Just because you know her name doesn't mean she's going to talk to you."

"It's one step closer. Thank you, Carrie. And if she talks to you about your message, you'll let me know, right?"

Carrie bit her lip. "You think this will help you find Sue?"

"I sure hope so."

"Okay, then. I'll be your double agent."

Delaney felt a little guilty involving Carrie in more trauma. She hoped neither of them ended up regretting it.

ELEVEN

Strong hands pulled Sue Wiley upright. Her entire body was shaking. She was weak. Cotton-mouthed. Her head was splitting open. All those things were bad. But the fear was the worst. The can't-breathe-can't-think fear. Fear of *him*. Of why he'd taken her. Of what he planned to do to her.

He smoothed greasy dark hair away from his beady-eyed face and licked cracked lips, exposing yellowed, crooked teeth. He was big. Twice Elijah's size. The same height but a lot heavier than her ex. Big bones, muscle, and fat. Fat that lapped over his belt. She'd even seen the white rolls when he changed shirts, from a dirty flannel button-up to some kind of sweater. She wished she had a sweater, but he hadn't offered her one. She was still in the T-shirt she'd put on to wear to school, and the way he was staring at her chest told her that the cold was getting to her and that he was a perv. The only heat was coming from a woodburning stove in the corner. A pot of something gamey and disgusting bubbled on its flat surface. Her mom's kitchen was like that after her stepdad went on a hunting spree. Steam rose from the rattling lid.

Stop staring at me.

"Where am I?" she whispered.

He moved closer and touched her cheek with cold, rough fingers. "Your new home. Our home."

Her home didn't look like this. Wasn't cold like this. Didn't have needlepoint versions of the Ten Commandments hanging in ten individual frames, with the only other decoration being pictures of white Jesus and some wooden crosses. "I don't understand."

"You don't now, but someday you will. I saved you from the filthy slaver who was disrespecting you."

"What?" That was crazy talk. Filthy slaver? Saved her?

"You're safe here. I will honor you and protect you."

"I don't need—"

"You will be my bride, my lovely Sue. Now and until death do us part."

"I don't know you."

"You are the chosen one."

"I'm too young to get married."

"Do you bleed each month?"

She wanted to lie, but his nod told her he'd already seen the answer on her face.

"You're a woman."

"No... Besides, I have a boyfriend."

"He's not worthy of you. Those corporeal relationships are fleeting. The feelings aren't real and will soon fade."

She shook her head violently.

He smiled at her like she was a little girl. "I hate to rush things, but I'm afraid we don't have much time. I have somewhere to be. We're going to exchange vows now, in front of God, so that he will bless our union."

Maybe if he was leaving, she could run away. *Please leave. Please leave.* "No! I can't!"

Something sharp jabbed her between the shoulder blades.

"What?" She tried to spin, to see what it was. Was someone else in the cabin with them?

The mountain of a man caught her wrist, kept her facing him.

"I—what was that? I think I'm bleeding."

"No matter. It's time."

The sharp thing pressed against her skin, not breaking it, but the threat was there.

"Repeat after me. I take you to be my lawfully wedded husband."

"No! Please no!"

The sharpness penetrated her skin. She fell to her knees, screaming. She raked the wood floor with her nails, looking for something to grab. There was nothing. She reached for a table leg. The man yanked her back to her feet. She dragged the table with her a few inches, but her grasp broke.

The man was scary calm. His fingers dug into her arms, though. "Say it."

"I... I... can't!"

"Say it," he roared.

His breath nearly gagged her.

The pain sliced down her back. Someone was cutting her open. With a knife. Or a razor. Or... or... something.

She sobbed and writhed against the man's grip. "Oh, my fucking God that hurts."

The pain before was nothing—NOTHING—compared to what she felt as the sharp object pushed in and twisted in her back.

She went limp, moaning and retching. Bile spilled from her mouth to the floor. To her feet. When had she last eaten that her stomach was so empty? *I'm disgusting. Maybe he'll stop now.*

But he didn't seem to notice. "Thou shalt not take the name of the Lord thy God in vain!"

* * *

Everything went black. And then it wasn't black anymore. She was lying on the floor, her head on the wood. Big feet in work boots were inches from her face. She was dizzy. Nauseous again. She didn't know how much time had passed. Maybe she'd fainted. Maybe she was losing it.

The man put a hand under her elbow. "Let me help you up."

She was too scared now to resist. She let him lift her. When she was on her feet, she swayed. *I don't know how much more of this I can take.*

"I don't like seeing you hurt. But legal matrimony is the only way I can protect you. Please do as you've been instructed. Say the words."

It was hard to talk through her hiccups and tears. "Are you going to kill me?"

He scowled. "Thou shalt not kill."

If it's the only way to get through this, what does it matter if I say it? I don't mean it. I say things I don't mean all the time. To Samuel. To Mom. Even to my friends. I can do this. It means nothing. "Can you repeat it?"

"I take you to be my lawfully wedded husband."

"What is your... what do I call you?"

"You will call me your husband."

"No, I mean what is your name?"

He stood taller. "You can call me the Mountain Man."

She couldn't do it. She couldn't use that name. Afraid of whatever, whoever was behind her, she didn't cross her eyes or her legs or her fingers or toes. Just choked out, "I take you to be my lawfully wedded husband."

"And I take you, beautiful Sue, to be my lawfully wedded wife. Forsaking all others. Now you say that."

Tears spilled and ran down her face and off her chin. She felt their wetness on her chest. "Forsaking all others."

"In sickness and in health."

This can't really be happening. "In sickness and in health."

"As long as we both shall live."

"As long as we both shall live." But how long would that really be, with this crazy man and whoever was literally stabbing her in the back?

"And now the important part. Sue, you know the commandment, 'Thou shalt not bear false witness'? You know what it means?"

"No."

"It means that our God has commanded you not to lie. And the very worst is if you lie *to* Him. Do you understand?"

"Yes, sir."

"All right, then repeat after me. So help me God. That means that everything you've just said is a promise to God."

Lightheaded, she fell forward, hands on knees, back heaving. "So... so... so help me... G-g-g-god."

He nodded, beaming. "So help me God. In the eyes of the Lord, we are now husband and wife. Or almost. There's just one thing left to do to make it official before I go."

Sue hugged her arms around her chest, feeling the blood trickling down her back and sides as she stretched the skin. *No. This can't be happening to me.*

But the hand gripping her wrist was hot and strong and all too real.

TWELVE

FIVE YEARS EARLIER

"Skeeter Rawlins, have a seat." The short man set his big hat brim up on the credenza behind his desk. With the Kermit voice and bowlegs, Sheriff Coltrane Fentworth reminded Skeeter of a frog.

Skeeter lowered himself into the chair. He'd exchanged a handshake with the sheriff, and he was sure he'd just transferred a load of sweat to the other man's palm. He watched to see if Fentworth would wipe his hands on his pants. He didn't. He took it as a good sign. Just like the fact that the sheriff had invited him in. Skeeter was going to get the job. He knew it. He'd been so sure when the sheriff called to set up the meeting that Skeeter had given his buddy the thumbs up on investing with him. He'd even mailed him the check. He was officially on the ground floor with one of the hottest companies his buddy had ever seen and on his way to making big bucks.

Fentworth took his own seat. He tented his hands, fingertips drumming each other. "I wanted to take a moment to express my thanks to you for applying to work for the department. You've been quite diligent in your follow-up."

"The Army taught me that, sir."

"The Army, yes. Very good. I'm going to be straight with you, son. You failed our medical exam. We can't hire you."

Skeeter couldn't process what the sheriff was saying. It didn't make sense. "But I'm in good shape."

"It's your back. I'm sorry to say it's his opinion that based on the injury you sustained and your current condition that it just won't stand up to the rigors of being a deputy."

"But I'm healing up good. I'm fine." Sometimes his back went out on him, it was true. When it did, he couldn't walk for a few days. But it hadn't happened during the exam.

The sheriff scribbled on a piece of paper then tore it off the yellow legal pad. "Here's what I recommend. There are a couple of companies in the area that use security guards. Call this fella here and see if they won't let you put in an application. I'm not promising anything. They still require a medical exam. You'd have a better shot at it. Or almost any other job. But we can't hire you here. I'm sorry, but that's the bottom line."

It was like Skeeter was teetering on the edge of a well. That the piece of paper Fentworth was extending was the lifeline that was supposed to save him. He leaned over and snatched it. But he still heard an echo in his ears and the sensation of falling as he walked out of the sheriff's office.

THIRTEEN

As soon as the disgusting pig man—she refused to call him her husband—was gone, Sue started thinking about how to escape. She was on her back on a wooden table, naked, without a mattress, a sheet, a blanket, a pillow. Nothing. Cables bound her by the ankles to the table, biting into her skin. The wound on her back burned and occasionally she could feel it bleeding. The worst pain was in her mind, though. The pictures flashing through it. The memories she'd spend the rest of her life trying to forget. His smell. His heavy body. His awful breath. She wished she could turn her brain completely off. She needed it to get out of this awful place, though. When she was home, she'd numb it with whatever it took. Elijah always had something for that.

The Mountain Man had been in such a hurry and so focused on the gross things he did to her that he hadn't noticed her stealing his pocketknife. Not stealing it really. It had fallen out of his pocket and into her hand. She palmed it and, after he stood up, slid it under her thigh. Then he got ready to go and kissed her goodbye like they were in love or something before he cabled her to the table and left. As if. She knew what love was. She'd been in love. So in love it had taken her breath away and made her take crazy chances. When she'd lost him—when he'd broken things off with her—she'd nearly killed herself more than once. Still thought about it sometimes. She'd tried dating other guys to make him jealous. She'd really believed he would change his mind when he saw her with other guys. Especially a creep like Elijah.

But he hadn't. No matter how many notes she wrote and stashed where only he would find them. No matter how many texts she sent with sexy pictures. No matter how many times she said she'd kill herself or begged or threatened. He insisted he was too old for her. That it was wrong.

But he wasn't nearly as old as this gross Mountain Man. Wrong was what *he* did to her. She'd come close to using the knife on him when he was on top of her. There were so many places she would have liked to stab him. To cut him. But she was more scared of the person who'd cut her during that awful, fake ceremony than she was of him. For all she knew, they were watching, hidden somewhere. By the time she hurt the Mountain Man, they'd be on her. She'd pretended like she'd fainted when the Mountain Man was on her.

A loud engine started outside. Soon the sound faded. The Mountain Man was gone. It was one on one now. Her against the mystery person. She had to be ready to use her knife. To escape. Because no one could stay awake all the time. No one could hold it forever. She would get chances. First, to figure out how to unfasten her ankles. Then to make a run for it while it was still daylight.

Soon after he left, the other person approached her. She didn't see them. She *heard* them. She heard them *breathing*. It was a rattling, a gasping. Wet and heavy. Like Darth Vader with pneumonia.

A finger poked her. She didn't move. Then a hand was rubbing something cold and wet on her. All over her. *All* over her, which made her want to scream. Then the sponge bath stopped. A soft tip moved across her skin. It smelled like Sharpie. Whatever happened next, she wasn't sure, because a cloth was draped over her face, and she drifted away. Blessedly, blissfully to somewhere else.

* * *

When she woke, she was alone. She knew she was because the weird, heavy breathing she'd heard earlier was gone. Was a hooded figure watching her from the window though? Were they standing outside the door listening for the slightest sound, ready to dart back in and slice her to ribbons?

It didn't matter. She had to move quickly. She pushed herself to a seated position. Her arm hurt and she looked to see what was wrong with it. She gasped. Someone had tattooed her arm. Her skin was red under the black ink, which read 1P31. Or IP3I. Whatever. She had to *move*. She turned her attention to her ankles. The cables were snug but not tight. It looked like the cables went into holes in the wood and fastened on the other side. She was so glad for the years of dance lessons and gymnastics at the community center where her teachers had called her Stretch Armstrong. She was freakishly flexible. Less than she'd been at nine, but still enough that she was able to bend forward and grasp the cable. If only she hadn't also been freakishly tall, she would have stuck with it, but she was knocking on six feet. Instead, she spiked volleyballs, which she didn't love but might get her into college someday. And mugged racehorses for the Indian Relays, which wouldn't get her a scholarship but was the most fun she'd ever had in her life.

If she survived the Mountain Man and the mystery person.

She pulled on the cable holding her right ankle. She needed

slack to get her foot free. Slack or to cut the cable itself. Opening the knife, she sawed at the cable from behind her ankle, where it wasn't touching her. The knife cut through the plastic on the outside quickly but then rasped against metal.

"Crap, crap," she said aloud but softly.

There'd be no way she could saw through that. She closed the knife and secured it under her leg. She clutched the rough plywood edge of the table, across her legs with her left hand on the right side. She pulled with her long arms to deepen the stretch, then she felt around on the wood underneath her ankle. What was holding the cable in place? When the Mountain Man had put the ankle restraints on her, he'd adjusted them. Whatever he'd adjusted, she could un-adjust. As her fingers slapped and crawled, a splinter wedged itself under her fingernail. She ignored the sharp pain. Willed her body to bend further. Stretch farther. Then the very tips of her fingers touched the long tails of the cable.

And she felt it.

Something metal. Not a screw. Some kind of clasp. She pulled harder, straining her back, hips, butt, thighs, even her arm and shoulder. It was enough. Her fingers locked on the clasp. She dug her pointer fingertip around the edges, trying to picture it. It was like a sideways triangle. A skinny one with the fat end sort of open and the pointy end shut tight like a mouthful of teeth. She had an idea. Instead of trying to pry it open, she pushed the fat end. The closed pointy end released for a moment and let out some cable. She gained an inch of beautiful slack around her ankle. She rotated her foot. It was enough slack to pull her foot out.

She gasped with excitement. No time to celebrate, though. She had to free both feet or this was worse than worthless. The mystery person would find her and, well, she didn't want to think about what would happen.

She changed sides, repeating the process of stretching,

finding the clasp, pushing it, opening it, and loosening the binding on her feet.

Oh, my god. Oh, my god! She wanted to weep with hope and joy and desperation.

Just before she pulled her foot out, the doorknob turned.

She stuck her other foot back through the cable, let go of the table, and flopped onto her back, eyes closed. Had she been fast enough?

The door scraped open, then shut loudly. Slammed, really. Like the monster who'd come in wanted her to wake up. Wanted a reaction.

Footsteps approached the table. The horrible breathing noise advanced on her. She felt sick like the time she'd drank too much Scotch with Elijah and barfed all over herself and him. Hot breath hit her face. Even worse than the Mountain Man. A smell like rotten meat. She knew rotten meat. Their game freezer had burned out last year and her mom and stepdad had forced her to clean it out. She had—no lie—vomited then.

She could not throw up now. She had to pretend to still be passed out even though she felt like she had her head in a bag of stink.

A finger touched her face, then the person pinched her nostrils, cutting off her nose breathing. Nothing had ever been harder than holding still was at that moment. But she switched to mouth breathing. It was better anyway. The smell wasn't as bad that way.

The hand moved away from her face. Footsteps receded. For several minutes, Sue heard noises. Things opening and shutting. Clattering. Thumps. The doorknob turning, the door scraping open again, the door closing.

Sue didn't move. For long seconds she held her position, listening.

And she heard the breathing. The rattling, rasping, gasping, sucking wet breathing. They had faked leaving. Sue felt like her whole body was trembling. She'd been so close to sitting up and making a break for it.

The door opened and closed again.

This time, there were no breathing sounds. She opened her eyes, turned her head, looked for a face peering back in a window.

Nothing.

Whimpering, more scared than ever, she sat up and worked one foot out, then the other. The table underneath where her ankles had been attached was stained maroon, almost brown. She shuddered. Flicking the knife open, she gripped it in her hand and ran to the windows one by one, searching for a person.

She saw no one.

She had to go now, while she had a chance. She didn't see any vehicles, although she'd heard the Mountain Man leave in one earlier, so she'd be on foot. Clothes would be good. Shoes would be even better. She looked around but didn't see hers. She opened a trunk by the foot of one of the two beds. Women's dresses. Ugly. Like prairie style ugly. Old and worn. She didn't care. She jerked one over her head. For a minute she searched for shoes, then gave up. It would be quieter to run barefoot anyway.

Making sure she had a good grip on her knife, she closed her eyes and sucked in the biggest breath she could, then opened the door and checked that the coast was still clear. It was surprisingly cold out and smelled like pine trees, which made sense, because forest was all around her. She saw no one, so she pulled the door shut behind her and stepped outside.

Dusk was falling. It wasn't ideal, but she had no choice. She had no idea where she was and which way to go, but she decided to follow the two-track away from the house. This would have been the road the Mountain Man left on. If he came back while she was on it, she was in deep, deep trouble.

She took off running, as fast as she could. Before she'd gotten a few steps, something hard hit her in the back of the head. It knocked her to the ground.

No!

She scrambled on her hands and knees to her feet and ran again, without looking back. Was it her imagination, or could she hear the wet, sucking breaths behind her? The skirt was slowing her down, so she gathered the long folds of fabric in her hands. Rocks thudded to the ground on either side of her. That's what had hit her head. A rock. They were chasing her. Throwing things at her.

Don't stop for anything!!!

The road was getting gravellier. The stones hurt her feet and were slowing her down. She had to run on softer ground. She cut across a meadow. Her feet didn't like it any better. She ran through a patch of snow, over prickly grass humps, through mud, and into the forest on the other side where pinecones and rocks tripped her up. They hurt her feet, a lot. She wanted to cry, but she didn't dare. Rocks were still pelting the ground, but not as close to her. She was doing good. She was pulling away. If she could get far enough in front so she could lose them, she could rest and figure out where she was.

Darkness was falling fast. She could barely see to keep from slamming into trees. It was lighter ahead, and she pushed toward the light. If she could break from the trees, maybe she would get a clear view of the terrain. Then she could figure out the best direction to take. She pushed harder, faster, digging deep for her reserves, her lungs burning harder than they ever did running wind sprints for volleyball practice. If the coach could see her now, how surprised she would be. Sue wasn't known for being the hardest worker on the team.

But no one had ever made her run for her life before.

With only a few yards to go to the light, she snuck a glance behind her. In the distance, she thought she saw a form behind her, but it was impossible to be sure. She turned back around just as her foot missed the ground. Missed it completely, and then she was jumping off the high dive at the pool in Buffalo, which felt completely wrong.

Suddenly, it felt like a collision, and then, nothing at all.

FOURTEEN

Delaney put her hand on the elbow of the hiker, or she thought she did. She mostly got a handful of the shock blankets the traumatized woman was wrapped in. The woman's pupils were so round and large that Delaney couldn't identify their color. Her nose and eyes were red. Tears had ravaged her cheeks.

Her tranquil Friday morning on the mountain—she'd been solo trekking—was anything but. "It was symbolic for me to get an early start. You know—a clean slate. A new beginning. A fresh start." Her lip twitched. She was holding back more tears. "I've just been through a divorce. Then a recovery program. Moved here from Colorado. It all felt right. And then—and then..." Her words petered out. Her lips quivered. Her jaw flexed.

"It's okay. Take your time."

Beside her, Leo was nodding. He looked hollow-eyed. Like he'd had a late night involving cocktails and another flavor of the week gumball from the dating app machine. She brushed the uncomfortable thought away.

"I wasn't paying attention to the trail because of the sunrise. It was like the sky was on fire," the hiker whispered. "I nearly stepped on her before I saw her. At first, I thought it was a downed tree. Then I saw it was a girl. I assumed she was asleep for a second. But there was no way. The mud and cold. Her neck. Her legs. Her head." She touched her own head on the last words. "I didn't know what to do. I-I-I checked her, you know, to see if she was breathing or had a pulse. Then I ran back to my car and called 911."

"Thank you. That was very helpful. Did you see anyone else out here this morning?"

"There were trucks and trailers in the parking lot. Empty when I was there. I heard some engine noises while I was hiking. People going up and down the road, I think. No one on the trail."

"Did anything—besides finding the girl—seem unusual?" Leo asked, his voice empathetic but professional.

"No." Tears spilled from her eyes. "Everything was peaceful. Nature. Birds. Like nothing had happened. It doesn't make any sense."

Delaney understood how wrong it could feel for the world to move on as if nothing had happened, when the very worst of things had happened.

Leo said, "Thank you. I think that's all the questions we have for now. We have your contact information, and you have ours. We appreciate you sticking around to talk to us."

Delaney added, "And we're very sorry this happened to you. Do you have somewhere you can go? Someone you can be with?"

"I'll call my friend." She walked a few steps back toward the parking lot a mile away. "Do you want your blanket?"

"No. That's okay. You keep it."

The woman nodded and disappeared around a curve in the trail. Leo crossed the yellow crime scene tape to stand near the body. Delaney joined him, careful with her footing in case of evidence, but she found she could barely stand to look at the girl. Sue Wiley's battered face was clearly recognizable. Her long dark hair was caked in blood. To Delaney, she seemed disturbingly similar to Kat.

Leo let out a shuddering breath. "No doubt on identification this time. This isn't the type of clothing I expected her to be wearing, though." Leo put his hands on his hip. "Does Kat have anything like this? Or could it be cosplay?"

Flowered fabric bunched around Sue's waist, voluminous and worn. The bodice was loose with a high neckline. The sleeves hung long, all the way to the wrist. "This doesn't seem like any cosplay I've seen. That tends to be more cartoonish. Or at least more modern. Some girls are into prairie style right now, but this dress is worn out and doesn't fit her."

"No underclothing. Would she have worn a bra?" Sue's body was nude beneath the dress. The lack of panties was obvious with her dress ridden up. Her braless state was revealed by a tear across the chest.

"She was old enough and developed enough for a bra. But she's also missing her shoes. Look at her feet. Toenails ripped off. Blood on the soles."

He nodded, thinking, then gestured at the rock cliff above the trail. "It's surprising there aren't more falls here."

"There was that young woman last year. The one who fell while watching the sunrise."

He winced. "I remember. She died. Very sad."

"But this is odd even for a fall. She should never have been up there dressed like this."

"Agreed."

Delaney held her eyes closed for a minute, allowing a moment of sadness in. The death of young people somehow always cut deepest and didn't get easier with experience, at least not for her. "I can't believe she's dead. Her poor mother." Peg Littlewolf had killed herself in the wake of losing her daughter. How would Jayla Russo react? Delaney would have given almost anything to have found Sue and returned her to her home before this happened. She couldn't help but feel they'd failed her.

Leo rubbed his eyes. She could see he was fighting emotion, too. "That isn't going to be an easy conversation."

"And another Crow girl. Two in one week, both on the eastern side of the mountains and ending up like this."

"Marilyn was five miles south of here."

"Sue disappears and then turns up dead in a dress that isn't hers with no underclothing or shoes, falling from a mountain cliff she isn't dressed for, the same week Marilyn dies in a similar fashion near here. They're connected all right."

"I hear you." He came to stand beside her.

Delaney felt her emotions building layer upon layer. "And there's still the matter of the horrific abuse to Marilyn."

"Yes. We'll see what Dr. Watson thinks about Sue on that front as well. Meanwhile, I've got to update the FBI's team and help coordinate a search. At least this time we don't have a mudslide working against us. That search hasn't turned up anything."

She went on almost like he hadn't spoken. "We have to stop the abuser, Leo. And make sure this doesn't happen to other girls." *Like my own beloved daughters. Their friends. Any girls.*

FIFTEEN

The Mountain Man threw open the door and pounded inside. "Where are you?"

There was no answer.

"I know you're here somewhere!" The snuffling, rattling sound of heavy breathing drew him behind one of the beds. *There you are.* "Get up. Get up and face me."

The figure hunkered tighter on the floor, curled into a ball.

"I heard it on the news. You let her escape. No—you didn't let her. You drove her away, didn't you?"

Raw sobs—a metal file rasping across iron—rose from the hunched back.

"What did you do to her? What did you do to my bride?!"

The body uncurled and scuttled across the floor, trying to escape him.

He blocked their forward progress with a huge, booted foot. "You know the punishment." He opened the standing closet and extracted a scourge. The multi-thong leather device was the right tool for the job. He ripped off his own shirt, then closed his eyes and said, "Don't forget, you're the one who made me do this."

He flicked the scourge to get a feel for it, then began the flogging. With each thud of leather against flesh, they moaned with him.

"My bride," he whispered. "My God-given bride."

When his strength was spent, he collapsed to the floor beside the other figure and wept.

SIXTEEN

Delaney dragged ass into the station on Monday. After the awful notification visit with Jayla Russo about her daughter's death on Friday, Delaney had gotten home late to relieve Skeeter. She'd asked him how he was and told him he was worrying Kat, but mostly he'd blown her off. For the rest of the weekend, she'd balanced working on Sue's case—joining in the search for evidence, interviewing classmates, contacting BIA law enforcement for the Crow reservation, updating her MMU contact about Marilyn's case possibly dovetailing with Sue's, and coordinating with Leo about the arrival of the feds—with some time with Kat and Carrie. Unfortunately, the call to the BIA had been a bust. Or fortunately, depending on point of view. They didn't have helpful information, but they also hadn't had any similar cases, which was a positive for the girls on the reservation. Clint had checked in with her, too, and his contacts in tribal leadership echoed what she'd heard from BIA.

Delaney felt so lucky. Both of her daughters had been kidnapped before. Both had nearly died. But they hadn't. They were with her now, and she was going to enjoy every single second she could get with them. Carrie especially was traumatized by recent events. Delaney had been charmed when Carrie had friends over to game Friday night and that Kat had wanted to talk endlessly about Freddy and Ashley. *If I hear Taylor Swift sing "You Belong With Me" one more time, though...* Saturday afternoon, she'd let Carrie drive the three of them to Billings in Shotgun Shelly to shop for summer clothes, where they'd caught a movie in a real theater and indulged in hamburgers, fries, and milkshakes at The Burger Dive. On Sunday evening, they'd hiked up to their special hilltop spot at the homestead after Delaney had finished working and picnicked while crazy Dudley chased butterflies and his own piggy tail.

She should be feeling at least a little refreshed now. But as soon as the girls had bounced off to bed the night before, the carousel and happy music had jerked to a stop. Grim thoughts of Marilyn and Sue had taken over. She'd tossed and turned all night, woken by nightmares when she did fall asleep, sometimes about Marilyn and Sue, but sometimes about Kat and Carrie, too.

She stopped in the breakroom to top off the coffee in her travel mug. Sipping as she walked, she was almost to her desk when Clara's voice stopped her.

"Delaney? I have a young man out here who wants to talk to someone about Sue Wiley. Leo's not in yet. You're working on the case, right?"

As was the police department, but she didn't say so. She was so hungry to work on this case that she almost snarled her answer. "Yes. Who is it?" She took another slug of coffee.

"Elijah Campbell."

Delaney nearly spit out her brew. The too-old-for-Sue boyfriend she'd been trying to track down for days. "Put him in the conference room. I'll be right there."

"Of course." Clara lowered her voice. "He seems very upset."

"Okay. Thanks."

Delaney fast-walked to her desk, texting Leo to join her if he arrived in time. She put away her purse and hung her jacket on the back of her chair, then took her coffee, phone, notepad, and pen into the conference room.

A pale, lanky teenager slouched in front of the pictures of dead sheriffs, chewing a thumbnail. He was wearing a ball cap with the brim popped, and when he turned to look at her, she was struck first by his acne scars, then by the tattoos up his neck. A flannel shirt hung open revealing a white muscle T but no muscles. A skull and crossbones hung from a chain connecting his belt loop to something in his pocket. A wallet, maybe.

"Elijah Campbell?" She set her things on the table and motioned for him to take a seat. "I'm Deputy Investigator Delaney Pace."

He sat, hunched over, and nodded. His body bounced slightly. *Jiggling a knee,* she thought.

Delaney took her time walking to the credenza. "Want some water? Or a coffee?" Most kids drank it these days, a change from when she was in high school. Maybe in the bigger cities they had even back then. But there hadn't been a trendy coffee shop on every corner in Kearny.

"Nah. I'm good."

She grabbed a bottle of water and set it in the middle of the table anyway. "You've been hard to find."

"I-I'm sorry. I was wrecked that Sue was gone. I thought maybe she'd, uh, run off."

Which doesn't explain where you were the morning she disappeared. Delaney decided to follow this kid wherever he took the interview, though. To just let it flow. "Is that what you think happened?"

"She talked about getting out of here a lot. We all did. I'm leaving the second I graduate." He patted his front shirt pocket, which sagged with the weight of a pack of cigarettes. Old-school cigs, not the popular e-cig kind. But he caught himself, seeming to realize without being told he couldn't light up in here. "I was really into her." He wiped dry eyes. "If she hadn't—if she'd lived, I would have stayed and waited for her."

"You think she would have run off without you?"

"She hated her stepfather. She had some friend who moved somewhere in California. I thought maybe she'd just taken a break to go see her."

"What's the friend's name?"

"She moved away before I met Sue. I mean, she's told me about her and stuff, but I don't remember her name."

"Do you know where in California she lives?"

"Nah."

"So, now that you know Sue is dead, what do you think happened?"

"Man, I have no idea. I'm, like, freaking out. And she was here this whole time. Or not far away."

"Did she have a reason to be up in the mountains that you know of?"

"No. She wasn't into nature and shit. She wanted to move to New York City."

"What about you? Are you into nature?"

"Hardly. I want to live somewhere with a good skate park."

"How long had you and Sue been together?"

"We've been hanging out a couple of months."

"Were you exclusive?"

"Hell, yeah. I would have crushed any dude who came near her. She was so fine. They could look, but they couldn't touch."

"Did some try to get close to her?"

"All the time. White and Indian. Grown men especially. She was like a geezer magnet."

"Any whose names you remember?"

"You mean other than her teachers and all her stepdad's skeezy friends?"

"How did she handle it?"

"She just ignored them. She was used to it."

"Did she date anyone before you?" The girl had only been fourteen years old, but it didn't hurt to ask.

"A few guys, but no steadies. When I got with her, she was pure as the driven snow."

"So, the two of you were having sex?"

"Like that's any of your business."

Delaney drilled his eyes with hers.

He finally squirmed and said, "Yeah. But we used protection. I didn't want to knock her up or anything like that."

"Did you guys get along?"

"Yeah, I mean, that's why we were hanging out."

"How about fights? Did she fight with you much?"

"Not really."

"Did you fight with her? Like about other guys?"

He shrugged.

"Is that a yes?"

He frowned. "Are you trying to say I was jealous and killed her? Because I didn't. I loved her. And I haven't seen her since I dropped her off at her place the night before she disappeared."

"I'm gathering information, because I don't understand why I wasn't able to talk to you before she died. In case something you tell me helps us understand what happened to her. And for your sake I'm hoping none of it would have saved her if you'd talked to me before, because it would suck to have to live with that. For you."

He jumped to his feet. "I'm not the one you should be talking to. I only came in because my rents said you've been up in their grills about me, and it was going to look bad if I didn't. I've been at my dawg John's house. We were skipping school the day Sue disappeared and then I just hunkered down when I heard about it because I felt like shit that she was gone." He stalked toward the door. "But I don't have to talk to you, so I'm out of here."

"John who?"

He flipped her off. "Rails. John Rails. Feel free to call him. He'll tell you."

Then the important part of what Elijah had said hit her. "Who is the one I should be talking to, Elijah?"

He grabbed the door handle and yanked.

"You loved Sue. I hear you. I get that. So, tell me who I should be talking to."

At the last second he turned and caught the door, sticking his head back in. "Nelly Hillmont. This is Indian shit, lady. Mark my words. Indian shit."

* * *

Delaney took the offered visitor badge at the middle school office. "Thank you." She peeled the backing off and pressed it onto her uniform shirt. Beside her, Leo did the same thing. After she'd updated him on her meeting with Elijah, they'd hurried over to the school together.

"You're welcome, ma'am." The girl making the badges was familiar, but Delaney didn't think she was in Kat's grade. Probably a ninth grader.

With the security hurdles and hoops these days, it seemed funny to Delaney that the person printing and passing out the badges was a minor. She made a mental note to follow up on the topic with the administration. Kat still had two more years at this school.

Principal Rickets ushered Delaney and Leo into his office. His back was almost as stiff as the gray buzz cut hair on his head. *A reflection of his bubbly personality.* "Deputy Pace. Sheriff Palmer. An unexpected pleasure." His voice wasn't warm. He and Delaney'd had run-ins before, most recently over Kat, and dating back to Delaney's own school days in his biology class.

"Good day, sir," Leo said, his voice solemn. By prior agreement, Delaney would be taking the lead.

"I assume there's a purpose for your visit."

Delaney hadn't given him any information on the phone. "Principal Rickets." She sat before he'd offered, in a too-small chair facing his desk and a wall of bookcases. Leo took the matching one beside her. Her nose wrinkled a little from the smell of the place. Bleach and deodorizers failing to cover the odor of dirty gym socks and adolescent boy sweat. She hadn't liked it as a kid and still didn't now. "Do you have a student by the name of Nelly Hillmont?"

His eyes cut down and to the left. He pulled at his lower lip. "Uh, why do you ask?"

"Her name came up. You know we're investigating the death of Sue Wiley?"

"I thought it was an accident? That she fell off a cliff? The girl lived on the edge. From what I heard, she ran with older boys and there was talk of alcohol and drugs."

"Nelly Hillmont?"

"Oh. Yes. She's in the ninth grade."

"Great. What can you tell me about her and her family?" Delaney could have just asked to meet with Nelly but chose not to. While she had the legal right to talk to her alone unless she considered her a suspect, Delaney wanted a responsible adult present. Ideally, that meant her parents, if they were available and not the types to ruin the interview. Principal Rickets would suffice if necessary. "Just general background."

He got up and shut the door then sat again, lowering his voice. "Nelly is a very angry young woman." His head dropped, then he opened a drawer in his desk and pulled out a file. He waved it. "Fighting. Destruction of school property. Truancy. The only reason she hasn't been expelled is because her parents are even angrier than she is."

"What do you mean?"

"They thwart every attempt to hold her accountable for her actions. They blame everything and everyone but her. Her father can be quite frightening. And litigious. The teachers don't dare fail her. Not just because of her parents, but because if they do, we might have to keep her here longer, when we are —thank the good Lord above—done with her at the end of this month when she graduates middle school."

Delaney didn't like hearing her daughter was going to a school where the administrators allowed themselves to be bullied into keeping a dangerous student on campus. But she'd get nothing from Rickets if she went on a mama bear rampage. She needed him to sit in on a meeting with Nelly—no way was Delaney going to ask him to call the parents now. "Did Nelly have a beef with Sue Wiley?"

He threw the file on his desk. "She had a beef with everyone. But I had heard she and Sue had a few particular disagreements."

She remembered Elijah's parting words. *This is Indian shit, lady. Mark my words. Indian shit.* "Over what?"

"The story I heard was that Sue was an up-and-comer for the Indian Relay Races, which Nelly thought she had locked up."

Delaney was a huge admirer of both the equine and human athletes in the Indian Relays. Each team consisted of three half-wild racehorses, one bareback rider, one horse catcher, aka mugger, and two holders. For horse nations like the Crow, the sport kept their heritage alive. The Indian Relay is modeled on the practice of warriors changing out their mounts for fresh horses during battle. Half the local Crow kids had relay dreams, although until recently it had been mostly a male sport except for "maiden" races, which were supposedly less dangerous. But lately the girls wanted to be like Logan Red Crow of the Siksika Nation. Girls were infiltrating boys-only teams, and some events featured a women's relay now. She'd taken Leo to the

WYO rodeo the previous summer to introduce him to the sport, so she was pretty sure he'd follow the conversation now.

"Are Sue and Nelly riders?"

"Believe it or not, they're muggers."

The mugger was the toughest member of the team without the glory that went to the rider. If all went well in a race, a rider rode one horse bareback around a racetrack, then leapt onto the back of a second horse and did it again, and then again onto a third horse for the last lap. The transition from horse to horse was a terrifying, dangerous spectacle of timing, luck, and the fortitude of the mugger, who had the job of bringing the running horse to a stop so that it didn't keep the rider from mounting the next horse or, worse, breaking free into the track and causing a high-speed pile-up of horses and riders.

After what Delaney had heard about Nelly, she wasn't surprised to hear she aspired to be a mugger, but this was a revelation about Sue. She modified her image of Sue to include athletic, brave, and tough.

Delaney said, "Wow. Did she beat Nelly out of a spot?"

"She did. Now, it's only a teen girl team. Not a championship team. But Nelly sees it as her future."

"And this was recently?"

"In the last few weeks."

"I need to talk to Nelly."

He blew out a long breath. "Could you do it offsite?"

"I was hoping I could get you to sit with us and do it here."

He was already shaking his head and actually scooted his chair back. "No. No way. I'm sorry, Laney, but that's not safe for me or the school."

She hated him reverting to her childhood nickname. There was a lot of heavy baggage in that one word. "Would there be anyone else here who would have the balls to do it?"

Red exploded across his face. "That's not fair."

"Sue Wiley is dead."

He pointed at the door. "This is not the police station, and I don't work for you."

Leo cleared his throat. "Sheriff's department."

"Whichever it is is immaterial, Sheriff. If the two of you aren't here to arrest her, or to talk to her alone, then I can't help you."

Delaney stood and brushed off the legs of her pants, even though they weren't dirty. "Rickets, calm down. No one has a gun to your head. You were helpful. We appreciate that. But think about it. Two girls dead in a week."

"In accidents."

"You want to bet the lives of more girls on that?" She crossed her arms. "Both were your students before they disappeared. It seems to me like that's a much greater risk to your students than just making Nelly and her parents mad."

Rickets looked down at his desk, fingertips pressed on Nelly's thick file. "Have a nice day."

Leo got up. "You, too."

He and Delaney marched out. She held her head high, but inside, she was seething.

SEVENTEEN

Leo looked across the desk at Delaney half an hour later, shaking his head. Like her, he was bothered about what was going on at the middle school. Freddy was in Nelly's class. "What do you want to do about contacting Nelly's family to set up an interview?"

"I thought we could surprise them together after she's home from school."

"Parents might not be there."

"If so, we can regroup, but I'd like to try to talk to her as soon as possible. Maybe six? Right at dinner time might be our best bet."

"We'll do it your way."

"Only thing is I pulled her dad up in the system. A few arrests for disorderly and one for assault for a bar fight. Supposedly, he's a roughneck. Mom works in a dive bar."

"The Loading Shed?"

"Ha ha." The Pace's bar wasn't upscale, and the local nickname for it was the Loading Shed, as in "where cowboys go to get loaded." In actuality, it was named after loafing sheds, which are the three-sided shelters livestock often loaf around in. "No, the other dive bar. It's downtown. The Moonbeam. Which is way too fancy a name for the place. Draws a rowdy crowd."

"Sounds like we need backup."

"That's what I was thinking."

"Who are you and what have you done with Delaney?"

"Double ha ha."

"I'll extend an olive branch to the chief and see if she wants to send officers with us. It'll give me a chance to update her as well."

"Great." Delaney stood to go as his phone rang.

He answered on the first ring. "Sheriff Palmer."

"Dr. Watson. I'm ready to update you on Sue Wiley."

"I'll put you on speaker with Delaney." He probably should have patched Chief Yellowtail in as well, but he decided the call would go better without her. He would just include this information in her update.

"Hello, Dr. Watson," Delaney said.

"Delaney, you can call me Louise if you'd like."

"I know, and you're sweet."

"What about me, Dr. Watson?" Leo winked at Delaney.

"Ask me in a year."

"Would you like us to come to you?"

"You can buy me lunch. I'm cheap. I'll take Buns in the Barn."

"See you there in fifteen."

On the walk to Delaney's truck, Leo said, "I still don't have my truck back. I'm in the mood to arrive alive. What do you say?"

She rolled her eyes at him and tossed him the keys. Leo grinned.

The drive to Buns in the Barn was peaceful and involved no terror or white-knuckle grips. Leo carefully parked, then they walked to the restaurant door. He reached it first and held it open. One thing he appreciated about Delaney was that she was secure enough not to be offended by the gesture. But if he started the list of things he liked about her, he'd get sidetracked. And right now, he wanted all his focus on the tiny woman standing to the side of the front counter and what she had to tell them. Dr. Watson. He waved.

"I saw you drive up. I've already ordered," she said. "But I told them you were paying. Just let me wash my hands and I'll meet you at a table."

"Sounds good," Delaney said.

A very pregnant young woman in a red smock looked between them, seeming to confirm that Leo wasn't going to object. Her hand was poised over the register.

"Add chicken fingers and fries to that, please," he said. "And a large iced tea. And whatever the deputy is having."

Delaney leaned back, reading the lighted menu hanging from the ceiling. "I don't know why I bother to read this thing. Cheeseburger and fries, as always. Iced tea for me, too."

Leo paid, then pointed at a booth in the corner, far away from other occupied seating. "Is that table okay?"

"Suits me."

He walked over and set his jacket on it. After they'd filled their drinks at the drink station, they returned to their table. Dr. Watson joined them.

"You ready to crack this one wide open?" Leo asked.

"You're feeling that optimistic, are you?" Dr. Watson's eyebrows quirked.

"I'm feeling that desperate. Half of me is terrified you'll suggest this case is related to Marilyn—whose identity we just confirmed, by the way—and the other half is afraid you won't. What I'd love most of all is a clear-cut accident. No ambiguity."

"That's not on the menu today, I'm afraid."

The cashier delivered Dr. Watson's food, balancing the tray on her belly. "The other two will be right up."

"Thank you, Mevanee," Dr. Watson positioned the salad squarely in front of her but didn't start eating. She tilted her head toward the cashier. "She graduated with my youngest. Want to cover Marilyn's dental records first?"

"That would be great," Leo said.

"I've had a chance to review Dr. Sharp's records for Marilyn Littlewolf and compare it to our first victim. The last time Dr. Sharp saw her, Marilyn was eleven years old. Her second permanent molars were coming in. Now, our victim has all her permanent teeth, although her wisdom teeth had not yet erupted. She has no orthodontic correction, no pulled teeth, and two filled cavities plus additional unfilled cavities. I'm able to match up the fillings in number five on the upper left and number twenty-one on the lower right with those Dr. Sharp did for her. Those were permanent teeth, not baby teeth. The teeth overall are not an exact match, but the differences seem consistent with age and wear."

"Sounds good. What is your opinion, then?" Delaney said.

"I'd be willing to attest that I believe it to be much more likely than not that a comparison of old dental records with our victim's teeth shows her to be Marilyn Littlewolf."

Delaney was nodding, her eyes alight. "That's exactly what we needed to hear to move this forward. Thank you."

Leo said, "Unfilled cavities. Untreated broken bones. Marilyn lived in Hell."

Delaney's chin jutted forward. "And we're going to find the person who put her there. I promise you that."

Dr. Watson rotated her salad. "I have complete faith in the two of you. Now, about Sue. Let me run through the pertinents. First, she died from a broken neck, which is not surprising given that she tumbled off a cliff. The debris on her body was consistent with the prevailing soil and flora on the eastern side of the

Bighorns in May at seven thousand feet in elevation. Absolutely nothing surprising there. Here's where things get more interesting—she definitely showed signs of recent abuse."

"The same as Marilyn."

"In one respect. The cable marks on the ankles. They weren't as serious or pronounced, but they were there. Oh—and she had a nasty stab wound in her back. It looked like someone twisted the blade once it was inserted."

Leo winced.

"Oh, my god!" Delaney said.

Dr. Watson nodded with a sad look in her eyes. "There are a few more similarities. One is that her stomach contained elk meat."

"Wild game. With Marilyn, it was rabbit, which is also highly likely wild game. Was this someone who loved game meat?" Leo mused.

"Or only had game meat? Or served it symbolically for some reason?" Delaney said.

Dr. Watson shrugged. "Excellent items for you to ponder. Sue had a homemade tattoo so recent that excess ink was still on her skin."

"How recent is that?" Delaney asked.

"Since her last shower. She'd only been missing two days. Teenage girls, in my experience, shower frequently. I'd guess at least in the last twenty-four hours since her disappearance. The tattoo would have been sometime in the last three days, but I would have guessed in the last twenty-four hours. The excess tends to rub off on fabric, too."

"What did it say?"

"It read 1P31. I think. Or those ones could be Is or a combination thereof. Definitely a do-it-yourself job."

"Another homemade tattoo." Leo groaned. "Okay. Letters and numbers, like Marilyn."

"But not the same number of digits," Delaney said.

"Not a phone number. Not a license plate."

Dr. Watson held up her hand. "I have a few more things, before you start off on a tangent. Sue had recently had unprotected sex. I've sent the semen off for DNA testing."

"That's huge!" Delaney's fist thumped the table. Dr. Watson's silverware bounced.

Leo eyed the counter, looking for their food. "If we get a match, it's huge."

"If not, it'll be huge to match with the suspect when we ID him. Was it consensual?"

"The only thing that makes me say no is the ankle injuries. Without them, I'd be telling you I saw no bruising or tearing. But it's possible the sexual intercourse occurred consensually prior to the binding of the ankles."

"How long before?"

"Semen can be found up to five days after sex. Based on the amount, I'd say less time had elapsed than that, but volume is dependent on any number of things."

Leo said, "So, it's possible she had sex before she disappeared."

"Yes."

"Like with a boyfriend."

"With anyone male."

"Good point."

"We need DNA from the boyfriend to rule him out," Delaney said. "Or any male suspects we can identify."

"Any other physical evidence on her?" Leo asked. "Fingerprints? Fibers?"

"Fingerprints from around the tattoo, which you'll have in your inbox when you get back. A few hairs that are possibly not hers. Again, I've sent them in for analysis. But, for someone who had recently been in close physical contact with a man, she was very clean. Like she'd been washed. Not her hair, but her body.

I'm thinking wash cloth. I found some fibers that are common in bath towels."

The fingerprints would be easy to follow-up on. "What color were the hairs?"

"Black and gray—they were pubic hairs."

"Excuse me," Mevanee said. "Chicken fingers and fries for the sheriff, cheeseburger and fries for the deputy." She set one tray in front of each of them.

"Thank you," Leo said.

Delaney didn't even look at hers. She waited for Mevanee to retreat, then leaned forward. "Black and gray doesn't sound like her boyfriend. He's a senior in high school."

Leo felt sick. "It sounds like rape. There's no such thing as consent between an underage girl and a man old enough for gray pubes."

EIGHTEEN

Delaney stared at the two whiteboards in Leo's office. He'd gone to *beard the dragon in its den* in his words, otherwise known as "update the police chief." Delaney hadn't had the heart to tell him that Daniel had bearded the *lion* in its den not a dragon, a story based on 1 Samuel 17:35 where the shepherd Daniel pursued a lion into its den and caught it by its beard after it had stolen a lamb. She'd memorized the verse kneeling on rocks at the feet of her grandmother. *All the ways in which having religious nuts in the family benefits me now,* she mused. Today was one of many days she was glad not to be sheriff. After Leo met with the police chief, he was sitting down with the FBI agent the bureau had sent.

The whiteboards were her murder boards—more like a tragedy board in this case, as they still didn't have enough to call either case anything more than horrible and suspicious. Each girl's name was written at the top of a board. Below it, she was writing in the evidence and people connected to their cases. The similarities were obvious. The abuse. The homemade tattoos. Their gender, age at disappearance, race, and similar place of discovery. Even method of death was enough alike to make Delaney's pulse beat faster.

The differences were stark. Recent sex with an older guy versus a pregnancy but no recent sex. The tattoos were both homemade but different. One girl had been gone only days. The other, years.

Delaney drew asterisks by the names *Nelly Hillmont* and *Patricia Cox*. She couldn't believe how bare Marilyn's board was, but she'd barely had time to pull the files out of the records on Marilyn's case before Sue had disappeared. It was time to give the two of them equal attention.

"Where did the two of you go? Did someone take you? And why?" she asked.

Leo walked in. "You know I've already input all of that into an investigation plan? I uploaded it through the cloud. You can get it off the records system and update it."

Delaney waved him off. "It helps me to write it out by hand. It helps me even more to see it on the board. Things on the screen don't do much for me."

"Speaking of things on a screen, I was able to hack into a database at the gaming company that owns the *Phantaztik Beaztz* game."

"That sounds illegal."

"Gotta keep those skills that landed me a sweet stay-out-of-jail card into the Coast Guard sharp."

"I rest my case."

He grinned. "I was able to locate Patricia's login and see that it's been tied to a particular IP address and link that to a town in California."

"I forgive you for your sins. What town?"

"Ferndale."

"I guess if we can't find her any other way, soon, I can connect with local law enforcement there for an assist. Thanks."

"You can repay me by bailing me out if the caper goes sideways."

She found herself smiling back. "How'd it go with the dragon lady?"

"A little louder for the people out in the parking lot."

"Sorry." She put her hands around her mouth like a megaphone. "How did it go with—"

"Stop." He laughed. "About like you'd expect. She's sending Caitlin and her partner as backup with us to the Hillmonts, though. And she called a status conference for the first thing tomorrow morning."

"The only update we'll have is Nelly."

"I tried telling her that."

Delaney tapped her phone screen. "It's five-thirty. Time to rally our brethren in blue?"

But a knock at the door interrupted the thought at the same time as Leo's annoying, insulting dating app notification chimed. Delaney threw him a slit-eyed look then turned. Caitlin Porter and Devon Peele stood in the doorway, stone-faced. Caitlin stood a head taller than her partner, but he was twice that and more her girth, and blond to her auburn.

Did we say anything that's going to get us in trouble with the dragon?

"Chief told us to report for a joint operation on the Sue Wiley case. A witness you've identified." Caitlin's lips barely moved.

"Deputy Investigator Delaney Pace identified the witness." Leo flashed his Hollywood grin and put his hand out to the man behind Caitlin. "Sheriff Leo Palmer."

The officer stared at the hand and hesitated a full second before giving it the briefest of shakes. "Peele."

"You know Delaney?"

He gave a curt nod. Delaney didn't bother playing catch-up on old times. Devon had been on the fringe of her brother

Liam's group when they were kids. Several years older than Delaney. She hadn't seen him since middle school, more than twenty years before.

She matched Leo's wattage. "Great to have you with us. Elijah Campbell showed up unexpectedly this morning."

"And we're just hearing about it?" Caitlin said.

"I put interview notes in the records system before lunch." Delaney turned up her smile. "Anyway, he said he was skipping school with a buddy at the time Sue disappeared and stayed with him since then. He claimed his trauma and sadness are why he didn't make himself available for interviews earlier."

"Did his alibi pan out?"

"You'll be shocked to hear I haven't been able to reach his alibi witness."

"We'll follow up." Caitlin crossed her arms.

"Be my guest," Leo said.

Delaney had no intention of letting that ball drop. Two follow-ups were twice as good as one. "Besides the deep and reciprocal love in his meaningful relationship with Sue, Elijah also told me that he originally thought Sue had run away. He claims she wanted to split town because she hates her stepfather. And that the real person we should be talking to is Nelly Hillmont because"—she made air quotes—"'this is all Indian shit.' His words not mine. Leo and I ran over to the middle school and talked to my good buddy Principal Rickets. He gave us an earful about what awful people Nelly and her family are, then said Sue had beaten Nelly out of the mugger spot on the girls' Indian Relay team, and that Nelly was really upset about it."

"The what?" Peele said.

"I'll explain later," Caitlin told him.

"Rickets refused to sit in an interview with her and us. He most definitely did not want the parents to come to the school for an interview either. Thus, we are left with attempting to catch her at home with a parent. Lana and Nelson Hillmont, by the way. Those are the parents' names. Leo went to your boss to ask that we work together on a six p.m. visit, and the rest, as they say, is hysteria."

"You mean history," Caitlin said.

"No, I really don't."

She waved at the boards. "What's all this?"

"Our work on the cases."

"You're working Marilyn Littlewolf?"

"Your boss didn't tell you?"

Caitlin and Devon shared an angry look.

Delaney sighed. "Why don't I fill you in when we're done with Nelly?"

NINETEEN

Because four officers at the Hillmont front door was overkill and likely counterproductive, Caitlin and Delaney faced a sullen-faced teenage girl together while Devon and Leo waited in their respective vehicles. The girl was stocky and medium height for her age. She had long dark hair in a single braid, a flattened nose, and dark eyes. Delaney hoped Caitlin stuck to their agreement—on this interview, the sheriff's department would take the lead.

Delaney said, "I'm Deputy Investigator Delaney Pace. This is Officer Caitlin Porter."

Caitlin corrected her. "Sergeant Porter."

Delaney nodded. *Someone's had a recent promotion.* She made a split-second strategy decision to minimize opportunities for Nelly to avoid talking to them. "We're here to talk to you, Nelly."

Nelly's eyes were flat. She didn't deny her identity or tell them to leave her alone, which was good. "Why?"

Caitlin said, "Because—"

Delaney couldn't let her finish that sentence, even if it angered her temporary partner. "Is a parent home with you?"

"Why?"

"Please get your parent, and we'll all talk together."

Nelly stared at Delaney, ignoring Caitlin. She made a disgusted noise, turned, and shouted, "Mom. Cops at the door for you." Her voice was deep and penetrating. She inspected her nails. Leaned against the door frame. Picked at a scab.

Meanwhile, Delaney felt the heat of Caitlin's angry gaze. She'd apologize and explain later.

An elongated version of Nelly appeared. "I'm getting ready for work. What is it?"

Delaney repeated the introductions, correcting Caitlin's title. "May we come in for a few minutes? We'd like to talk to Nelly with you present."

"What the hell did you do?" the woman hissed at her daughter.

"Nothing." Nelly didn't whine. Didn't question. *She's a cool customer.*

To Delaney the woman said, "This had better be quick, and you'd better not be targeting Nelly for some bullshit or I'm calling my husband."

"Just a few questions." Delaney thought a smile would be too much. "And your name is?"

"Lana Hillmont. Who's that?" Lana waved at the two law enforcement vehicles.

"Our partners are waiting on us." Delaney moved forward optimistically.

Lana and Nelly made room for the officers and led them into an eating area with four chairs around a metal-legged table. Delaney and Caitlin sat.

"Nelly, when was the last time you saw Sue Wiley?" Delaney asked. She was trimming the fat out of this interview, to achieve the speed Lana had asked for, and because her instant read on Nelly was that the girl would do better with direct questions.

"At school last week. Before everyone was freaking out that she was gone. Before she jumped off a cliff."

"Were you at school the day she was first missing?"

Lana stood, hands on hips. "Wait a minute—you think she had something to do with that girl killing herself?"

Delaney held up a hand. Interesting that twice in this household people mentioned Sue taking her own life. She would follow up on it. But not yet. "I'm trying to learn what happened to a girl who died. Let's see what your daughter knows."

"Yeah, I was there," Nelly said.

"That's what the attendance records will show?"

Lana pulled out her phone. "I'm calling my husband. This is racist. This is harassment."

"Please feel free to call him if you'd like. But I would like to hear Nelly's answer."

Nelly snorted. "How would I know? But I was there. I had a history test that morning and since I was already there, I stuck around all day."

"You haven't seen her since she disappeared?"

"No. It's not like we hang out."

"You had a falling out, in fact, over Indian Relay."

"Is that a question? I didn't like her. She also beat me out of my relay spot. The two things aren't related."

"Why don't you like her?"

"Well, I really hate her perv stepdad more than her."

"Samuel Russo?"

"Yeah. Piece of work." She gave her mom a hooded look. "If I'm allowed to say that." But her mom was on the phone and not listening.

"Why do you say he's a perv?"

"Because he has a thing for girls his stepdaughter's age."

"Did he do something inappropriate to you or around you?"

"If by inappropriate you mean did he try to touch me or ask

me to do stuff, no. But he did it to my old girlfriend. She used to hang out at their house."

"What's her name?"

"Patricia Cox. She moved though. I think partly to get away from him."

"Are you in touch with her now?"

For the first time, Delaney saw a flicker of pain in the girl's eyes. "No. She ghosted me."

"I'm sorry."

Nelly shrugged.

"Do you have any tattoos?"

Nelly frowned. "No. I'm scared of needles."

"Did Sue have any?"

"I hadn't seen any."

"Were any of the kids in the middle school into homemade tattoos? DIY stuff?"

She shuddered. "I hadn't heard of that. Maybe. I don't know."

Delaney changed gears. "You mentioned that you think Sue jumped off the cliff."

"Didn't she?"

"Why would you think that?"

"It's what people are saying. And it made sense."

"Why?"

The front door flew open and slammed into the wall. The man that entered was a tank. If this was Nelson Hillmont, she could see where Nelly got her build from. "What the fuck are you doing in my house questioning my daughter like she's some kind of murderer?"

Leo and Devon hovered outside the door, hands on their holstered weapons.

Delaney nodded at the angry man. "Nelly has been very helpful, and your wife has been present the whole time."

"A fat lot of good that did us, having Lana here."

Lana had backed away, toward a hall. "You think you can do better? Be my guest. You should be thanking me for calling you. I'm out of here."

"I'll deal with you later."

She flipped him off and slammed the back door as she left.

Caitlin stood.

Delaney did not. "Nelly, you were telling me why it made sense to think that Sue killed herself?"

Her father advanced on the girl and jerked her to her feet by her elbow.

Now Delaney moved, standing but not advancing. Escalation was the last thing she wanted. "That's quite enough, Mr. Hillmont. Unless you want to accompany us to the station in handcuffs. I'd think you'd want to avoid more time in the county jail for assault."

"It's okay, Dad." Nelly had gone limp. "I wasn't going to tell them nothing."

He released her arm. "Go to your room."

Nelly shot Delaney a look as she left the room. It was hard to read. Did she blame her? Did she want her to intervene? Did she have something more to tell her? But so far, Mr. Hillmont hadn't crossed a line she could arrest him for, although he was getting close.

"I'd like you to think carefully about your actions toward your wife and daughter this evening. You've got the attention of four law enforcement officers."

He pointed a sausage finger at Delaney, stopping several inches shy of her nose, but the action still felt intimidating. Delaney held herself stock-still. "Get the fuck off my property and don't come back without a warrant."

Now Delaney indulged in the smile she'd withheld throughout the visit. "If I do, it won't be for Nelly. Good evening, Mr. Hillmont."

Then she motioned a wide-eyed Caitlin ahead of her. Delaney had waved a red flag in front of a bull, and she didn't want to stick around to see how sharp his horns were.

TWENTY

Leo jabbed his keyboard with frustrated finger strokes as he worked on the investigation plan for Sue Wiley. The plan for Marilyn Littlewolf was open on his tablet, which he'd propped up beside his laptop. He'd been trying to crack the code of their tattoos all day. First, by talking to Jayla Russo—who claimed Sue hadn't had a tattoo before her disappearance and that she didn't recognize the ones in the pictures—and next by talking to other students, starting with a heart-to-heart with Freddy over breakfast.

"Uncle Leo," Freddy had said. "I don't hang with kids who are into ink."

"But do you know any who have tattoos like these?" He'd showed them to Freddy.

Freddy's face was at first curious, then blank. "Make those make sense."

"I'll take that as a no, that you haven't seen any like them before. And that you don't know what they would mean, either."

Freddy had shot a finger pistol at him and winked. *Cheeky little sod.* "Ashley's meeting me for coffee before school. If I'm one minute late she'll be super freaking out. She's like into rules and studying." He said it like the concept was mind boggling.

Leo thought the girl was a good influence on him. And a preacher's kid to boot. He wasn't standing in the way of that friendship. "Good talk."

And that had been that.

Delaney said she'd asked Kat and Carrie about the tattoos the night before, but that it had yielded similar results. So had interviewing Sue's friends.

Live human intel is a bust. That left the internet and code-breaking applications. He was barely ten minutes into that when his phone interrupted him with a dating app notification. He didn't bother looking at it. The women weren't making him forget about Delaney. And the notifications and dates were almost as annoying to him as they were to her. *But is she annoyed or jealous? Maybe it's a good sign if she's jealous.* He hadn't signed up for that reason. He'd been trying to help himself. Maybe... just maybe... he was, even if not in the way he'd expected?

"Any progress on the tattoos?" Delaney poked her head in.

He put his phone on silent. He'd turn the notifications off altogether later. "Nothing yet other than updating the investigation plans. I was just starting on the internet. Oh—and I asked the agent from the FBI to take over coordination with the BIA police and the MMU. He's on the way out of town, though."

"Thank you. I've still got more than I can do, so it doesn't hurt my feelings."

"I figured it wouldn't. Want to take the 'two heads are better than one' approach on the tattoos?"

His offer lured her in. How could her presence be exciting and calming at the same time?

She sat in front of his desk. "All right. What does our friend Google tell us?"

"Ah, but it's more complicated than that. My first step was

to generate all the possible alternatives of what the actual tattoo represented. In Marilyn's tattoo, I see ambiguity in this character." He switched to a spreadsheet, turned his screen to face her, then rolled his chair to join her on the other side of the desk. His knees bumped into it. Tactical error. The other side was better for working. It also looked too cozy for the two of them, so this would have to do.

The first cell contained EP522.

"The S?" she said, reading the ambiguous character as a letter.

"Or a five. Marilyn's tattoo isn't too hard, as that generates only two alternatives. But Sue's has two ambiguous characters." He pulled up a second spreadsheet, with the cursor in the first cell. It read 1P31.

"The ones."

"Or Is. And with two ambiguous characters in that tattoo, it generates four alternatives. But what if we're wrong on any of the other letters? You can see how the options start to become exponential as you introduce more possible errors."

"You're giving me a headache."

"And there are no other similarities."

"Besides that, they were home jobs of number and letter combinations on the wrists of teenage girls who turned up dead near each other after disappearing and suffering abuse?"

He smiled. "When you put it that way. But they don't have the same number of characters. They don't contain the same characters, with only one character seeming to repeat. The order of letters versus numbers is different. There's no pattern that I see yet."

"I don't disagree."

"Even just starting with the two alternatives for Marilyn's tattoo, Google is not making this a cakewalk." He typed in the first alternative. "EPS22. That gets us a lot of types of foam."

Delaney's eyes were scanning the search results. "Replacement parts for a record player."

He grinned, catching her energy. "Flatware."

"Electronics. Styluses."

"Anything that screams 'tattoo'?"

"Nothing."

He typed in EP522. The results popped up on the display.

"Batteries. Auto parts. Embossing powder," Delaney read aloud as he scrolled. "Those don't sound significant or promising." Then she leaned in. He leaned with her. *We are always in sync.* "What about this? Episode 522?"

"Yes. And if you put a space between the EP and the 522 that becomes an even more viable alternative. But an episode of what? And how does that relate to 1P31?"

She read show names aloud. "*One Piece Anime. Rumbleverse. The Film Stage Show. Maximum Fun. Press Your Luck. More Important Issues. The Invention of the Economy.* Oh, here's one. *The Cruz Show* talking about Drake and Kanye. Possibly relevant to teens."

"Anime might be, too."

"Not big in Kearny, Wyoming, though."

"But Drake and Kanye are?"

She shook her head, dismissing their line of discussion. "But if these tattoos were done to them, it's not about the relevance to *them*, but to the person who chose and created the tattoo."

"Maybe."

"Either way, I'm not feeling it with these options."

"Let's switch to the other tattoo."

"Let's crack open that bottle of Excedrin I know you keep in your top drawer."

Leo got it for her. While he was up, she took over his keyboard. He returned and handed her the pills. "Delaney in the driver's seat."

She dry swallowed them. It hurt him to watch. "It's my natural position. Okay, using the letter I in the tattoo, we get Idea-Pads. Page after page of them. And the most promising alternative from the other tattoo was episodes. I'm not seeing any crossover."

"If at first you don't succeed..."

"I'll try it with the letter I and a one then a one and letter I." She hit enter, then nodded. "IP ratings. Island Packages. Ingress Protection." Her eyes moved rapidly. "See anything?"

"Nothing."

She changed out the one and the letter I and read the onscreen results aloud. "Oh, my god. Crystallization of Nucleo-some Cores?" She made gagging sounds. "Way too sciencey for me to understand."

"You're not into biology?"

"Not the kind with big words that require graduate degrees to understand." She stood and grabbed a half-drank water bottle.

"Help yourself to my water."

"Don't mind if I do." She chugged it all, tossed it in the trash, and started typing again. "Now on to ones only."

Leo shook his head as he read the search results. "More science. Chromosome deletions."

"We're not getting anywhere."

"Nope. I'm going to run through some codebreaker software I kept on my laptop from back in the day."

"How long will that take?"

"Not long once I get it set up. If I come up dry, I'll outsource it."

"But even that won't work if it's significant only to one person or a handful of people. Because then it's not a code."

She was right.

"Let's hope for the best. How did things go updating the chief with Caitlin and Devon this morning?" Leo had been at a Meet the Candidate breakfast with the Young Republicans.

"Fine. I had a chat with them after we left the chief's office. We're on the same page now, at least. Skipping the chief might help relations. Or, from their perspective, skipping you."

"Do you think I'm the problem?"

"Your existence, yes. But I'm honestly not sure what Yellowtail's problem is."

"She seems protective of Caitlin."

Delaney waffled her hand.

"Have you had any thoughts about what Nelly was going to spill last night?"

"Only that whatever it was, her dad was in on it or knew about it."

He feared it might be more general, given Nelson Hillmont's troubled criminal history. "Or just objects to the police in general. As in no snitching ever."

"I find it interesting kids are saying Sue killed herself. Why is that the gossip instead of that she was murdered or had an accident?"

"Do you believe she took her own life?"

"Zero percent."

"Yeah. Same here."

"I want to explore whether there's a connection between Nelson and Sue."

"Or him and Marilyn?"

She nodded. "Or both."

Her fingers started punching at keys again. Her typing style was awkward and deliberate. It was funny as compared to her driving style, which was intuitive and fluid, aggressive but graceful.

"Nelson Hillmont—funny, Nelly may be named after him—has a long history of knocking heads with the law. But it's all for inability to control his temper and his fists. Nothing stalkerish or sexual."

"Let's go back to Google. His name with Sue's."

"One step ahead of you, Sheriff." She shook her head. Typed again. "Nope. Not with Sue or Marilyn." Then she smiled. "Maybe the tie is between Nelson and Sue's mom. Jayla." She typed.

They leaned forward to read together. Nothing. They sighed in tandem.

"That didn't work," Leo said.

"There's one more family member. One that came up prominently in the interview with Nelly."

"Samuel Russo."

Delaney typed, nodding. "Well, there's definitely a connection between Samuel and Nelson. They went to high school together in Dayton. Some of their misdeeds appear to have been interconnected, always on the same side of the altercation."

He pictured the two men. Nelson, a Brahman bull. Samuel, short with his lopsided gait, the weakest steer in the herd. "They're an unlikely pair. I would have thought someone like Nelson would have bullied a guy like Samuel."

"There has to be a reason for it."

Leo's phone alarm went off. "I have to pick up Freddy. Adriana is working late."

Delaney stood. "I thought you were going to say you had a date."

He did. But that was after his middle school pick-up run. "I'll take the codebreaking home with me."

"I'll explore Nelson's connection to our cases. Hopefully when you come in tomorrow, I'll have a clear roadmap for us."

"Extra points if it doesn't involve talking to Nelson Hillmont again."

"No promises." She winked.

And just like that his date for the evening didn't stand a chance.

TWENTY-ONE

Delaney walked beside Caitlin down Main Street canvassing for witnesses along Sue's route to school. She would have preferred to do this with Leo. Or alone. But Leo had asked her to pair up with Caitlin. It helped keep Caitlin and Devon from tattling to their boss that the sheriff's department wasn't sharing the toys. In the end, that helped Leo's campaign and ultimately helped Delaney. She loved the general idea of a female sheriff, but only if Leo wasn't running, and not if the choice was Mara. The chief had done Delaney and the sheriff's department dirty when, acting on the word of a sole informant, she'd raided the Pace home without giving Leo a heads-up. Bygones could be bygones, but they didn't win Delaney's vote. Maybe Mara would season into the kind of law enforcement boss who honored the spirit and value of collaboration placed on them by Wyoming statute. Until then, Delaney would take care to stay off her bad side.

"So far, everyone is coughing up the same answer they did the first time I did this, last Thursday," Caitlin said. "That they hadn't seen Sue the morning she disappeared."

"Today is a Wednesday—the same day of the week she

vanished. Maybe some places repeat the same schedules every week. We might get lucky and talk to the right people this time." Delaney pushed the door to the Java Joint open.

"What can I get for you, officers?" a bespectacled man asked, adjusting his sweater vest.

"We're wanting to see if this girl was in your shop last Wednesday." Delaney handed him a picture of Sue.

"Sue. Yes. She had her before-school usual. An iced caramel macchiato. Drinks it all year, no matter how cold it is."

Delaney felt a surge of excitement. The possibility of a breakthrough. "Who was she with?"

Caitlin pulled out a small notebook and pen, which she set on the countertop. Her handwriting strokes were tight, her penmanship tiny.

"She was alone. She was always sweet on her way to school. She was a different girl when she was with her friends at other times. Not so nice. That group is insufferable."

"Did you talk to her that morning?" Delaney asked.

"I think I asked her how she was doing. She said fine. That was it."

"How did she seem emotionally to you? Anything off?"

"One hundred percent normal."

"Not scared or depressed?"

"No. Not in my opinion."

"Was anyone watching her or following her?"

He gave a pained look. "I was slammed. I wish I'd paid closer attention to her, given what happened, but I didn't. She paid, she left, that was it."

Delaney handed him her card. "This was helpful. Is there anything else I should have asked you but didn't?"

He tucked the card into his wallet. "She used to be a lot more outgoing. About the time her mother married that guy—oh, what's his name? He comes in here some days around nine a.m."

"Samuel Russo."

He rolled his eyes. "Him. About the time Jayla and *that man* got married, Sue shut down."

"When was that, approximately—that you noticed it?"

"Around Thanksgiving of this last year." He frowned. "Right before. I remember I was putting up some decorations for Christmas when she came in with puffy eyes like she'd been crying. She didn't even look at me when she ordered."

Delaney turned to her temporary partner. "Caitlin, anything you'd like to ask?"

Caitlin nodded, pen poised. "Have you ever seen Sue in here with a man? Not an older boy, but someone you'd consider an adult?"

"She's in here in the afternoons with that Elijah Campbell. He's a menace to downtown. Always stealing little things."

"What about her stepfather? Or someone his age?"

"Oh, she's been in with Jayla and Samuel. I think maybe with the parents of some of her friends, too. I've seen her talking to a teacher or two in here, but nothing like coming in *with* an older man."

"Would you remember which teachers?"

"One was the basketball coach. I'm blanking out on the other. There might not even have been one."

"Thank you," Caitlin said.

"How about one large coffee, black, to go?" Delaney said.

"What kind?"

"The house blend." When he stared at her blankly, she added, "Barista's choice. Dark roast."

He lifted a cup off a stack and pulled the lever on a dispenser. "I've just brewed some Death Wish. I hope you like it."

She put a ten-dollar bill on the counter as he handed her the cup. "Thanks. No change necessary. I suspect we've scared off a few teenagers this morning."

"God bless you."

She and Caitlin hit the street again.

"That was valuable," Caitlin said. "We now know she left her home at a normal time and was headed on her usual route toward school."

Delaney blew on her coffee through the tiny hole in the lid. It made a whistling noise. "And disappeared somewhere in the next three blocks because she never made it through the doors of the middle school."

"The city park takes up half that route, too."

The two of them stopped in the remaining businesses on both sides of the street but didn't uncover any more sightings of Sue. They headed to the park where kids on their way to school were walking, bicycling, and riding by in cars with adults. They stopped each of the walkers and bicyclists and asked about Sue. None could remember—or would own up to—seeing her. Then the rush to get to the middle school before the tardy bell was over. The park was quiet. The traffic on the street thinned out.

Delaney finished her coffee and tossed the cup into a trash barrel. She and Caitlin took a seat on a picnic table.

"Maybe a UFO picked her up in the middle of the park," Caitlin said.

"Is this what it was like on Marilyn's case?" Delaney asked.

Caitlin looked away. "Yeah, I think so."

"If you can remember details that far back. It was a long time ago."

"Tell me about it. I was a rookie."

"Did she disappear on the way to school?"

"Maybe. We were never sure. And then we learned she'd run away, so it didn't matter."

"Maybe."

Caitlin shot her a glare. "What's that supposed to mean?"

Delaney kept her voice non-confrontational and her gaze into the middle distance. "She was tortured and had multiple pregnancies before she was nineteen. I still haven't been able to reconcile in my mind how a fourteen-year-old pulls off running away like that only to be found dead in our mountains. Not on the streets of Denver. Or Vegas. But here. Almost like she never made it out."

"Well, I guess Delaney the wonder cop will find out and tell us all about it." Caitlin was on her feet. "I'll see you back at the station." And just like that she was gone, walking at a brisk pace, not toward Delaney's parked truck, but toward their building. It was at least a mile away, but Delaney didn't go after her.

For a moment, Delaney wondered if Leo would be unhappy she hadn't kept things cordial with Caitlin. She called him on FaceTime.

"All done downtown?" he said, looking puzzled. "Where are you?"

"We confirmed Sue grabbed a coffee three blocks from the school. I'm at the park trying to figure out how she disappeared between the coffee shop and the school. Two heads are better than one."

"What about Caitlin?"

"She had to go. So will you be my other head?"

"All right. What are you thinking?"

"If Sue was skipping first period, where would she have gone?" Delaney turned the phone to show Leo what she was looking at, panning from the picnic table, across the park, and up into the leafy treetops.

"She was drinking her coffee. She could have been sitting at that picnic table. If I was her, I'd rather be there than class."

Delaney took a slow look around the park. It was empty, but in her experience it wouldn't be for long. The moms of younger kids would be out here soon enjoying the gorgeous spring weather. She squinted at movement. The park wasn't empty after all. A woman was pushing a grocery cart slowly through the public parking lot.

"See her?" Delaney zoomed the phone and tried to show Leo.

"Yeah. She looks familiar."

Delaney had seen her many times before. Everyone in town knew Sandy Two Toes, as people called her, since she had a habit of carrying her shoes around her neck tied together by their laces when it was warm. Her bare, dirty feet would be on full display, and one of them had only two toes. The big one and the pinky toe.

"It's Sandy Two Toes. Kids are scared of her. Kat acts like the poor woman's the wicked witch of the west. I've never heard of Sandy doing anything worse than shouting at people. But she does shout. Kat says especially at girls."

"Girls. She shouts at them. She notices them."

"Yeah."

Delaney approached Sandy, keeping her phone low. "Sandy, may I have a word?"

The woman didn't react.

"Sandy, can we talk?"

The cart rattled onward.

Delaney raised her voice and used the nickname. "Two Toes—I'd like to talk to you."

The cart stopped. Sandy turned her head and touched her chest. Her voice came out cracked and low. "Talk to Two Toes?"

"Yes. Hello." Delaney introduced herself. "And I'm talking on the phone to my partner. Sheriff Palmer. He's listening."

"I seen you. I know you."

"Great. I have a picture of a girl to show you. To see if you know her and have seen her." She held the picture of Sue where Sandy could examine it.

Sandy moaned and backed into her cart, nearly tipping it over. "Oh, no. I seen her. I know her."

"Do you know her name?"

Sandy put hands on both of her temples. She shook her head violently. "Girls shouldn't act that way. No, no."

"Like what?"

"Showing her private places. Touching. Getting in cars. No, no." She began moaning, rocking. She looked distraught. More than distraught. She seemed borderline unhinged.

Delaney could see Kat's point of view now. Sandy took girl behavior very seriously. But might that be because she valued girl *safety*? A heavy weight settled in Delaney's gut. Maybe because someone hadn't valued Sandy's safety when she was a girl? *What has this woman been through? And what would those experiences make her do?* For the first time, Delaney wondered if Sandy was capable of violence. Toward girls or toward people who hurt girls.

She merited more attention, and a compassion Delaney hadn't accessed with her before.

"I understand. When was the last time you saw her?"

Sandy's mouth opened, revealing a dentist's worst nightmare of discolored, broken, and missing teeth. "Going with that man. Going with him. Going away with him."

Delaney tried not to show her excitement. She needed to stay calm for Sandy. "That's good, Sandy. Thank you."

Someone who didn't live by a calendar—and whose mental capacity was likely impaired—might have difficulty with the concept of time. But Delaney could at least try to home in on the details of the man and vehicle. Maybe even whittle the time frame down. "What kind of car did he have?"

"No car."

"A motorcycle?"

Head shake.

"A truck?"

Head shake.

"Did they walk away together? Or ride bicycles?"

Another head shake.

What else could there be? And then Delaney reminded herself to think like she was in Wyoming. In Florida, the next option was a golf cart. But in Wyoming it was an off-road vehicle. "Was it an ORV, you know, one of the loud little vehicles?"

Sandy wailed. Then she threw her fist in the air and hopped. "Yes."

Elation flooded Delaney. "What color was it?"

A frown.

"Red?"

Head shake.

"White?"

Head shake.

"Yellow?"

Head shake.

"Black!"

Another hop and fist pump. "Black, black, black."

Delaney hated suggesting the answers. Sandy was not suggestible, though. She was rejecting any alternatives that didn't match what she thought she'd seen. *Sue left in a black ORV with a man. This is progress.* "Here? You saw her and him here?"

Sandy pointed at the street next to the park. The side street.

"This street? By the park?"

She nodded.

"Was it a boy? Someone Sue's age?"

"No. Old man." She whispered, eyes terrified. "Bad man."

"Did he have white hair?"

"White face not white hair." She pointed at the asphalt in the parking lot. "Like that."

"Dark. But with gray in it."

"Bad man. Bad man who walk funny."

"What kind of funny?"

Sandy rocked back and forth.

"Like this?" Delaney repeated the motion.

"Yes."

How to narrow down the time? Delaney decided first to test her against an impossibility, to see if she could trust her. "Was this today?"

Sandy hugged herself and shook her head.

"Yesterday?"

She paused, seeming to think. "No?"

"Was it a long time ago?"

"No?"

Change of tactic. "Was it snowing?"

"No snow."

"Was it raining?"

"No rain."

"Was it nighttime?"

"Day. Same time. Always day. Always morning. I come here."

"You come here in the mornings?"

Brisk nod. "Then I go river. Then I go sleep."

"It was a sunny morning. Not too long ago. Not today. Before today. And Sue went with an older man in a black ORV that was loud."

"Yes. Loud." Again, she dropped her voice. "Bad, bad, bad."

"Did he hurt Sue?"

"He made her sleep."

The elation Delaney felt earlier when she first realized Sandy might have useful information turned to sadness. It sounded like Sandy was describing an abduction. Empathy for Sue, empathy for Sandy—both washed over Delaney. The woman before her had clearly been traumatized by seeing it happen. Seemed to relate to it. "Did he make her bleed?"

Sandy shrugged.

"You don't know?"

"Don't know. Maybe no?"

Delaney hoped Leo was getting all of this. "You've done so

good, Sandy." Delaney wanted to keep her talking. She also wanted to thank her. "Would you like something to eat?"

Sandy's eyes glowed, but there was a wariness. "Eat what?"

"What would you like?"

"French fries. I eat french fries."

"Come on, then. I know just the place." Into the phone she said, "Leo, meet us at Buns in the Barn?"

"Sure," he said.

Delaney left him on FaceTime. As she walked with Sandy, Delaney thought of another question. "Did you ever see Sue after she left with the bad man?"

A single tear dripped from Sandy's eye. "No. That's what happens when go with bad mans."

TWENTY-TWO

Leo hurried to Buns in the Barn in his personal truck—a Toyota—after ending the call with Delaney. He was becoming quite the regular at the burger joint. Sandy Two Toes was standing outside watching him suspiciously as he walked up, then averted her eyes when he nodded at her. Delaney waved to him from inside, where she was just being handed paper bags of food. The bell on the door dinged as he entered.

"Can you grab a Coca-Cola for Sandy?" Delaney indicated the cup being held out by the cashier. It was the same woman as earlier in the week. Still pregnant.

"Thanks," he said to her. "Sure," he said to Delaney.

Delaney's phone buzzed. She read a text and said, "I can't deal with this now."

"What's the matter?"

"It's Mary. Skeeter is drinking a lot. Every night."

"I'm sorry."

"It's okay. I tried to talk to him about it Friday night, but he blew me off. Said everything was fine. I wanted to believe him, but I just don't. As soon as we find the monster who's hurting these girls, I'll see what I can do to get him to open up."

Leo nodded. “I’ll meet you outside.”

A minute later, he brought the drink. Sandy had taken a seat, cross-legged, and was eating fries with an expression of bliss on her dirty, weathered face.

Delaney was unwrapping a hamburger for her. “Sandy was a big help today. I was thinking maybe she could ride back to the station with me. Maybe work with a sketch artist to draw a picture of the bad man. What do you think, Sandy?”

Sandy didn’t pull any attention away from the fries.

To Leo, Delaney added, “I’d like to get her a shower. Maybe some clean clothes and some bottled water to take with her.”

“I’ll call Clara to set it up.”

Inside Buns in the Barn, there was a commotion. A man and a woman were having a loud fight. Food splatted against the window. A soft drink followed it.

“I’ll be back.” Leo trotted to the door and re-entered.

Jayla and Samuel Russo were screaming at each other. Rather, Jayla was screaming at Samuel. He was yelling, “Stop,” and ducking as she grabbed every item she could get her hands on from every table in the restaurant. Guests were cowering and running out. The pregnant cashier was filming.

Jayla picked up a squeeze ketchup bottle. This time, instead of hurling it, she squirted it at her husband, dousing him in red. “If you touched her, I’ll kill you!”

“If you touch me again, I’ll kill you, bitch! Enough!” As Samuel wiped ketchup from his face, he caught sight of Leo. “Oh, shit.”

“Mr. Russo, Mrs. Russo. Let’s take a walk outside together.”

Jayla’s screams turned to sobs. She sank to the ground with her face in her hands.

Leo put a hand under her elbow. “Mrs. Russo, let’s go outside where we can talk and let the other customers return to their meals.”

The cashier said, "Who's paying for all this food? And who's cleaning it up?"

Leo gave Samuel a hard look.

He took out his wallet and put five twenties on the counter. "Will this cover it?"

"It should. Except for the clean-up part."

Jayla stood. She lifted her chin. "I'll do it. If the sheriff will let me."

"After we talk. And assuming that neither Mr. Russo nor the owner of Buns in the Barn want to press charges."

"Shit," Mr. Russo said again. "No."

"I'll call Martha," the cashier said. "I don't think anything's broken, though."

Leo held the door open. Jayla exited first, then her husband. She made a right, heading toward the side of the building where Delaney was with Sandy. Leo followed them, his mind turning over the words Jayla had screamed at Samuel.

But the scream in his mind was replaced by a new one. And it was coming from Sandy, who was pointing at Samuel, hiding her face, and chanting, "Bad man. Bad man. Bad man."

TWENTY-THREE

FIVE YEARS EARLIER

Skeeter twirled on his barstool. It had been a while since he'd gotten loaded, but what better place to do that than somewhere called the Loafing Shed? He'd driven past this place fifty times since he'd moved here and never stopped. He wouldn't make that mistake again. It was perfect for him. A little run-down, a little overlooked but with a bright neon sign that said it was thinking it was more than it would ever be. And the bartender was one foxy lady. He liked his women short, curvy, and dark-haired. Well not *his* women. But in the general population of women that ignored him he thought the hottest ones were short, curvy, and dark-haired.

"Gimme a shot," he said, smiling at her.

She glanced at the door in the back of the bar. It looked like it led to a hallway. "Gotta tell me what you want in it."

"Whiskey."

"House or well?"

"What do you recommend?"

"Wyoming Whiskey. Because your accent says you're not from here."

"Wisconsin." He thumped his chest. "Packers for life. Where you from?"

She held up a Wyoming Whiskey bottle and he nodded. She splashed the amber liquid into a shot glass and set it in front of him. "Southern California."

"What happened—did you take a wrong turn somewhere?"

"Love."

That was disappointing. Just when he thought they were hitting it off.

A man opened the bar flap and entered the inner bar. He filled a glass with ice, added two fingers of bourbon, then covered the empty spaces with Coke.

"Liam," she said. "Do you need me in back?"

"Lila's got things covered for now. I have someone coming in later for a meeting. Can you take care of him?"

Skeeter wasn't much for noticing other guys, but even he could see that Liam Pace would be considered good looking. The green eyes were hard to miss. He felt a twinge of jealousy.

"Who is it?"

Liam winked. "Our next senator from the great state of Wyoming."

"Okay."

He nodded at Skeeter. "Haven't seen you in here before."

"First timer."

"Glad to have you."

From the back of the room, a woman called out, "Liam? A word?"

Skeeter turned toward the sound of the voice. A black woman, so beautiful and polished that she looked like she should be anywhere but Kearny, Wyoming, was standing with her arms crossed over her chest, foot tapping.

Liam rolled his eyes. "What about, dear?"

"Our daughter. You know, Kateena Pace. The one who acts just like you?"

"If it's not one thing, it's Kateena or her mother," he said to Skeeter. "Coming, honey."

Skeeter wasn't sure what he'd meant, but he got the general idea that Liam thought his wife and daughter were crosses to bear.

Liam said, "On second thought, Mary, since I'm going to be otherwise occupied getting my ass chewed, could you go out back and sign for the shipment?"

"Yes, sir." She tapped the bar top in front of Skeeter. "Need anything? I'll be gone for five or ten minutes."

Skeeter threw back the shot. It burned. He liked it. But he needed something more substantial. "A Bloody Mary. Two shots of vodka in it. And a snit of beer to chase it."

"Are you sure you don't want the whole beer to pace your two shots? What if it takes longer than I expect back there?"

Skeeter laughed. "World's best bartender. Sure."

A minute later, she pushed both drinks in front of him and then left the room.

"Thanks," he shouted after her.

The front doorbell jingled. A grizzle-faced man peered around the bar, squinting through eyes Skeeter could tell were glassy from all the way across the room. The man waved. Since Skeeter was the only other person currently in the bar, there wasn't much else to wave at. He waved back. The old man shuffled across the room and climbed unsteadily onto the barstool next to Skeeter.

"Howdy, young fella. How's the air up there?" the man said.

It took a second, but Skeeter realized he meant that Skeeter was tall, and the other guy was hunched and short. "Good enough, sir. How are you?"

"Thirsty. Have you seen Mary?"

"She had to do something in the back."

The old guy stared at Skeeter's untouched beer. "You drinking that?"

I was gonna. But Skeeter pushed it over to him. "Help yourself."

The stein didn't have far to go to reach the man's mouth. He pulled half of it down, smacked his lips, then said, "Name's Post. Yours?"

"Skeeter."

"Both of us got unusual names."

"I reckon we do."

"What do you do with yourself when you're not contributing to the cirrhosis of my liver?"

Skeeter's sole purpose in coming to this bar had been so he wouldn't think about exactly that question. "Army for a while. Roughneck for a bit. Thought I'd go into law enforcement, but it doesn't look like that's working out. Running out of money, so I'm trying to figure out what to do next."

A yellow-toothed grin spread across Post's face. "This may be both our lucky days."

"Why's that?"

"I'm looking for someone unemployed but ambitious. And if not ambitious, I'll take desperate. Are you either of those?"

"I expect I'm both."

"How would you like to be a private investigator?"

"I'd say it's right up my alley other than I don't have a license."

"Which you don't need in Wyoming. Just another reason to love this great state."

"You're kidding?"

He shook his head. "I've been building up my agency for years, but I'm ready to ride off into the sunset. It's a younger man's game. You interested?"

Skeeter's jaw literally dropped. He'd been looking for work in all the wrong places. "You bet I am."

TWENTY-FOUR

Kat Pace had never been more miserable in her whole life, and it wasn't just because it was meatloaf and peas day in the school cafeteria. It was because of the super pretty, super sweet, super smart, super everything girl sitting beside her. Ashley Klinkosh. Her new bestie. Because she couldn't be best friends with Freddy unless she BFFed with Ashley, too. She was surprised they even wanted her as a third wheel. A tagalong. A shadow. Could Ashley not tell how into Freddy Kat was?

Maybe she was better at hiding it than she thought.

Across the table, Freddy was listening to Ashley talk. The goofy, moony-eyed look should have been for Kat. If she was a guy, though, she would have wanted to date Ashley, too.

"The new cheerleading uniforms for next year are like so *extra*. I mean, c'mon, they have sequins on them. Sequins! Can you believe?" Ashley pushed her straight black hair over her shoulder.

"They'll look great under stadium lights." Kat smoothed her own hair, which would never look smooth and silky like Ashley's. She'd tried out for cheerleader, too, but she hadn't made it. She wished Ashley would talk about something else.

"And you are a smoke show no matter what you wear." Freddy blew at the barrel of a pretend gun.

Just kill me now.

Ashley's face fell. "And then I think about Sue, and I feel bad for worrying about something dumb like sequins on a sweater."

Sue. Everyone was thinking about Sue. Kat couldn't believe she was dead. A girl from their school. Kat hadn't been friends with her, but she knew who she was. She'd eaten in this cafeteria. Walked these halls. Had the same teachers last year as Kat had this year. Everyone was saying she'd jumped off that cliff. That she'd killed herself. But according to Aunt Delaney, whatever happened to Sue between when she disappeared and when she died seemed awfully close to what happened to the girl who'd disappeared five years ago.

"My uncle Leo was quizzing me about tattoos this morning."

"I *hate* tattoos," Ashley said.

Kat thought some were kind of cool, but she didn't offer that up. "Aunt Delaney asked the same."

"Oh, my god! Did Sue have one?"

"Yeah, but they're not sure if she got it before or after she was, uh, gone. I do know that Aunt Delaney asked me not to talk about it."

Ashley made wide eyes and a zipping motion over her lips. "But what was her tattoo?"

"Homemade. Weird letters and numbers." Freddy leaned across the table and held out his hand. Ashley took it.

Kat wanted to throw up.

"Why would anyone want a tattoo like that?" Ashley asked.

Freddy dropped her hands and went back to his food. "No clue."

"What do they think happened to her, really?"

Freddy was chewing, so Kat answered her. "I'm not sure,

but my aunt Delaney is *hovering*. And Skeeter is even worse. Like he's so panicked someone will take Carrie or me. I don't get it."

"If they're triggered, they have to believe she was kidnapped and murdered. You guys. She was Crow, like me. That's legit terrifying."

Kat could understand her feeling that way. "Yeah. I can see that. But I'm not Crow. I'm like whoa, back off, Skeeter and Aunt Delaney."

Ashley's head tilted as she studied Kat. "They're right to be worried. With your hair straightened, you could pass as Native American. Maybe Crow, maybe mixed nations background."

Kat shivered. She'd never thought of that.

Freddy thumped his chest. "You're my most important girls. You've got to both be careful."

Ashley simpered at him.

Their science teacher, Mr. Randolph, took the seat beside Freddy. "Two of my best students sitting together. It goes to show it's the company you keep."

"My science brain is rubbing off on them." Freddy had never had Mr. Randolph's science class because he'd already been in eighth grade when he moved to Kearny.

"Thanks, Mr. Randolph," Kat said.

Ashley had gone back to eating her meatloaf. *She's braver than me.* Kat was making do with mashed potatoes and gravy today.

"Ashley, I've regraded your last test. I'd like for you to come by after school and get it. Would today work?"

"Um. I can't." Ashley didn't look up.

"Could you come now?"

"Now?"

"It should only take us ten minutes to go over it."

Kat had made an A-plus on that test. She and Ashley were usually battling for the top score. She wondered what Ashley had messed up on and felt a little thrill that her rival wasn't perfect.

Ashley was frowning. "All right, I guess."

Mr. Randolph stood. "Great. Let's go together now."

Ashley grabbed her things and stood, leaving her food unfinished. She waved at Kat and barely looked at Freddy. "I'll see you after school, Freddy."

"See ya then."

She walked away with the teacher.

"I wonder if I should go with her?" Freddy said.

"She would have asked you if she wanted you to." The words came out even though Kat didn't believe them. If it was selfish to want a few moments alone with her best friend, then she was selfish.

She just wanted her gone.

TWENTY-FIVE

Back at his office, Leo rifled through his deep desk drawer. That had been an interesting lunch. And not just because of Delaney's information, the fight between the Russos, and the outburst from Sandy Two Toes. Or even because Jayla swore she'd only screamed at her husband that if he'd touched "her," she'd kill him because she thought he was cheating on her with a friend of hers—an accusation Samuel flatly denied. Samuel was sober, but Leo was fairly certain alcohol had played a large part in Jayla's meltdown. The two had left together, with both Samuel and Martha, the owner of Buns in the Barn, refusing to file charges against Jayla.

No, to Leo lunch had been most interesting because Delaney hadn't ordered food for either of them, just for Sandy. Who went to Buns in the Barn and didn't get anything? He was so hungry he was getting the shakes.

His drawer search became more frantic. He'd become addicted to Wyoming Authentic Meat Sticks and kept them here so they wouldn't gross out his vegan sister. His fingers grasped something tubular. He pulled it out. His favorite—Wild Ginger flavor. He tore off the wrapper, stomach growling hangrily, and wolfed it down. It wasn't enough. He searched again and found two more. Scarfed them, too.

Now I can think. Where was I?

Codebreaking. Leo had tried and failed to make sense of the tattoos with his own codebreaking software the night before. Time to call in the big guns. He'd contracted with someone a few times when he was still with the Coast Guard. The guy had been a literal child back then. At thirty-ish now, he was an old man in the high-tech world. Leo started typing an email.

> Wolverine: This is Slater. I have two tattoos I hope you'll analyze for me. I suspect they're related to each other in some way and have significance that might help identify someone who kidnapped, tortured, and tattooed two teenage girls who died suspiciously. They look like DIY "stick and poke" jobs. Both girls were Native American—members of the Crow Nation. We have no suspects, although there is some evidence that one girl was taken by an older white man who drove an off-road vehicle. Wish I had more for you. Can you see what you can come up with?

Leo felt ridiculous using code names. His was in homage to Kelly Slater, one of the best surfers ever. Not that Leo had ever been any good himself. He loved surfing, though. It was one of the things he missed about San Diego. The endless power of the ocean, the perfect climate, great seafood, and surfing. SoCal could keep the rest of it. He typed in the possible variations of the tattoos and explained the ambiguity about the letters versus numbers, then hit send.

His phone chimed with a text. It was from Carrie. Delaney's Carrie.

Patricia will FT u but no Delaney cuz scary.

Leo jumped to his feet and shouted. "Yes!" He texted Carrie back.

Great, thanks. I can talk anytime.

From his doorway, Delaney said, "I heard that from my desk. What's going on?"

"Patricia Cox is going to FaceTime with me."

"Awesome!" Her forehead scrunched. "Weird that Carrie reached out to you instead of me, though."

Leo smirked. "Apparently, Patricia is scared of you."

Delaney put her hand on her chest. "I'm the least scary person I know."

"And yet I'm scared of you, too."

"When are you going to talk?"

"Could be any second. You shouldn't be here."

"I have to go anyway. I'm neck deep in ORV registrations after talking to Sandy, but I have a call in a few minutes to talk to a guy who's interested in Gabrielle."

Delaney had told him she was selling Gabrielle. Leo knew the pros and cons. "That's great. Except I know she means a lot to you."

Delaney's throat bulged. She was walnut-shell tough on the outside, but when it came to her girls, including the automotive ones—Shelly and Gabrielle— she was a vanilla cream center. She waved him off.

"Before I go, I need to give you a heads-up. Caitlin and I got sideways this morning after we talked to the owner of the Java Joint." Delaney had filled him in about that earlier on the phone while he was driving to Buns in the Barn. "We were talking about Marilyn's case. I sort of questioned her judgment. It needed to be discussed, but she got her nose out of joint and walked back to the station alone. She wasn't present when I talked to Sandy. I wanted you to know in case the chief mentions it."

He nodded. "I'll be ready." He was curious about something else, though. Delaney had hung around with Sandy Two Toes at Buns in the Barn after Leo had moved the Russos out of sight. "Did you get anything else from Two Toes after I left?"

"Not much. She was too upset to make sense and she refused to go anywhere with me. Short of arresting her, there was nothing I could do. At least she gave us the leads."

"I keep thinking about the bad man with salt-and-pepper hair and how that could have been why she was upset when she saw the Russos. Samuel matches that description."

"He could have seemed like a bad man to her. It seems pretty likely she's suffered abuse herself."

"Or looked like the one who took Sue."

"That's worth pursuing. Of course, he might not have been the trigger at all."

"True."

"I'm going to contact all the businesses and homeowners in the area where Sandy said Sue was taken. Maybe someone has video or pictures from their cameras."

"Why don't you get one of the patrol deputies on that—you've got a lot on your plate."

"Sounds like a plan."

"Good luck with your buyer."

"Thanks." Delaney waved and left.

Leo watched her. Then he saw an email from Wolverine.

Challenge accepted.

No promises on outcome or timeline. Leo knew better than to ask. Any help was better than none.

His phone rang. Caller ID said FaceTime with Carrie. He

answered and enabled his video. The girl's face filled his screen. "Hey, Carrie." Things between the two of them had started out tense then moved to awkward but lately had improved to comfortable and friendly. Carrie had been involved the year before with an older man who she'd believed loved her. Leo knew that kind of grooming and manipulation had lasting psychological impacts that could lead to difficulty navigating relationships with adult men. According to Delaney, Carrie was still seeing a therapist.

"Hey, Sheriff Leo. I'm going to add Patricia in a second."

"She gave you her number?"

"Yes. And, if she says it's okay I'll give it to you when we're off. But I wanted you to know she's very nervous. She wants me to stay on the call with you guys. I think something happened to her."

"It's good you'll be on."

"Will this help you figure out what happened to Sue and Marilyn?"

"I hope so."

Carrie nodded. "Okay. Let's do this. Hang on."

Leo waited longer than he expected to, but, within a minute, Carrie came back on. This time another caller joined them, although her video was turned off. A round image with the letters *PC* in the middle was all that was showing for her.

"Hey, Leo. This is Patricia. Patricia, this is Leo," Carrie said. "He's the sheriff, but he's also a good family friend. He really helped me, and I trust him. He and my mom are going to find out what happened to Sue."

Leo brushed aside his surprise at hearing Carrie call Delaney her mom. It was sweet, and he'd have to remember to tell Delaney. "Hi, Patricia. Thanks for agreeing to get on this call with Carrie and me."

"Hello." The girl's voice was soft. It sounded like she was crying but trying to muffle the sound.

"This is a sad thing to talk about. I hate to make you do it, but I think you can really help us figure out what happened to your friend. And keep it from happening to anyone else."

"Okay."

"We'll start with easy stuff. When was the last time you talked to Sue?"

"The d-d-day before... you know. She had a date with Elijah that night. We talked after she got home."

"Was anything wrong then?"

"No. She was normal."

"How did the two of you communicate?"

"Through Discord."

"Why did you use Discord instead of a phone?"

"She didn't want her stepdad to see it. He peeps her phone and her laptop and goes through her purse and drawers and shit, uh, I mean stuff. The dude is weird and obsessive."

"Gotcha. We can talk about him in a minute. Besides Mr. Russo, was Sue having problems with anyone else?"

"Nelly. Nelly Hillmont."

"Over Indian Relay?"

"Well, a little, maybe. But really, I think it was because of... of... of me."

"Tell me about that."

"Last fall, before I moved, I spent the night with Sue. I did a lot. I went into the bathroom. Mr. Russo was in there, but he left the door open. And he was *naked*. Looking at himself. Touching himself... there. I must have made a sound because he turned to me and smiled and said, 'I was just thinking about you.' I ran back to Sue's room. We locked the door. I called my mom to come get me, but I didn't tell her what happened. I just told her I didn't feel good. I never went back after that. Never. Sue came to stay with me instead. And then we moved."

Leo clenched his fists. "I'm sorry that happened to you. It shouldn't have. Thank you for telling me." He'd be making it his business to get up in Samuel Russo's from this point forward. At a minimum, the guy was a sicko who was harming kids psychologically.

"You're welcome."

"Why was Nelly upset?"

"Nelly and I were kind of hanging out. I told her about it. She wanted me to report him to someone. Like the police. I said no way. So, she went to Sue behind my back and told her she was a piece of shit for having me over around a perv like him and for not doing anything about it and her mom was a piece of shit for marrying him and it just got real ugly from there."

"I see."

"And then I broke up with Nelly about it, and she accused me of picking Sue over her."

Leo's heart went out to the poor kid. That was grown-up level hard stuff. "I'm very sorry."

"It was bad. So, when my mom said do you want to move away—my dad had gone to prison—I was like yes, please. Right now, as far away as we can go. And now I feel guilty about it."

And her story just kept getting worse. "It sounds like you made a good choice for you. You shouldn't feel guilty about that."

Her voice rose in pitch and volume. "But what if Mr. Russo started doing things to Sue again without me there? I kind of think that when I was there, I was a witness, and he couldn't. Or he could bother me instead of her."

An icy coldness ran through Leo. "What do you mean, 'again?'"

The screen image changed from the round ball with PC in it to video of a girl. A pale, hollow-eyed girl with stringy blonde hair. "Because last fall I found birth control pills in Sue's room and a bunch of disgusting notes. I mean really, really disgusting. To her. About her and what someone wanted to do to her. Was doing to her. And a pair of dirty underwear. Like, why was she keeping dirty underwear with those notes? She was really upset at first. Mad at me, but the pills fell out of a T-shirt I was borrowing. It's not like I was snooping. I think she was mostly embarrassed. I kept asking her what was up, who the notes were from, what was up with the panties, why she needed birth control pills." Patricia pressed her palm over her mouth. She was crying. She held up one finger with the other hand, asking for time. After a few seconds, she was able to continue. "I went home. Later, after she calmed down, she called me and told me it was her stepdad and that no one could know because her mom married him for security. If he went to jail, her mom would have nothing. And her mom would hate her and never believe that it wasn't her fault."

Now tears streamed down her face. She didn't bother to wipe them away. Carrie was crying, too.

Leo felt like he might join them. "What happened next?"

"She told me she could handle it. That she'd find a way to make him leave her alone. And now she's dead."

She buried her face in both hands and sobbed.

TWENTY-SIX

Delaney made it home later than she intended to Wednesday night. She wanted to talk to Carrie after what Leo said had been a disturbing call. But she'd been lost in research, trying to progress the seemingly interwoven cases of Marilyn and Sue. The ORV registrations. Looking for connections between Nelson Hillmont and Samuel Russo. Getting two deputies started on the hunt for a photo or video of a man in a black ORV from last Wednesday morning. And she'd been distracted worrying about Sandy Two Toes. Why had meeting the Russos upset her so much? Was she okay and was there anything Delaney could do to help her? The clock had advanced faster than she'd expected.

She pushed the door open with her foot. "Hello, everyone. I'm home."

Skeeter and Dudley were sitting on the couch. The little bulldog spared Delaney a short look then returned his gaze to the potato chips Skeeter was eating. Drool hung in a long chain from his wide mouth.

"Hey." Skeeter's voice was listless.

"Where are the girls?"

"Doing homework." Skeeter popped a chip into Dudley's mouth. The dog went after it like a great white shark. She was surprised he didn't swallow Skeeter's whole hand. "That was the last one. No more for either of us." Skeeter crumpled the bag and stood amidst a lot of huffs and snorts from the dog.

Delaney set a bag of Thai food—a favorite of Carrie's—on the kitchen table. She needed to lock her Staccato handgun in the gun safe, but this was a perfect chance to talk to Skeeter. "What's been up with you lately?"

"Nothing."

"Any exciting new cases?" Skeeter worked small PI cases while the girls were at school. Leo and Delaney referred a lot of business his way, mostly background checks and skip traces.

"Not really."

Delaney leaned against the table. "You seem a little down. Is there anything I can do?"

He was on his feet like a jack in the box. He made quick work of grabbing his keys and jacket. "I'm fine."

Delaney moved closer to the door. Not blocking him. Well, maybe a little. "Mary said you've turned back into her best customer."

His forehead bunched. "I got a right to enjoy myself when I'm not working for you."

Delaney dialed it back. His quick offense was unlike him. "Absolutely. I just want you to know that if there's anything wrong, I'm here for you. Mary, too." She touched his elbow, feather light.

Carrie appeared with Kat right behind her. Carrie's delicate nose was twitching like a rabbit's. "Thai food? Did you get me drunken noodles?"

"And potstickers."

"What about me?" Kat said.

"Chicken pad Thai."

Kat did a little dance, palms pulsing upward. "Yes!"

Skeeter stepped around Delaney and out the door, which slammed behind him. Delaney winced. He hadn't said goodbye to any of them. The bag of Thai food had their complete attention, and they had Dudley's. They were soon having a chirpy discussion about chopsticks versus forks—a mixed vote—and whether to warm up the potstickers—no. Containers were set on placemats, and they all took their seats.

Delaney dug into her spicy eggplant. "Delicious," she moaned.

The chattering ceased as they ate. Dudley whined. His drool was pooling on the floor.

"Gross, Duds." Kat took the last potsticker.

"That's mine," Carrie said.

Delaney's phone rang. As the girls debated potsticker ownership, she checked caller ID. It was the ATF guy. Again. She had to talk to him sometime, but she decided family dinner was not going to be that time. She sent the call to voicemail. While she was still messing with her phone, she saw a text message from Igor, the guy she'd talked to earlier about Gabrielle. He wanted to test drive her the next day. She agreed and sent him the address for Gabrielle's storage unit.

"No phones at the table, Aunt Delaney." Kat's smile was all teeth. She'd won the last potsticker victory and was getting to gloat at her aunt.

"Sorry. I was just setting up an appointment for a guy to test drive Gabrielle."

The sudden silence was sharp. Delaney looked up. Both girls were giving her death ray vision.

"Test drive her, *why*?" Carrie finally said.

Delaney chewed the inside of her lip. Had she not told them she'd put the tractor on the market? "He's thinking of buying her."

"You're not going to sell her, though, right?"

"She's worth a lot of money now but less every year. We

could use that money. For things like college." She jostled Carrie with a soft elbow.

"I don't want to go to college."

"Don't be ridiculous. Of course you do."

"Of course I *don't*."

They were not having this discussion in front of Kat. "Well, this will also mean Gabrielle gets used for what she was built for. It's a crime to leave her in storage with her lubrication gumming up."

"It's a crime to have never taught me to drive her." Carrie's voice was strident, bordering on hysterical.

"I didn't know you wanted to learn."

"You never ask anything about what I want."

Her tone of voice was grating on Delaney, wearing down her patience after a long day. A long week. "How can I when your nose is always in a game?"

Carrie jumped from her seat and ran to the door. For the second time that night, someone Delaney loved slammed it after talking to her. *I'm on a roll.*

Kat shook her head. "You've really stepped in it now."

"Did you know she wanted to learn to drive Gabrielle?"

Kat nodded, eyes wide and solemn.

Dammit. "I'll be back."

Delaney didn't grab a coat, just ran out after Carrie. She regretted it the second she stepped outside, but she wasn't turning back. The sun hadn't set completely, but it might as well have in the eastern shadow of the Bighorns. Most of the time the ranch felt far enough from the hubbub of town, but close enough that they weren't completely cut off from civilization. Tonight, it was so quiet it seemed like the end of the earth. Their closest neighbor wasn't within shouting distance, and they'd had unwanted visitors before. Granted, that had usually been Liam, but he was worse than anyone. And once an old boyfriend had shown up trying to win Delaney back, with no success. She was sure Carrie and her friends snuck in and out. People could and did make it onto their property without detection.

With someone out there who was doing awful things to teen girls, this was a chilling thought. While both girls had been of Crow heritage, assumptions were dangerous. Their race could be a coincidence, not a pattern or even a preference. Delaney couldn't let her guard down where her girls were concerned. Not for a minute.

Not even on their own property. Their isolated, rugged property.

"Carrie," she shouted. "I'm sorry. I love you. Let's talk."

An enormous shadow drifted across the parking area beside Delaney's department truck. She tensed, then an owl hooted. The night made everything bigger, scarier.

"Come on, Carrie. It's not safe out here alone. Girls are disappearing. Just let me come sit by you."

Carrie's answer drifted to her, but from not too far away. "Like you care."

Delaney strained to get a fix on Carrie's location from the direction the sound had come from, but it had been too diffuse. "I do care. I care so much."

"Relax. I've already been taken once. I don't want to go through that again."

Gravel crunched near the barn. Delaney was careful not to react. She saw movement—Carrie walking toward hay stacked on the far side of the barn. Delaney slunk after her, slowly, silently. When she neared the stack, she heard rustling as Carrie situated herself. If she'd relied only on her eyes, she would have never seen her. But her soft breathing. A sweet but peppery garlic smell. The slightly darker negative space where hay bales should have been.

Delaney perched a few feet away from Carrie. Hay poked through her uniform trousers. She ignored it.

"I can't ever get away from you." The girl's voice didn't sound unhappy. Maybe a little frustrated, but with a note of relief.

"Never get adopted by a cop."

"Now you tell me."

"I'm sorry I hadn't told you about Gabrielle. I thought I had. I've been pretty tied up with the cases and these girls."

Carrie snorted. "Tell me? How about ask me what I thought? You treat me like what I think doesn't matter."

The punch of her words took Delaney's breath away. "I don't..." She stopped. Took a deep breath. "I'm sorry I've made you feel that way. What you think matters to me a lot."

"We're not related by blood. Not like you and Kat."

Delaney couldn't believe this had never come up before, and now was only hours after Leo had just told her that Carrie referred to Delaney as her mom to Patricia. She had thought she was ready to discuss it with her. The context wasn't what she'd expected, though.

"Carrie, I barely knew Kat or her mother before I came back to Kearny. And you know Liam has done nothing to endear himself to me as a brother. I love Kat for Kat. Just like I love you for you. In fact, you don't come with all the negative associations I have with my family. You and I started with a beautiful clean slate. But I can see how sometimes it would feel like blood matters more than it does."

"It doesn't matter to me. I just wonder if it does to you."

"No, but I think the weird part has been that Kat had a family name for me already. Aunt Delaney. She'll never call me anything different. But you don't."

"I guess calling you Delaney works."

"It does. But you can call me whatever you want to. You can make up your own name for me." *But you called me your mom earlier.* She hoped maybe someday Carrie would feel comfortable letting Delaney know that. Let her hear the word from Carrie's lips.

Carrie laughed. "Let's stick with Delaney. The other ones I can think of you might not like."

Delaney closed her eyes, holding onto the moment like a hug. Even if she never got a "Mom," this conversation and their reconciliation was more than enough. "Do you think we can go inside now? I'm getting kind of cold."

"Wimp," Carrie said, but she stood and headed back. She was easier to see walking toward the light than she had been away from it.

Delaney followed her, fighting a surge of love and emotion that was replaced almost immediately by unease. The cost of love was so high. The fear. The risk of loss. *Big Guy up there, help me not screw this parenting thing up.*

TWENTY-SEVEN

Bright and early the next morning, Delaney buffed a spot from Gabrielle's shiny black hood. The pace of the current cases was brutal, and she felt guilty for even these few minutes taking care of personal business, but it was her sleep she sacrificed, not her work time. As she waited for the potential buyer who would possibly fund college for her daughters, she relived the memories she held with this hunk of metal and enormous engine, many of them good. When she'd realized a few years into her first stint with the sheriff's department that her father's killer still eluded her and might always, she'd run from that pain. Run as far and as fast as the ten wheels on the truck could take her, plus eight when pulling a trailer—hence the commonly used name eighteen-wheeler. She was free, she was alone, and she didn't have to face the loss and failure that had smacked her in the face every day in Kearny.

Now, she was back. She knew who had killed Rudy Pace. She was tied to the town for at least six more years. Selling Gabrielle was the right thing, financially, but it still hurt. Like she imagined a divorce would. Or cutting off her right hand at the wrist.

"Nice rig," a gruff voice said.

Delaney turned, pasting on a smile, and praying she didn't have tears in her eyes. "She took good care of me for a decade, so I took even better care of her back." She stuck the rag in her pocket and offered her hand. "I'm Delaney Pace."

"Igor Salazar."

Kearny and the rest of Wyoming had a burgeoning Hispanic population, but Delaney suspected Igor was Basque, which she supposed was pretty close to Spanish in origin, yet culturally and genetically distinct. Igor had a flat nose, pale skin, prominent chin, and dark hair—albeit going gray—a look she was accustomed to from her childhood and the sizable, insular Basque communities in this part of Wyoming. Salazar, too, was a familiar last name for the same reason. He was a tall man, a large man. And a familiar one. Not in a generic sense, but in a literal sense. "Do I know you?"

He shook his head. An earring caught the sun. Jesus on a cross. She remembered it more clearly than his face. Had never seen one like it before or since.

"North Dakota. You got jumped in a bar." The fight replayed in vivid flashes of detail in her mind. Several black truckers had gone after Igor at once, and Delaney and anyone else with half a brain had stayed well clear of the fracas. Sprays of blood. Broken teeth on the floor. Just as it looked like they'd kill him, a big group of skinheads had turned the tables. Igor had been carted off in an ambulance. The police had hauled away a fighter or two from each side. The next day she'd taken off with a load and never thought of it again, until now.

His eyes betrayed nothing. "Huh. Maybe."

"You're still driving then?"

"You're not?"

"No, I had to retire to take care of family."

"Your uniform." He moved his fingers. Not pointing. Not exactly. But similar.

"I'm a deputy."

He nodded, not in agreement. More like he was stalling.

"What can I tell you about Gabrielle?" Delaney pointed at the name in delicate cursive on Gabrielle's driver-side door.

He backed away. "Your ad said twenty years old and make your best offer. It was more than I needed, but I thought it was worth the trip because I expected something a whole lot rougher. Something more like what I could afford. Now that I've seen it, I know I can't. Driving her will just make it even worse. Show me what I can never have. Thanks, though." He turned to go.

Delaney had mixed feelings. She didn't want to sell her truck. She didn't want her in the hands of someone who wouldn't utilize her optimally and, well, *adore* her like Delaney had. But she also didn't like having her time wasted, time she could be getting closer to finding out what had happened to Marilyn and Sue. Everything about this rig had been in her Marketplace post, including pictures. And, yeah, it hurt her feelings that he could be confronted with the brilliance and perfection of her baby and wouldn't even test drive her or make a lowball offer. Which, of course, would have hurt her feelings even more.

She gave it one more try. Because Igor was the only person inquiring, so far. "If you're sure. I'm motivated to get her back out on the road."

Igor walked away, down the block. He'd arrived on foot, which was weird. *I hope he gets a blister for wasting my time and dissing my girl.*

TWENTY-EIGHT

Leo dropped by the police chief's office when he arrived at the station on Thursday. Mara was on the phone. She turned her back on him when he poked his head in. He took the hint and held up a wall in the hallway where he could hear every word of her side of the call. She was making lunch plans with a friend. Frankly, he didn't want to be here. But after sleeping on the evidence from Sandy Two Toes and Patricia Cox for a night, he was convinced they had a viable suspect in Samuel Russo. He'd conferred with Delaney the previous afternoon. They'd tied those pieces to the sexually explicit notes Delaney had found in Sue's room. One of them made mention of their age difference and not letting her mother know. Another was signed SR. All were in the same handwriting and referred to times, places, and specifics of trysts. *SR is Samuel Russo.* While Delaney didn't see it as clear-cut as he did, she didn't disagree on next steps. It would be enough for probable cause for an arrest warrant, just barely, and then they'd have two days to gather more evidence for the county attorney to charge him. He knew another SR—Skeeter Rawlins. But that was just noise—all signs pointed to the stepdad, so he wasn't going to raise that issue. He and

Delaney had updated the records system, but it was time for the sheriff's department to collaborate with police.

Five minutes and much laughter later, Mara got off the phone. She didn't call for him to come in.

He repeated the process of putting his head in the door. "Good morning. I have big developments and a time-sensitive issue. Do you have a minute?"

"Try calling ahead next time. I've got meetings."

Leo gritted his teeth. He couldn't risk her recording him or giving her something to misquote later. "I'm going to arrest Samuel Russo for the sexual assault of Sue Wiley today. I'm hoping we can charge him with that and much more."

"What? Why wasn't I informed of this earlier?"

"This is earlier. And Delaney and I entered all the evidence gathered through last night in the records system. Are you getting notifications with updates?"

"You're arresting him when?"

"That's why I'm here. To see if you'd prefer to make a joint arrest or that our department handles it solo."

"Caitlin should be there," she snapped.

"That was my thinking as well. I'd be happy to pair her with Delaney."

"Absolutely not."

"Why not?"

"Caitlin informed me of Deputy Pace's bad behavior, accusing her of mishandling the Littlewolf case. Get me another deputy."

"Deputy Pace informed me that she and Caitlin spoke about the Littlewolf case and that Officer Porter took offense over a discussion necessitated by current facts. I'm not pulling Delaney. They're grown-ups and professionals. They can work it out for the mutual benefit of our organizations, community, and victims."

"You can't dictate to me."

"Nor you to me." Leo seethed as he held eye contact, willing his face to remain relaxed. "I'll have Delaney reach out to Caitlin and the two of them can make a plan together. If they can't reach an agreement that results in that arrest moving forward in the next hour, then Delaney and I will do it without the police department." When he thought he was capable of it, he smiled. "Thanks for your time."

He was pressing speed dial for Delaney as soon as he crossed the threshold to leave Mara's office.

Standing on Russo's front porch with Caitlin, Leo had to admit that Delaney had come up with a better solution for handling the arrest. She voted that Leo replace her, while she focused on tracking down the black ORV and on the elusive Hillmont and Russo connection. Her worry—and his—was that any delay created by her friction with Caitlin was time critically lost. Russo might do a runner. If he went on the lam and he was sexually abusing young teen girls, he could disappear and continue unabated. Right now, it was possible he was hanging around to avoid looking guilty, thinking no one was on to him. That could change in an instant. It only took one whisper from the wrong lips.

And Delaney had promised to throw up no roadblocks to working with Caitlin in the future. The bonus? He got to participate in the arrest of a real asshole.

"Ready?" he said now to Caitlin.

Samuel's truck was at the curb, the best evidence they had that he was home. There were two patrol deputies behind the house in case Russo resisted his way out the back door.

She nodded and raised her fist to knock. Samuel pulled the door open before her knuckles made contact. The shock on his face when he saw them was comical. The scowl that replaced it seemed heartfelt.

"I'm on my way to work. Jayla is asleep. Unless you've solved the mystery of why her daughter is dead, please don't bother her." He started to push past them.

Leo and Caitlin closed ranks to block his path.

Leo said, "Samuel Russo, you're under arrest for the sexual assault of a minor female. I'm going to cuff you then read you your rights. Please put your hands behind your back." He tensed, expecting a fight.

Samuel spat. "You're kidding me, right? This is a joke?"

"I can assure you, Mr. Russo, that it is not. Hands please."

"Who did I allegedly assault?"

"Sue Wiley."

"My own stepdaughter? That's total bullshit."

Leo said, "We can talk at the station. Hands behind your back."

Shaking his head, Samuel did as instructed and even turned for Caitlin to snap the cuffs on.

Leo read him his rights. "Do you acknowledge that I have read these rights to you?"

"Oh, I acknowledge you read them to me. For all the good that will do anyone. They won't mean squat for me. I'll probably be killed in prison while the person who hurt Sue is on the outside, laughing. Maybe he'll even come for one of your girls next. I hear Deputy Pace has a few he might like."

Leo pushed Samuel's face into the front door. "Is that a threat, sir?"

Samuel laughed. "Call it what you want. I call it a prediction."

TWENTY-NINE

Delaney shook her head at the long list of multipurpose vehicles—of which ORVs were one body type—registered in Kearny and adjacent counties and identified as black in color. Samuel Russo's name wasn't on the list of registrants. With Leo and Caitlin arresting him at that very moment, she hoped, it was critical that within the next two days they bring enough evidence to the county attorney that he'd be willing to charge Samuel. Wyoming gave them only forty-eight hours after an arrest to hold someone without charging them.

A knock sounded on the cubicle wall beside her. She turned her chair to find a surprising sight—police officer Devon Peele.

"Can we talk?" he said.

She raised her eyebrows. "I guess. Okay." Devon's chilly reception to her the week before didn't make her feel warm and fuzzy now. But the sheriff's department was collaborating with police on these cases. She slipped on her sunglasses, strapped on her duty belt, and led the way. "How about we take this to the conference room where it's more private?"

He nodded, and she walked ahead of him. They passed Leo's empty office. Delaney hoped the arrest was going smoothly. Law enforcement officers encounter high octane situations every day. Traffic stops. Serving warrants. Arrests. Domestic disputes. Any have the possibility of erupting in violence. She never took her safety or those of her fellow officers for granted, but she felt a lot better about it when she was present. When she could help control the outcome. It bothered her more than she'd expected that Leo was out there right now without her as backup.

When they got to the conference room, she waited for him to take a seat. "Want me to go first?"

"Sure." He kept his eyes straight ahead.

"I guess first I want to know if there's any bad blood to clear between us. You seemed unhappy to see me a few days ago. I can't recall us interacting since I was a little girl. A very little girl. If I have a situation to fix, I'm unaware of it."

Devon pulled at the collar of his shirt. "I don't like your brother."

"Didn't like."

"If you're nothing like him, me and you are okay."

"I'm *nothing* like Liam." She prayed nightly to the God she sometimes didn't like very much that she was not. But the similarities were there, and it scared her. A willingness to skirt the law to suit their own purposes. Always taking things *past* too far. Unafraid of death or causing it. Delaney had to believe her *why* for her actions were essentially good and that Liam's were rotten to his core. Hopefully, the way in which they were different was the important thing.

"Then we'll be fine."

"All right. Your turn."

"You and Caitlin..."

Delaney jumped into his pause with both feet. "She was overly defensive to the detriment of frank and important discussions about how to find a monster."

He raised both hands in surrender. "She's under a lot of

pressure. The Marilyn Littlewolf case is a black eye for the police department. I'm just asking you to cut Caitlin some slack."

"Pretend her tantrum didn't happen?"

"Well, yeah."

"But I still need to talk to her about the case."

"I'll make sure it happens."

"In the meantime, how about you help me on the cases?"

"Now?"

Delaney pointed at him in the chair. "Stay here. I'll run get the list of black ORVs in Kearny County. We need to start figuring out how the owners are connected to our persons of interest."

"What do you mean?"

"I mean Samuel Russo doesn't own one. We need to figure out if he had access to one."

* * *

Delaney had texted Leo what she was up to, so she wasn't surprised when he checked in on them mid-afternoon. "How's it going?"

Delaney explained their task. "You didn't happen to see a black ORV at the Russos' house?"

"No. Samuel lawyered up in about two point five seconds and refused to tell us anything. But he did break his silence long enough to say he had no black ORV and hadn't been driving one when we asked him about them."

"Honestly, if he'd admitted to having one, I'd be crying with joy right now. This project isn't a lot of fun."

"Well, don't let me stop you. We need this. I'll check back later—gotta go. I just got a message that the team is done executing the search warrant." He stepped out.

Devon hadn't spoken the whole time Leo was there.

"You got a problem with Leo, too?" Delaney asked.

"He seems all right. My boss doesn't like him. I need my boss not to dislike me. Getting chummy with him seems like a bad strategy."

"Mommy and Daddy need to figure out how to get along. It's hard on the kids."

Devon smiled and got back to his ORV list.

Delaney was making good progress on her half of it when she got a text from one of the deputies who'd been on the hunt for photo or video of Sue in the black ORV from the week before.

Emailed you the only thing we've been able to find, and we've exhausted everything in the search grid we put together with you. Let us know if you need anything else.

She pulled up the email, which explained that the attached video was taken by a security camera at a private residence across from the park.

Looks like the capture was triggered by a bird flying in front of the camera at the right time. Vehicle was too far away to activate the motion sensors.

Delaney opened it. "We have video from last Wednesday."

Devon rolled his chair closer so he could see her screen.

She clicked to play it. A bird swooped in front of the camera as a grainy black and white vehicle jerked across the screen. A dark ORV drove along the opposite side of the street, at least forty feet from the camera. A man was driving, his face turned away. His large body blocked their view of the passenger seat. The video didn't capture the front or back of the vehicle, as it ended before the ORV had passed by.

"That's it? Shit!" Devon said.

Delaney replayed it several times. "Well, I agree with Sandy Two Toes that it's a man who isn't young and has dark hair that looks like it's silvering. His skin is light. But I couldn't see his face."

"Assuming it's our guy, it does help clarify that he is male and that we can probably target an age range between forty and sixty."

"And Samuel falls within that." Delaney nodded. "I'll see if we can get the video enhanced, but without a face view or license plate view, I'm not hopeful."

"Stop. Can we at least identify the make and model of the ORV?"

Delaney froze the video. "Yes. Polaris RZR."

"Agreed. That helps a lot."

"If it's our guy."

She typed an email to Leo with what they had learned and a request for assistance and hit send, then thanked the deputy via text.

They returned to their task with renewed energy. By the end of the day, the two of them had shortened the list to about fifty registered black Polaris RZRs, eliminating another hundred. They'd mapped all the connections to Samuel that they could identify. It was still daunting, but it was workable. Delaney hadn't been surprised to see several guys she knew on the list. This was Wyoming, after all. ORV ownership was a man card requirement, followed by a travel trailer and a hunting rifle. Leo had none of the above, but based on the way her pheromones were reacting to him, he was carrying his card.

"I'm crossing off Deputy Joe Tarver and Skeeter Rawlins. Neither have connections to Samuel, and I can vouch for both of them," Delaney said.

"And I'm putting two stars by Nelson Hillmont. He acted like he had something to hide," Devon said.

"We've got to figure out how he's connected to Samuel. I didn't find anything today."

Devon nodded. "And we need to cross-reference everyone mentioned in Sue's and Marilyn's files to this list."

Her phone rang. It was Kat. "My niece. Or, um, my daughter."

Devon gave her a confused look.

She didn't have time to explain. "I have to take this." She stepped into the hall. "Hey, Kat. How was your day?" She'd been meaning to text the girls and Skeeter that she'd be home late anyway.

"Fine until now."

"What's wrong now?"

"I'm standing outside the school like a mo."

"Why do you feel like a moron?"

"Because everyone has gone home, and Skeeter never picked me up."

Delaney's stomach plummeted. Skeeter. His drinking. *Oh, my God. Is he at the Loafing Shed? Or passed out on his floor?* "Have you tried Carrie?"

"Yeah. She hasn't answered my texts or calls."

"I'll come get you." She could call Skeeter on her way to the school.

"Could you, like, hurry? I'm all by myself. It's super weird."

"Can you go back in the school?"

"I guess, but it's creepy in there this time of day."

"Okay. I'm on my way."

They hung up. She texted Devon where she was going as she went to her desk and grabbed her purse. She had to come back after she took Kat home, if she could find someone to be with her. Or if Skeeter showed up sober. She'd almost made it to the lobby when her phone rang with a call from Leo.

"Hello," she said, too loud and slightly out of breath.

"We've got another girl missing. Where are you?" His voice cracked.

She stopped short. A girl? What girl? She thought of Kat telling her that Carrie hadn't answered her phone. "In the lobby. I was on my way to the middle school to give Kat a ride home. And to find Carrie."

The call dropped just as she reached the doors.

"Leo? Leo?"

Clara called to her from the front desk. "I heard about the missing girl. Did I hear you say Kat needs a ride?"

"Yes."

"I was leaving anyway. I can pick up Kat if she can come with me to my place."

Things were moving so fast. It was hard for Delaney to get her bearings. She had to find out about the girl. About who the girl was. "Uh, yes, that sounds great. Thank you. Thank you so much, Clara."

Footsteps pounded down the hallway, then Leo was in front of her. His face. The look on his face. It seemed to confirm her worst fears.

"Oh, God, Leo. Tell me it's not Carrie!"

"What? No. No. But it's a middle school girl again." His face was ashen, his voice thick. "It's Ashley Klinkosh. Freddy's girlfriend."

THIRTY

Ashley Klinkosh dawdled on the way home from school, stopping to inspect the first buds on the spring flowers in a yard at the end of her street. She'd cut out of her study hall as soon as the proctor had taken roll. The woman never checked back in on them. Ashley had thought having a study hall during the last period of the day was the best schedule ever until creepy Mr. Randolph started showing up most days to talk to her. To ask her to go with him to his room. He'd told her he could make her his aide. Instead of study hall she could hang out with him and grade papers. *No, infinity.*

This was her favorite time of day. She loved seeing her friends and Freddy at school. She blushed. Freddy. He'd kissed her by her locker before study hall. She still couldn't think about it without giggling, which she realized she was doing now, all by herself.

She loved having the house to herself with her border collie Slick and no parents or little brother around. She loved to make cheese burritos in the microwave. Thick slabs of cheddar melted into a flour tortilla with heaps of sour cream and salsa. Her mom bought the fixings just for her. "I don't know where you learned to eat like that growing up Crow in Wyoming," she would tease. Ashley didn't play the dumb online games like most of the kids her age did. She used the quiet time to read or finish her homework, Slick curled up beside her, calm and quiet for once.

She also loved when her parents got home from the church, bringing crazy Len with them. She could not believe she had a four-year-old little brother. What had her parents been thinking? But he was super cute, and they all adored him.

She even loved bedtime, that delicious feeling of putting her head on the pillow, imagining all the great things in store for her the next day as she sank into dreamland.

But she loved her walks from school most of all when she was completely alone with her thoughts. She would imagine traveling. Someday she wanted to go to Paris. She wanted to swim in the Mediterranean Sea. She would see whales off the coast of California. Ride the London Eye Ferris wheel. Bask in the glow of the bright lights of New York City. And she did it, every afternoon, in her mind. Her dad called her a dreamer. He was probably right, but that was okay.

She left the flower behind, reluctantly. She'd have to hurry now, or she'd be late. Her mom freaked out if she didn't get a Ring camera notification that showed Ashley arriving home safely at exactly the right time every day. Next year, she'd be later, of course, because she'd have cheerleading practice after school. She frowned. It might be too late to walk home. She'd miss this.

A black ORV ran up on the curb out of nowhere. Ashley jumped out of its way and fell to the ground. Her ankle twisted as she went down. Pain shot through it, and she grabbed it.

A man jumped out of the ORV and ran to her, looking like he was about to fall himself. A big man with salt-and-pepper hair. "Are you okay?"

"I hurt my ankle."

"I'll get you to a hospital."

"That's okay. I think I can—"

He scooped her into his arms and deposited her into the front seat of his ORV. He smelled bad, like rotten meat, and she nearly gagged. "Buckle that seatbelt, we can't have you falling out and getting hurt worse."

"No, really, I can just go home and take a Tylenol." Ashley had a bad feeling about this. Her parents had told her never, ever to take a ride with a stranger. It didn't matter that she'd been hurt. *And he was the one who ran me off the sidewalk.*

"Well, I'll at least give you a ride there. You can't walk." He reached over her and pulled the seatbelt across her body and snapped it into place. She shrank back from him. "There. I feel better about that."

She looked back down the street toward the turn to her house and felt a pang in her chest. She didn't know what to do. This was all happening so fast. She reached for the seatbelt, but the driver smashed down the accelerator. The ORV shot forward. The loud engine drowned out all sound. Her head fell back against the seat, and her hand missed the seatbelt latch.

He missed the turn to her house. Panic exploded in her chest.

She yelled as loud as she could. "My house is back there." She shouted the street name.

He turned and smiled at her, but he didn't turn at the next street or the one after that.

"I'd like to get out now." He acted like he hadn't heard her, so she screamed at the top of her lungs. "Let me out right now!!"

They raced past the city limit sign and toward the mountains.

He slowed just a little. He finally spoke. His voice was deep and booming. Even with the engine noise, she heard him—*felt* his voice, down to her bones. "I can't let you go. You're my chosen one. We're destined for eternity together."

Ashley had to get out, even if it meant hurting herself. She grabbed her seatbelt's buckle and mashed the button. It wouldn't budge. She mashed it and mashed it again. Stricken, she looked up at the man.

He reached out and stroked her face. She jerked her head away. Slapped at his hand. Grabbed the belt and yanked it over and over.

"I'm sorry, my sweet. That one requires a key to unlock."

That was the moment Ashley was very, very sure something horrible was about to happen to her.

THIRTY-ONE

Leo kept a tight grip on the armrest. Delaney was taking traffic laws as a suggestion on their way to the Klinkosh home. For once, he wanted to tell her to go faster. He'd let Freddy down. He'd let Ashley down. He'd let the whole town down. He'd known Crow girls were at risk. He hadn't solved the case fast enough, and now that sweet girl was somewhere out there with God knows what horrors being done to her. He had to speak with her parents; they had to find her while the trail was fresh.

His rational brain tried to slow his thoughts. *She might be at a friend's house. She might be okay.* But in his gut, he knew that wasn't true. Had Samuel gotten to her before they'd taken him in, on the way to school like Sue?

Leo's phone chimed with a notification. In case it was related to Ashley, he pulled it up immediately. But it wasn't about the case. It was about his love life. Before he could press the button to black out his screen, he recognized the profile photo of a "Caitie" who was expressing an interest in getting to know him better. Caitie looked a lot like Caitlin Porter. In fact, it *was* Caitlin Porter. But why would she approach him through an app?

Delaney shot him a look. "Could you please turn off those notifications? Maybe you can set aside a special time each evening to review your haul from the day."

"I thought it was about the case." And he would turn them off. He wanted to. He'd just forgotten to do it during the last few days. Now it had distracted them both from their mission and pissed off Delaney. *Great.*

They reached the Klinkosh address, and Delaney nearly ripped out the transmission throwing her truck into park before it had stopped. They were out and walking in tense silence half a second later.

Leo checked his smart watch. They'd arrived within ten minutes of Mrs. Klinkosh's call.

Mr. and Mrs. Klinkosh were waiting for them on the porch. They were both tall, long-limbed. He had dark hair, hers was light. His arm was around her shoulders, holding her tightly against him. Their faces were tight. Hers was tear stained.

Quick introductions were exchanged. They retreated into the house around a beautiful solid wood kitchen table that looked handmade. A black and white border collie paced around from the kitchen to the living area and back in figure eights.

"Tell us what happened with Ashley," Leo said.

Eliza Klinkosh rubbed the back of her long neck. "She's never late. She's a good girl. Very mature and responsible. She always tells me if she needs to be somewhere after school. A practice. A friend's. She was supposed to be home. Only she wasn't."

"When did you first know?" Leo said.

"I was sure by four-thirty. My Ring camera notifies me when she gets home. She always waves or makes a funny face." A sob escaped her. She clapped her hand over her mouth.

Delaney spoke in a gentle voice. "Do you have any reason to think she was sad or depressed?'

"None. Ashley is... pure sunshine. Otherworldly." Nevada wrung his hands, his big shoulders bunching with muscle. He looked more like a linebacker or steer wrestler than a priest. "Honor roll. Athletics. Now cheerleading. Nice to us and her little brother. God gave us a perfect child. Now someone has taken her."

"She is a great girl," Leo said. "My nephew Freddy is friends with her, and I've had the opportunity to spend time around her. She is a very positive person."

Delaney nodded. "I'm Kat Pace's aunt. Kat is one of Ashley's classmates. That's been my experience with Ashley, too. So, did you know of anyone who had a beef with her? Or made her uncomfortable? Was following her? Was jealous of her? Basically, any bad vibes lately?"

Both parents shook their heads.

Eliza said, "I'm sure some people were jealous. She's pretty and popular. Smart. She dresses nicely and the Lord has provided well for us."

"Ransom?" Delaney asked.

"Not that well," Nevada said, with a rueful smile. "We both work for the church."

"What are you doing to catch this person?" There was an edge to Eliza's voice. "This is the third girl, if I'm not mistaken."

"We have no reason to think we can't find Ashley. We've amassed evidence that will help us."

"But what if it's not fast enough?"

It felt premature to disclose information, but maybe it would jar something into consciousness for the Klinkoshes. Leo gestured at Delaney.

She picked up the inquiry seamlessly. "We have reason to believe a large white man with black hair going gray took Sue. He may have been driving a black ORV in town near the city park. Does any of that resonate with you?"

"No," Eliza said, wide-eyed.

"No one like that has shown up on your Ring camera?"

"No. And I always check the notifications."

"We'll canvas between your home and the school and see if we find anyone with video of them." Too bad that path didn't take them by either of the road cameras in town.

"Who is this guy?"

Delaney shot a look at Leo. "We, uh, we have a suspect in custody. But based on the timing, it's unlikely he took your daughter, unless she skipped school?"

Nevada shook his head. "We already checked with the school. She was in all her classes."

Leo's disappointment was crushing. *Samuel didn't take Ashley.* "I want you to know that we've confirmed Freddy's whereabouts. He was at school, then his mom drove him home."

"We never suspected him. He's a good boy," Eliza said.

"I appreciate that, but I caution you not to rule anyone out. People can sometimes fool you. Speaking of which, I hate to ask this, but it is protocol. Can we get your fingerprints, a DNA sample, and your whereabouts? That way we can close off that line of inquiry and focus on what's important."

Nevada glowered. "You can't be serious."

"I am. I have to be. Most often a family member or close friend is the one who does things like this. Thus, we have to, in every case like this one. But I want to stress that this is about clearing you early, so we devote our resources to real suspects."

"Fine. We were both at work at the church. I assume you'll want alibi witnesses?" Nevada said.

"It would help."

"The church secretary can provide all the details you need." Nevada gave a name and phone number.

Leo captured them in his tablet. "We can set you up to meet with Clara at our department in the morning for the fingerprints and DNA swab. Someone will take your statements then, too."

"Thank you."

Delaney said, "Did Ashley have any tattoos?"

"Absolutely not! We've raised her to respect her body and herself," Eliza said.

"We might have even gone overboard about it. She's pretty judgmental about them on other people," Nevada said.

Delaney asked. "Do any of her friends have them?"

The Klinkoshes looked at each other. Both shook their heads.

Eliza said, "Not that we've seen. I'd be surprised if they did."

Delaney showed them photos of the tattoos on Sue and Marilyn. "Have you seen anything like these before on anyone you know?"

Eliza and her husband grabbed each other's hands.

Eliza said, "Are these on... is this...?"

"Sue and Marilyn. Yes. I'm sorry. But the context—how the tattoo is done and where it's located may be important. What it means if you have any idea."

"Yes. Yes. I understand. It's just... they were so young, and now they're gone. These photos." She pressed her knuckles to her lips.

Leo swallowed, trying to minimize the lump in his throat. Eliza's and Nevada's pain was palpable.

Nevada took the phone from Delaney and studied the photographs. Eliza leaned over for another glance, then sat back in her chair as if unable to take any more of the sight.

He said, "Before I became a priest, I worked in printing. T-shirt printing. In some ways, it's not so different from tattooing. It's very obvious these were done at home and that the tattooist didn't have decent training, if any. Black ink. You can see the needle stick marks. A poor man's Picasso."

"The method, the numbers and letters. Do they mean anything to you? Bring anything to mind?"

A knock on the door drew their attention away from the photos.

Eliza leapt up. "Maybe it's Ashley!"

"She wouldn't knock," her husband said, intercepting her at the door. "Let me get it." He opened it, and his eyebrows shot up. "Another officer" To the newcomers, he said, "The sheriff and one of his deputies is already here. May I help you?"

It was Caitlin and Devon. Heat bloomed in Leo's face. Caitlin had just sent him a message through a dating app. "Mind if we join the party?"

"It's far from a party. Our daughter is missing."

"My apologies," she said. "Bad phrasing on my part. But if we join you now, you won't have to answer the same questions twice."

Leo knew the Klinkoshes would be answering all these questions in quadruple or quintuple fashion. "Caitlin. Devon." He nodded.

Delaney stood, offering her seat.

Both of the officers shook their heads, and Delaney sat back down.

Eliza said, "I have to go pick up our son soon. Len is four. He's still at the church daycare."

Nevada put his hand on her shoulder. "Could you ask your sister to look after him?"

"Good idea." Eliza pulled out her phone and typed a message. "Okay. Sent."

Leo said, "We weren't too far from done. Caitlin and Devon, if you don't mind Delaney and I finishing up?"

Devon nodded. "Fine by me."

Caitlin gave him a heavy-lidded gaze that felt extremely inappropriate under the circumstances. "Go ahead."

He ignored her. "Before Freddy, did Ashley have any boyfriends or admirers? Maybe someone who got his feelings hurt?"

"No. Freddy is her first crush," Nevada said.

"She didn't mention any boys before then," Eliza added.

"Did Ashley have a relationship with either Marilyn or Sue?"

"Sue is a grade ahead of her—was—and I think Ashley felt like Sue was too wild. She didn't have activities with her. And none of us ever knew Marilyn."

"Do either of you have any dealings with Nelson Hillmont or Samuel Russo?"

Nevada said, "I know them."

"Always, like you've known them since childhood?"

"Yes. Different years in school, but close enough for me to know to stay away. Both of them had a way of finding trouble."

"What was the connection between them?"

Nevada said, "They're foster brothers. I think it was off and on because Nelson's parents were still in the picture. They lived with a family outside of town that had a big herd of foster kids. All those kids were rough."

"Do you remember their name?"

"No. Sorry."

Leo and Delaney shared a look.

Delaney said, "I did time in the Kearny foster system. Enough to understand the bonds that can be formed."

Leo imagined the two men as boys. Survivors in a sad, lonely, and likely very hard world.

Nevada frowned. "Why are you asking about them? Do either of them have something to do with Ashley being gone?"

Before Leo could stop her, Caitlin said, "We think so. In fact, Russo is in jail now."

"Was he in jail when Ashley disappeared?"

"N—"

"Yes," Leo cut in, interrupting her.

Caitlin and Devon looked at them in surprise.

"Ashley was at school all day. Past the time we took Samuel to jail."

Nevada said, "But Hillmont wasn't in jail."

"No," Leo admitted.

"Excuse me then." He snatched a keyring from the kitchen counter and barreled toward the front door.

Leo said, "Mr. Klinkosh. Father Klinkosh. Please stop. We will handle Nelson Hillmont. Your wife and son need you here."

Nevada stopped at the door, his big body nearly blocking it from view. "Like you've handled Marilyn and Sue? The one who needs me right now is my daughter." He nearly yanked the door off its hinges.

"Nevada, noooo," Eliza moaned. "He may be a priest, but he has a temper. He was a boxer in high school and college. A good one. And he's not scared of anyone with the Lord on his side."

After a split second's thought, Leo said, "Caitlin, Devon, go after him." It was the more efficient use of resources. He and Delaney were almost done talking to Eliza. Caitlin and Devon would simply start over with her from ground zero.

Caitlin didn't move. "I'm sorry, Sheriff, but we don't work for you. We need to talk to Mrs. Klinkosh."

"And if he kills Hillmont while you wait on your boss?" Leo pulled out his phone and held it up. "What if we need Hillmont in order to find Ashley?"

After a few awkward moments, Caitlin and Devon turned and ran out after Nevada Klinkosh.

THIRTY-TWO

Parked outside the station after the interview with Eliza and Nevada, Delaney strategized next steps with Leo.

He rattled off ideas rapid-fire. "I called the FBI. They're sending the agent back. I'll send Joe and a few patrol deputies door to door and camera to camera," Leo said. "The cops checked in. Nevada and Nelson Hillmont had a screaming match, but Nevada went home. They stayed and interviewed Nelson, who had an alibi that they'll check. They're going to start interviewing Ashley's friends and teachers. Wyoming DCI is working with statewide law enforcement to extend our search for the black RZR being driven by a man matching our description. I'll be working on Ashley's electronics and digital trail." Eliza Klinkosh had given them all of Ashley's logins and her laptop. Her phone had been with her but appeared to have been turned off—or destroyed.

Delaney said, "I think we should call Search and Rescue. They could organize a search. I'm sure the Episcopal Church congregation and the community would come out in droves."

"Good idea."

Delaney bit her lip. "I hesitate to bring this up, but I have to. Kat went with Clara because we can't get Carrie to answer our calls. I have to find Carrie. I can call Search and Rescue on the way." She felt like she was being torn in half. For her, two girls were missing. She was sure Carrie was all right. She had to be.

"You think Carrie's missing, too?"

"I don't know. I just know I have to find her."

"What about Find a Friend on her phone?"

"Apparently she turned that off last night when we had a big argument about Gabrielle."

"Run that by me again?"

"Find a Friend is not an option right now."

"What about Skeeter?"

"That's why Kat is with Clara." She held up her phone to show him her string of unread texts and switched to show her unanswered calls. "No Skeeter either."

"Delaney, I had no idea. I'm sorry."

She turned to face the mountain view. "They're fine. I'm sure they're fine. I just need to hunt Carrie down and check on Skeeter and then I'm one hundred percent on this again."

"Between us, DCI, and the police, we're on it. I'll call Search and Rescue. And if I need more bodies and heads, I'll contact the state police."

The knot in Delaney's gut eased a tiny bit. Leo would handle Ashley. She'd make sure Carrie and Skeeter were all right, then rejoin him. It would be okay. "Thank you."

"The safety of all our citizens is our job. That includes our families."

"I'll be back as soon as I can."

"Keep me posted in the meantime?"

Delaney nodded. Leo left her truck, and she pulled out of the parking lot, her heart racing with a panic she'd been trying to keep at bay.

. . .

Delaney left the homestead, fuming. Partly at herself, partly at Carrie, partly at Skeeter. Dudley was missing. She assumed one of them had left the dog out, since she could see no sign that he'd dug under his dog run. A Frenchie of his size was too big for most birds of prey, but he was a great meal for a mountain lion, coyote, or wolf, and he was no match for any of them. If he ended up eaten by a predator, Kat would be devastated. Now, not only did Delaney have to find Carrie and Skeeter but Dudley too, before Kat ever learned he'd been gone. Kateena Pace might not ever forgive anyone who put her beloved Duds at risk.

She switched out cars to Shotgun Shelly and revved the engine. She felt more powerful behind the wheel of her beautiful baby, the only real legacy from her dad. The homestead had been handed down through generations. Her dad had lived there, but it hadn't been his heart. The bar had passed first to her brother and thus bore his mark. But the Chevelle—Shelly had been special to her father, and he'd shared that love with her. Driving Shelly on the search felt like having him with her. So much so that she slid his 38 Special tape into the eight-track player. Something about their music felt right for the moment.

She took a quick second to check for responses to her many calls and texts to Carrie's friends. They couldn't all be missing, but they were all electing not to answer her at the same time. It was highly suspicious behavior that led her to believe Carrie was missing on purpose and getting her friends to cover for her. But she couldn't be sure until she found her.

Delaney put her phone away and accelerated with just enough speed to satisfy her emotions but not so much that she peppered the undercarriage with gravel. Honestly, when she found Carrie, she was grounding her. Again. It had gotten to where she couldn't remember when the girl was grounded and not. *The definition of insanity is doing things the same way and expecting different results.* Time for new carrots and sticks.

She steered toward the near side of town with a singular destination in mind. Carrie and her friends had been crowing about the sick new gaming setup Downing Bailey had at her place. A big screen TV with a super sound system and gaming chairs. It had been a seventeenth birthday present. Since she'd heard about the gift, Delaney was no longer as big a fan of Downing's parents.

Driving along Downing's street, Delaney passed Carrie's Toyota pickup, an inheritance from her deceased twin brother. It was parked three houses away from the Bailey residence. Relief and anger flooded Delaney at one time, threatening to overload her emotional system.

She parked and ran a caress across Shelly's hood. "Thanks for coming along, Dad. And Shelly."

As she approached the house, she could hear raucous shouts and high-pitched laughter. She pressed the doorbell. It took three tries to get an answer, then it came in the form of a voice over the Ring camera.

A giggly voice said, "Downing can't come to the door, she's—"

Delaney held up her badge and interrupted the girl. "Send Carrie out."

Silence. Then, "She's, uh, not here right now." Scuffling. Whispering.

Delaney leaned toward the camera, pointing her finger at the lens. "Carrie, this is not a joke. It's not a drill. Meet me outside. You have thirty seconds."

And then, while her attention and emotion was focused on Carrie, she let her guard down. Just for a second. Maybe two. But it was enough.

Out of nowhere, something hooked her around the neck and pulled her backwards over the porch railing. She landed hard, half on the yard, half on what felt like someone's leg. The person behind her—under her—landed harder, with an explosion of hot breath on top of her head. Her brain was on a delay. She'd been wrapped up in Leo and Caitlin. Worried about Carrie and Ashley. Unless she snapped into the present and quickly, God knew what this person would do to her. If they'd used a weapon, she'd already be dead. A knife to the throat. A kill shot from point-blank range. A blackjack to the temple.

She shot her fingers up, going for a surprise attack instead of an escape move. She found rubber—a mask?— and the shape of a nose, pulled her hand back, rotated her wrist, and shoved a fist into it. The sound of cartilage and bone cracking was gratifying. Encouraging. Especially with the padding of the mask. *Score one for adrenaline.* The person snarled and began to writhe and try to jerk their head away. Delaney arched her back, pushing off her feet, and dug her shoulders into their chest. A reverse pin. She pounded at the nose again, then on the next strike opened her fist and used two fingers to go for the eyes. It took her several tries but finally she found tissue that yielded under her jabs. The guttural scream that accompanied her strike was further good evidence.

It was time to subdue her attacker. She didn't have surprise working for her, but she did have training and quickness. What she needed was to put them on their face on the ground with her on top. She sensed them relying more on the right side of the body. Sliding her arm through the crook of their left, she dove away from the dominant hand and twisted the left wrist and shoulder. Her goal was to drive them up and over, away from the pain, then rebound with both her knees in their back.

It was working well, too, until she heard a girl's voice. "Aunt Delaney!"

Carrie. Carrie, screaming. Carrie, tackling, flailing, pounding. The sentiment was admirable. The result, catastrophic. The action took away Delaney's advantage. Now, she had to fight to protect Carrie instead of to capture the suspect.

"Carrie, no," she grunted. "Stop. I've got this."

Carrie did not stop. Carrie was a girl on fire. Half her blows landed on Delaney, and they were surprisingly strong for someone as slight as her new daughter.

Delaney was on her stomach now, pushing at Carrie and trying to get hold of the assailant at the same time. She had a clear view of a thick body on a tall frame. A chest that while not hard was not feminine. Dark hair through a round collar below the mask. He was male. And he was scrambling away from them.

"You are under arrest. Stop fighting." She was out of breath, but she spit the words out anyway. "I don't want to have to use more force on you."

The man struck blindly, scuttling on his back. His fist connected with Delaney's face. She grunted.

Carrie redoubled her efforts. Delaney ignored her smarting cheekbone. The girl's tsunami attack continued to thwart Delaney's efforts to safely subdue the suspect. The man flipped and crawled out from under the teen. Delaney lunged after his feet, landing on her adopted daughter, who screamed again. The man was up, stumbling, running.

Delaney ran after him, but he disappeared into the night.

* * *

Delaney leaned on her knees, breathing heavily. What had just happened? Who the heck was that? She pictured the big, soft body, her mind replaying the fight. It was almost like the guy had tried *not* to connect with Carrie. She touched her own cheek. He'd landed a good punch that rattled her teeth but was just low enough that she'd have a bruise but not a shiner. A traitorous thought entered her mind. *Skeeter*. But no—there were lots of guys with this body type. Nelson Hillmont for one. Numerous past perps. Other random thugs. She wouldn't think that about Skeeter. Couldn't. He had no reason to hurt her. Not that she knew of.

She turned to Carrie. "Did he hurt you?"

Carrie rolled onto her back, knees up, a forearm over her face. "No. He didn't touch me. Who was he?"

He could have been anyone except Samuel Russo. But *who* wasn't the only question. The other was a big fat *why*. The attack might mean she was getting close to something important, but she had no idea what.

"I don't know." She leaned down and put two fingers on Carrie's forehead. "When I tell you to stop, you have to stop."

"He was hurting you."

"I know it seemed like that. But it's my job. I was about to arrest him."

Carrie sat up. Delaney saw her feet. Socks without shoes. "You're welcome."

"Thank you for trying. I love that you wanted to help me."

Carrie stood, shaking her head. "You're so embarrassing."

"Because I got attacked in your friend's yard?"

"No. Because you showed up here and pulled me out of a game like I'm a two-year-old."

Their interaction was going downhill fast. It wasn't going to improve. Delaney was unhappy with Carrie's choices. *She's my daughter. I will* always *go after her.* "Skeeter no-showed. You turned off your Find My Friends. And another middle school girl went missing. All within the same five minutes. And now, because of your choices, instead of hunting for Ashley, I'm chasing you down."

"Wait. Ashley? Not Ashley Klinkosh?"

"Yes, Carrie. That Ashley."

Carrie's legs buckled.

Delaney caught her before she crumpled back to the ground. "What's the matter?"

Carrie tilted her head up to face Delaney. Her skin was ashen. "Ashley and Sue. The things I've heard."

"What are they, Carrie? Just tell me."

The girl gulped a big breath and nodded, then started to talk a mile a minute.

THIRTY-THREE

Ashley had lost track of where they were. Far back in the mountains was all she could tell. The man had pulled the ORV into an open area in front of a cabin. A lived-in cabin with smoke rising from a chimney. She'd never dreamed people lived up here. It was May and there was still a lot of snow. She was freezing in the short-sleeved shirt and sandals she'd worn to school.

"Home sweet home," the man said. "I hope you'll be very happy here."

This was beyond freaky. She didn't know what to say to his nonsense. "Please take me to my real home now."

The scowl on his face made her recoil. He was smiling one minute and scary the next. The scowl went away, but she didn't relax. "Home is where the heart is. Ours are here, together. Forever. Just as God planned."

Ashley's parents were religious. Her dad was a priest, and they went to church all the time. She felt confident talking about God and his plans, and she did not agree with him. "I'm thirteen years old. Only God knows his plan for me."

"And me. Because he showed me the bad path you were

headed down. He told me to save you and make you my own. You'll understand someday."

"I'm a good girl. I really am."

He shook his head, his eyes pitying. "I know you think you are. But I've been watching you, hoping you'd resist temptation. You've made bad choices."

"We've barely even kissed! I haven't done anything."

"Lucky for you, things didn't work out for me in my last relationship, and I got to you in time. Enough talk now. We have business to attend to. Happy business."

"What is it?"

"Our wedding!"

He came around to her side and cuffed her arms behind her back. It hurt her shoulders. "Just a precaution. Until we get used to each other." Then he unlocked her seatbelt. "Come with me, Ashley dear."

She didn't see any choice but to obey. She swung her legs out and stood. Her legs felt weird, like she was going to fall down. He gave her a little push between her shoulder blades toward the door. She walked to it unsteadily.

He opened it in front of her. "Wait."

She stood, afraid to move.

He swept her off her feet and into his arms, giving her an up close on his stink again. Literally, like a bride in every movie she'd ever seen, he carried her over the threshold into the cabin. But only after the wedding when the married couple was heading into the bridal suite. When she'd gotten her period, her mother and father had told her about what married people did. Not that she hadn't heard all about it already from kids at school. Was that what he was going to do to her? Bile rose in her mouth. She turned her face as far away from his stench as possible.

Inside, he kicked the door shut and set her on her feet. She gazed around the one large room. It smelled like her grandmother's stinky cast-iron skillets that she never washed. Greasy, gamey. There were two beds. Maybe the bride thing was all make-believe. On every wall were framed religious prints. Ten Commandments stuff. And she thought her parents had a lot of God stuff in their house. That was *all* this man had decorating the cabin.

He saw her looking at them. "We will live within God's laws here."

"Okay."

"Let's begin our ceremony."

In a panic, she blurted out the only thing she could think of to slow things down. "Where's the minister?"

"I'm ordained."

She knew what that meant. He had the power to marry people. "But you can't marry us yourself."

He stood tall, his chest puffed out. "Are you questioning me?" His eyes were narrowing. His voice growing louder.

"You're, uh, older than me. I'm sure you're right. Maybe you can, uh, teach me."

He nodded, calming. "Yes. That will be our way."

"But a wedding is supposed to be special. It may be my only one."

His brows furrowed. "I can assure you it will be your only one."

She held back a whimper. "I'd like a wedding dress."

The puzzlement on his face would have been funny if not for her predicament and the menace radiating from him. "A wedding dress?"

"Yes. I always dreamed my father would give me away—"

"Impossible!"

"So, if I can't have that, I'd like a white dress. And some cake."

He went to a large trunk and pried up the lid. She thought about making a run for the door, but she knew she could never get away from him. Her arms were bound behind her. He was bigger and stronger. She had no idea where she was.

After pawing through the trunk for a minute, he shook his head. "I don't have a wedding dress."

Ashley gave in to the tears of sadness and fear. "No wedding dress?"

The man paced back and forth. He stopped and built up the fire in the wood stove. Ashley's teeth chattered and she eased closer to it, hugging herself. The man picked up a box from a shelf and came back to her. He removed the top, revealing two gold rings. Her mouth went dry as sand.

He said, "I will get you a dress. In the meantime, I'd like us to wear our rings as a sign of our betrothal. Hold out your hand."

She'd managed to stall him. Thank you, God. Thank you, thank you. She gave him her limp hand. He slid a gold band onto it.

"We'll have the ceremony when I return with your dress. The sooner I go, the quicker I can come back. I'll leave in the morning. You can make the cake for our celebration while I'm gone."

The thought of him leaving her up here alone was almost as terrifying as him staying. But if he was gone, she had a chance to run away. "Thank you, sir."

"You may call me the Mountain Man. Now, since we aren't marrying yet, I forbid you to tempt me. We'll need to change your clothes and put you to sleep."

"Something warmer?"

He went back to the trunk and returned with an old metal contraption and a lock. It was odd and had a small round piece with jagged teeth in the center. "We'll put this on you."

"What is it?"

"A chastity belt. And this." He threw a voluminous dress at her feet.

"I can't put it on with my hands cuffed. And I don't know how it works."

He uncuffed her, stopping to sniff her hair. He groaned.

She stepped away. "I'll put the dress on over my clothes."

"A good idea."

She pulled it over her head. The sleeves and skirt were long. While it wasn't thick, it still helped a lot.

"Much better." Tension seemed to ease from him. "Although you are still beautiful. And a virgin. You are a virgin, aren't you?"

I'm only thirteen! "Y-y-y-yes."

"The belt now."

She picked up the contraption.

"The belt goes around your waist under your skirt. We lock it into place once you have the protective device positioned correctly over your, um, lady place."

Now she understood where to put it. She hiked up the skirt and put the belt around her waist outside her jeans. It took her a few tries, but she finally aligned the metal properly. She was one hundred percent down with the chastity belt. She didn't like his sniffy sniffing or the hungry look in his eyes. She locked the belt.

"Give me the key."

"Doesn't that defeat the purpose? I should give it to you as a wedding gift, don't you think?"

"Do *not* contradict me again. Do you understand?"

She was starting to. "Yes, sir."

"Lastly, we'll put you to sleep."

There was no way Ashley could sleep, but she could pretend to.

He went to a cupboard and pulled out a bottle. He shook out two capsules with white powder in them, then poured water from a pitcher into a metal cup.

"Take these."

"What are they?"

"Something to keep you asleep until we're ready for our union."

This is not what she had in mind. She couldn't fight back if she was asleep. She couldn't run away. "But I'm not tired."

"Do not argue with me," he roared. "Wives obey their husbands. You shall start that now. Open your mouth."

She did as she was told.

He put the two pills on her tongue. "Swallow them." He tilted the metal cup to her lips.

She swallowed the water and the capsules.

"Now get in bed."

She walked to the smaller bed. "Here?"

"No." He pointed at what she'd thought was a wooden table. There was no sheet. No pillow. No cover.

Just stains. Brownish stains. Stains that looked like the ones on the table her dad used during hunting season, when he was dressing the deer or antelope or elk he'd harvested. Maybe that was the gamey smell in the cabin. The Mountain Man was a hunter. Or maybe not...?

She looked away. She didn't want to think about the stains anymore.

THIRTY-FOUR

Once Delaney had stashed Carrie with Kat at Clara's ranch, she walked back to her car. A phone call came through, and she answered it without looking. *Maybe it's Skeeter. Or Carrie.*

"Delaney here."

"Delaney, it's Caitlin."

Delaney sighed. She didn't have the energy for the woman's drama now. "I don't have much time. Sorry. What's up?"

"Are you and Leo a thing?" Caitlin asked.

Delaney took a step back from Shelly's door. She'd expected a rehash of their disagreement. "Why do you ask?"

"I don't want bad blood between us over him."

Delaney bent over, the closest she could get to putting her head between her knees. Leo and *Caitlin*? "You're asking for my blessing?"

"Forget I asked."

"No, I mean, I have no claim on Leo. Go for it. Him." She couldn't picture the two of them together. Leo didn't seem like Caitlin's type. Neither did the two women she'd seen him with in the last week. *I'm his type. I don't want him to find another type.* She recalled the words typed over and over in his date tracking spreadsheet. *Not Delaney.*

"Okay. Thanks. And about the park. Marilyn's case. Maybe we should go over the file together. I might have missed something."

"Yeah, sure. Thanks."

"Okay. Bye."

"Bye," she muttered.

When she was sure she wasn't connected anymore, she said, "Jesus, Delaney, don't be an idiot. You pushed Leo away. What did you expect?"

But it made her want to call Leo. Hear his voice. Forget Caitlin's call and the dating apps. She got in the car and FaceTimed him.

"Tell me good news," he said as his greeting.

"Carrie is safe." But Carrie had no idea where Skeeter was or what had happened to Dudley. She swore that Dudley had been in his pen outside when she left for school with Kat that morning. He'd had plenty of shelter from the sun in there, and the run had a chain link roof. He should have been safe. *Someone let him out. The question is who was that someone. And another—why?* Carrie promised not to tell Kat yet, to give Delaney time to find the dog.

"Thank, God! That's great," Leo said.

"And... I was attacked in front of Carrie's friend's house. Completely blindsided."

"What? By whom?"

"Some guy. He had on a mask, so I don't know. He was big. Heavy. I was going to arrest him, but Carrie jumped into the fray, and he got away."

"Shit. I'm sorry. Do you think it was random?"

"Could be. But I'm inclined to believe it means we are getting closer than we realized. I suspect he followed me."

"And it wasn't Samuel."

"Yep. Anyway, I'm fine, and Carrie had a lead for us."

"That's great. What did she say?"

"The girls in her gaming group heard rumors about a middle school teacher with a thing for his students."

"Who?"

"She didn't have a name. It's pretty thin, but..."

"Thin is better than nothing."

"Right. What she heard is that at least Sue was involved with the teacher and that the teacher had been pursuing Ashley."

"Jeez. That's potentially huge."

"Yes."

"Are you going to pursue the lead?"

"It has to wait for daylight, I think. Although, we have a list of men in the target age range who have black RZRs. It's in the record system."

"I think you're right on waiting for daylight, unless we get a hit we can pursue tonight."

"I have one more problem, though."

"What's that?"

"Skeeter. I still haven't been able to find him."

"Again, no Find My Friends?"

"Not on his old phone. I'm going to check the Loafing Shed and his apartment. That should take an hour. Then I'll get back to the office and work that RZR list against the middle school staff."

"All right. Good luck. Stay in touch."

"Thanks."

She hung up the phone, took a deep breath, and put Shelly in gear toward town. "Where are you, Skeeter Rawlins? And what the hell are you up to?"

. . .

Delaney pushed through the front door of the Loafing Shed half an hour later. Skeeter's apartment had been a bust. His vehicles weren't in his parking spots, he wasn't home, and there was no sign that he'd been planning to leave. His toothbrush was lying on the bathroom counter half smeared in dry toothpaste. His dirty clothes were on the floor, and his suitcase was at the top of his closet.

Inside the bar, her eyes adjusted quickly. She zeroed in on a bulky body sitting on a stool in front of Mary at the bartop.

When she reached the man, though, he turned an unfamiliar face in her direction. She ignored the furrows between his eyebrows and took a seat a few stools away from him.

"Delaney! What brings you in?" Mary's smile was megawatt. The woman was a great bar manager and even better friend.

"Have you seen Skeeter today?"

"No. He closed me down again last night. I had to drive him home myself. His car's still out back."

Delaney frowned. "He never came to get it today?"

"No. And normally he walks back for it. Or if the weather's bad or he's in a hurry he drives his RZR, which he leaves for like *days* at a time. But no sign of him today. I just assumed he decided to go open air with the RZR in carpool line."

Delaney nodded. He'd been known to take the RZR to the middle school on occasion. Kat loved it. It sort of made sense, because the RZR hadn't been parked in its space at the apartment. Except for the part where he'd never shown up at school or their house. "Would you have him call me when he rolls in? He no-showed today. I'm worried about him. And potentially a little bit upset, but don't tell him that." She stood, preparing to leave.

"Sure." Mary lifted the bar flap and came out to join her. "I'll walk with you."

"Okay."

They headed toward the door together.

Mary said, "I know Skeeter has his faults, but this isn't like him. He cares, you know? Like sometimes he cares too much."

"I know. I'll admit, I'm concerned."

"Will you call me when you find him? I'm going to worry now, too."

"Of course."

They parted at the door. Delaney walked slowly out to Shelly. There was nothing else she could do to find Skeeter at this point. He was an adult. If he wanted to torpedo his life, that was on him. If he didn't turn up tomorrow, she'd do a deeper dive. Until then, her only objective would be finding Ashley.

She put on her seatbelt, expecting to feel the familiar resolve and sense of rightness that single-minded pursuit of goal gave her. It didn't come. Instead, she was uneasy. Filled with disquiet. Free-floating anxiety filled the interior of the car and hung in the air. She backed out and accelerated on the highway toward town, 38 Special blasting her ears.

She didn't like this. Ashley. Sue. Marilyn. And now, in a strange twist of fate, Skeeter. She didn't like it one bit.

THIRTY-FIVE

Delaney burst into Leo's office. "Tell me you've found Ashley."

Leo put down his tablet. "I wish I could. Pull up a chair—let me tell you what we have so far. Any sign of Skeeter?"

She flipped a chair and straddled it. Now was not the time to notice the effect she had on him, so he looked away.

"None. Skeeter's car is at the Loafing Shed. His RZR isn't home. Tomorrow I'll check bars, hospitals, and jails. Dudley's missing, too."

He snapped his fingers. "I talked to Adriana a minute ago. Freddy, you know. He's taking this business with Ashley really hard."

"No other way to take it."

"She said she chatted with Skeeter in carpool line today. As in, 'It was just a normal day. Skeeter and Dudley were making me laugh, and yada yada yada'."

She cocked her head. "Skeeter had Dudley and they were at the school! Did you ask her whether she was sure that was today?"

"I did. She was."

"That makes no sense. He was in line, then he left Kat there alone. Why?"

He hated saying this. It killed him to do it to her. But it was his job. "I have absolutely no idea. But I'm getting a bad feeling."

She put a hand to her temple. "Me, too. And there's something else. The guy who attacked me was wearing gloves, so I doubt we'll be able to identify him for sure. But I feel very sure he was after me, not Carrie."

"Could it have been Skeeter?"

"I can't say it wasn't, although it makes no sense. And he took great pains not to hurt Carrie."

"Shit. We have to rule him out, or we have to tell other law enforcement."

"I gave his apartment a once-over, to see if he was there. I could go back and look deeper or stay here and help."

"Go. Search and Rescue has a night search starting in town and another one queued up for first light. We've got teams out questioning Ashley's friends. Deputies are going door to door between the school and the Klinkosh home. I'm working on coordination and technology. We're covering it. The Skeeter piece is critical now."

"Are you going to release Russo?"

"We didn't arrest him for kidnapping Sue. He may be guilty of the rest."

"You're weak on proving assault. Not without video or audio evidence."

"I don't disagree. Deputies searched the Russo home after we took him in. They're still working through the evidence, but it's not looking good." He pushed hair off his forehead. It was sticky with sweat. "Today has been out of control."

"Tell me about it."

"I'll talk to the county attorney, but I plan to hold Russo as long as I can in an abundance of caution. I'll be the biggest idiot in the state if I let him go and then we discover he did kidnap Sue and has an accomplice like Nelson Hillmont who took Ashley."

"Understood." Delaney dismounted the chair in a graceful athletic move. "Pretend you don't know I'm going in Skeeter's place without a warrant. I have a set of his keys, and this is a welfare check."

Leo put his hands over his ears and closed his eyes, but he reopened them for one last look as she left.

"Call me if you find anything. I can be there in five minutes," he called after her.

THIRTY-SIX

Delaney unlocked Skeeter's apartment and let herself in, struggling to tamp down her emotions. Guilt that she was even taking a second look. Fear that she'd misplaced her trust. Dread at what she might find. Hope that it would be nothing. "Skeeter? Are you here?" She'd checked Skeeter's parking spaces, and his vehicles were still not there, so she didn't expect an answer and she didn't get one. She'd even called the Kearny County jail on her way over just in case he'd turned up there without her knowing, but no luck.

"I know this is an invasion of privacy, and I'm sorry," she said, as if he was there. *But you brought this on yourself.*

She took a deep breath through her nose and got a whiff of ripe garbage. He'd been at the school that afternoon, so she chalked the trash up to slovenly housekeeping. She wasn't sure what she was looking for, but since she wasn't constrained by a search warrant, she could freestyle. What was important was to be methodical and do nothing as a concerned friend that would invalidate a later official search, if necessary.

First, she walked the space, taking a visual inventory. The one-bedroom bachelor pad seemed hardly large enough to contain Skeeter's oversized body and personality. A living area with the ubiquitous big screen TV, a couch, and a recliner. A laminate coffee table with two corners broken off. No shelves, no books, no magazines, no newspapers on it. Just a remote control, a collection of empty beer bottles, and a large plastic bowl with popcorn kernels and a wadded-up potato chip bag in it. She slipped on latex gloves and lifted cushions where she found pens, coins, and paperclips.

The walls were bare except for a photograph of a very young, fit Skeeter in camo with other men and women his age. She peeled it off the wall—it was hung with Scotch tape—and read the back of the photo. *Fort Sill, 1994 Sam Smith, Ed Greene, Leslie Harbond, me, Sasha Tribiana.* He'd underlined Sasha's name twice. Skeeter's arm was around a statuesque brunette with great cheekbones. Sasha, she guessed. Was Sasha Native American? She looked like she might be. *God, please don't let this be evidence that Skeeter has a type.* She felt a stinging sensation in her eyes. *Dammit, Skeeter.* She took shots of the front and back of the photo with her phone and rehung it.

She moved on to the kitchen with its tiny pantry and washer-dryer stack. She was meticulous and went through every shelf, drawer, and nook. His silverware and cutlery was mismatched and could seat three people, tops. He had no cookware to speak of. Or cleaning supplies. His pantry held cereal, and his refrigerator stocked beer and mold. The dryer was empty, and there wasn't any soap for the washer. The freezer was the saddest of all to her. Frozen meals, Banquet and Stouffer's. Inexpensive, big portions, very little variety.

Her phone buzzed. A text. She read it quickly. Another feeler on Gabrielle. She couldn't think about that now. But there was another text there as well. ATF Special Agent Clark Applewood.

You don't return calls. Let's see if you respond to texts.

Typing no was redundant, so she didn't.

She took a seat at Skeeter's little table—a two-top with one chair. She'd been to Skeeter's apartment before today. Once, maybe twice? She hadn't gone past the entrance, and she couldn't even remember the reason for the visits. When she had a check or a gift for him, she gave it to him at her house. Which he was at five or six days a week. He was completely immersed in all things Kat, Carrie, Duds, and Delaney. How involved were they in his life? His *real* life? Speaking just for herself, that would be... very little.

She felt an urge to sob. *No.* She stood. *Be a professional.*

Shaking off her guilt and sadness, she decided that she'd tackle the worst of the two remaining rooms next. The bathroom. Earlier, she'd peeked inside it to assure herself he wasn't stranded or dead in there. It had been foul. Worse than the stinky trash, which she'd discovered in the kitchen under the sink, overflowing. Now, she had to spend enough time in the bathroom to search it thoroughly.

She opened the door with one gloved hand under her nose. It was like stepping into a fraternity house bathroom the night after a big party. A bottle of Wyoming Whiskey with the top off, half full. Beer cans, some smashed and lying on their sides on the counter and floor. Toothpaste droplets dried on the mirror, hairs stuck inside the sink. Cap off the deodorant spray—she hadn't even known people still used spray. No hand towel, no soap by the sink. One empty roll of toilet paper on the yellow-stained floor. A dirty towel thrown over the shower curtain rod. Mildew stains on the curtain. Under the sink, a spare towel, a multipack of Irish Spring soap, and three extra TPs. She lifted the toilet tank lid. Nothing but hard water marks.

She backed out. How could he keep her house so clean and live like this?

The final room. She hoped it held more clues to Skeeter's secret life. Or any life outside his work with her daughters.

What she'd seen so far was banal and depressing. She'd have run from this existence, too, if that's what he'd done.

But then she had an uncomfortable thought. While Gabrielle was far cleaner, isn't this what her life was like for a decade? A small life in a small space? Thank God for Kat and Carrie. And even Dudley. Now she had the department and Leo. *Me and anyone with access to a dating app has Leo these days.*

The bedroom was similarly spartan, and riffling his drawers and closet yielded nothing. But under his bed she found flat boxes of file folders. She slid them out and perused them, considering each for its potential relation to his whereabouts or those of Ashley. The general contents were unsurprising. Personal identification documents. Banking records. Tax files. Tedious PI cases similar in simplicity. Following cheating spouses. Skip traces. Even some collections of bad debts.

She pulled out the banking records. Flipping through statements, she noticed that he made a payment of $500 every month to Gene Hawkins. Month after month, every month, the same amount to the same person. A sick dread filled her. He'd never mentioned the guy. She took pictures with her phone. Hopefully it was payments on an old loan.

She put the banking records away carefully. Several envelopes addressed to someone named Betty Crowheart were marked *Return to Sender*. Skeeter's name was in the return address. She withdrew one and unfolded it. Skeeter's familiar handwriting filled the page. In the letter, he threatened to come after Betty, who he said had dumped him and unfairly accused him of stalking when all he had done was love her. Three more envelopes, three letters like the first one.

Everyone has a past. Everyone has relationships that end badly. But the girl's name. It was Native American. And it sounded so ominous, revealing a side of Skeeter she'd never known. Again, she took pictures. She replaced the letters and envelopes in the box.

And then she saw the word MARILYN on a file folder.

Her mouth went dry. She slid the file out. *Please be a different Marilyn.* She opened it. The top document was notes of an initial meeting with Peg Littlewolf. About the disappearance of her daughter Marilyn and the lack of progress made by the police. She read the contents hungrily, every word of them, cringing when she came to a handwritten description of Marilyn as a "super fine Indian girl" as well as Marilyn's well-thumbed middle school annual for the year before her disappearance, filled with notes and comments from her friends.

He shouldn't still have this.

"Oh, Skeeter, why didn't you tell me?"

But he hadn't.

Peg had hired Skeeter to find her daughter. And despite Marilyn's death being big news in their small town over the last week, Skeeter hadn't mentioned it to Delaney.

THIRTY-SEVEN

"Betrayed. I feel betrayed." Delaney didn't like the whining tone in her voice, but dammit, she felt like whining. She hoped Leo couldn't see that she'd been crying on their FaceTime connection. "And a little panicked."

"I can understand that." Leo's eyes were soft and kind. His voice, too.

"I left my kids with him."

"And he hasn't hurt them."

"I trusted my home to him."

"All you can do is move forward. Try to figure out what this means. Did you go through the rest of his files?"

"Yes. And I took photos of everything. I'm not going to lie. There were some troubling things. Regular payments—substantial ones—that I knew nothing about to someone named Gene Hawkins. Letters to someone named Betty Crowheart that were returned to sender. I'll text one to you. He sounded a little unhinged, honestly."

"Did anything make you think he's *involved* in some way with our cases?"

"You mean did I see homemade tattoo tools or ankle

restraints? No. But what possible reason did he have to hide this case from me?"

"We're going to have to get a search warrant for his place."

"I gloved up, and I put everything back like I found it. Honestly, Leo, this place is so devoid of anything personal that it's like Skeeter doesn't exist. Not the Skeeter I thought I knew. My God, am I just a terrible judge of people?"

"Don't think that. Do you think he has another place to go?"

She closed her eyes. "It crossed my mind. A place where the real Skeeter resides."

"You've never heard him talk about one, though?"

"He's talked about favorite places, but not a place of his own."

"So, what are his favorites?"

"Mountains. He grew up a lake rat, but when he moved here, he found his peace in the mountains." Delaney walked back to the living room. She saw the personal photo of his Army buddies again.

"All right. You headed home after this?"

"Yes."

"Promise me you'll sleep. I need you to play the long game here. I have people on shift working the case through the night."

"I'll try. You, too."

They ended the call.

She sighed as she gave the apartment a last look to be sure she'd set it to rights. Like she could promise Leo she'd sleep. All she could do was get in bed. Sleep wasn't likely to follow, and she knew she'd have her laptop open and be following up on every detail she could think of, into the wee hours.

Suddenly, it was all too much. The tiny space felt oppressive. Her emotions resurfaced, overpowering her senses. Betrayal tinged with her own guilt. What had she been missing about Skeeter all this time? Had she put her girls at risk? She'd come into the apartment thinking she'd let Skeeter down, and she was leaving thinking maybe she'd been enabling someone who was a danger to their community.

She locked up and bolted down the stairs, stripping off her gloves as she ran to the ground floor. Within a few steps away she was out of the illumination from the stairwell lights. She put her hands out but didn't slow down. Shelly was just down the sidewalk, along the curb. Despite all the upgrades she'd made on the Chevelle when she'd refurbished it, it still had old-school manual lock and key. She fumbled for a moment at the door, her fingers numb and refusing to hold the key steady.

A sharp bark at her feet made her jump. Twice tonight she'd been snuck up on. The man who attacked her could have killed her. But this dog didn't sound dangerous. It yapped on repeat. She started to tell it to shut up when she recognized the bark.

"Come on, come on." She finally got the key to work and unlocked the car. Then she turned on her phone flashlight.

Her hands were shaking as she shone the beam at the noise-maker. Black and white fur. A barrel chest. Short legs. A piggy tail. Smushy face. And right now, that face looked pissed.

It was Dudley. Miles from home. By Skeeter's house. She picked him up and hugged him. He slathered her face in kisses and snorted like he was telling her everything that had happened in his eventful day. Then he started wriggling.

She set him in Shelly's back seat.

"Oh, Dudley. How I wish I could understand what you were saying. I was afraid I'd never see you again."

The dog panted and squirmed.

"Wait here just a minute. I have one more thing to do."

She walked over to Skeeter's parking spots.

They were still empty.

Where did he take you, Duds? How did you end up back here? And where is he now?

THIRTY-EIGHT

Ashley woke to the driest mouth she'd ever felt in the purest dark she'd ever experienced. *Where am I?* A deep, wet snore rumbled through the room, and she remembered. The cabin way up in the mountains. With that awful man. It made sense now why it was so dark. There were no streetlights. No house-lights. No headlights. No electricity. She squinted into the darkness. It seemed like there were blackout curtains or shutters over the windows. She glanced over at the woodburning stove. It was quiet. No sound of a crackling flame, which made her aware of how cold she was too.

The snore rumbled again. *He's still here.* From the sound of him, he was between her and the stove. She had to be quiet. If he was asleep, he couldn't hurt her. Or decide to rush her into marrying him. She tried to turn over, but she couldn't. Her ankles were tied up or something. She pulled at them but whatever was around them didn't budge. A scream resounded in her head. She didn't dare let it out.

When the scream had passed, she tried to calm down. That was when she became aware of how thirsty she was. The insides of her mouth felt like they were sticking together. It was so dry, she couldn't even swallow. *Water. I need water.* But none was coming. Another wave of panic hit her. This time, it was so intense that she forgot about being cold and thirsty for a minute.

And then it passed again. She wondered if her dog Slick had missed her. He slept in bed with her. He would have been so lonely. Little Len wouldn't go to sleep without one story each from her and her parents. And her parents—were they as terrified as she was? Her dad always seemed so in control as a priest, but in their house, he said her mother was stronger. What would they tell her to do right now? The answer to that was easy. They'd tell her to turn to God. *But what if the man who has me thinks God is on his side?* She knew he couldn't be right. God would never condone kidnapping girls and forcing them to get married. The man was crazy. That was all there was to it. God was on *her* side.

She closed her eyes and prayed, doing it like her dad had taught her. "Don't pray for outcomes. Pray that you have what it takes to achieve them on your own. God wants his people to do for themselves and others. And always, always thank him. No matter how bad things seem, they could be worse." *Dear God, help me be smart, brave, and tough. Thank you that he didn't marry me yet or kill me. I'm trusting you here. You've always had my back. Amen.*

She felt a little better, but groggy. Very, very groggy. Then she remembered the pills the man had given her. He'd drugged her. She pressed a hand to her mouth. If she'd been drugged, then what had he done to her while she slept? Her clothes were still on. She patted her waist. All of them, the big, baggy dress over her clothes. She prodded at the belt. What had he called it? The chastity belt? It was where it was supposed to be. Now that she thought about it, it was really uncomfortable. The edges of the piece between her legs were digging into her private places, even over her panties and jeans. The metal was rough and when she shifted, she felt it snag on her jeans and the dress.

He had kept the key. She had to wear the thing until he took it off her. No matter how uncomfortable it was, she was willing to keep wearing it if it meant that he left her alone.

She became aware of pain in her arm. The inside of her forearm. It was hot and prickly. She probed it with her fingertips. It was swollen. Sore. Her eyes had adjusted to the light enough that she could see writing on her arm, although she couldn't read what it said. Maybe he'd marked her up with a Sharpie. But a Sharpie wouldn't burn and hurt.

She bit down on her lip until she tasted the sharp tang of her own blood. Again, the man snored. Maybe he had passed out from drinking, and she should try to get out of here? She jerked at her foot restraints again.

Just as she was gearing up to try to work her feet out of them, she glanced up. She felt something odd. A presence behind her. But the man was snoring in front of her. It had to be nothing. She tilted her chin up to look behind her and licked her lips.

A pair of beady, unblinking eyes were staring back at her.

THIRTY-NINE

Leo took a mug of black coffee to Delaney's desk the next morning. It was before seven. He felt as bleary as she looked. "Tell me you slept."

She was braiding her hair at her desk. *Delaney, I don't know how to quit you.* Even at a time like this with a girl missing and two mysteriously dead, she mesmerized him with the simplest of things.

"Don't make me lie to you," she said. Her voice was hoarse.

"Then show me something spectacular you figured out."

"I found three male middle school teachers with black RZRs. I already left a message for Principal Rickets letting him know I'll be by for interviews later this morning. It's an in-service day at the school, so it shouldn't be a problem."

"That is pretty spectacular. Come get me and I'll go with you."

"Okay. And that reminds me—Clara is hanging out with Kat and Carrie today. She promised me she had plenty of paid time off days to use."

"It's fine. Most everyone will be out working this case on the ground today. Speaking of which, I just got back from search headquarters. The morning shift has started. I put out the call for bodies last night. We're getting help from neighboring jurisdictions, so the search area is expanding."

Done with her braid, Delaney rubbed her eyes. "Good. And I called around this morning looking for Skeeter. His phone again. Area hospitals and jails in neighboring counties. I'll try bars when they open. But... I found Dudley."

"That's great! Where was he?"

"Loose at Skeeter's apartment. I dropped him with the girls last night at Clara's. I wish he could speak English. Or that I'd let Kat buy him the GoPro camera she wanted him to wear. He'd be our star witness, I suspect."

"Man, nothing about this case is making sense. Even Dudley's reappearance is weird."

"Right? I also found this last night." Delaney pulled up a picture on her phone and handed it to him. "The picture is from Skeeter's basic training days in the Army. The woman with him is named Sasha Tribiana. Does she look like our victims to you?"

Leo stared at the picture then handed the phone back like a hot potato. "Far too much. And Skeeter looks completely different."

"I'm going to try to find her. Maybe something about the younger Skeeter would help us find him or Ashley. Another thing. I did some research on Betty Crowheart. The one Skeeter wrote those crazy letters to."

"Yes?"

"She is a missing person."

"You're kidding me!"

"I need to follow up on the case. I left a message with the police department in Wisconsin where her parents filed. I haven't heard back yet."

"That's troubling."

"I couldn't figure out who this Gene Hawkins is that Skeeter's sending money to, though. I have a long list of them to go through before I can figure out whether he's relevant."

"No wonder you didn't sleep. I have news, too. The DNA profile on the semen sample Dr. Watson pulled from Sue Wiley is delayed."

"That's extremely disappointing. You sent off for a DNA profile of Samuel Russo, too, right?"

"I did but it won't be back before we have to decide whether to charge him or not. I still think we can prove he's guilty of something. The search turned up the dirty underwear and birth control pills Patricia mentioned. We sent the panties off for DNA testing, too."

"Okay." Her tone infused that one word with every ounce of doubt she could muster. He knew she had her doubts about Russo's guilt. "Caitlin called me last night."

Why had she called Delaney—weren't they on the outs? During the night, Caitlin had submitted a match for him on three additional dating apps. He was beginning to think she was trying way too hard to get his attention. Unease lapped at him.

"Oh? What about?"

Delaney gave him a funny look, then it grew funnier, and then he realized her eyes were bugging out of her head for a reason that was probably synchronized with the reason for the rictus of a smile on her face.

"Caitlin?" he mouthed.

She gave one nod.

He turned. Caitlin was two paces away and closing fast. The woman had a bad habit of sneaking up on him.

"Good. I caught you both," she said. "Delaney, you said you wanted to go over Marilyn's file with me. I wanted to get that out of the way first thing this morning. Having Leo near to be the arbiter of good sense would be ideal."

Delaney snorted. "Comment on good sense withheld because I have some."

Leo withheld a comment of his own. He didn't want any part of being in a room with Caitlin and Delaney.

FORTY

After fifteen minutes to track down a number for Sasha Tribiana and leaving her a voicemail, Delaney met Caitlin in a conference room on the police side of the station—different only from the sheriff's in the pictures on the wall of chiefs instead of sheriffs. The review of the Littlewolf case with Caitlin was less contentious than Delaney had expected it to be, at first. Caitlin walked her back through what she remembered, using the old records to jog her memory. Delaney had the copy she'd made of Skeeter's investigative file in front of her as well as the list of registered black RZRs, ready for comparison to each other and the police file when the time was right.

Caitlin was sitting ramrod straight, hands in her lap. "When I look back on the case now, I can see it's thin. But that's because Peg let us know her daughter had moved in with a relative in Montana."

Delaney kept her face neutral. "I'm making a timeline. How long after Peg reported her missing did she let you know Marilyn was with relatives? I couldn't find a notation in the file."

Caitlin's lips thinned. "I don't remember. Are you sure it wasn't in there?"

Delaney moved on to her next question. "Okay. So, who did you consider your top suspects at the time?"

"Well, we really always thought she'd run off. She had a history of it."

Delaney had seen that Peg admitted her daughter had run off before. "Who were you working the case with? I only saw your name."

"It was mostly me."

Delaney locked eyes with Caitlin and waited. She urged her lips into a tiny smile.

Caitlin looked down at the papers on the table. "Mara Gipson helped from time to time."

Delaney's eyes narrowed. "You mean Chief Yellowtail?"

Caitlin arranged the papers so that the corners lined up neatly. "Mm-hmm. Before she was married, obviously."

"I didn't know she worked on it." Alarm bells were clanging in Delaney's head. After working alongside a dirty cop the previous year, she knew anything was possible, even if she hated believing it. Why would Mara and Caitlin by trying to keep Mara's involvement a secret?

Caitlin tapped a square-tipped nail on Skeeter's file. French manicure, Delaney noticed. "I never knew this private investigator Skeeter Rawlins was working on the case."

Delaney let the issue of the chief's involvement slide for a moment. "He identified potential suspects. Lots of witness interviews. It's a very different type of file from the police records, which as you know was basically family and friends. He identified some people we need to talk to, ASAP." She pulled out a spiral bound notebook marked MARILYN on the front and placed it on the table. "Bull Lawrence. He was a home health care worker in and out of Marilyn's home. Skeeter was also looking into and talking to some of the middle school teachers. He thought Sandy Two Toes was suspicious. And a boyfriend of Peg's named Sammy B, although I have no idea who that is."

Caitlin flipped through the notebook, reading Skeeter's notes and taking her time. When she was done, she leveled a cool gaze on Delaney. "Again, once we learned she ran away, there were no suspects."

"For me, that's the sticking point. That call from her mother and what she actually said. Do you remember talking to her?"

"Uh, no."

"Who did?"

"I'm not sure."

"Chief Yellowtail?"

"Maybe."

"I want to know who that relative was that Marilyn moved in with. And that's difficult since her mother isn't around to tell us anymore. If we can confirm Marilyn actually lived with someone, then there's no reason to pursue Skeeter's suspects. But if we can't, then I don't think we have a choice. Not now that Skeeter is missing."

"Isn't Skeeter being missing more of a reflection on him and his actions than on anyone else involved in the case?"

Delaney had been fighting off that conclusion all morning. "I wish I knew how he came to be hired in the first place. What his entry point was. Maybe if we can find the relative Marilyn lived with, they'd know?" She hated to admit it, but she almost felt the need to utilize one of Leo's fancy investigation plans to manage this case. It was getting too complicated. She'd hoped to track down relatives with the copy of the birth certificate in Skeeter's file, but the father hadn't been named.

Caitlin tapped the notebook. "I wonder why all those pages are torn out of the back?"

Delaney slid the notebook back over and flipped to the end

and found the telltale fringe left from ripping pages out of a spiral bound notebook. "That's odd."

"And he doesn't wrap the case up, that I can see."

"There seemed to be a lot of that going around."

"Did he intentionally remove part of his own notes? Did Peg tell him about the relative in Montana, too?"

"There's so much we don't know."

"There's so much that stinks about Skeeter. Who's to say he didn't become involved as a sick game because he was the one who took Marilyn?"

"Then why did Peg believe she was with a relative?"

Caitlin shrugged, her eyes sparking a challenge. "I guess we'll have to ask your buddy Skeeter when we find him."

Delaney had been biting her tongue through their entire conversation, about something she needed to say, if she and Caitlin were going to collaborate. The charge building between them had brought the issue to a boiling point. "One more thing."

Something in her tone caused Caitlin's pupils to constrict. "Yes?"

"I make a great ally unless you keep me from doing my job."

Caitlin's cheeks pinked. She saluted her with limp fingers. "Understood."

Delaney caught the disrespect. She didn't want to work with the woman. She didn't want Caitlin to be with Leo. She also didn't want to suspect Skeeter. She didn't want girls in their town to be at risk. But if she had to accept the rest of those things, at least she'd laid her cards out on the table.

She and Caitlin were square, for now.

FORTY-ONE

Kat stroked Ringo with a brush, removing the salty sweat from his coat. Clara had let her ride the beautiful bay Quarter Horse that day. Kat hadn't known the coloring was called bay, but Clara had told her about it. Reddish-brown with black points—which meant Ringo had a black mane, tail, and lower legs, and even black outlining his ears. Clara knew tons about horses. She'd been an actual rodeo cowgirl most of her life. Kat had barely even ridden a horse, even though she'd lived in Wyoming her whole life. Her parents had said they didn't have time for horses. Aunt Delaney said horses ate money. But Clara loved them, and Kat did, too. Ringo's head dropped almost to the ground. His eyes closed as he swished his tail.

"This is the best day of my life so far. No school and Ringo." Kat felt a little guilty after she said it. It wasn't that she'd forgotten about Ashley being missing. She was worried about her. Scared for her. But for an hour, riding Ringo had taken her to another world.

Carrie was brushing a horse that was mostly reddish with a white stripe on its nose. Gypsy was a sorrel Quarter Horse.

"You're easily pleased." Clara had taken their saddles back to the tack room, so Carrie whispered. "There are flies everywhere. It smells like horse poop. And the WIFI and cell here sucks."

"I don't care. I think this is my destiny."

"To shovel poop and brush sweaty horses?"

"Rodeo."

Clara returned. "Looking good, girls."

Kat said, "Do you think I have what it takes to be a rodeo cowgirl, Clara?"

Carrie let out a rude laugh. Kat socked her in the arm.

Clara put a hand on Kat's shoulder. "If you work at it. You need a lot of time around horses and on horses. You also have to be fearless."

"She's crazy," Carrie said. "Is that the same thing as fearless?"

Clara smiled. "You're nice and small, which is good for the horse as long as you're strong."

Kat struck a pose, making a bicep muscle and kissing it.

"Not just strong in your arms, but all over strong. And flexible. You have to be even stronger in your mind than your body, though. A horse is a lot bigger than you. You have to make one thousand pounds of animal believe you're large and in charge."

"I can do that."

"And you have to be okay with dirt, sweat, bugs, sunburn, cold, wind, rain, snow, sleet, hail, and falling. You'll fall off a lot. That ground is a long way down and surprisingly hard."

Carrie said, "I'm out. I'll stick to things with wheels."

Kat grinned. "I'm good with all of that. Now I just need a horse and someone to teach me."

"You'll have to get to work on Delaney. Now, let's take these guys to their pasture."

Kat and Carrie untied the lead ropes from the hitching post

and followed Clara out of the barnyard and to the pasture gate. They led the horses through and, at Clara's instruction, released them. Ringo took a few steps and his legs buckled.

"Is he okay?" Kat said.

Ringo hit the ground, where he rolled and kicked his legs, then reversed to his other side and repeated the thrashing there.

"He's great. He's taking a dirt bath to scratch his itches." Clara motioned them out and shut the gate behind them. "Remember that if you can open a gate with one hand, a horse can open it, too. We always double latch." She showed them how. "Now, about your rodeo training. Are you serious?"

Kat skipped along beside Clara as they walked back to the ranch house where Clara lived with her husband. He was a rancher. "Yes!"

"Maybe I can help you out. You'll have to convince Delaney, though."

"No problem. Thank you!"

Kat ran ahead and into the kitchen for a drink of water. Dudley met her at the door and gave her a thorough sniff-over. She'd left her phone on the counter. She picked it up and saw she had a text from Freddy.

this sux can't stop thinking bout ashley

"Boots by the door," Clara said.

Kat forgot about the water. She went back to the door and pried her boots off using a boot jack. The boots hoovered her socks off. She left them hanging out the tops. Then she flopped into a living room chair.

She typed quickly.

So sry

shes smart & tuff shell b ok

Delaney sez it's dangerous 2 b a grl

She watched the three dots, waiting for his answer. She wanted Freddy to notice her and like her like she liked him, but not because something bad happened to Ashley. She and Ashley had always gotten along, but they'd never been close friends. Ashley was the tallest girl in their class and Kat the shortest, partly because Ashley was the oldest and Kat the youngest. Ashley was a whole year older in fact. This year they had science together with Mr. Randolph. The same Mr. Randolph who was old, like Skeeter-old, but kind of hot at the same time. Last semester, everyone had said Sue Wiley had a crush on him. Some people even said they'd seen them together. That she was *with* him. It was too gross to even think about.

Kat stared at her phone. Freddy's reply hadn't come through. Maybe he wasn't sending one. She'd give him just a little bit longer. Her mind suddenly latched on to Mr. Randolph again. This time she saw him in the cafeteria at lunch a few days before. Kat had been eating with Freddy and Ashley and trying to pretend like her heart wasn't broken in two by how gaga Freddy was over Ashley. Mr. Randolph had walked up and said something to them.

No, he'd said something to *Ashley*. She'd left with him. Kat's mind's eye zoomed in for a close-up on Ashley, replaying the scene one more time.

She sat upright, troubled by the memory. Ashley hadn't wanted to go with him. If the gossip was true, Sue was connected to him in a creepy way. If Kat could believe what she'd seen, he'd made Ashley feel yucked out.

She switched out of her texting with Freddy and typed one to her aunt Delaney.

Ashley didn't like our teacher

Then she deleted it. What did she really have to tell her that she could explain in a text? Instead, she typed:

call me when u can

and hit send.

FORTY-TWO

After she finished reviewing the Marilyn files with Caitlin, the women split up for Caitlin to attend a meeting. Delaney updated Leo, then he joined her on the hunt for Bull Lawrence. It didn't take many calls to identify the company Bull worked for—there were only two home health care outfits in Kearny County. Delaney was transferred to a supervisor who had said Bull was with patients, but surprisingly, they'd coughed up his schedule as soon as Delaney had explained this was about getting Bull's help in finding Ashley Klinkosh. They caught up with Bull fifteen minutes later.

Delaney hopped from her truck just in time to trot after the burly, crew-cutted man as he was leaving a patient's home.

"Mr. Lawrence?" Delaney said.

He turned. His eyes made comical Os. "Am I speeding, officers?"

Delaney smiled. "You do walk fast! Can we have a minute?" She introduced herself and Leo.

"I'm always rushing from one patient to the next." He checked his smart watch. "I have five or ten minutes. Oh, and I think you know I'm Bull Lawrence."

"Yes, sir. We can just talk here, then, if you don't mind?"

He flashed a charming smile. Dimples. "How about my car so I don't look like the target of a multi-agency criminal investigation?"

It wasn't normal protocol, but she could empathize. Their meet-up wasn't a good look for someone people trusted in their homes. "Fine by me. Sheriff?"

Leo nodded. "We don't want to cause you any unnecessary trouble."

Once inside the car, Delaney's phone buzzed with a text. She glanced quickly. Kat. She'd read it later. The girl was in good hands with Clara, who would call if there was an emergency.

Delaney said, "I'll get straight to the point since we're short on time. Your name came up in an old investigation that we're revisiting. The disappearance a few years ago of a teenage girl named Marilyn Littlewolf."

His features sagged. "Marilyn. I saw she was found dead recently. So sad. I used to help her grandmother. She died a few weeks after her daughter, Peg. I want to say that wasn't too long after Marilyn left. They all lived together, you know. In Peg's house. I think the old lady would have hung in there, but Peg killed herself. It was all too much for Mama Wolf. Heart attack. She was gone in an instant. I really liked her." His eyes were moist.

"I'm sorry. It must be a tough part of your occupation. Losing patients."

"It isn't for the faint of heart, that's for sure. But if it ever stops mattering to me, I'll know it's time to do something else."

Delaney admired his attitude. "Do you remember how Peg found out what happened to Marilyn?"

He closed his eyes, squeezing them tight. When he opened them he was nodding. "She got a call that Marilyn had moved in with a relative."

"Do you recall which one?"

"No, but whoever it was, it upset her so much that she refused to discuss it. Mama Wolf, too. The investigator may have told them, but if he did, I'm not sure if I ever knew."

"The investigator?"

"Yeah. Peg didn't feel like the police were doing enough to find Marilyn. No offense."

"None taken," Delaney said quickly. "Do you remember the investigator?"

"I talked to him once. Real fit ex-military guy. He was checking out my alibi." He smiled. "I was at the Littlewolf house when they figured out Marilyn was gone and with patients the rest of the day, so I was in the clear."

Delaney gave him the dates and time ranges for Sue's and Ashley's disappearances. "Where were you then?"

He held up his hands like he was being arrested. "Before I tell you that, let me volunteer something that will save us all some time. I'd be looking at me, too. I worked in Marilyn's house. I helped Sue's mom Jayla after she had surgery, although that was about two years ago. And recently I took care of Ashley Klinkosh's grandfather when he was recovering from a stroke. So, I've had connections to all of their families."

Delaney was surprised. Leo was typing notes into his tablet. "Thank you for your openness."

"You're welcome. But I didn't take these girls. I have a pretty packed schedule. Mornings are very hectic. On that first date—that's when Sue went missing?"

Delaney nodded. "Yes."

He pulled a business card from his console along with a pen. He scribbled a name and number. "I was here. You can verify with my patient." He drew a line under the first name and number and wrote another one. "And on that afternoon date, this is the patient I was with. I also submit time sheets, but honestly those can be falsified. They don't check up on us unless there's a complaint."

"We'll do that. Did you talk to Skeeter about anything else?"

"Skeeter! Skeeter Rawlins. That was his name. We talked about whether Marilyn might have run off, whether she had a boyfriend, whether anybody weird was hanging around."

This jived with Skeeter's notes. "Tell us about that. Whatever you can remember."

He ticked his pointer finger. "She actually seemed pretty normal to me. A little serious, maybe. I had a younger sister. Middle school and high school can be rough with girls. But Marilyn had run off a couple of times, just overnight to friends' houses. I didn't know that at the time. Peg told me later. So, I didn't have anything new for Skeeter there, but I guess there's no one else to tell you now."

"Thanks. Did she have friends over a lot?"

"Not really. Mama Wolf's bedroom was the living room. She was Marilyn's grandmother. Marilyn liked to hang out at her friends' places."

"What about a boyfriend?"

"She was so young. I don't think she had one. She never talked about boy crushes around me. Of course, I was a grown man, she might have just been embarrassed. But there was one thing that came up a lot in the last few weeks before she left. Apparently some older guy had been making her feel uncomfortable. Peg was very upset about it. I got the impression it was a teacher, because once I heard her say she was going to get him fired. Marilyn wanted her mom to let her handle it herself."

"Did you ever hear them use a name?"

"No. They'd always hush if I came into the room. I think they were embarrassed about it. I told Skeeter. He seemed really interested. But honestly, I think Peg wanted to keep it quiet."

"Did you ever talk to the police?"

"No. I always wondered why, since I was at their house nearly every day. But, whatever. Peg and Mama Wolf were there, too. Anything I knew, they knew and could tell the cops."

"Okay, so back to Marilyn and her relatives. How again did Peg find out where Marilyn went?"

"The investigator called her. I was there. She was real happy at first. Then she was even more sad. Marilyn was alive, but she refused to talk to her or come home. She felt like she'd been a bad mother, which wasn't true. She was a good mom."

"Did Peg talk to the relative?"

"I'm—I don't know."

"Would anyone else know about where Marilyn went?"

"Well, Mama Wolf, but she's gone."

"Wolf as in Littlewolf?"

"Yeah. But they called her Mama Wolf. I did, too."

"Littlewolf was Peg's own last name then, not a husband's?"

"Right. I don't think she ever married Marilyn's dad. He wasn't in their lives when I was taking care of Mama Wolf."

"There was a boyfriend. Peg's boyfriend. Do you remember him?"

"Sure. Sammy B." His belly shook with a quiet laugh. "Like he was some white rapper. I couldn't ever imagine him on stage —he had this funny limp—but Peg said he had recorded some songs. Was pretty good."

"Do you have any idea how we can get in touch with him?"

"Oh, he's still around. Married Jayla."

Delaney couldn't believe what she was hearing. "Sammy B is Samuel Russo?"

He slapped his leg. "Yeah, that was his name. Samuel Russo." He snorted, shaking his head. "Sammy B. He said the B was for badass. What a dumb shit."

There was a roaring in Delaney's ears. Neither Samuel nor Jayla had mentioned his connection to Marilyn Littlewolf.

It was time to have another chat with the man who used to call himself Sammy B. But first, Delaney had an appointment to keep chasing down possible pedophiles at Kat's school.

FORTY-THREE

The Mountain Man gazed with yearning at the long, lithe body asleep on the table. He hadn't wanted to restrain Ashley—she was *the one*, he was sure of it—but he couldn't take any chances until they were married. Just like he couldn't trust her yet, he couldn't trust himself either. So, the chastity belt had been as necessary as the restraints. He wouldn't disgrace himself with God, who had given him this amazing creature.

He'd tossed and turned most of the night, drawn to her, knowing she was there. So much so that he'd slept late that morning. He'd given Ashley the chance to attend to her necessaries then given her another dose of the sedatives, witnessing her swallowing the pills. She'd been quiet over breakfast until she fell asleep with her head by her plate. He'd returned her to the sleeping table, refastening her restraints before he went outside and tended to the chores. Things were easier now that the weather was warming up. The patches of snow were shrinking before his eyes.

Now he touched Ashley's hair. *So silky.* She didn't move, so he lay the back of his fingers against her cheek. She would be different. She would understand he had protected her, rescued her. He would love her, and she would love him back. She was young and sweet and would give him another chance at children. Their marriage would be a gift from God. Their *love* would be a gift from God.

He swallowed a lump in his throat. Such emotion just from looking at her sweet face. He leaned down and whispered in her hair, "I wish I didn't have to go. I was supposed to do this last week. Then, things went wrong. I hadn't realized you would come into my life so quickly."

For a moment, he thought about throwing away the job and staying with his bride. But he couldn't. Too many people were counting on him, for different reasons. His clients. His so-called boss. And the people he *really* worked for. If he didn't show up, he'd bring unwanted attention to himself. To his lifestyle. What if someone showed up at his door? How could he explain what he and Ashley were to each other?

No, he had to leave and get this job done. Short-term sacrifice to secure their long life together.

"I will return as quickly as I can with a wedding dress. You will be the most beautiful bride. While I am gone, you will be in good hands. And you will have help making our wedding cake."

He pressed a gentle kiss on her lips. She didn't stir. Telling himself it was just to be sure she was okay, he rested his hand on her chest. Her heart thumped against his fingers. Her lungs rose and fell under his palm. His own pulse thrummed in response.

She was alive. She was his.

FORTY-FOUR

Leo paced an empty middle school classroom where a slight formaldehyde smell lingered in the air. Principal Rickets had set aside the science lab for Delaney, Caitlin, and Leo to use for interviews. Caitlin had met them at the school after her meeting. She and Delaney seemed tense with each other but not openly hostile. Apparently, the kids had been dissecting frogs in biology the day before. Various live specimens—a guinea pig, a rat, a snake, and some frogs—were munching and napping in their enclosures on a countertop that ran the length of one side of the room.

So far they'd questioned two of the three male teachers Delaney had identified as having black RZRs and were waiting on the last one now.

Delaney's phone rang. She turned from her tall stool to show him Kat's picture filling her screen. "She's been texting me, asking me to call her."

"Grab it. You can always join us in a minute," he said.

Just as Delaney said, "Hey, Kat," into her phone, the door opened, and a teacher walked in.

"I'm Steve Randolph. You asked to speak to me?" He stood

eye-to-eye with Leo's height. Leo would guess Randolph was a decade older, based on his wrinkles and salt-and-pepper hair. His clothes were fairly youthful, though, and he was a good-looking guy.

Delaney walked out, holding up a finger to indicate she'd be back quickly.

"Hello, Mr. Randolph." Leo introduced himself and Caitlin, who was rotating back and forth in the teacher's chair. "Have a seat."

"What's this about?" Steve pulled a stool away from a table and half-sat, half-leaned on it, his arms crossed over his chest.

Leo raised his eyebrows. Two girls missing within a week, one dead. One Randolph's former and one his current student. "What would you think it would be about? If you had to guess?"

"Rickets didn't say. My guess would be you're talking to Ashley Klinkosh's teachers."

"Close enough. Let's start with Sue Wiley. Where were you before first period a week ago Wednesday?"

"Here. At school. I arrive by 7:45 most mornings."

"How can we confirm your arrival time that morning?"

"Um, maybe someone saw me in the teacher's lounge? I usually get a coffee before I head to my classroom to grade papers and prepare for the day. My first class is second period. Until we heard about Sue the next day, it was just a normal day. It never occurred to me I'd need—what—an alibi?"

"And yesterday after the last period ended—where were you for the next hour?"

"I stayed after to help students with their assignments. I can get you names of kids who will verify that."

The door flew open. Delaney swaggered in, her cheeks rosy-red and green eyes glowing and intense. She exuded a strange electricity. Leo's energy reacted to hers. Something was up.

"This is Deputy Investigator Delaney Pace."

Delaney stopped, hands fisted on her hips, examining Steve

like a mountain lion eying a baby deer before breakfast. "We know each other. He's my niece's science teacher. You know Kat Pace, right? She's friends with Ashley Klinkosh."

"Yes. Kat. She's one of my best students."

Leo leaned forward. Delaney was getting ready to pounce. He could feel it.

"Kat mentioned she was having lunch with Ashley last week. She said you asked Ashley to come meet with you alone in your classroom."

Steve licked his lips and glanced at Leo, then Caitlin. *There's no one coming to save you.* Leo couldn't help the smile that eased up the corners of his mouth. The hint of malice to Delaney's words, Steve's reaction? They were closing in on him. Delaney nodded at Leo.

He cleared his throat. "We were just going over Mr. Randolph's alibis for the time Sue and Ashley disappeared."

Caitlin raised her hand from the teacher's desk. "Uh, Leo? He doesn't have one for Sue."

"True. We were going over his lack of an alibi for Sue and gathering potential witnesses to verify his alibi for Ashley."

"Wait a second. You're making it sound like—"

Leo pointed at the teacher. "Make a list, please, of everyone who can vouch that you were at the school in their presence last period through four-thirty yesterday."

"Um, okay." When Leo stared at him, Steve said, "Now?"

"We can wait."

Steve nodded. He took out his phone and started typing. A minute later, he said, "Can I text it to you?"

Leo gave him an email address. Steve appeared to send the list, then set his phone on the table.

"Now, let's talk about your RZR."

"My razor?"

Leo understood the confusion. "You have a black Polaris RZR, do you not?"

"Oh, yeah. It's been in the shop for the last few weeks, though. Getting tuned up for summer." His phone vibrated on the table in front of him. "Um, can I take a break to go to the bathroom?"

"This shouldn't take that much longer."

"I'm sorry. This is embarrassing. But it's an emergency."

Delaney's lips had tilted up in a malevolent smile. She was still standing with her arms crossed, blocking Steve's route out of the classroom. "I can escort him."

Leo almost laughed. "He's not under arrest."

"We're mid-interview. Humor me."

"Okay, but I'll shadow him. Male bathroom."

Delaney shrugged.

Steve's eyes were saucers. "Um, okay."

He exited the room ahead of Leo, but they walked side by side in the hallway. They passed the boy's bathroom.

"Where are you headed?" Leo said, pointing back at it.

"I have to grab some medication from the teacher's lounge, then I'll use the bathroom there. Teachers avoid the student bathrooms at all costs." His laugh was high-pitched.

Leo grunted. He could imagine. He followed Steve into the lounge.

The teacher went to a locker and retrieved a bag. "I'll just be a minute."

He disappeared down the hall. Leo stood at the end of it. There was a male and female bathroom on either side of the corridor and what looked like a closet at the far end. Leo glanced at his phone. He wanted to text Delaney and ask her what she was so fired up about. But then he decided that while he was there, he might as well use the facilities, too. He went into the bathroom. Steve was not at the urinal. Leo chose the bigger of the two stalls, eschewing the urinal which he'd done ever since campaigning for public office although it had never bothered him before. But as he unbuckled his belt, he sensed something off. The lack of something. The energy of a human presence.

He leaned over and looked under the stall. No shoes. "Steve?"

No answer.

"Shit!" He texted Delaney.

SOS. Steve did a runner.

Then he sprinted out of the bathroom. He had to be methodical, so he checked the women's bathroom first. "Steve?"

No feet. No body. No answer.

He checked the third door in the hall, the one that he'd assumed to be a closet.

It was not a closet. It was an alternate access point to the lounge. *I'm an idiot!*

He tore down the hallway, footsteps resounding. A teacher jumped out of his way, dropping a stack of papers.

"Sorry!" he yelled.

Others poked their heads out of classrooms. A few called out to ask what the matter was. One said, "Do you need help?"

Leo didn't have time to acknowledge any of it. His mind was racing faster than his feet. If he was Steve and was trying to make a getaway, he would take the nearest exit and get to his vehicle. Leo headed toward the front entrance, which let out on a circle drive that adjoined a parking lot. It wasn't a large school, and he found his way to the doors quickly. Delaney was ten feet ahead of him, already pushing the doors open and flying out. A cluster of teachers broke apart and pushed their backs against the walls.

"Excuse us!" he shouted.

He and Caitlin burst out and hit the sidewalk at the same time.

"She's a damn cheetah," Caitlin gasped.

Leo didn't answer as he surged ahead of Caitlin and began gaining on Delaney. She was fast, but he was faster. An engine roared to life, and he saw the flash of running lights. Delaney cut through a row of parked cars. Leo did the same, gaining on her. They were only four car-widths away from the rumbling engine. A Subaru began backing out of its space. The back end swung away from them.

Steve hadn't seen them. He'd be pulling forward right at them.

Leo knew what Delaney was going to do before she did it. "No!"

She launched herself onto the hood of a dark blue Subaru. Leo had a split-second view of Steve's shocked expression through his front windshield.

Leo drew his gun, flicked off the safety, and pointed at the ground in the low ready position. With any luck, Steve would stop when he saw it. Or he'd pull forward close enough for Leo to open the door if it was unlocked. Knock the window out with the butt of his gun if not. He didn't want to shoot a gun in a school parking lot, even on an in-service day, not with Delaney on the hood. Not unless it was a last resort.

He reached the driver's window just as the Subaru surged forward. Steve wasn't going to stop. Out of the side of his eye he saw that Caitlin had run up behind the car. There wasn't time to thumb the safety off and try to bust the window. As the car passed him, he whirled and shot low for first one back tire and then the other. He heard the satisfying thud and hiss from each. Direct hits. He knew the trajectory of his bullets was too low to hit Delaney on the hood, but he worried about ricochet off the pavement for her. Shrapnel for him and Caitlin. Before he could be certain he'd caused no harm to any of them, the bumper crushed into the back of a parked car.

Delaney!

Leo sprinted past Steve to the front of the Subaru. Somehow, his partner—the woman he was crazy about—had managed to wrap her fingers around the top of the hood. Her body was splayed full length with her feet dangerously close to where the Subaru had made impact with the other car, but she'd hung on. He switched his gun to his left hand and stuck his right out. She clasped it, and he pulled her up and off the hood with so much force that she landed upright on both feet.

Then he turned to Steve as he switched his gun back to his right hand again. Through the window, he saw the teacher's face. Blood was running down his forehead into his eyes. Leo walked up to the side window. Steve wasn't wearing a seatbelt.

Leo held his gun in down ready, standing slightly toward the back seat and facing the teacher with his back toward Caitlin and Delaney to his left. "Get out of the car with your hands where I can see them, Mr. Randolph."

Steve groaned.

Delaney reached over and tried the door handle. It was locked. "Open the door. Now."

Steve pressed the unlock button. Delaney jerked the door open.

"Watch for a gun," Leo said.

She nodded, keeping the door between her and Steve. A second later, she said, "His hands are empty and in his lap."

She reached in and turned off the ignition.

Caitlin had moved to stand beside Delaney now, breathing heavily. "What can I do?"

Leo didn't answer her. He spoke to Steve. "Come out now, Mr. Randolph."

Still without speaking or making eye contact, Steve finally climbed out.

"Arms behind your head, fingers interlocked."

He complied, turning to face his car.

Delaney was searching his car.

"Caitlin, can you pat his midsection and pockets for

weapons, then cuff him, please. I'm covering." His personal arrest strategy was to ensure there were no weapons in the easiest to reach areas where offenders commonly stashed weapons, then cuff them before doing a full frisk.

Caitlin nodded. She searched Steve's waist area and pockets but found nothing. Leo kept his gun in the down ready position.

"Nothing." Caitlin used Flex Cuffs and secured Steve's hands behind his back.

"Do a full pat down now, please."

As Caitlin frisked Steve more thoroughly, Leo holstered his gun and Delaney backed out of the car. She was holding a handgun and a knife. Leo would have been more surprised if she hadn't found the common weapons in a vehicle in Wyoming. They could make sure the gun was registered later.

Delaney said, "I have a question for him before we take this any further."

"Go ahead."

Delaney stepped into Steve's line of sight, a foot from him. He cut his eyes down toward the ground. "When did your affair with Sue Wiley end, and did you break it off or did she?"

That was why Delaney had the gleam of a hunter in her eye earlier. She hadn't mentioned Steve and Sue being involved before the interview. Then she'd gone to the hall to talk to Kat and come back on fire, making an insinuation about inappropriate conduct toward Ashley before Steve bolted.

But she hadn't mentioned Sue and a possible relationship until now. Leo stared at the man, almost holding his breath waiting for an answer that didn't come.

The teacher was frozen. He didn't blink. His chest didn't even rise and fall, and the silence spoke volumes. *Kat had known this teacher was preying on her friends.*

Delaney wasn't done yet, though. Her voice was laced with barely controlled fury. "Why was Ashley Klinkosh uncomfortable being alone with you? For that matter, why did you ask her to meet alone with you during her lunch period?"

Steve licked his lips.

And suddenly Leo understood Delaney's rage was about more than Sue or Ashley. It was about Kat's vulnerability and proximity to a predator. Had Freddy known, too? He wished the boy would have told him. Maybe they could have protected Ashley before this happened. But then he realized something. Steve hadn't seemed concerned about his alibi holding up for when Ashley had disappeared. He hadn't seemed overly panicked that he didn't have an alibi yet for the time of Sue's disappearance, which suggested he felt sure of where he'd been and that he could find others who could corroborate his location for him.

Could it be possible that he was a sexual predator but not involved with any abduction or torture?

And if he was a sexual predator in Sue's life, what did that mean about Samuel Russo and his stepdaughter, if anything? What were the odds the girls were being preyed on by two older men? And the initials on the letters. SR. They could just as easily mean Steve Randolph as Samuel Russo. For that matter, what if the connection between the indigenous girls was an irrelevant coincidence?

His head felt like it was going to explode.

But Delaney was still going strong. "What did you do when Peg Littlewolf threatened to report you to the cops if you didn't quit hitting on her daughter?"

Steve spoke in a raspy croak. "I think, I, uh, I need an attorney."

Leo became aware of sweat rolling down his neck and back. Of his shirt sticking to it. He was so angry, he was close to combustion. "Are you sure? We haven't arrested you." *Yet.*

"I want to invoke my Fifth Amendment right against self-incrimination."

"That only counts if you're under oath. Which it sounds like you should be. Mr. Randolph, let's take a ride to the station, shall we?"

"You said I wasn't under arrest."

"I said not yet." He pretended to think about it for a moment. "Delaney, did this man have sex with a minor?"

"I think we'll be able to match DNA evidence to sex notes and to the underwear in her room to Mr. Randolph."

"That's good enough for me. Steve Randolph, you're under arrest for statutory rape. And for assaulting an officer with a deadly weapon."

"What? I didn't assault any—"

"Your car. My deputy." Leo couldn't help but notice that Steve hadn't argued against the statutory rape allegation.

He felt sick to his stomach as he cuffed the man and walked him to the truck.

FORTY-FIVE

Delaney's pulse still felt elevated, half an hour after booking Steve Randolph and sending him to cool his heels in lock-up. She stared out the window of the conference room, hands wrapped around a coffee mug, not even seeing the green mountains in the distance. Her mind was locked on the horrible knowledge that Kat had known—whether consciously or not—that her science teacher was preying on students, as had other kids. Yet none of them had felt safe or *right* in coming forward about it. Her own niece. Her own adoptive *daughter*, who lived in a law enforcement family and who had been victimized before.

What else were their youth keeping to themselves?

A knock at the door broke her out of her worries. It was Caitlin. "Leo asked if you could meet him in the interview room? He has Samuel Russo and his lawyer there."

Without a word, Delaney set her mug down and fast-walked past Caitlin, but she felt the other officer pivot and follow her. The two women entered the interview room. Delaney closed the door behind them.

A blonde woman dressed in a hot pink silk shirt and black

suit stood. "I'm Jenn Herrington. I represent Mr. Russo." She was short—tiny—but she projected an aura of personal power.

Delaney had heard about the attorney. She had burst onto the northern Wyoming legal scene recently. A few months before, she'd had a great experience with Wesley James, Jenn's associate, when he'd represented first her and then Skeeter when they were falsely accused of fencing stolen property. Wesley had been impressive if a bit goofy. She'd just heard that Jenn was former deputy Tommy Miller's counsel in his upcoming criminal trial. Jenn had a rocky road ahead of her in that one as the dirty cop was guilty of multiple crimes with a mountain of evidence against him. The Kearny County Attorney was licking his chops, but Delaney felt sure Tommy would take a deal. Unfortunately for him, law enforcement officers didn't usually fare well in the prison population, so no matter what deal he took, his future was bleak.

"Nice to meet you, Ms. Herrington. I'm Deputy Investigator Delaney Pace. I know your associate, Mr. James."

"Kid." Jenn smiled. "He's great. And he spoke highly of you."

Caitlin introduced herself as well.

Delaney took the seat nearest Leo, and Caitlin sat on the other side of her, with Samuel and Jenn across from them. Samuel's face was beet red, and a vein pulsed in his temple.

Jenn flipped shiny blonde hair off her face. "I hope we're here to talk about my client going home today with an apology."

Leo said, "Not so fast. We have questions."

Samuel made a disgusted sound.

Jenn put out a hand to settle him. "Exactly what charges do you intend to level against my client?"

"We have a few more hours to make up our mind about that."

Now it was Jenn who snorted. "Come on, Sheriff. You've had another girl disappear since my client has been in jail. And

I just heard from a little birdie that you arrested one of Sue's teachers for an inappropriate sexual relationship with the girl. After conferring with my client, he assures me he has done nothing against the law."

Delaney wanted to choke out the little birdie.

"Maybe, maybe not. But as Sue's stepfather and a member of this community, I would think at a minimum he would like to help us find Ashley Klinkosh."

"Of course. But what is in it for him?"

"Besides doing the right thing and proving his good intentions to law enforcement? His answers might fully clear him. We won't know until we know. But I can assure you I have no interest in anything except bringing Ashley home safely and stopping a monster."

Jenn narrowed her eyes but nodded. "Go ahead, for now. I will of course jump in if you overstep."

"As is your duty." Leo dipped his head at her with respect. "Now, Mr. Russo, it's come to our attention that you were dating Marilyn Littlewolf's mother at the time Marilyn disappeared."

"Yeah, so?" Samuel said.

"I don't think it was a secret that when you were questioned about Sue we were interested in any information that would lead to finding her, especially in light of our obvious concern that she was missing only days after Marilyn was found dead. Marilyn Littlewolf was front and center from day one. And then Sue was found dead, similar to Marilyn. Why didn't you tell us about your relationship with Peg Littlewolf?"

"You didn't ask."

"Correct. But there are times when withholding information makes you look like you're hiding it. What are you hiding, Mr. Russo? And is it about Marilyn, or Sue, or both girls?"

Jenn threw a hand in front of her client like a mother

protecting a child in a car. "This is the first I'm hearing of this. A moment to confer with my client?"

Delaney grinned. "Seems like your attorney agrees with us, Samuel."

Samuel lifted his handcuffed wrists, then dropped them heavily in his lap. "I don't want a minute. I ain't done nothing wrong. Not with Marilyn, not with Sue. I didn't tell you about Peg. I don't like to think about her. About what she done to herself. People make like it's my fault. Like I wasn't enough after Marilyn ran off. You should be worrying about what happened to Sue, not harassing people like me who've got their hearts broke twice now. Three times, really."

"We are very worried about what happened to Sue. And to Marilyn. And now Ashley. I think you can help us," Leo said.

"Yeah, how?"

Jenn sniffed. "To reiterate what I said earlier, the bigger question is how will helping you help him?"

Leo said, "I'd love nothing more than to release Mr. Russo based on what we learn today. And I'd say it's a real possibility, but we've got dots to connect."

"What dots?" Samuel said.

Jenn motioned for Leo to continue, but he nodded at Delaney.

She took over. "Let's start with Marilyn. Did you ever suspect or hear that Peg suspected Marilyn was having problems with sexual attention from a teacher?"

"Not specifically." He frowned. "Marilyn was a pretty girl. Real mature for her age. She got a lot of attention. But she was shy. I don't think she liked it. I know it bothered Peg a lot. And Marilyn did skip school a fair amount. I never heard it was because of a teacher bothering her, but it wouldn't surprise me none."

"Did she ever mention a Steve Randolph. Or a Mr. Randolph?"

His face colored so fast Delaney worried he was having a heart attack. "Steve Randolph is a sick fuck."

She spoke quickly in a surge of excitement. "So, Marilyn did have problems with him?"

"No. Sue did. When I found out she was seeing him, I threatened to get him fired and tell her mother unless she stopped."

Confirmation! She felt Leo shift beside her. Delaney wanted to scream in triumph, but she kept it under control. "Sue was... seeing him?"

"I saw them together." He looked at his attorney. Jenn sucked in a breath between closed teeth, but she didn't stop him. "They were in his car, her shirt was off, he was on top of her. Her science teacher! So, I stopped them. Threatened them both real good."

"And you never told anyone?"

"Look, all I cared about was that Sue would stop. She coulda gotten knocked up. This guy was gonna ruin her life. If people found out, they'd talk about her and she woulda never been able to get past it. And it woulda broken Jayla's heart, too. Sue mighta been a pain in the ass, but she was the most important thing in the world to Jayla, and Jayla is the most important thing to me."

This wasn't sounding like a man who'd sexually molested his stepdaughter. But she had to be sure. "Really? Because I heard you were just jealous that she was with him because you wanted her all to yourself."

For a few seconds, Samuel seemed to be processing her words, then he exploded upward, chains rattling. He jabbed one finger across the table at Delaney. "You fucking bitch. Are you saying I was having sex with Sue? Is that what you're saying? You're sick! Sick! I was trying to save her from filth. I never touched her. Never wanted to."

Leo had run around to the other side of the table to restrain him, but Jenn was already on her feet and pushing him back into his chair.

The attorney's voice was calm. "Samuel, that's enough. Don't let her get to you. You haven't done anything wrong, but they have to figure that out for themselves."

Leo stood back, letting Jenn handle it. Samuel muttered and shifted in his seat. Finally, his anger sputtered out. Delaney sat stock-still. Samuel collapsed on the table with his face on his arms, sobbing. Delaney and Leo shared a long look across the table. His said *not a predator* and hers said *I agree*.

When Samuel lifted his head, his face was wet and blotchy. "He was doing it to Marilyn, too? Is that why you asked about a teacher?"

Leo came back around and took his seat by Delaney.

"Maybe. Do you have any evidence of Sue's interactions with Randolph? With her gone, we need something to make this stick."

He glanced at his attorney, then back at Delaney. "You should have found the letters he wrote her in her room. And she saved this pair of underwear. I asked her about them, and she said they were special. I figured they were evidence if I ever needed to go after him. I tried to get to all of that stuff before you were in there." Tears had pooled on his craggy cheeks. "She was going to grow up someday and want to be somebody. Love somebody. Have babies. I didn't want that following her around. My mom—" his voice broke. "She had me real young. I never had a dad. It was some older guy. People called her names. I thought..." His voice trailed off, and he shook his head.

The letters they'd originally thought were from Elijah, then believed were from Samuel. They were from Steve. "We found the letters. Birth control pills. The under garment." She nodded at Leo. He nodded back. Again, they were in sync, knowing they'd use the fingerprints and DNA evidence from them to question Steve now instead of Samuel. If they had to, they could do handwriting comparisons, too. "Thank you, Mr. Russo. I'm sorry for making you talk about something so difficult, but you can see, I think, why this is important, and why what you've just told us will be very helpful."

He nodded and his shoulders rounded and slumped.

"Just a few more things. Back to Marilyn."

He looked defeated and shook his head from side to side. "I'm sorry. I'm sorry I didn't tell you about Peg and me."

Delaney waved it off. The spigots were open and flowing. She didn't want to dam him up. "Peg hired a private investigator."

"Skeezer Ralston," he said.

"Skeeter Rawlins. Did you ever meet with him?"

"Yeah, some. With Peg there."

"Do you recall how Peg came to learn Marilyn had run away?"

"Sure. Skeeter said he'd tracked her down at a relative's in Montana and that Marilyn said she was fine and didn't want to come home."

"Do you remember the name of the relative?"

"I feel disloyal saying."

"It's okay. Peg, Mama Wolf, and Marilyn are gone now. But what you know might help us work backwards to a predator."

He closed his eyes. "Her father."

Delaney bit the inside of her lip so hard she tasted blood. *Now we're getting somewhere!* "What was her dad's name?"

He shook his head. "I don't remember. I may not have ever known. But Peg had just moved Mama Wolf and Marilyn to Kearny a year or two before that. They'd lived up on the Crow reservation. That was what broke her, hearing that Marilyn didn't ever want to talk to her again and had gone to her father. Peg didn't have a nice thing to say about that man. He refused to take responsibility for Marilyn. Never helped with a cent. Wouldn't have no relationship with his own daughter. Peg was always worried she'd done something wrong to drive Marilyn to a man like that. I tried to tell her she was a good mother, but she couldn't never believe it after that. Now I wonder if it was that teacher. Randolph." He said his name like he was hawking up phlegm. "If he was the reason Marilyn run off. Peg killed herself a year later, but she was dead from the moment she heard Marilyn went to her dad."

"I'm so sorry for your loss. For all of your losses."

His lips pressed together in a white line, and he nodded.

"Did Peg try to track Marilyn down after that?"

"Peg pushed me away, but Mama Wolf said she did. They never found him, though."

Damn. They had resources at their disposal that citizens didn't. They would find him. Could he be their monster? Or could he be a critical juncture in the trail to finding the real bad guy? But talking about Skeeter made her remember she had other questions to resolve about him. "Do you remember how Peg found Skeeter to hire him?"

"Oh, she didn't. He came to her. Showed up at her front door one day and said he'd heard her daughter was missing and that he thought he could help her find her. Told her he was a private investigator."

Delaney tried not to let her emotions show. She really hated that answer. Really, really hated it. Her elation about the lead to Marilyn's whereabouts after her disappearance diminished. A horrible thought struck her. Skeeter was the source of the information about where Marilyn had gone, but it wasn't in his file. It should have been there. And now she was hearing that he had sought out Peg Littlewolf as a client after Marilyn vanished? Skeeter, what was going on with you then? And what the hell have you done now? She swallowed and gave herself a moment of quiet breathing to re-center. "Let me ask you one more time, to be really sure I understand. Peg never spoke to Marilyn again —she never spoke to Marilyn's father or anyone else who confirmed they knew where Marilyn was and that she was okay?"

"I don't think so."

"How could she be sure Marilyn really did run away then?"

His face folded. "I don't rightly know. But what reason would that investigator fellow have to lie about it?"

Indeed. And Delaney felt like she was going to throw up.

FORTY-SIX

FIVE YEARS EARLIER

Skeeter sat on his uncomfortable couch in his depressing apartment and dialed the phone again. Why didn't Sam have an answering machine? Or maybe pick up his phone once in a while. Skeeter had called fifty times in the last week alone. No exaggeration—fifty times. He knew Sam had received the check for Skeeter's disability money, because his bank statement showed it had been cashed and deducted from Skeeter's account. Sam, his Army buddy going all the way back to basic at Fort Sill.

When they'd been in the Army, Sam had always seemed like the smartest guy he knew. He was constantly coming up with ideas on how he would make money when he got out. He was also the best at staying in touch after they got out. So many of his friends disappeared. He didn't blame them. He wanted to forget about a lot of it, too. But Sam stayed tight. And then when he'd told Skeeter about the killing he was making on investments in cryptocurrency, Skeeter had been jealous. He'd asked how he could do it with his disability payout, and Sam had offered to invest it for him. His cut was only going to be one percent, which Sam said would be more than enough because Ethereum and Bitcoin were hot, hot, hot.

Skeeter had thought about doing it on his own, but when he'd researched it, he'd found out fast it wasn't for him. Everything about it was confusing. He wanted a piece of that easy money, though. It was great to have a friend like Sam.

He dialed again. There was no answer again. He texted. The text bounced, like it did when a text went to a landline number.

He sent an email to Sam. Skeeter wasn't big on technology or email, but this was serious. His contract with Sam had an email address on it. He typed it in, added his message, and hit send. Seconds later, he got an email back. But it wasn't from Sam. It was an error message letting him know he'd emailed an invalid address.

How the heck could it be invalid? He checked it carefully against what was on the letter. He'd typed it right.

He'd even emailed the whole gang from back at Fort Sill, minus Sam. Bared his soul. *I invested with Sam. He's disappeared. Anyone know where to find him?*

The replies were embarrassing. *He's a crook.* And *Can't believe you fell for his shit.* The worst, from Sasha: *The rest of us cut him out of our lives years ago. I thought you were smarter than that.*

This was bad. Really bad. His old friends thought poorly of Sam, but that didn't mean he'd for sure taken Skeeter's money. Maybe something had happened to him? A car accident? Or was he in the hospital sick? Or had he left Denver to take care of a sick mama or something?

It took Skeeter a while to decide what to do next. He wrote a letter on a piece of notebook paper then grabbed his wallet. He didn't have envelopes or stamps, but he could get them at the post office and mail the letter to Sam's address.

Sam would have an explanation for this. He was a smart guy and a good friend. All Skeeter had to do was find him.

FORTY-SEVEN

Leo felt good about making Steve Randolph spend a few hours in jail before attempting to interview him again. Samuel Russo had been released that afternoon, so they didn't have to worry about Sue's stepfather finding a way to assault the teacher. But in his experience, time to reflect in the right environment softened people up. Encouraged them to talk.

Delaney marched in beside him, her face resolute. "I vote we bluff him hard on the DNA and fingerprints. Nothing Sue said or that other kids say amounts to anything, and I'm sure he knows it."

"Agree. But I also want to focus on things that will lead us to Ashley." He hadn't had time to confirm Steve's alibis for the times of Sue's and Ashley's disappearances yet.

"Even if he didn't do it, he could be an accomplice."

"Yes. Or he might know things from his relationship with Sue or his proximity to Ashley and Marilyn."

Delaney nodded. Her face was pale and her eyes hollow. She looked like she needed sleep. He couldn't give her that, but he wished he could. He wanted to wrap his arms around her and carry her off to someplace safe and peaceful where she could forget all of this. Of course, he didn't want a black eye, so he didn't. He was glad they were tackling this interview without Caitlin. The cop had swung by his office earlier, after the interview with Samuel. It had been awkward to be alone with her, to say the least. It was like she was waiting on him to acknowledge all her dating app advances. *No way in Hell.*

"This feels all too familiar." Leo opened the door and stood back to let Delaney into the interview room first.

Wesley James stood and bowed at the waist. The young attorney was comically earnest. "Sheriff. Deputy. Nice to see you again."

Steve did not rise. He'd aged twenty years since they'd booked him.

"Hello, Wesley. We just saw your partner." Leo took the seat he'd vacated only a few hours before.

"Boss. I'm her associate. And I'm representing Steve Randolph."

Delaney pointed at Steve. "My niece is in your class, you jerk."

Delaney won't be taking the good cop role, apparently.

"And we're off!" Wesley said. "I think you'll find that Mr. Randolph is eager to speak with you. There's no need for hostility."

"He's a pedophile in my niece's school. There's plenty of need. And he should be eager. We have the soiled underwear Sue Wiley saved from their encounters and all his deviant 'love notes' to her. She was only thirteen years old, for Pete's sake!"

Steve jerked like she'd slapped him. "She was very mature for her age."

"You didn't just say that." Delaney glared at him.

Leo put his arm in front of his partner. "All right. It's safe to say that we'll have no trouble making charges stick for the statutory rape of Sue Wiley. The county attorney is salivating for a chance to take this to court." That exaggeration bordered on a lie. He hadn't talked to the county attorney yet. And most times the entire staff in the county attorney's office avoided trial like asking it of them was akin to sending them on the Bataan Death March. But he knew it was what they would have wanted him to say.

"Let's wait on the evidence," Wesley said.

But Steve's eyes were bugging out of his head.

"What we want to focus on for the moment is how we find Ashley."

Steve leaned forward with his cuffed hands stretching across the table. "I don't know! I swear! I never touched her!"

Delaney snorted and rolled her eyes.

Leo said, "Where did you take her, Mr. Randolph?"

"Nowhere! I didn't take her."

"But you know who did."

His eyes begged Leo to believe him. "How would I know that? I have no idea!"

"Just tell us where she is."

"I don't know. I swear I don't know."

"Then how about this. You give us your best guess."

Steve clasped his hands and thumped them on the table in time with his words. "I don't know."

Delaney said to Leo, "I can't believe he expects us to fall for this garbage."

"It's not garbage." Steve was blowing spittle now. "I had nothing to do with any of that. The girls disappearing. What happened to them. Where Ashley is. Nothing!"

Leo decided to take it down a notch. Try another tactic. "You were involved with all three girls. Marilyn Littlewolf. Sue Wiley. Ashley Klinkosh." He held up a hand as Steve started to protest. "Your involvement with each might have differed, but you were in a position to see who they interacted with and potentially learn things directly from them that others might not. We want to know what you know. And we'd like to start with Ashley."

Steve shook his head rapidly. "Nothing. I swear. Ashley was quiet. She didn't say anything to me except the shortest possible answers to direct questions. I knew less about her than my other students."

Delaney stomped Leo's foot. He wasn't sure if there was a message in it or if she was just frustrated, but he was, too, and he wasn't letting up.

"Okay. What do we need to know about Sue?"

Steve sighed. "She was a nice girl."

"Did you ever see any men—besides yourself—who showed inappropriate interest in her? Followed her? Approached her? Watched her, stalked her? Or did she tell you of anybody like that?"

"No one in particular. But you've seen her, or seen pictures of her, right?"

Leo didn't even nod in response.

"She was"—his Adam's apple bobbed—"effervescent, maybe? She glowed. She was beautiful and womanly in a girl's body. She attracted that kind of attention all the time. But there was no one that she complained about to me. And I never saw anyone crossing the line and following her around."

"Did you ever feel followed when you were with her?"

Steve shot a look at Wesley.

Wesley said, "Asked and answered. You asked if anyone followed her. As to any other implication in your question, I'm instructing my client not to answer it further."

"All right. Marilyn is a little different. She disappeared a long time ago. Her family was under the impression she'd run away. In fact, they thought she had run to get away from *you* for a while."

Steve's jaw worked for a moment. Leo let him stew in the silence.

"Then they were told she'd gone to live with her dad in Montana. Given your... *proximity* to her, did you have any reason to think she was looking for her dad?"

Steve was nodding rapidly. "She was definitely looking for him. We were talking about DNA in my class. The traits that are passed down through genetics. Later she told me that she wanted to find her father to learn more about herself."

"Did you tell anyone else this?"

"No one asked me."

"A girl goes missing and you know she wants to look for her father, but you don't think that's relevant?" Delaney asked.

Steve looked at the table.

"Did she tell you his name?" Leo asked.

Steve cocked his head, closed his eyes. "It was a long time ago. I do think she told me."

"Take your time."

Steve nodded. "She said he used to live on the reservation. That she would see him around. But that he moved north. Roundtop. Round Rock. Somewhere in Montana."

"Roundup?" Delaney asked.

He snapped his chin down. "That's it."

"It's north of Billings," Delaney said to Leo.

"Geno?" Steve said.

Leo frowned. "What?"

"I think she said his name was Geno. I don't remember the last name."

Leo cut his eyes to Delaney. She was already up and heading out the door. He turned back to Wesley and Steve. "That will be all. For now."

FORTY-EIGHT

Sitting in Leo's office, Delaney bounced her knee. The night before, she'd made locating Geno her insomnia project. She'd been so energized when she left the jail. Unfortunately, it didn't take long to find the one and only Geno of the age to father Marilyn Littlewolf with ties to the Crow reservation. Geno, a nickname for Gene, last name Hawkins. The name of the man who Skeeter had been mailing monthly checks to for years. She called and woke up Samuel Russo to see if he recognized the name from Peg. After Samuel cussed her out, he said, "That's the SOB all right."

That would have been great news if one of the first documents she'd found about him online hadn't been his obituary from a month before. In a car wreck in Kansas, not Montana. She'd broken the bad news to Leo first thing that morning along with the full story.

They would not be talking to Marilyn's father.

She leafed through Skeeter's Marilyn Littlewolf file for the thirtieth time. She'd read every document thoroughly, scanned them, and touched them. And she couldn't find a single mention that Skeeter had talked to Marilyn or any of her

Montana relatives. Not a word about Marilyn's father. Just the bank records. She hated looking up at Leo, admitting what she'd found.

"Nothing," she said to him. "And he did a decent job of documenting his other steps and interviews. Talking to Peg, Mama Wolf, Samuel formerly known as Sammy B, Bull Lawrence, Marilyn's friends. He noted that he intended to talk to her teachers, but it appears he wrapped up the investigation before he did that. He even has an investigation plan"—she held up a piece of paper—"and although it's not the work of art that yours are, it's a solid effort."

Leo said, "Maybe it got lost. Like fell out of the file. Or was misfiled."

The sadness and hopelessness she felt were overpowering. "Maybe. But his plan didn't mention the Montana connection either. Leo, he kept a running track of his hours in his notes. I compared them to his final invoice to Peg. If he talked to Marilyn or her dad or other family in Montana, he didn't include any extra time for that. His totals add up to the records he kept in his notes. And there are pages torn out of the back of his notebook. Plus the checks he's been sending Geno Hawkins for years."

"That doesn't sound great."

She pushed baby hairs back from her face. They were suddenly irritating her skin. Everything was bothering her. Her uniform felt tight. The chair was uncomfortable. Her eyes burned like she was coming down with something. She didn't have a lot of people she counted on. Leo. Mary. Skeeter. Now it appeared her faith in Skeeter had been misplaced. What did that say about her ability to read people? It was a cornerstone of her profession. If she'd been this wrong about Skeeter, could she trust her judgment about Leo and Mary? Or anyone?

"Let's look at Skeeter's availability to commit these crimes."

"I doubt seriously we'll be able to figure out where he was at the time Marilyn disappeared."

"Did he have a job then?"

Delaney actually knew the answer to that. "Skeeter was unemployed when he moved to Kearny. He didn't start working until he became a private investigator."

"Sounds like his schedule would have been pretty fluid then."

Delaney pulled out her phone. She saw a text from her ATF buddy.

No reply to texts either. At least you're consistent.

She ignored it and hit Mary's record to initiate a call. "Mary might know. She worked for my brother at the Loafing Shed back then."

Mary picked up on the second ring. Delaney immediately heard Ian Munsick's voice at a glass-rattling volume. She recognized it. "Long Live Cowgirls." In the modern West, cowgirls was a term for females that included Native Americans—a big advancement from the days of "cowboys versus Indians." It gave her a sad twinge as she thought of Sue and the girl's passion for the Indian Relay Races. "Hi, Delaney. We're getting a little early happy hour rush here. Business is booming!"

"All thanks to you. I'm putting you on speaker with Leo. We have a Skeeter question."

"Okay."

"Did you know Skeeter before he started doing PI work?"

"Yeah, sure. He was trying to get into law enforcement, but no one would hire him. When that didn't work out, he met an old PI—mostly a drunk if you want to know the truth—who talked him into working together, just before the old guy croaked."

Delaney hadn't known Skeeter had tried to be a cop. She

felt a frisson of sadness. "Do you recall him talking about working on the Marilyn Littlewolf case?"

"Do I ever! It was literally the first case he ever landed on his own. He was over the moon about it. That's *all* he talked about for a while."

"Did he ever mention speaking to Marilyn herself or to her dad or any of her family out of state?"

"I don't think so. Or at least I don't remember."

"Before he took the Littlewolf case—was he working any other jobs? I'm trying to figure out how busy he was."

She guffawed. "He kept office hours here. No, he wasn't working any other jobs. I mean, he was trying. When I first met him, he was working out and applying for jobs and all kinds of things. Then that stuff just kinda tapered off and died. He started drinking more and put on weight."

Delaney looked at Leo.

He said, "Thanks, Mary. We appreciate it."

"You guys go find Ashley Klinkosh."

"Will do."

Delaney hung up the phone. "I'd say we'd need to consider that a probable lack of alibi for Marilyn. Sue was taken right before the start of a school day. Carrie drops Kat at school. Skeeter doesn't start with us until mid-afternoon when he runs a few errands for me and picks up Kat."

"So that's probably no alibi for Skeeter regarding Sue either."

"And then there's Ashley." Delaney literally felt sick.

"After school."

"When Kat called me to tell me Skeeter hadn't shown up."

"No alibi."

"Oh, Leo." She gripped her hands together, squeezing hard.

"You've run his background before, right?"

"Yes. When he came to work for me. Criminal and professional references. There were no red flags."

"And if we were investigating Skeeter—"

"Which we are."

"Which we are. The person we'd come to for information about him would be you."

"Yes."

"So, we've exhausted that line of inquiry. Next we'd look into his past."

"The background check."

"Leaving us with... what?"

"That he owns a RZR like the one Sandy Two Toes saw Sue being taken in. That he matches the description she gave."

"That he is someone Ashley knew and would have trusted."

Delaney winced. "We have a few more leads I've been tracking down. I'm waiting to hear back from the police in Wisconsin about the woman he wrote to there. Betty Crowheart. Then there's a woman in his basic training picture."

"The one who looked like the girls who have been taken. You showed me."

"Sasha Tribiana. I left her a voicemail. I didn't hear back." Delaney stood. "I'll follow up with those again and let you know if I get anything."

"I've got a piece of good news. Devon found Sandy Two Toes and coaxed her in to work with a sketch artist. They should be done soon."

"That's great! Did you—"

"Make sure she gets a shower, change of clothes, a meal, and some water to go?" He saluted her. "Yes. I channeled my inner Delaney."

She smiled. It was a good thing among a lot of very bad things. "Thanks."

Back at her desk, Delaney left another voicemail for a detective in Wisconsin. Then she scrolled through her Recents and dialed the South Carolina number for Sasha Tribiana. She'd gotten lucky finding the woman's number so quickly. Tribiana wasn't a common last name in the US, and she found only one Sasha. Verified her through her social media—age, looks, military background— and was able to track her right down to where she lived and get a number. The outgoing voicemail identified Delaney as having reached the number for Sasha and to do her thing, which she had. Sasha just hadn't done her thing back.

But this time, the call was picked up. "Hello?"

"Hello. My name is Deputy Investigator Delaney Pace of the Kearny County Sheriff's Department in Wyoming. I'm calling for Sasha Tribiana."

"Speaking. What's this about?" The woman's voice was clipped. The accent was definitely *not* southern. More like Wisconsin. Or Minnesota.

"We're investigating the disappearance of some teenage girls. I found your name on a picture at the home of someone whose name has come up in our investigation."

"That's creepy. I don't know anyone in Wyoming. Where'd you say you are again?"

"Kearny. The name of the person is Skeeter Rawlins. You're in a picture he kept from basic training in the Army. It's a group photo."

"Yeah, I have that picture, too, I think. But wait—is he missing? No, you said missing girls. Did he get into trouble?"

"We don't know. I'm sorry."

"I don't know how I can help. I haven't seen him since basic training. We were on some of the same email chains, back when that was more of a thing. You know—dumb jokes and Christmas letters. But he didn't chime in much. And I never see him on social media or anything." Her voice was less clipped, but her tone still held Delaney at arm's length.

"I'm going to level with you, Ms. Tribiana. Skeeter is a

person of interest, but he also works for me. He helps me run my household, I guess you'd say. While he does some private investigator work part of the day, the rest of it he spends keeping my tween and teen girls in line. I know him very well. Or I thought I did. But I don't know about who he was as a younger person. You struck me in that picture because you look like the girls who are missing." And because Skeeter seemed taken with her. Underlining her name twice. His arm pulling her into him.

"What do you mean?"

"The young women are Native American. With your dark hair and eyes and striking features, you could be related to any one of them."

"Ah. I have Italian ancestry. Not Native American."

"Makes sense." It didn't change her similarity or the possibility that Skeeter had a type, though.

"Is that all?"

"I was wondering if Skeeter had any trouble with the opposite sex? I don't mean getting dates. I mean did he ever get too aggressive or fixated or obsessed? Did he ever scare someone or make them nervous?"

"You're asking if he was a perv?"

"In so many words, I guess so."

"Hold on." Delaney heard her put in an order for a green smoothie. "Okay. So, um, did Skeeter ever mention me?"

"No."

"Does he see anyone from basic?"

"I don't know."

"Because anyone who knew us would have told you that the person he obsessed about and made uncomfortable was me."

Delaney closed her eyes. "What happened?"

"We went on a date. If you can even call it that. I wasn't into him. He was way too into me. He was talking about marriage and babies and protecting me from all the bad guys out there before we had dessert. It freaked me out."

"Did he ever take you anywhere against your will? Restrain you? Hurt you?"

"No. I met him for our one and only date."

"Did he stalk you?"

"No. He just moped. Called me when he was drunk. You know. The usual. He didn't scare me. He just made it hard to be around him and our friends."

"Did you ever hear of him doing anything like that with other women?"

"Nope. But there weren't a lot of women in basic with us."

"This was very helpful. Is there anything else we should have asked you or that you'd like to tell us?"

"Just, when you talk to Skeeter, tell him that I appreciate that he kept his word. He never contacted me again after basic. Other than in the group emails, and that was fine. As far as I'm concerned, what happened back then is history. You asked, so I told you about it, but otherwise, it was done. Oh, and you can tell him he's a giant sucker for giving Sam his money."

The name rang a bell, but was it only because of Samuel "Sammy B" Russo? "Sam? Who is he? And what do you mean?" But even as she asked, her mind fixed on the group photo from Fort Sill again. There had been a Sam in the photo.

"Get Skeeter to tell you. Better yet, don't. I shouldn't have said anything. It doesn't have anything to do with women or girls. Just Skeeter being a dumbass. I hope you find those girls, and I hope he didn't have anything to do with what happened to them."

You and me both. "What does your gut tell you?"

Delaney heard a quick intake of breath, then Sasha ended the call.

FORTY-NINE

No sooner had Delaney walked out of his office than a call came for Leo. The sketch artist. Leo answered with, "Apollo, how did it go?"

Apollo Nichols did not hail from Kearny, Wyoming. Sketch artists were still an integral part of police work, but with the greater prevalence of public and private cameras, there was less need for them. Often camera images were too grainy, or the lighting or weather made them unusable. Most witnesses could only remember five or six features, but a sketch provided a starting place for officers when trying to identify witnesses, suspects, or even objects. Apollo lived and worked as a law enforcement consultant in Cheyenne, but, thanks to technology, the sheriff's department was able to benefit from his talents.

"Not the easiest witness." Apollo talked in a robotic buzz. Since having his voice box removed due to cancer, he used an electronic larynx to create his voice.

"Sandy Two Toes is a legend around Kearny. I've never held a fully coherent conversation with her. I would imagine doing it over Zoom exacerbated the problem."

"Definitely. The issue was her fascination and inexperience

with the technology. Well, and focus. But she got a good look at this person. She felt strongly about remembering his traits. More decisive and confident than most people I work with."

Leo would never have thought of the woman that way. She had ultimately fled the scene at Buns in the Barn despite the hot lunch she left behind. But that had been fear for her own safety, from what he could tell. This was a very different situation. "I wish we had someone who could give you a second description of the guy."

"Maybe you'll track one down with my sketch."

"True. And Sandy agreed that your drawing was a good likeness?"

Apollo laughed. "She said, and I quote, 'that's the bad man that take the girl.'"

"Good. You'll get your invoice to us?"

"You know it. Sending it now with the file."

"Thanks."

"One more thing. She kept talking about this ORV the guy was driving, so I sketched that up for you, too. Black four-seater. More sport than utility. Some white trim colors. And I think one of those after-market fabric covers with the fiberglass windows and windshields, I think."

Leo compared it in his mind to the video. It seemed like a possible match. "That's great. Consistent with a Polaris RZR? We had some grainy video that we thought might be it."

"Yeah, it could be. I didn't get the feeling she remembered the make or model. But it gets better. She felt very sure this one had a bumper sticker on it. FEAR GOD, she said."

"Fear God? I don't know if I've ever seen one like that before." *A homerun if this information is reliable.* Leo was ashamed he'd assumed Sandy didn't read. "Thanks, Apollo."

"No problem. Good luck finding the girl, man."

Leo ended the call and pulled up his email through his laptop. Apollo was fast. There was already an email with an attachment in Leo's inbox. He saved it to his hard drive, then to the record system. Finally, he opened it.

He looked at the image. Staring at it was like having a bucket of ice water thrown in his face. Pure shock. The painful kind.

The guy Sandy had seen? He knew him.

FIFTY

Delaney whirled in her chair when she heard Leo's heavy footsteps coming down the hall. Was he running?

"Delaney, I have to show you something," he said.

"And I have something to tell you. I talked to Sasha."

Leo seemed not to hear her. "I just emailed you the picture from the sketch artist. Pull it up."

Something in his voice scared her. She was already trembling when she turned and pulled up the email. Clicked to open the picture. As she zoomed in, her hands were shaking convulsively. Leo had pulled a chair up behind her and taken a seat.

"First impression. Do you know this person?" Leo asked over her shoulder.

"You know I do." She hadn't meant to snap the words. It was that or sound defeated. She'd rather keep fighting. "It's Skeeter."

"Okay. Second impression. Keeping in mind this is a sketch done by an artist from a sole witness who has mental health issues. Alternative explanations. Alternative identifications."

Delaney returned the drawing to its original size. "First, she could have seen Skeeter a million times in town and be remembering him from them."

"True. Keep going."

"She could have had a negative interaction with Skeeter and because of that, be fixated on him."

"Also true. More."

"She could have seen Skeeter actually helping Sue. Whatever happened to her could have occurred later."

"Although I would have expected him to let us know about that interaction, if it occurred."

Delaney shrugged. "Yes, except he hadn't been telling me anything lately. That's all I have for alternate explanations for why Sandy saw Skeeter. Alternate identities—it could be someone that just looks a lot like him."

"How would you describe that?"

"Caucasian male. Forty to sixty. Short dark hair going gray. Dark eyes, no glasses. Skin tending toward ruddiness. Tall, burly. Muscular. No visible scars or tattoos. No facial hair, although that can change."

Leo nodded. "A lot of that can. Hair can grow, be cut, or be colored. Contact lenses change eye color. Glasses can be added. Lifts can be put in or taken out of shoes. Clothing can change body appearance. Scars or tattoos can be covered or even drawn on."

She heaved a sigh. "Yes. Which means that someone could have disguised his appearance to look more like this when Sandy saw him or have changed his appearance since. Maybe someone who wanted to look like Skeeter."

"There are a lot of variables, it's overwhelming. I could do a spreadsheet of possibilities."

"Please don't."

"The artist did one more sketch."

"Another person?"

"Another thing. The ORV." Leo pulled it up on his phone and showed her.

"Looks like Skeeter's." Her eyes and voice were flat.

"Does his RZR have anything like this?" He showed her the FEAR GOD bumper sticker.

"Fear god? Hell, no. He has one with the Wyoming Whiskey label." Hope sparked in her chest. "Leo, it's not his RZR."

"A sticker can be added or covered."

"Let me have my one good moment."

"Sorry, but it's true." He reached out like he was going to touch her shoulder. Their eyes met. He dropped his hand.

She shook her head and brushed hair behind her ear. "You're wrong. You'll see." She took a deep breath. "There's something I learned talking to Sasha, though. First, that she and Skeeter had one date and he was obsessed with her but more lovesick than creepy. Second, that he lost a ton of money with an Army buddy."

"What do you conclude from that?"

"What if Skeeter was desperate for money and he made a bad choice. Maybe he was paid to look the other way with Marilyn. Or, and this is worse, but maybe he sold information about her. So, he kept it out of the file."

"You're basically saying he sold Marilyn to a monster."

"No! That's not what I'm saying! Besides, it makes no sense in light of the payments he made to Marilyn's father."

"That doesn't explain Sandy seeing him. Or why he's missing now, just when Ashley disappeared."

"If Sandy even saw him! It's not his RZR."

"Maybe it isn't. Maybe it is."

Delaney wanted to put her head down on the desk and sob. After she took a hammer to all the electronics on her desk. "I disagree."

"Where does this leave us?"

Seconds ticked by in Delaney's mind. Where did it leave them? Without Skeeter in her girls' lives—or in her life. The old Skeeter was dead if these facts summed to a figure she feared they did. As the clear suspect to pursue in a horrific case, with two girls dead and one missing. With...

No.

I do not accept it.

Skeeter did not do this.

Delaney felt herself swaying forward and backward. No, rocking. She was rocking. Breaths away from keening and weeping like a child.

"Delaney?" Leo's voice was tender. Compassionate.

And she hated him for it. She hated him for being worthy of her love and yet the wrong person to receive it. She hated him for moving on from her rejection of him. She hated him for being good at his job and understanding as she struggled to accept the mounting evidence against her friend.

Her emotions—her inverted love—exploded out of her. "You can chase after Skeeter if you want. I see how this looks. I accept that. But I don't accept the conclusion." Her words came out like a barrage of machine gun fire.

Leo's head tilted. He looked confused. Hurt. A little frightened. "Come on. We're a team."

She was spinning out of control, her emotions overloading her system. She knew she wasn't making sense. That she was acting irrational. She didn't care. "Not on this. If you need me to take a leave of absence, I will. Unpaid. But I'm going to find Skeeter. Because there's one conclusion this evidence points to that no one has mentioned. Not even me, I'm ashamed to say. But it's the true one, and I'll prove it." She sucked in a deep breath. "Skeeter is a victim in this, too. I don't know how, but that's what my gut is telling me. He needs my help. I'll find

Ashley. I'll find him. When I bring them both back alive, you'll see."

Leo put a hand out, tamping down her objections. "I hear you. I don't need you to take off work. We're heading in the same direction."

She stood, pointing at his office. "We're not. Your gun is drawn and pointing at Skeeter. Mine is pointing away from him, at whatever the danger is that we haven't figured out yet. Go, Leo. Do what you have to do, but just go."

He pushed back in his chair but didn't stand. "You have an idea? Something new to pursue? Because whatever *reason* you have for tracking Skeeter, you still have to find him. Me, too. And I'm out of ideas."

She had been without a clue until that second. Then she turned to the brilliantly colored maps lining the inside walls of her cubicle. Why hadn't she thought of them before? Her whole life she'd believed in the power of geography. The curious happenstance of life forces on raw materials. Heat, pressure, water, rock, minerals. The creation of topography. The confluence of location. And there, on her maps, was an answer. She just didn't know what it was yet.

She grabbed a wax pencil from her drawer and drew an X on the spot where Marilyn's body had been found. Did the same thing where the hiker discovered Sue. Then she drew arrows upward from each X. The inflection points. Where their deaths had become inevitable. Up in the Bighorns atop cliffs and hillsides. Then, with a flourish and long experience eyeballing distance onto maps, she drew circles. One around Marilyn's fall location, the other around Sue's. She scribbled out the downhill sides, not bothering to explain her reasoning, hoping Leo followed. That left a wide area within the circles that was up in the mountains, with a small overlapping slice between the two of them.

She stabbed her finger at the overlap with one hand and

swiped away tears with the other. "There. I'm going to start there." She owed it to her girls. To Skeeter. Hell, she even owed it to herself, to the little girl who'd been more lost than anyone had ever realized, right in plain sight. Under her watch, no one was going to be left behind. Not other people's children, and not her family.

FIFTY-ONE

Delaney took a deep breath, reining in her big emotions, and gestured at the circles she'd drawn on her maps. "If the girls were staying or being held up there somewhere—like in a cabin or a travel trailer or even a tent—we might be able to identify where. They might have just been passing through, but that seems like an awfully big coincidence. It seems like we need to explore the first alternative."

Leo was nodding. "Looking for a place up there makes sense. Sue had been gone for days and Marilyn for years."

Delaney nodded and pulled up aerial maps for her search area. Her wall maps were good for topography, elevation, and roads, but she wanted images of what actually existed in the space now. Leo leaned over her shoulder so close that his breath fanned her neck. *Why can't I not notice him, dammit?* They studied the screen together, Delaney's skin tingling.

"What's that?" Leo pointed at a bit of shine in an otherwise endless expanse of trees.

"Could be a rock formation. There's plenty of them in the forests and there's lots of sparkly bits in them. Or it could be a roof."

He nodded. "Or a travel trailer or vehicle."

"True." Wyomingites loved their travel trailers and dispersed camping. In this part of the state, actual organized campgrounds were few, which was confusing to out of state camping visitors. One look at the national forest maps cleared it up though. Rules specified where to pitch a tent or park a vehicle—how far from a road, how far from a riparian area. Delaney loved that it scared off all but the hardiest of campers. *Let them camp in California or Colorado.* "Although I don't see any roads that would make that a feasible camping spot."

"It's crazy to think someone might own property up there."

"What do you mean?"

"To build a cabin."

"It's unlikely they do. There are pockets of private property, but most of the cabins you see up there are built courtesy of hundred-year leases with the federal government."

"Then who owns the cabin?"

"Well, the government, if it's still standing at the end of the lease. Until then, the people who built it or bought it, but honestly, it's pretty risky. The government can invalidate or revoke the lease. They can refuse to let people rebuild if their cabin burns down in a forest fire."

"I can't believe people build them."

"You'd be shocked. Those are some of the most sought-after dwellings in the state. Forget the mansions in Jackson Hole. With enough money, you can buy whatever you want, except lease cabins. People hold onto these like precious gems." Delaney did a screenshot. "It's hard to see with all the trees in the way."

"I've got an AI tool that identifies construction."

"How does it work?"

He shooed her with the back of his fingers and settled in at the keyboard, fingers flying. "From what I understand, it looks for signs of things that are man-made. That don't occur in nature. Like perfect ninety-degree corners." He hit enter. "There. Let's see what it finds."

"How long does it take?"

"Exactly that long." Leo grinned. "We've got results." He pointed at them. "Here. Here. And here. It thinks those are buildings." He zoomed in as close as he could get. "Two of them seem like clusters of buildings. This last one... hard to say. Looks really decrepit."

"There's logging, mining, and cattle grazing history around there. It could be the remains of old shelters. But what there isn't much of is private property. Those other two that look to be in good shape—I'll bet they're forest service lease cabins."

"How do we find out?"

She hit speaker on her phone and accessed a number from her contacts. "You call your favorite employee in the regional U.S. Forest Service."

"And our favorite employee is who?"

When she heard a hello on the other end, Delaney said, "May I speak with Trish Flint please? This is Deputy Investigator Delaney Pace calling."

"Hi, Delaney. This is Trish. I haven't talked to you for a while."

"Since that fire out at Pete Smithers's place."

"That spread up into my forest. Don't remind me. I hope you're calling with something better today."

"I need to identify the owners of some cabins on forest service leases."

"Oh, you want Moira Hilton, not me. I'll connect you and let her know to treat you right."

"That's great. I know Moira. Thanks, Trish." Once upon a time long ago, Moira had worked at the church Delaney's family attended.

"Take care."

A few moments later, an older, high-pitched voice came on the line. "It's me. Laney, sweetheart. How are you?"

"I'm good, Moira. How are you?"

"Well, Lorne passed on in February. I've just come back to work, and I don't mind telling you, it's been a struggle. The commute feels longer all the time, thinking about him and missing him on those drives."

"I'm so sorry to hear that. You two were a wonderful couple."

"Thank you, dear. But you didn't call for that. Tell me what this is really about."

"Forest service cabins, or what I believe are cabins. I've identified some from aerial photos. I need to find out who owns them and get in touch with the owners."

"You don't have names?"

"I don't have names or plot numbers or addresses. I've got map dots."

"You don't ask for much, do you?" Moira laughed.

"This isn't even a brain teaser for you. I'm going to show you these drawings and you're going to know instantly."

"Send me over what you do have to my email." She recited an address. "I'm sure I can help you out."

"Thanks, Moira."

"Kiss that sweet little niece of yours for me. I miss seeing her and her mama at church. You know, the door's always open. You used to spend a lot of time there and look how good you turned out. It would be so nice to have you back."

Delaney tried to block out most memories related to her ultra-religious grandparents, of which compulsory church attendance on Wednesday nights, Sunday mornings, and Sunday nights were a major part. But not everything about the memories was bad. Not all the people there were like her grandparents, Moira being a prime example. She went with a simple, "Thank you. Talk soon."

Leo had hijacked her keyboard while she was on the phone. He already had an email queued up with attachments and an explanation of what they needed.

Delaney raised her brows. "That doesn't sound like me."

"You're welcome. And, by all means, edit away."

She hit send. "This may take her a second. There's something else I wanted to show you about the overlap in our circles I drew up in the mountains."

"What's that?"

"We need to go to a map that shows the roads. I think I remember a place in that area from when I was in high school."

"What kind of place?"

She navigated to the Wyoming State Parks, Historic Sites, and Trails website and retrieved their ORV map for the Bighorns. "It's some springs that have significance to the Crow. I can't remember the name. I only went by there once—I felt like I was trespassing, even though people used to go there to party. But I think I'll recognize the roads if I see them." She traced the screen with her finger, lips moving.

"Something like Medicine Wheel?" Leo was referring to a ring of stones around a rock cairn high in the Bighorns that was sacred to Native Americans.

"Not in the sense that it's man-made. I think it's just a place that people revere. Honestly, it could just be a makeout spot for all I know. I'm going off what I believed as a kid." She tapped the screen. "I think this is it. Bison Springs." She hit a speed dial number on her phone.

"Who are you calling now?"

"Clint." The call went to voicemail. She left a message asking him to call her. "I can go by and look at it. I'm just thinking it's another possibility. Both Marilyn and Sue were young, they were Crow. The person who abducted them was drawn to them. Maybe he or she was drawn to this place, too. It's worth visiting."

"Do you really have the time? What do you think you'll find?"

His words and tone crawled under her skin. She scowled at him as she stuffed her phone in her pocket. "It's called investigating. I'll know it when I find it. One way or another, I'm heading up there soon."

His voice was sharp, his response quick. "Not alone."

She whirled on him. "Not with anyone who's got preconceived ideas about Skeeter. Or is carrying an arrest warrant."

Leo threw his hands in the air. "Ashley is a teenage girl. She's much more vulnerable than Skeeter. She has to be our first priority."

Her face felt hot. "Are you saying I don't care about her? Because I do. I happen to have daughters. To be a woman who was an at-risk girl. I care a lot."

His sigh shuddered. "I know that, Delaney. I do."

She turned her face toward the window. Joe quickly averted his gaze. She and Leo were making a bit of a scene. She sighed, too, and, when she did, her shoulders sagged. This was all so hard. "These things can co-exist. But I want unbiased team members by my side."

"Are you saying I'm not?"

"I—no."

"We go *together*." Leo stomped off, but the heat had left his voice.

"Fine," she whispered, knowing he couldn't hear her.

Almost immediately, her email notified her of an incoming message. She opened it to find Moira had come through with two cabin owners, noting which was which on the map Delaney had sent. She'd even included contact information. That was above and beyond. Nothing Delaney couldn't have researched herself, but having the last known addresses and phone numbers of the owners saved her time and gave her a comparative in case she found the information out of date. Moira had also noted that the dilapidated roofs were miner's cabins, validating Delaney's hunch.

She was feeling stir crazy. She could make calls from anywhere. She printed the email and its attachments and headed out to her department truck. She wished she had driven Shelly, but even a drive in the truck was mind expanding. She motored out of the parking lot after syncing her phone via Bluetooth and calling the first property owner.

Jared Salazar. The name rang a bell with her, but she couldn't place it. She dialed the number Moira had provided. She got an "out of service" recording. Since she was driving she decided to move on to the second cabin owner instead of researching Jared.

Nickel Burde. Again, she dialed. It rang only twice before a woman picked up. "Hello?"

Delaney introduced herself and explained who she was looking for and why.

"I'm Sherlynn. Nickel was my dad. Nicky, actually. I don't go up to the cabin much anymore. None of us in my family do. I live too far away. But we have such great memories of the cabin from our childhoods, my stepbrother and I can't bear to give it up."

"Does anyone use it?"

"We've thought about fixing it up and renting it out, but it's so remote that it would be really hard to manage cleaning and problems. We don't let anyone else use it, and I don't think any of us have been up there since we spread my parents' ashes up there five or six years ago. I can't believe they're both gone." Delaney heard a sniffle. "Sorry. For some reason, your call is stirring up all my feels."

"I'm sorry about that."

"It's okay."

"There's another cabin not too far from there. Possibly owned by someone named Jared Salazar."

"Salazar. Yeah, I remember that name. It was on the sign above their door."

"Did you know them?"

"I think maybe my parents did. I remember their kids were younger than me and the family was kind of weird. I didn't hang out with them. My stepbrother did a little, maybe?"

"Boys or girls?"

"One boy and one girl, I think. Very close in age. Maybe even twins. I don't know."

"So, you don't know how to get hold of them?"

"I'm sorry. I don't."

"We're trying to find a missing teenage girl. There's a chance we need to enter your cabin. I wanted to let you know that's a possibility."

"Oh my gosh! You think she's there?"

"Maybe. We need to rule it out."

"By all means. Do what you need to do. And let me know."

"Of course. If we enter, we'll make sure it's secured when we leave."

"Thank you."

Delaney gave Sherlynn her contact information and hung up the phone. While they'd been talking the sun had fallen behind the mountains. Her stomach growled. She realized she hadn't seen Kat and Carrie in two days. A girl was missing. But she couldn't find her in the mountains in the dark and she was out of ideas. She headed toward Clara's ranch and her daughters.

She'd be up at Bison Springs tomorrow at first light.

FIFTY-TWO

Leo walked out to his car lost in thought. *You know you're working late when the stars are out as you leave your day shift.* Even sheriffs are no good without occasional food and sleep. What choice did he have about the long hours, though? Ashley Klinkosh was out there somewhere, going through God knows what. She'd officially been missing for more than forty-eight hours. While there was no direct evidence she'd been kidnapped, the circumstances were grim. Community searches were ongoing but had yielded nothing. His department, the police, and Wyoming DCI were all working to find her.

Due to the high-profile nature of the case, help was coming from neighboring jurisdictions now, too. Leo and Mara had decided the best use of the new manpower was reviewing footage from every security camera, public and private, they could find in town. Going door to door for information, with Ashley's picture and the sketch artist renderings of the suspect and the RZR. Extending the search to neighboring towns. Contacting every morgue and police station in the Rocky Mountain states. Plastering Ashley's pictures everywhere.

It would help. He hoped it would be enough.

"Leo." A cold voice jerked his mind back to the present.

He was standing at his car door. Just standing there. How long? He turned to Mara Yellowtail to find her with Caitlin. *Awkward.* Caitlin hadn't said a word to him about all the messages she'd been sending through the dating apps. But her hair was down and straightened. She was wearing more makeup. Her vibe was different—longer eye contact, licking her lips. Honestly, it was uncomfortable for him. And the fact that she'd asked Delaney if it would be okay to date him? That was over the line. Maybe if there'd been only one message to him and no call to Delaney he would have gone for a coffee with her. But as soon as these cases were done and dusted, he was setting her straight. There was zero chance he would ever go out with her.

"Yes?" he said.

"Are you ducking my calls?" Mara said.

"What are you talking about? I haven't been ducking anything." He checked his phone. It had thirty-seven percent charge on his battery. The sound was on and up. He had no calls from her in his Recents. "Did you call my cell or the department line?"

Mara shook her head. "Have it your way." *Nonresponsive.* He began to sense a trap. A show for Caitlin's benefit.

"What did I miss?"

"We got the sketch artist renderings."

"Good."

"I think it's time to issue an arrest warrant for your boy Skeeter Rawlins."

He'd been expecting this. "I think we're still at the person of interest stage. Everything is circumstantial."

"That's for the lawyers to worry about later."

"Well, obviously if you disagree with me, you can pursue this on your own."

"But without your support."

"I strongly support finding him. But yes, without my support for an arrest warrant. We have forty-eight hours to charge after an arrest. I don't like having to cut a suspect loose for lack of evidence."

"Like you just did with Samuel Russo."

"As a matter of fact, yes."

"So, you're being indecisive because of your record of mistakes. That's exactly the type of public endangerment voters need to hear about and make up their minds based upon."

"We'll see when this is over."

"Or sooner. Who knows?"

"It would be a shame to create a distraction for political reasons, but I can't stop you. For now, I'm all about finding Ashley and solving this case."

"More like coddling your girlfriend."

Caitlin, who'd been impassive until this point, made a strangled cat noise.

"I'm not coddling anyone, including a nonexistent girlfriend. I'm happy to hold a fully transparent press conference and tell the public that Skeeter is a private investigator who has done work for the sheriff's department, takes care of my deputy's kids, and did work for the family of a recently deceased teenage girl related to this case. I'm not embarrassed by the truth. Nor will I be pushed into premature action because of it."

"I'd prefer you leave Marilyn out of it."

"Really? Why? Because you worked the case?"

"Caitlin's actions stand on their own."

Again, the strangled cat sound from Caitlin.

Leo said, "Is this all because you don't want to look indifferent about young Crow women?"

"I was not indifferent. My name is nowhere in that file."

A warm certainty built up and spread from his center outward. It was her careful wording. That *her name* was not in the file. Why wasn't it? Had it ever been? And how could he find out? He grinned. He'd have Joe Tarver pull the revision history on the Marilyn Littlewolf files from the records system while he was in the mountains with Delaney tomorrow. He felt a little guilty loading Joe up with all the research. He'd already asked him to dig hard into Skeeter's background. Interview everyone he could find from his past. Childhood. Army. Roughnecking. Kearny days. Follow-up on Betty Crowheart in Wisconsin. He wasn't sticking Joe with grunt work because the deputy was running for the sheriff nomination against him. It was a legitimate division of labor. Someone had to go with Delaney, and that someone was Leo.

"Isn't that an issue for the voters to hear about and make up their own minds based upon?" Leo smiled at her, enjoying her discomfiture.

And if Joe's research didn't find anything, maybe he would do coffee with Caitlin after all. He wouldn't lead her on. He'd just give her a chance to open up about her boss. If she thought she could impress him with information, he owed it to Ashley to let her try.

FIFTY-THREE

Delaney turned down the forest service road, leaving the brilliant sunrise in her rearview mirror behind. Ruts from spring runoff jerked her steering wheel back and forth on the two-track. Every few rotations, the truck clambered over exposed rocks and sent Leo toward the ceiling. His tall coffee mug had a lid, but he kept lifting it higher.

She envied his coffee. She'd opted for a few more minutes of sleep over making her own before she left. The house had been quiet as death without the girls. She hated it. Her visit with them the night before at Clara's had seemed too short, even though she'd stayed until they were yawning and ready to go to bed. She missed the life she had now, one she'd never realized she wasn't living before Kat and Carrie came into it.

"If it weren't for my seatbelt, the top of my head would be mushed flat," Leo said.

"Almost there."

"You're sure?"

"Close to it. Clint talked me through the directions last night."

"Oh, that's good."

She shook her head. "Your voice any time I mention him. He's a good cop and he's helped us out many times." *And it was only a few dates.* Really, though, was she any better about Leo's suddenly active dating life?

"Did your good buddy have any insight to share?"

Delaney stomped on the brakes and took a fork to the left. The trees crowded the road even tighter in this section, scraping the sides. "He liked the idea that the person who took the girls might be attracted to coming here. Might have even brought them here. He said it's a spiritual place."

"Religious?"

Religion versus spirituality. The church versus Delaney. She'd thought about her childhood church days that morning on her way to pick up Leo. Her grandparents used to make them all get up and take care of the animals extra early on Sundays so they could devote the day to the Lord and to spending it in church. The day of rest. Except that it never felt restful. It was the most exhausting day of the week. Maybe if their version of faith had been more life-affirming she would have found renewal in it. What she and Leo were doing certainly didn't honor the day of rest concept. But just as the care of livestock and children was a required exception to rest on Sundays, so was the rescue of innocent young girls. She sent a message heavenward. *I feel you looking down on me with approval from up there. Don't try to deny it.*

"No. It's a spring. A gift from the earth and God or the gods if you will. Native American spirituality is very in tune with nature. I grew up with it, so it's second nature to me. They believe all natural elements, like the mountains, water sources, and animals, possess a spirit that should be respected and honored. Clint said, to him, Bison Springs represents an awakening of gratitude to nature for all it provides. He took an offering of tobacco up there when he was a teenager."

"Like a sacrifice?"

She rolled her eyes at him. "No. More like a payment. 'Thank you Great Spirit for the gift of fresh spring water. In return, I'm giving you this tobacco.' Those are my words, not his."

"Why tobacco?"

"I didn't grow up Crow. But I was always told that it's a sacred plant. He said we'll see all kinds of offerings tied to trees up there. Little bags filled with herbs. Antlers. Ribbons. Sage from smudging. You know, for cleansing rituals."

"I actually do know what smudging is." He sounded proud of himself.

The trees opened onto a clearing with a formation of rocks at the far end. She recognized the place. "See?" She pointed at colorful trinkets tied up in trees. "Offerings." Another car—this one old and low to the ground—was parked to the left. *Wyomingites get the unlikeliest of cars into the toughest places.* Delaney pulled up beside it. "Let's go take a look."

She and Leo exited and followed a footpath around the rocks. It was chilly, damp, and still fairly dark back in the shadow of the rock. The loamy smell reminded Delaney of childhood camping trips with her dad and brother. She pushed the memory away. Then she heard someone singing. The words. It wasn't English—sounded Native American. *The person from the car*, she supposed. Given the spiritual nature of the springs, she hated breaking the singer's peace. But at least between the path and the voice, she felt certain about the direction of the springs. When she'd been here before she'd been paying more attention to her friends than the surroundings.

"Hello," she called. "I don't want to startle you."

The singing stopped. Then a tentative, "Oh. Okay." The speaking voice sounded younger than the singing voice had. More than one person?

She saw a teenage boy now, through the trees, around a slight bend in the trail. The spring was before him, protected by rocks on three sides. He was crouched at the edge of it but stood when they drew near.

She raised a hand. "Sorry to disturb you." She introduced herself and Leo.

"I'm Brent Allen." His last name surprised her. Not just because of his singing, but because with his strong chin, slightly hooked nose, and high, broad cheekbones, he looked like the portrait of Crow Chief Plenty Coups as a young man hanging in Big Horn's Brinton Museum. As if used to that reaction, he said, "My dad's the whitest dude in town, but apparently he has wimpy DNA."

Delaney laughed. "Do you live in Kearny?"

"Yeah. I'm in my first year in high school."

"My daughter Carrie goes there. She transferred from Sheridan."

"I know who you're talking about. She's a hotshot gamer. Won a big tournament last month."

Leo took a seat on a boulder. He seemed content for her to run with the conversation.

"Really?"

He grinned. "She smoked everybody."

"Yeah. She loves it."

"She's *good*, man. Really good."

Delaney felt a twinge of pride, something she'd never associated with Carrie's gaming before. "You game?"

"Some. I'm nowhere near as good as her."

"Listen—we're up here on a case. Looking for Ashley Klinkosh."

His face fell like all the muscles in it quit at once, leaving skin hanging off spectacular cheekbones. "That's why I'm here, too."

"You're looking for her?"

"No. I'm, I-uh, I wanted to get closer to the source of it all and ask for help. You know, God and stuff."

She did. And she felt sorry for him. "Did you know her?"

"Since we were little. I'm a year older than her. But she was sick when she was supposed to start kindergarten, so her mom held her back a year. We're two years apart in school."

"Did you know Sue Wiley, too?"

"Not as well. But it's sad about her. I don't want the same thing to happen to Ashley."

"Have you heard anything that might help us find her?"

"Not where she is or nothing. I heard people saying she ran away. So many of my friends take off. Sue maybe I coulda seen it. But Ashley, no way."

The longing in his eyes. This boy had a crush on Ashley. She shot Leo a look, hoping he understood she didn't want him to speak now no matter what. She pushed at a tree root with her toe. "Does Ashley know how you feel about her?"

Instead of denying it, he picked up a rock and chunked it into the trees. She heard it thud against a trunk. He threw another. That one cracked against a rock. Then he turned to her. "Yeah, she knew. But she went white for a boyfriend. All the best-looking native girls do."

She felt Leo shift as the boy referenced Freddy. But Brent didn't sound like he meant it in a mean-spirited way. In a sad way. And in a true way. That hadn't been a common thread they'd explored. Marilyn was being pursued by a white teacher. Sue—who had been involved with that teacher—was dating Elijah, who was white. Even their mothers had dated the same white man. And now Ashley and Freddy. Of course, this boy was mixed race by his own admission. Several of the girls were, too. *Maybe it comes down to us all being who we believe we are.* A thought for another day since Delaney wasn't always sure about herself.

She handed him her card. "Thank you, Brent. If you hear anything or think of anything, can you let me know? We want to see Ashley home safe."

He nodded and took it. Leo looked a question at her. She jerked her head toward the clearing and their truck. She wanted to give this boy space to do what he'd come here to do.

As they put the rock formation between themselves and Brent, Leo whispered, "Was this worth the visit for you?"

"Not for finding her. But for understanding what's happening here, maybe."

"You think he knows something?"

"I don't think he realizes it, but yes, I think he does."

White men and boys pursuing native girls. Multicultural dating was common in today's society. It might mean nothing. She rolled it around in her brain for a moment and was suddenly very convinced that it did not.

FIFTY-FOUR

Ashley cradled her arms against her chest and shivered. The Mountain Man had been gone for at least one night. Maybe longer. It was hard to keep track with no outside light in this awful place.

She'd cried herself to sleep when he left, after she'd been unable to break out of the restraints. When she'd woken up, she'd been wearing a blindfold. Her hands had been tied together. Not down to the board like her ankles, but in front of her body. *Those intense eyes I saw the first morning—they came back*. Whatever she was tied up with felt rough, like rope, and it dug into the sore spot on her arm. She'd struggled against the binding for a moment then decided it was better to get the blindfold off first. The eye cover was tight around her head and cheeks. Painfully tight.

When she reached up toward her face, though, something had struck her forearm and wrist. Some*one* had struck them, very hard.

She'd screamed, her heart-thumping terror amped up by the shock of the blow. Caught in the panic of her blindness and immobility, she hadn't sensed the person standing beside her.

What had they hit her with? It didn't feel like a hand. It wasn't scratchy, not soft like skin or cloth. As much as it hurt, she didn't think it was as hard as metal. As she replayed the horror in her mind, she remembered it as whiplike.

Through it all, the person hadn't spoken.

When Ashley had stopped screaming, she'd heard them, though. A horrible, wet, raspy breathing sound. Like a St. Bernard dog. Like Darth Vader with asthma. Like a creature from a nightmare. It wasn't far away from her either. She tried to picture it. Level with her own chest. Maybe the person was sitting in a chair. Close enough to strike her with something, so only a foot or two away? So close she could smell sweat and body odor. Bad breath. All the awful things.

"Hello?" she'd whispered.

The breathing was her only answer.

She tried to swallow. Her mouth was so dry that it took several tries and made her feel like she was going to choke to death. She didn't. Then she flexed her fingers. Luckily, her bones didn't seem broken. Hyperaware of the heavy breathing beside her, she knew she wouldn't try to remove the blindfold or wrist restraints again. Not while they were around.

Later, she'd been given toast. Water. The person had unfastened her ankles and led her blindfolded to an outhouse. When she'd returned, a shove had been enough to communicate they wanted her to get back on the table. They resecured her ankle restraints. Tighter this time. Cutting into her skin. Sat down and panted in her face again.

She must have fallen asleep, as impossible as it had seemed. Had they given her more sleeping pills? She woke to an odor that wasn't unpleasant. It smelled like... cake? They had been baking. And the sound was different. Atonal. Not a voice. A buzzing. Maybe humming overlaid with the horrible breath noises?

Then the significance of the odor sank in. A cake. They

were making a cake for her wedding. Because he was coming back.

She didn't know which was worse. Fearing his return or enduring his absence with the faceless, voiceless menace lurking near her. She bit down on her lip to keep from crying out. She wanted to pray, but it didn't seem like the God her parents had taught her about was listening. *What if my prayers just go to the horrible god the Mountain Man believes chose me for him?*

God would either help her or He wouldn't. Then she remembered one of her dad's favorite mottos. *God helps those who help themselves.* It wasn't even from the Bible, but he loved it. God couldn't help her if she didn't help herself. How could she do that, though?

After thinking about it for a while, she had come up with some things she could do. She had to stay alert. Mentally sharp. She had to keep from swallowing anything else. Pills. Food. Water. Anything that could be drugged, for as long as she could hold out. She had to think about something else besides being scared. She thought about her parents. Freddy. Her friends. Imagined them here with her. Challenged them to an imaginary alphabet game. "Name a place that starts with A." Wasn't sure if it was only in her head or whether she said it out loud. "I'll start. A is for Amsterdam. Name a place that starts with B."

No one else came up with anything of course, so she took all the turns. Her lips kept moving, and she kept cycling through the letters, over and over, thinking of all the places she was going to visit when she got away from here. Not if. But when.

She refused to die like this. There was so much out there to see. Places to visit. Things to live for.

"Q is for Quebec. R is for Rotterdam. S is for..."

FIFTY-FIVE

"We square?" the Mountain Man said.

The other man saluted. The gesture fit his flat-top haircut, his camo fatigues and tactical boots, and the AR-15 rifle slung over his shoulder and held across his chest with his free hand. "Boss man said to tell you he can forgive late once but don't make it no habit."

The Mountain Man had told them he'd been ill. He couldn't explain the real reason he'd been late to show up with the cash pickups from drop locations all over Wyoming, South Dakota, North Dakota, and Montana. The donations from devoted followers were the lifeblood of the group. Kept them armed. Kept them ready. Gave them the freedom to think strategically.

But he'd brought the cash now—all of it—hidden among the supplies he also delivered weekly. "Yeah, I get it. I'll waive my fee for the aggravation this time. See you in a few days."

He eased past a barricade lifted by a second man. Two others stood on either side of the dirt road. The compound was in the backcountry, a densely forested area bearing little resemblance to modern civilization. The population of the encampment had more than doubled over the last year.

The Mountain Man didn't miss it. It had been five years since he'd moved on from this life. Back when he'd convinced the leader he'd do more good for the cause on the outside. Back when he could no longer resist the voice in his head promising him a bride for the taking.

He radioed ahead. "Checkpoint Alpha. All clear or do I need to make a safety stop?" He was only allowed to drive out if no vehicles were passing for five miles in either direction. His old compatriots took privacy and security very seriously.

A voice answered him. "Clear."

"Ten-four." He'd need to radio two more checkpoints before he could breathe freely and feel reasonably certain he'd escaped their net again.

He shifted up. His rented rig was okay, but not nearly as nice as owning one. Especially the one he'd visited with that deputy. Of all the luck. A deputy owned the truck he had his heart set on. Not only a deputy but one who had been a trucker and remembered him from the road. This trip would have been easier if he'd bought it, but there was no way he was entering into a transaction with paperwork with a cop. He would find a different truck someday. The Lord would provide. The Lord had always provided.

He rested his palm on a package close beside him on the seat. He had stopped at a thrift store in Rapid City and bought a wedding dress for Ashley. She was going to be beautiful in it. If all went well, he would be there in time to see it on her tonight. They would exchange their vows the second he got home. He did have to stop in Kearny, but just to make a phone call. Not to the boss man the guard had referenced earlier—no, he was a clown. He wasn't the one the Mountain Man answered to.

He had to call his real boss.

The thought made his insides feel liquid. But assuming that went well—and it would because God was on his side—then... then he would claim his bride.

FIFTY-SIX

Leo gazed out the windows and up as Delaney turned off the engine. Clouds were rolling in. They were in front of an old, gray log cabin in need of a good chinking and fresh sealant. The roof was covered in debris. The slats of a wooden fence around a small yard lay crosswise on the ground. Those were the downsides.

He got out and turned in a circle.

The upside was immeasurable. A little creek, swollen from spring runoff, wove in front of the house. He'd been so entranced he hadn't realized they'd crossed a bridge—he was thankful it hadn't collapsed. From the front porch, the forest road was invisible. And over the treetops a rock cliff face guarded the cabin and surrounding forest.

If this dwelling was in Kearny, the city would be leaving official notices on the door warning about safety hazards. It would fetch the value of the lot it sat on minus the cost of demolition.

But up here—with this location and view? It was spectacular. He couldn't begin to calculate its value.

He said, "This wasn't exactly the easiest place to find." An understatement. It had taken hours of driving on horrible roads. They'd have been far better off in an ORV. Thank goodness Delaney had brought them sack lunches, something he hadn't thought to do. *She's always prepared.*

"Watch your step," Delaney said. "These boards are sagging. I'm not even sure why they put in a porch. They just rot up here under all this snow. Good old packed dirt works better." She knocked on the door.

When no one answered, Leo rapped harder and said, "Sheriff's Department. Is anyone home?" They hadn't expected it to be inhabited, of course. Sherlynn Burde had said her family hadn't been to the place in years. But empty houses attracted squatters, even up here.

Delaney reached above the door frame and patted around. "Ow. I found the nail that the key is on." She brought the key down. "Ready?"

Leo nodded.

"I'd stand back in case of animals." She opened the door and they both moved to the side. "Shoo, bears. Shoo, now."

The squeaking of rodents and their scurrying feet were the only sounds. Dust floated in the air. The scent of urine wafted out.

Leo peered into a dark interior. "I think we're good."

"Let's open the back door and let some light in. Just to be sure there's no evidence of occupation."

"I'll get it." Leo turned on his flashlight and shone it around the interior.

The place had been winterized by whoever had used it last, with oil cloth and plastic over every surface. Rodent droppings provided an additional layer of cover.

Delaney moved ahead of him. "Looks like a central room and two bedrooms. This being central. Woodburning stove, table, cabinets. A sitting area."

"What used to be a rug and became rat dinner."

"I don't see any signs of human footprints or usage."

"Me neither." He crossed to the back of the house and opened that door. A shed out there looked in better shape than the rest of the house.

Delaney was turning in a circle with a soft expression. "The place has a lonely feel. Like it was well-loved and waiting for that love to return."

"Delaney Pace, you're a romantic."

She snorted.

He felt it too, though. "How do you buy a place like this?"

"The first step is finding a motivated seller."

"I'd love to fix it up."

"I would, too."

"Want to see if the Burdes would sell it to us?"

"Who, you and me and one of your Tinder hookups?"

"I'm not on Tinder."

"My point stands."

"Friends share vacation properties all the time. Think of the fun our families would have up here."

"Now who's the romantic?"

He took a deep breath. "Delaney."

She cocked her head. "Hmm?"

He almost said it. *Please give this a try. Please give me a try.*

"Leo, what?"

"Nothing. I'll check the shed."

"I've got the bedrooms. Be sure you look up into the rafters and down. I can't imagine anyone digging a cellar in this rock, but just in case."

He nodded and walked to the shed, feeling like he'd just chickened out or dodged a bucket of ice water. One or both. Whether she wanted to go in on it with him or not, he was calling Sherlynn Burde to see whether the family was ready to part with it. It was crying out for love. He sighed, feeling pathetic.

When he reached the shed, he found a key on a nail above the door, there, too. But when he tried the knob, the door wasn't locked. He holstered his flashlight, drew his gun, and held it in the down and ready position, safety off. "Hello in there? Sheriff Leo Palmer. I'm coming in." He opened it and moved quickly to the side.

More rodents protested his interruption. No humans. He traded the gun for the flashlight. The shed had been picked clean, if it was ever full, which he assumed it was. Other than some used condoms and empty mini bottles of Fireball, the dirt floor was bare, which made it easy to see there was no cellar. He bagged the condoms and liquor bottles. They were dried up. Most likely from teenage partiers the year before, but he wanted to test them just in case. The low roof made an attic a no-go, too. He closed up, leaving it unlocked like he found it, and walked back in the house.

Delaney was coming out of a bedroom. "Family mementos and weather-damaged photos. Take a look at this one." She held out a framed picture of two kids, the older one roughly Freddy's age. A boy and a girl.

He took it from her. "The boy looks familiar."

"It's old. I'd imagine these were the kids of the owners."

"Sherlynn Burde and her stepbrother." He removed the frame back and pulled the photo out. Narrow, neat handwriting on the back read "Our cabin. 1995. Sheri and Steve." The hair rose on his neck. "Delaney, read this." He turned it toward her.

She took it from him. "Steve." Her eyes went squinty. She flipped the picture over and stared at it. "Son of a bitch. Is this who I think it is?"

"It is if you think it's Steve Randolph."

FIFTY-SEVEN

TWO DAYS EARLIER

Skeeter woke to the worst headache of his life. Like a knife was stabbing into the base of his skull at the same time as a mallet was pounding against his forehead. Hangover? He tried to remember where he'd been. The Loafing Shed, yes. But hadn't he spent the night at home? Well, then he'd gone back to the Shed for breakfast. Eating at home or alone in a fast-food parking lot was too damn sad. He'd taken his laptop and used Shed WIFI to run some background checks. That was stretching the truth. He'd mostly read articles online about Marilyn Littlewolf and Sue Wiley. But that wasn't current enough for him. Afraid he might be missing something, he'd gone home and listened to his police scanner, wondering if and when he needed to come clean with Delaney. Hating the thought of her disappointment so much that he'd convinced himself to put it off a little longer.

And then what? It got fuzzy.

He was starting to wake up more which was not a good thing. Where in tarnation was he? His face felt like it was smushed into mud, his hip was balancing on rock—something hard and sharp—and his hands and feet were numb. Damn. All of him was cold. Wet. And... he moved his hands to his legs. It was hard to be sure with hands like blocks of ice, but it seemed like his skin was bare. He ran his hand up his body. Was he naked? Naked out in the cold and the wet? Confusion was giving way to fear. He reached his neck, touched the back where it hurt. Brought his hand around and saw that his damp fingers were covered in something reddish-brown.

Hurt neck. Dried blood?

He tried to roll over, but it didn't go well. All he managed to do was turn his head and vomit. Excess bile pooled by his mouth, and he spit. He became aware of bad odors. The odors of him. His bleary vision focused a few inches beyond his face. All he could see was the wet pile of what used to be in his stomach. *Dear God, I've been unconscious a long time.*

He squinted. His vision cleared enough to see further into the distance. Trees. Lots of trees. Pine needles on a forest floor. Patches of snow, few and far between. Mud puddles everywhere. He tried to make sense of his situation. He was in trees, it was cold and muddy. There were rocks. Unless he wasn't in Wyoming, that meant he was in the mountains, because the only trees outside of them and the creek bottoms were telephone poles. He was naked and concussed. So, how did he get from his apartment to here? And when did it happen? Why and how did it happen?

Think, man. Think. Thinking hurt worse than anything. He rested for a moment then tried again. Pictures formed and then shifted others like he was watching TV. It was a pretty day out. His car had been at the Shed from the night before. He took his RZR to pick up Kateena, after stopping for Dudley. *Kat, my bad. Never Kateena anymore.* But he'd been early. He'd decided to cruise the neighborhoods and play the game of what house he would buy when he could afford one. The prices had been skyrocketing lately, though. Too many out-of-staters driving them up. People used to paying big city prices on the east or west coast. Driving the dreams of guys like him further and further out of reach.

His mental images flickered. *Come on.* They came back into focus. He'd seen that nice girl, the one who Kat's Freddy liked. Dumb boy couldn't see his best friend had a crush on him, and was there any kid cuter in the world than Kat? Skeeter didn't think so. Anyway, the girl had been walking through the neighborhood. For about two seconds he worried that he'd forgotten about early dismissal, but he knew he hadn't. Why was she out before school released for the day?

As he was thinking about it, a RZR a lot like his came from the opposite direction, ran off the road, and she'd fallen down. Had it hit her? The driver had jumped out and checked on her as Skeeter sped toward them. Then he'd picked up the girl and put her in the passenger seat. Skeeter had almost caught up with them when they took off. Skeeter assumed the guy was taking her to the hospital. He'd been glad.

He'd been behind them as they headed out. When he reached the school, he eased into the pick-up line. Chatted with Adriana. He looked up into the distance as the other RZR passed the turn to the hospital *and kept going*.

A knot formed in his stomach. He didn't like remembering this. He put a hand to his forehead and groaned, then forced himself to face his memories.

He'd driven out of the line and went after them. His plan was to just catch up with them and ask Ashley if she was all right. Probably by then the driver would have circled back to the hospital. He'd probably just missed the turn. Then Skeeter would go straight back to the school for Kat.

He'd pressed his accelerator to the floor. The other RZR was driving way too fast. So fast Skeeter could barely keep up. It passed the city limit sign. *He's not taking her to the hospital.* He gained on it. Whoever this was, he was headed for the mountains.

Skeeter wrestled with what to do about Kat. He checked his phone. He decided to text Delaney and let her know something had come up, that he was following Freddy's girlfriend into the mountains and why. She'd send someone for Kat, and she'd come help. He stopped and typed the message and hit send. If this panned out, he'd be the hero who *saved* a native girl. *Not like last time. Never like last time.*

Just before he accelerated, he looked at the passenger seat. Dudley was gone. When had the dog gotten out? And how? Kat would never forgive him if something happened to her dog. But Skeeter would never forgive himself if another native girl was hurt and he could have stopped it. He smashed the accelerator to the floor, fishtailing on the gravel.

He chased the other RZR for an hour. Skeeter prided himself on being a good driver, but the other guy managed to keep distance between them, even pulling away a bit. Finally, the kidnapper—because Skeeter felt sure now that is what he was—pulled into what looked like a driveway. There was a cheap gate across it anyway. A chain on the ground attached to a fence post on one side of the two-track.

The RZR parked. Skeeter raced up behind it. He was packing his handgun. He had a knife. He was ready. He put his own RZR in park and left it running. Put his hand on his gun.

The guy got out of his ORV and looked past Skeeter like he wasn't even there.

Why would he do that?

Skeeter couldn't see Ashley's face. *If this is her dad or grandpa I'm going to feel really stupid.* At least he knew that if things went sideways, he'd texted Delaney. She'd come looking for them, after she got Kat squared away.

He decided to approach the guy. He leaned to get out, and that's when he felt something hard contact the back of his skull.

That's why it hurts now.

The world went dark before he even hit the ground.

Yes. I remembered. Someone had attacked him from behind at a little mountain cabin. Where was he now, though? Where was Ashley? And the man who had taken her? And who the hell had clobbered him and left him for dead out here?

He had to get up. He had to get out of here in case whoever it was who threw him out here came back. He scrambled to his feet, retching again, but scared enough to no longer care. The world wobbled back and forth. He walked with his hands on the ground a few steps until he was able to stand, holding on to a tree.

He looked down. *Yes, definitely naked.* If they'd thought he was dead, why did they bother undressing him? Maybe to make sure he died of exposure?

He took a minute to look around and get his bearings. Bearings. Bears. At least no predators had made a meal out of him. He didn't see the cabin or his RZR. His guess was the man had driven him away from the cabin and dumped him where his rotting carcass wouldn't stink. *Joke's on you, sucker. I ain't dead.*

Which meant they wouldn't expect him. He looked up through the treetops. It was an afternoon sun. He had plenty of daylight left, but he had to get moving. He walked in circles, scanning for tracks until he found them. Tire tracks. They would take him back to the cabin. He had another chance to save the girl. To save a girl. To make up for the one whose death he blamed himself for.

Marilyn Littlewolf.

FIFTY-EIGHT

Delaney pulled her poncho around her shivering body as she climbed back into the truck. The hike into the old mining cabins had only been two miles from the parking area through the entrance to Cloud Peak Wilderness, but the weather had turned just before they reached them. They'd scoured the area in a deluge of rain and near darkness with lightning and thunder rattling the mountaintops above them.

It made the fact that they'd found nothing that much more bitter a pill to swallow.

Leo was about to strip off his poncho as he got in.

She started the truck and cranked up the heater. "I wouldn't do that. All the water ends up on the inside if you take it off. You'll be sorry then if you need it again."

He groaned. "Thanks."

As soon as he had shut his door, she whipped them into a circle and pointed back down the mountain. It was already starting to be more rocky river than road. There was no way she'd turn the driving over to Leo in these conditions—or anytime—but that meant she had to leave him in charge of the maps. "Remind me how far we think it is by road to the Salazar cabin?"

He held his tablet away from his wet outer gear then enlarged something on the screen. "I'd say ten miles."

She gripped the steering wheel as the suspension rode a series of jarring bumps. "So, as much as forty-five minutes in these conditions."

"If we don't get lost. How are we on gas?"

"Three-quarters of a tank. And there are snacks and drinks in the back seat."

"I still can't believe how quickly storms hit up here."

"The extreme changes in elevation hide the clouds so you don't see them bearing down on you." She rolled her shoulders, then relaxed her arms. It was better to dance with the road than fight it as it pushed and pulled the wheels. "I can't believe Steve Randolph is connected to one of the cabins. I still can't figure it all out, though. No one had been using it."

"I did find those condoms and Fireball bottles," Leo said.

"But our bad guy didn't seem to use condoms, if Marilyn's pregnancies and the semen collected from Sue are any indication."

Delaney felt it before she heard it. A vibration that grew stronger, then a loud clattering above them. Beside them. In front of them. She slammed on the brakes and then threw the truck in reverse, pushing the gas pedal to the floor and turning with her arm over the seat to get the best view she could of the road behind them.

"What is it?" Leo shouted.

Delaney concentrated on driving backwards up the mountain.

"Oh, my god," Leo said.

She knew what he was looking at in the road in front of them. Heard the rocks bouncing, cracking, breaking, rolling.

Felt them pelting her truck. Saw one land in the truck bed and literally believed for a moment that the roof was going to collapse as one made impact there.

"A rockslide. And if we'd kept going, that boulder would have crushed us."

Delaney gave it another twenty yards before she felt safe enough to stop. The rock sounds had stopped. The last rock to hit the road had been ten seconds earlier. Still, she held her breath.

"Say something, Delaney."

She pursed her lips and let the bad air out slowly. Then she turned to Leo with raised brows. "Let's not do that ever again."

"Deal."

* * *

Delaney and Leo spent the next half hour moving all smaller boulders out of the road. A big, heavy boulder in the center of the road still blocked their way.

"I can't get around it on the right because of trees. And on the left..."

"Straight down."

"Why do these things always happen on cliffs?"

She had to laugh. "Because that's where the rocks can fall."

"Forget I asked that."

She went back to her truck and got a chainsaw out of the back seat. "Essential in mud season up in the mountains. Roots lose their grip in runoff and the tree slides and falls across roads. You never know when you're going to have to muscle your way through."

Leo stared at her, hands on hips. "Uh, you know that won't cut through a boulder, right?"

She nodded. "But it will cut us down a tree."

"Which helps us..." He snapped his fingers, grinning. "Fulcrum and lever. You want to put the end of a tree under the big boulder while balancing the tree across a smaller boulder. We use the tree as a lever and the smaller boulder as a fulcrum. A pivot point. And the lever allows us to move a heavy boulder we could have never budged ourselves."

She winked and smiled back. "Simple mechanics. Work smarter not harder."

"I'm impressed."

"Does four inches in diameter and twenty feet long sound about right to you?"

He was nodding and turning, hand shielding his eyes from the water. He pointed. "There's a good candidate."

"Get us a fulcrum in position. Plenty to choose from."

Leo nodded and trotted off to the rock debris.

She turned on the ignition and set the saw on the ground. She put her left foot on the front handle, her right foot on the rear one, and pulled the starter cord straight up. It took four tries until the engine caught. Leo's choice on the tree looked fine to her, and it took her less than a minute to fell it and another couple of minutes to relieve it of its branches. She returned the saw to the truck. Leo was already dragging the tree into position. She caught up and together they maneuvered it into position with one end under the boulder and the trunk balanced on the fulcrum.

"Ready?" Leo said.

Delaney nodded and together they each grasped the tree on the other side of the fulcrum and began to pull it down.

It didn't budge.

"We're not heavy enough," she said. "I've still got a few fifty-pound bags of sand in the truck bed, and a lot of rope."

Leo was trotting over to the truck. He came back with two bags. She followed him with a long section of rope. She threw the rope over the tree trunk and adjusted it with equal lengths pooling on the ground on either side. Leo had in the meantime brought the rest of the bags.

"Two on each side?" he asked.

"Works for me."

Five minutes and several false starts and dropped sandbags later, they'd managed to secure the bags to the rope and push it out where the sand was suspended above the ground.

"Let's try this again," Leo said.

Delaney stood in front of Leo, who was standing in front of the sandbags. They both reached up, grasped, and pulled downward with all their might.

"Please don't let this son of a bitch break," Leo gasped.

Delaney felt the rock shift. "Shove it forward."

They kept pace with the rock, keeping their tree tip under it. They pulled again. The rock lifted. Shove. It lifted some more. Shove.

When they had the trunk at waist level, Leo said, "I've got it. Shove a rock under."

Delaney sprinted to a pile of rocks that it appeared Leo had gathered for exactly that purpose. *Smart thinking.* She shoved a couple under the boulder then sprinted back to her place under the tree. Leo was straining, puffing. She grabbed the trunk. They were pushing down now. Push. Shove. Push. Shove. And finally, it tipped on its side and rolled a giant rotation. Their tree lost its purchase. Delaney and Leo fell to their rumps in the mud. The tree whacked Leo in the head.

"Ow," he shouted.

Delaney stood and shook mud from her hands. She nodded with satisfaction. They hadn't sent the rock off the side, but they'd cleared a path.

Leo got up and put his arm around her. He pulled her in tight. "I'll take you as my partner any day and twice on Sundays."

She almost put her head on his shoulder. Instead, she

moved away. "Don't say that until I get us down from here and we find Ashley."

"Killjoy."

But she was already shaking off the tumult of emotions he'd stirred up in her. "Move the rest of that crap out of the way. We need to get out of here before Hell rains another boulder storm on us."

FIFTY-NINE

FIVE YEARS EARLIER

"Another round?" Mary asked.

Skeeter hit his shot glass twice on the bar and grinned at her. "If you ever ditch that boyfriend of yours, I'm first in line to ask you out to dinner."

"You mean the one who just wheeled a hand cart of boxes through here and would whip your ass if he heard you talking like that?"

"Correct. Except that part about whipping my ass. I'd never let that happen."

She patted her belly. "You're a little late."

"You already ate?"

"No, you big goofball. I'm pregnant. We're having a baby."

Skeeter sighed. "Well, I like kids. I'll make it a standing offer."

She poured another shot in his glass. "How's your big case going?"

Like shit, he almost said. Which he hated. Skeeter couldn't believe he'd landed the Marilyn Littlewolf case. The police hadn't made any progress, so he'd marched himself up to the door of the Littlewolf house and handed the girl's sad mother his card. Waived fees on his first ten hours and gave her half price on the rest, which meant he was basically working for free since as an apprentice to his buddy's investigation firm, he coughed up half his hourly rate anyway. It was the first really interesting case he'd worked on. For sure the most important.

He'd felt like a real cop working it. Except for one thing. He'd tried to update the police. That new East Coast cop, Mara Gipson, who got the job he'd applied for, had been rude when he called to talk to the officer working the case. He didn't want to be crosswise with them. He would have appreciated an update on where things were, and he would have been willing to share anything he found with them. But they hadn't called him back. It stuck in his craw. Made him want to solve it even more just to show them he had what it took, whether law enforcement wanted him or not.

Unfortunately, though, he hadn't found her. He'd talked to all the witnesses. He'd run down leads. He'd done everything they did on the cop shows. Her friends had said she was obsessed with finding her dad. So, he'd gotten the guy's name from Mama Wolf, the girl's grandmother, and tracked him to Roundup, Montana. When he'd shown up there flashing Marilyn's picture and asking about the guy, folks said he'd left town for parts unknown a few weeks before with a girl that might look a little like her. No one could even say what direction he'd headed. So, basically, it was nothing. *He* had nothing.

It wasn't just that it made him feel like a failure. The more time that passed, the sadder Mrs. Littlewolf got. She was a sweet lady. He wanted to give her closure. And he needed to close this case as a success.

"It's okay. I just want to help the family."

"What do you think happened to her?"

He said what most people were saying. "She ran away, I expect."

"I mean look at me, right? That's what I did."

Skeeter hadn't realized that. "Did you tell your parents?"

"Hell no. They hated"—she patted her flat stomach again—"my boyfriend. Told me I'd amount to nothing. Basically, called me a slut."

"That sucks."

She wiped the counter. "I only talk to my sister. Maybe I'll talk to my parents someday. If they want to see their grandchild."

"Well, I think you turned out just fine."

She held out an imaginary dress and curtsied. "Thank you, sir. And I think you're turning out just fine, too, Mr. Rawlins."

Not hardly. He had no personal life and hadn't been able to get a job as a cop or a security guard. He was barely making ends meet as a PI. Sam and his disability money had disappeared. Phone not answered. Email and text bounced. Letters returned to sender. He was going to have to accept the facts. His friend had stolen from him. What kind of dumbass did that make him? *I'll have to use my fancy new PI skills to try to track him down someday.* In the meantime, though, he needed a win if he was ever going to land more cases, or he was going to lose his apartment. Go hungry. Not be able to afford to come see Mary at the Shed. Wyoming was no place to live homeless.

And it was at the moment he knocked back his fifth shot that the plan formed in his mind. How he could be a hero and solve his own problems. Close this case. Let Marilyn—who really had probably run away—be free. Give her mother the peace of mind of believing her daughter was alive and only wanted what Mary and other kids like her had wanted. To get away and grow up on her own. I mean, isn't that what he'd done, basically, by joining the military? He'd been a few years older than Marilyn, but girls grew up faster. Matured earlier. Were more responsible.

So, he'd tell her mom he'd talked to her. That she'd gone to live with relatives back in Montana. He could even say it was with her dad since people thought they might have seen her with him in Roundup before he left the area. That would give her mom peace of mind. And it might be true. The more he thought about it, the more he was convinced that is exactly what she'd done—moved away with her dad. Skeeter was sure she'd be okay. Everyone would feel better. Wouldn't they?

He chased any doubts away with another shot.

SIXTY

Delaney was thankful the Ram had more-aggressive-than-standard tires and good four-wheel drive as she sped through the narrow opening they'd created in the rock debris. She drove in white-knuckled silence for about ten minutes. The descent leveled out to a gradual downhill. The weather didn't improve, but the hazards from uphill became less of a threat.

"Turn here," Leo pointed to the right.

Delaney took the turn. Thirty minutes later, they were back at the same intersection. "This looks disturbingly familiar."

"I guess our turn is further up the road than it seemed," Leo said. "Sorry."

"It was already going to be hard." The difficult navigation had become almost impossible with roads acting like rivers and terrible visibility. Delaney pointed her truck back onto the road leading down the mountain.

Another ten minutes passed. Another wrong turn led to another half hour wasted. Delaney was getting nervous. They were going to run out of light. And, while still fine, their gas wouldn't last forever. She didn't relish the thought of a night out here. The temperatures were going to plummet.

"This is it, I think." Delaney turned right. If anything, this road was worse than all the others.

"Do you think we need to pull over?" Leo asked.

Delaney accelerated on the edge of a road-wide puddle. Halfway through, the truck struck a large, submerged rock. The impact was hard enough to jar her neck. She bit her lip and drove out of the water. Hopefully they wouldn't be changing a tire out in this. Or worse. "I was about to say no and then that happened. But I still think we should keep going."

"I'm not sure we're even on the right road."

It was possible he was right.

"Honestly, I think we're close. And according to my memory of the map, if this is the right road, we shouldn't have any more turns until we reach the cut-off to the Salazar cabin."

"I don't want to have to requisition another new truck." As if to emphasize his point, hail began pelting them. Small at first then bigger and bigger. "Nice."

"At least it isn't rocks. But we're okay. We're not going fast enough to increase the force of impact significantly."

"Ashley may be out in this. Skeeter, too. We have it better off than them."

"Right. I've got this." She gave him a dorky thumbs up, which drew a smile.

The rain had melted most of the snow but within minutes piles of hail had accumulated. Their bouncing headlights glinted off white like they were trapped in a snowstorm. Actually, Delaney knew a snowstorm wasn't out of the question at this elevation. Not now—not in any month of the year, actually.

Another glint off the headlights startled Delaney, but this time it was a creature moving erratically through the trees. A light-colored creature. *Albino deer?* It was injured, if so.

"What's that?!" Leo had pushed his feet into the floorboard and his back against the seat.

The creature lurched into the road. For a horrified moment, Delaney thought she was going to hit it.

"Oh, my god. Is that a person?" Leo said.

"It is. It's a person."

"A naked man. Is this our guy?"

The figure toppled to the ground. Delaney jammed the truck in park and both she and Leo jumped out. The bracing wind and wet cold cut right to the bone. Delaney put her hand on her Staccato. She hadn't seen any weapons, but clubs and rocks could be lethal. She and Leo met in the headlights. The man crumpled in the road was shielding his face with a hand. He was big. Heavyset. His skin was so white it was blue in places and pink in others that had borne the barrage of ice.

They reached him simultaneously.

"Sir," Leo said. "I'm the Kearny County Sheriff. Let's get you into shelter." He took the man's arm.

Delaney gasped. As the man's hand moved away from his face, she recognized him.

It was Skeeter.

* * *

In the truck, Skeeter shivered so violently that his knees knocked into the glove box. He hadn't uttered a word. Delaney spoke soothingly to him, worried he was in shock. Leo wrapped him in a silver emergency blanket, which was good for warmth but non-absorbent. Delaney turned the heat and defrost on high. She took the opportunity to check her gas gauge again. They still had half a tank.

"We need to get him into some dry clothes," she said.

Leo leaned over into the back seat, pawing through his bag. "I don't have any. Not even on my body."

"I have an extra jacket and socks."

Skeeter started shaking his head. Finally, he croaked out

words in a voice that sounded nothing like himself. "The girl. We have to find the girl."

Leo and Delaney shared a glance. The time to aid was over. Now was the time to be a sharp cop.

"What girl?" she said.

Skeeter turned to her. His pupils were so enlarged that it made his irises look black. "Freddy's friend. Ashley something."

Leo swallowed, but he kept his voice calm. "What happened to Ashley?"

"Some man in a RZR ran up on her. Knocked her down."

"What does the man look like?"

Skeeter frowned, groaning. "Big old white guy like me. No beard. Lots of hair, wiry, going gray."

"Where did he take her?" Leo said.

"Somewhere. Up here somewhere. I don't know. I was unconscious. I've been looking for her since I woke, mostly. Maybe two days now? But the weather went bad."

Delaney asked, "How did you get here?"

"I saw it happen. I followed." He frowned. "I sent you a message, Delaney. Told you about it. That I couldn't pick up Kat."

His words were a blow. Had she missed a message from him? It was impossible. But technology might have failed them if he really sent it. "I didn't get a message."

"So, no one is looking for her?" His voice cracked, high-pitched, panicky.

Delaney put a hand on his arm. "Everyone is looking for her. And for you."

Leo said, "We need to get you to a hospital."

"No! I can't leave without her. I can't let her down. It was my fault. All my fault." He deflated, his head falling forward, shoulders heaving.

Confirmation. She'd believed Skeeter hadn't taken Ashley, but now she was sure. He hadn't hurt any of the girls. They were still a long way from proving it, but just this knowledge lifted a huge weight from her psyche. Skeeter might not be all good. He might do dumb things. He might have made some serious mistakes, but he hadn't hurt any girls.

Thank you, Big Man.

"What's all your fault?" Leo said.

"I told them—I-I-I told them she went to live with her dad. And now she's dead." He sobbed, loud and shuddering. "I couldn't find her. I thought I was helping. But it's all my fault."

Oh, God. Delaney's heart felt like it was being ripped from her chest. Skeeter had falsified information in Marilyn's case. She'd suspected it. She didn't understand why yet. But it was clear that it was a burden that was crushing him.

"Who?" Leo's voice was gentle but firm. They needed him to say it.

"Huh?"

"Who is dead?"

"Marilyn Littlewolf. I thought she would be okay. I really did."

"Is Ashley dead?"

"I hope not. We have to help her." His voice trailed off to a whisper.

"Does the same person have her?"

"I don't know." His shoulders rose, lifting the silver blanket, then they fell. "I just don't know."

"Okay, a few more questions and we'll go find her together, okay?"

A brief flicker of eye contact between Leo and Skeeter. Then Skeeter nodded.

"What happened to you? Why are you out here like this—naked and hurt?"

Because he was hurt. Delaney could see the abrasion and lump on the back of his neck. He still wasn't skinny, but he had dropped weight.

"I followed them to a cabin."

A cabin. Delaney put the truck in gear and mashed the gas pedal. There was only one other cabin up here within foot travel distance. She'd studied the Google Earth images carefully. She and Leo had confirmed no one had been to the Burde cabin in quite some time.

Ashley was at the Salazar cabin.

The truck fishtailed in the mud as she fought to keep it from smashing into the trees on either side. "Hold on. This is going to get rough."

SIXTY-ONE

Leo and Delaney huddled with Skeeter in the forest near the small Salazar cabin. Delaney had turned off the headlights and parked one hundred yards back up the road. Thankfully, she'd found a pair of baggy-on-her sweatpants in her preparedness bag. They were obscenely tight on Skeeter. Given that they would have had to handcuff him to get him to remain in the truck, though, it was a big improvement over no pants at all.

"Skeeter, we need you to stay out here. We'll send Ashley out to you. Your job will be to get her in the truck and keep her safe there."

Skeeter nodded. His glazed eyes were locked on the house in a resolute stare. He looked concussed, though. Add to that feverish and also likely in shock—the man needed to be in a hospital, not out in the woods being pelted by rain and hail. But his actions up until this point left no doubt Leo could count on Skeeter to lay down his life to protect Ashley.

Leo turned toward the cabin, a nearly invisible cutout in the forest. This close, a light gray curl of smoke gave it away, although the storm was beating that out of the air almost as soon as it left the chimney. He could see a faint glow around the windows. It looked like blackout curtains were blocking most of the light. To the right were several outbuildings. One looked big enough to garage vehicles. Another was likely a woodshed. A third he guessed held tools and equipment. Another had the shape of an outhouse. It took him a little longer to recognize the others as probable food storage and prep buildings—an icehouse and a smokehouse maybe?

This is a year-round dwelling. There was no electrical service up here, no telephone or cell, and no public water. He did see an elevated water storage tank. *How would they keep that from freezing? Maybe they don't fill it in the cold months.* Also, a line of propane tanks along one side of the cabin. Leo had heard some homeowners in the mountains hauled their own water and propane, but usually only for seasonal usage or very sporadic winter usage. He knew that other mountain houses received propane and water delivery during months when the roads were open. It was possible this cabin did, too, although hard to imagine.

Whoever lives here is hardcore off-the-grid. Resourceful. Probably a separatist, which he associated with paranoia and enough weapons and ammo to arm a regiment.

Delaney waved her hand around. "We're going to get a fight."

Leo had used a satellite phone to call in their location and situation half an hour before, along with a request for more officers. "I'm thinking we should wait."

Skeeter grunted. "Might be easiest right now. It appears only one of them's home."

Leo frowned. "What do you mean?"

Skeeter nodded at the garage structure. "The RZR is gone."

Now Leo could see the garage door was open and the building was empty inside. He felt a surge of hope. "So, you think Ashley is alone?"

"No. I think only one of them's with her."

There's more than one of them?! "I'm missing something. Start over with why you think there's more than one person."

"When I got out of my RZR here I could see the man who'd driven Ashley. Then something hit me in the back of the head. Knocked me out. Had to be another person."

"Was the second person a man or a woman?" Delaney said.

"Dunno."

"Might there be a third or more?"

"Dunno that either."

"Shit," Leo said.

"Shit," Delaney agreed. Then she gestured at Skeeter. "I'm with him. If we wait for the team, it's going to take hours. Ashley might not have hours. Who knows what's being done to her in there. And whoever is driving the RZR could show up, see our vehicle, and come in guns blazing."

Leo had a constitutional opposition to agreeing with Delaney's more risk-taking nature. He ground his teeth together.

Water dripped down her forehead and onto her nose as Delaney smiled. "You don't have to say it. Just nod if we're moving in now."

He gave one short, reluctant nod. They'd prepared their weapons back at the truck. He and Delaney had their handguns with extra clips of ammo on their duty belts as well as their clubs, multi-tools, and pepper spray. "Let's scout the house."

She made an OK symbol with her thumb and forefinger.

"Wait here," he said to Skeeter, who nodded.

Leo moved out ahead of Delaney, staying low and moving as quietly as he could in the mud and crunch of icy hail underfoot. The storm provided great sound cover and even good visual interference with their movement. A lightning flash illuminated the world around them. *So much for concealment.* The thunder crack was almost instantaneous and shook the ground. Within seconds he smelled ozone, sweet and pungent.

One good thing had come from the lightning—a brief chance to see the back of the house. Like most remote, hand-built cabins, it was rudimentary. A box with a slightly off-center door and two windows covered with blackout curtains.

He turned and motioned for Delaney to draw even with him. "I'll take the front."

"Are you going to knock and wait for an invitation?"

"We don't have visual confirmation that a crime is being committed inside. Or that Ashley is there. We only have Skeeter's word that he thinks this is the cabin a man parked at with Ashley in his RZR."

"Where Skeeter was attacked."

"All compelling circumstantial evidence."

"Knocking gives them time to aim a weapon at the door. Or use Ashley as a human shield."

"Or potentially causes them to surrender, whereas forced entry puts them in self-defense mode."

Delaney rolled her eyes. "I just love our little debates, honey."

"Pulling rank here. Give me five minutes."

"I won't be able to hear you."

He tapped his radio. "That's what these are for." They'd switched them to walkie-talkie mode back at the truck.

She nodded. "And, when they don't answer the door, how would you like us to enter?"

"I want you blocking their escape through the back door."

She frowned. "I was with you for a minute. How about—"

Then the back door to the house flew open and an enormous body stood backlit by firelight two feet away from him behind Delaney.

And it was holding a wooden club strapped with long metal spikes. A dangerous, medieval-looking cudgel.

Leo drew his weapon. "Kearny County Sheriff. Drop your weapon and freeze!"

The figure leapt toward Delaney, spiked cudgel raised to strike. Delaney ducked. The figure fell on her. Both of them rolled to the ground at Leo's feet in a tumult of fabric. The cudgel rose again, gripped in a meaty fist. Delaney was fighting back now. The two bodies were writhing, intertwined in a violent coupling. Leo held his breath. He couldn't shoot. He couldn't pull them apart without getting struck by the cudgel or putting Delaney at a disadvantage. But he had to do something and do it quickly. He danced around to their feet. He'd grab the other person by the ankles. Create a secondary front. Draw the fight away from Delaney.

But before he could, Delaney was on her feet. Somehow, in some way that defied imagination and he couldn't even follow with his eyes, she had broken free.

The other figure was up now, too, though. And he could see she was a woman. A very large woman with a bald head. A skirted sumo wrestler.

"Ma'am, drop your weapon and freeze. You are assaulting a law enforcement officer. That's a serious crime. You need to stop before someone gets hurt," he said. *Taser,* he decided. He would use the taser on her.

Delaney was circling the woman like the outclassed challenger in the match. But size wasn't everything.

The woman showed no sign she had heard him. She hadn't spoken. Didn't take her eyes off Delaney. But she was making a sound. A wet, rattling sound with each breath she took. She opened her mouth in a silent scream. Leo recoiled.

Her mouth was only darkness. The woman had no tongue.

She barreled at Delaney. Delaney drew her Staccato.

Leo was going to have to do it. He pointed the taser at her.

And like a ram, Skeeter charged into the woman and sent her flying out of the path she'd been on toward Delaney.

"Skeeter, no!" Delaney shouted, gun down and ready.

Leo swapped his taser out for his gun as well. Neither of

them had a shot. But that cudgel was lethal, and this woman was fighting for her life. She could kill Skeeter. A civilian who he should have anticipated wouldn't be able to resist entering any fight that threatened Delaney or Ashley. He should have handcuffed him to the steering wheel in the truck. If Skeeter died, he would blame himself.

Skeeter landed on his stomach in the mud. The woman rolled and ended up on her back, just out of Skeeter's reach. They were roughly the same size.

With shocking speed, especially clutching a club in one hand, the woman scrambled toward Skeeter and hit his ankle.

He let out an inhuman roar.

She scooted back on her bottom and cocked her cudgel like a bat ready for a pitcher to release a ball. Skeeter dove for her, headfirst.

She swung.

Skeeter ducked and the cudgel missed his head by the barest of margins. It crunched into his shoulder, and the man bellowed. The two fighters crashed into the ground with Skeeter's momentum rolling the woman to her side. The bulk of his body landed on her head, with her hand and cudgel under it.

Even with the cover of the storm, Leo heard a sickening sound. A crunch. But at the same time, wet. Skeeter flopped off of the woman, groaning and reaching for his ankle.

The woman didn't move.

Leo approached cautiously, expecting that she was playing possum and would whip the cudgel out and brain him with it. But she didn't move. The weapon was implanted in her temple. Blood was oozing beneath her head and something else, something he didn't want to think about. He took her pulse. Got what he expected. Turned to Delaney.

"She's dead. Landed temple-first on her cudgel."

Delaney leaned down, breathing hard. "Look at her tattoos.

They're all over her face, her neck, her arms. It looks like the same artist who did the ones on Marilyn and Sue."

Leo noticed scars on the woman's neck and shoulders where her dress was ripped away. He pulled it aside further and recoiled. Some of the marks were fresh and oozing. "She's been lashed."

Delaney shuddered. "We have to get inside. To Ashley."

Skeeter had rolled over and was sitting up. He tried to stand and fell.

"What's the matter?" Leo said.

"My ankle. It don't look so good. It feels even worse."

Leo was no doctor, but Skeeter's ankle was at an odd angle. Broken most likely.

"Stay off it," Delaney ordered. To Leo she said, "Help me get him inside?"

They each grabbed him under a shoulder. When they had him standing, he leaned on each of them like crutches and hopped into the house. They sat him in a chair just inside the door.

Delaney said, "Sit. I'll doctor you later."

He waved her off. "Take care of the girl."

And there she was, lying still as a corpse on a raised plywood platform. Leo rushed over to her. Her chest was rising and falling in a slow, steady rhythm. *Alive.*

"Ashley?"

She didn't answer. He pushed her long, tangled hair aside and checked the pulse in her neck.

"Her pulse is strong. She's dressed in some funny getup. Bulky layers. The top dress is like what we saw on Sue. Her wrists are tied in front of her."

Delaney was turning in a circle. "Needlepoint pictures of the Ten Commandments are framed and hung everywhere. Someone is into religion." She looked over Leo's shoulder at Ashley's ankles.

He saw the direction of her gaze. "Now we know why Marilyn's and Sue's ankles were scarred."

Frowning, she moved up to the table, put a soft hand on Ashley's knee. "You're going to be all right now," she whispered. She closed her eyes for a few seconds. When she opened them, she said, "These ankle restraints. I've seen something like them before in pictures."

Leo was busy trying to figure out how to unfasten Ashley's restraints. There was nothing on the front of the table, so he crouched under it and shone his flashlight at the back side, where the cables threaded through holes in the plywood. "What do you mean?"

"During the Spanish Inquisition, there was a torture ceremony. It was called the Act of Faith, I think. The idea was to keep tightening the straps around the limbs of victims until they confessed."

"And if they didn't?" *Bingo.* He pinched the metal clasp, and its teeth released the cable. He reached one arm up top and grabbed it. He pinched again and this time pulled the cable out several inches.

"It got worse from there and eventually the person died but probably not as soon as they would have liked."

He unfastened the cable around her other ankle. "How do you know these things?" He eased one foot away from the restraint.

"People like that were heroes to my grandparents. They took great glee in teaching Liam and me all about what the truly faithful did. With books and pictures no less."

He'd moved around the table and drawn her ankle out of the loop. "You think this was an Act of Faith?" He got out his multitool and uncut the rope on her wrists, taking care to pull it away from her and not abrade her skin by sliding the rope against it. "Look. She's got a brand-new DIY tattoo. Like the others."

Delaney studied it. Then her knees buckled. She grabbed the edge of the table. "Oh, my God. Why didn't I see this before?! What if these are Bible verses? The first letter. Marilyn's was EPS22 or EP522. That could be..." she mumbled, then nodded. "Ephesians, chapter five, verse twenty-two."

"If you say so."

"If you assume the Is are ones then Sue's was 1P31. First Peter, chapter three, verse one! What is Ashley's tattoo?"

"COL318."

"Shit. I'm right. That's Colossians, chapter three, verse eighteen. Oh, my God. Oh, my God."

"What is it?"

"They're all the same thing."

"Which is?"

"Wives, submit to your husbands."

"Oh my God is right." Leo looked at Ashley. The horror Sue and Marilyn had gone through. That Ashley had been enduring. "Time to get her the hell out of here."

Ashley's eyes fluttered open and focused on him. "Freddy's uncle?"

Leo smiled at her. "Yes. You're safe now. Kat's Aunt Delaney is with me, too. And Skeeter. Kat's, um, nanny. I'm going to pick you up now. We've got to go."

Ashley's eyes flew open wide. "The man. He's coming back to make me his bride."

Delaney shook her head. "It all makes sense now."

Leo slid a hand under her shoulders, "It's okay. We've got you, Ashley."

"No!" Her voice was urgent. "He's here." She raised her hand and pointed across the room.

Leo's eyes followed her finger in horror. *Is she pointing at Skeeter?*

SIXTY-TWO

The man standing in the open doorway to the cabin was no stranger to Delaney. She'd seen him only days before. The man who had come to look at Gabrielle. *What is his name?* The man she'd first seen in North Dakota, back in her ice-road trucking days. He was big. He was dark-haired-going-gray. He could have been Skeeter's biological relative.

And he was holding a wedding dress in a clear plastic bag draped over his arm.

"My bride!" he bellowed.

"That's him." Skeeter shouted and bucked in his chair. "That's him!"

"Freeze," Delaney shouted as she drew her gun into the down ready position. "Sheriff Department. Hands up where I can see them."

Igor. His name is Igor.

Igor dropped the dress. It floated to the ground. Then he whirled and was gone.

"I'm going after him," Delaney screamed.

"Don't leave me here," Ashley screamed. She tried to jump

off the table but crumpled to the ground. Tried to get up. Fell again. "I can't walk. My ankles. I can't get up."

Leo yelled, "We have to get Ashley and Skeeter to safety. Wait for us to go together. That's an order!"

"Take care of them and follow me."

"Dammit, Delaney. Don't go out there alone."

This man is a kidnapper and abuser of young girls. Nothing he could have said would have slowed Delaney down.

SIXTY-THREE

Lightning ripped across the sky. Delaney pictured Igor as he'd fled. Did he have a weapon, or had he grabbed one as he took off? She hoped not. *Who am I kidding*—the mountain provided all the weapons he would need. Rocks to bludgeon. Branches as clubs. Plus, he outweighed her by a good seventy-five pounds, so he could use his body as a literal battering ram. She was on his home turf. Dark and claustrophobic in the best of weather and broad daylight, the forest was rife with hiding places. Igor could wait her out until she ran out of steam or accidentally off a cliff. He could be watching her now. Lying in wait. Between the mud, snow, ice, water, vegetation, and obstacles on the ground, she was navigating a minefield. She'd be lucky if she didn't break her ankle or her neck. She'd be a sitting duck, lost, alone, and at his mercy. The man had already shown his depravity, kidnapping young girl after young girl, raping them, driving them to their deaths, and God knew what else. Maybe she should have waited for Leo. But would they have ever found him if he got a head start? She might not even find him now.

She stopped to catch her breath. How long had she been running? Was she chasing Igor or her own tail? For all she knew, she could have been running in a circle. Her head whipped around as she used the lightning to search for him. No Igor. But what she saw stopped her cold. Around her was a field of bright flowers of every color, all in bloom. Impossible. It's too early in the season.

The flash of light had passed, but the afterimage of the flowers burned in her mind. She examined it and realized many of them didn't even grow in the mountains. *Plastic. They're plastic flowers.* She was standing in a dark meadow of plastic flowers high in the mountains chasing a mad man as rain and hail beat down on her.

It was completely macabre.

And then she noticed something else in the afterimage. Little wooden crosses. Four of them. A graveyard. *Girls? Pets?*

But Dr. Watson had said Marilyn carried at least one pregnancy to a fairly late term. What if she'd had the baby? Or babies? What if they'd died? Or been killed? She spun, looking again for Igor as she fought an urge to throw herself on the ground in front of the little markers and weep.

A blur streaked across her peripheral vision. Movement? *It could have been an owl. A bat. A trick of light. Or...* She eased toward it, peering into the darkness. There was nothing moving now. *Still.* She took cautious steps toward the trees where she'd seen it, whatever it was.

A heavy weight hit her body from behind, knocking her to the ground, landing on her, exploding the air from her lungs.

"Oof," burst out of her mouth before she hit the ground. Something hard bit into her lip. She tasted her own blood.

Big arms wrapped around her, one *over* a shoulder, one *under* a shoulder, closing around her like a seatbelt. The weight shifted up, digging her torso into the dirt and pinning her arms beneath her body. Given that long teeth didn't rip out the side of her neck, she surmised her attacker was human and not bear or mountain lion. She writhed but couldn't free her arms.

"Okay, okay," she said, struggling to get enough air to speak, to not choke on mud and blood. "You've got me. I surrender."

Hot breath on her cheek. The voice of the man she'd spoken to at Gabrielle's storage unit. "You killed my sister. I saw her."

Well, that answered her first question. *Who was the woman at the cabin?* "I didn't hurt her. She fell and landed on her cudgel when she attacked us." An ugly vision of the spiked club buried in the side of the woman's head made her squeeze her eyes shut. "I'm sorry for your loss. What was her name?"

"Maria."

"Maria Salazar?"

His grip tightened. "How do you know that?"

She coughed for a breath. "Property records. Your cabin."

"You know nothing about me." His grip eased just enough.

She drew a deep breath. "Very little," she admitted. "Except that you told me your name is Igor when you came to look at my truck."

He drew back a few inches, panting heavily in her ear. She relaxed. Rested. When his guard was down, she could try to escape again. For now, if she kept him talking and gathered information, it would give Leo time to find her.

"You were going to, um, marry Ashley?"

"It was God's command to me."

"You and your sister. You seem very devoted to God."

He began to recite the Ten Commandments. "Thou shall have no other gods before Me. Thou shall not make idols."

Delaney interrupted him and took over, speaking rapidly. "Thou shall not take the name of the Lord thy God in vain. Remember the Sabbath day, to keep it holy. Honor thy father and thy mother. Thou shall not murder. Thou shall not commit adultery. Thou shall not steal. Thou shall not bear false witness against thy neighbor. Thou shall not covet."

"You know them in order."

"Yes. I suspect we were raised the same."

"Are you Basque?"

Now they were getting somewhere. She tried to shift her arms. Found enough room to ease them upward, inching them to where she'd have more mobility. "No. But I grew up here. The graves. Who is buried here?"

His breath caught. "The young'uns."

"Yours and Marilyn's?"

"Yes."

"Was she your first, um, wife?"

"She was the first one God commanded me to take."

"Were the babies stillborn?"

"No. My sister Maria said they didn't honor their father and mother. Screamed all the time even though Marilyn asked them not to. They broke a commandment. She buried them while I was gone."

Delaney's mouth went dry. Maria had murdered babies for crying. She wanted to cry herself. "She killed them."

She felt him shrug. "Because she also broke a commandment, I punished her."

"By tattooing her?"

His voice took on a disapproving tone. "She desecrated her own body with those. I allowed her to adorn each bride with one as well, because she said they were for their own good."

Maria was the one instructing the girls to submit. "How did you punish her then?"

"I took her tongue for the first time. For the second and all her other sins, she got the lash."

"There were two babies?"

"Yes."

"She was pregnant when she died. When she ran away."

For long moments, Igor didn't even breathe. Then he said, "Take that back."

Instead, Delaney changed the subject. "There are four graves." Who else had the Salazars killed?

"Two graves. Two markers. One each for Marilyn and Sue."

That was good, at least. Delaney remembered the scars on Maria's back. The fresh wounds. The recent punishment. "Did you not break any commandments?"

"I kept only one bride at a time. I did not commit adultery. God saved me from covetousness. He showed me the girls that needed my protection and instructed me to take them away from their situations."

"What situations were those?" She closed her eyes. Expecting to hear it. Dreading that she was right.

"A white man who wanted to perpetuate the rape and imprisonment that has been going on in this country since the Europeans came to America, with each of them. The way he chased after them. He wanted to defile them. I wanted to honor them. Make them wives. Give them families."

A white man—not teenage boy, like Elijah? "Are you talking about the teacher?"

His voice thundered and sprayed her neck and face with spittle. "I knew him as a boy. I knew his perversion. I watched it ripen and rot."

She fought back revulsion. "We're talking about Steve Randolph now. Just to be clear. Yes?"

Igor spat. Part of it landed on the ground. Part of it splattered on her check.

You're making it pretty hard to believe in you right now, God. A voice rang out in her mind. *That is him, not Me.* Did she actually hear the words? Or was she just going crazy? "That sounds covetous to me." Delaney wished she could take it back as soon as it left her mouth.

"Let she who is without sin cast the first stone? What about you? It's the Sabbath and are you keeping it holy? No, you've come after me."

Was it Sunday? Then she remembered that technically the Bible identified sundown Friday through sundown Saturday as the Sabbath. Which meant, since it was after sundown, she was in the clear. But she doubted he cared about that distinction.

"What about drugging the girls? The torture? The marking of their bodies with tattoos?"

"That was not me. Maria had her weaknesses. But I had to be gone much of the time. She kept my brides safe in my absence. I had to allow her some latitude."

His easy justification of his sister's atrocities was breathtaking. She sensed a physical and mental change in him. Something about the slackness of his body told her the time to resist had come. She took a split second to rehearse mentally. *Flip him onto his weak side and push up and out of his hold. Then get my gun and draw on him until he submits. Hope it doesn't go any further than that.*

What she really hoped is that Leo had gotten Ashley and Skeeter to safety and would show up to help her at any second. But she could only rely on herself.

Go time. With an explosion of adrenaline-fueled strength, she threw her weight against the side of his body that was holding her from under her arm. She needed that arm pinned and immobile.

She felt his hesitation and then his weight shifted. *Didn't see that coming from a girl, did you, asshole?* She bridged her hips, pushing with her thighs and glutes, straining against his heavy body. Everything had to go perfectly now, or he'd turn the tables.

He released his strong side grip. It was exactly what she'd hoped for—that with his size and strength, especially in comparison to hers, he would rely on brute force instead of technique. That he would show his lack of knowledge of the basics of hand-to-hand combat. She scurried up, shooting out from under him like she was being reborn, then bear-crawling away as fast as she could. When she calculated she'd gone far enough, she stopped to draw her weapon.

It was a costly misjudgment.

He grabbed her ankle and jerked her toward him. "Get. Back. Here."

She was sliding on her stomach, eating and breathing mud, bucking and fighting but soon to be at the mercy of his bulk again.

It's now or never.

She jerked the Staccato from her holster and swept the thumb safety off. *Just shoot him. He's a monster.* But she couldn't make herself do it. She was facing away. If she had to fire on him blind—behind her back, even—at point blank range, she might blow his damn head off. He hadn't killed anyone that she knew of, although his sister had. He hadn't even tried to kill her. Her brain told her deadly force wasn't justified, even though she wanted to use it, wanted to with every cell in her body. In the end, getting away dead was too easy for him. He deserved to spend the rest of his life in prison and everything that would happen to him as a child rapist there. She'd fire one warning and hope it was enough.

Her gun boomed as she shot into the air in front of her.

He jerked at the report. His hands loosened.

It was enough. She pulled free and jumped to her feet, keeping a grip on her gun. She whirled around, Staccato up.

Igor had leapt up as well. He was crouched, ready to spring at her.

She spit mud on the ground. Aiming at his center mass, she forced calmness into her voice. "I wouldn't do that if I was you."

The whites of his eyes shone in the dark. She watched as he mulled his options. She saw it the second he decided. He stood up. Squeezed the knuckles of one hand with the other. "God will punish you."

"Maybe. But he knows I was just following his Eleventh Commandment."

"There is no such thing."

"You don't know it? It's Thou Shall Not Let Any Sick Bastards Hurt Little Girls."

He lowered himself again. He was preparing to rush her. He was going to make her shoot him. She adjusted her footing, relaxed her shoulders. She was prepared to do whatever she had to do.

"Delaney!" It was Leo's voice. Then his footsteps, pounding nearer. Sweet, sweet sounds.

She bared her teeth at Igor in something like a smile. "I think the sheriff just saved your life."

Leo splashed up to them and stopped five feet to her left. "I heard a shot. Are you okay?"

She didn't take her eyes off Igor. "I'm fine. We both are. Cuff him, please. Hands and feet. I want him immobilized until backup arrives."

"Agreed."

Leo stomped over to Igor. "Hands behind your back."

Arms out, Igor leaned his head back and bellowed to the heavens. "Save me, God. I've done your bidding. I am your servant."

Leo snapped a metal cuff around one wrist, then jerked that arm to spin Igor around. He grabbed the other arm and cuffed it, too. Igor did not resist. Leo put a hand on his head. "Sit."

The big man sat. He continued praying or chanting or maybe just babbling out insanities as Leo used Flex Cuffs on his ankles.

Watching with her weapon down ready, Delaney experienced a moment of utter clarity. Call it the voice of God or an epiphany or whatever, but the words reverberated in her head. *You may have trouble believing in Me, but can you at least believe in yourself and the goodness of the people I've put in your life?*

She holstered her gun and stood there, frozen. If she answered the voice in her head, did that make her more or less crazy? She decided more, but no one could hear her, so she did it anyway. *I can work with that.*

Leo stood and backed away from his secured prisoner. He nodded, apparently satisfied Igor wouldn't get away. Then he turned and strode over to Delaney like he was going to walk right through her. He put his hands on her shoulders, stopping only inches away. Rain plastered his hair to his face and coursed down his cheeks.

"I heard the shot. I thought he'd killed you." His voice broke. "I thought I'd lost you."

The electricity. The emotions. The feelings. She couldn't fight them anymore. Didn't want to. She reached her hand behind Leo's head, stood on her tiptoes, closed her eyes.

She pressed her lips and body into his.

SIXTY-FOUR

Leo hung up the phone with the county attorney Monday morning. He'd been given the green light to charge the Mountain Man—Igor Salazar—with three counts of kidnapping a minor child. The county attorney had promised to add additional charges later. Statutory rape. Torture. Administering drugs to commit felonies. He'd sworn on his dead champion border collie's life to Leo that they'd throw the book at him. They'd even found a stash of highly illegal fully automatic weapons locked in a chest in one of his sheds, something that had seemed to interest the FBI as much as the other crimes. Their agent had left town an hour before, after assuring Leo that all relevant parties with the BIA—police and MMU—were up to speed. Leo's job now was to continue to gather evidence in cooperation with Wyoming DCI.

But not the police department. Because Joe Tarver had sat Leo down that morning and traced the digital footprints in the records system for him. Three hours after the girl's body had been found, the name Mara Gipson had been removed from all of Marilyn Littlewolf's records. To Mara's credit, when Leo had taken the evidence to her an hour before, she'd kept her chin up, admitted what she'd done, and thrown herself at his mercy. He'd told her he'd get back to her. He wanted to take a minute to ponder how much mercy he was willing to give.

And, on the subject of mercy, Steve Randolph would be getting none either. The DNA results from Sue Wiley's panties had come back and matched his sample. Other women and girls had come forward with their own tales about his despicable behavior. In a conversation with Steve and his attorney, Steve had vomited up everything he could remember about Igor Salazar and professed to be horrified about how and why Igor had chosen his three brides. Reading between the lines, Steve believed that Igor had stalked him over the years because Steve had ended the friendship over Igor and his family's religious practices. Two wrongdoers did not make a right.

The one wrongdoer they'd been shocked to learn about was Nelson Hillmont, whose friend Samuel Russo had ratted him out to Leo as having attacked Delaney in retaliation for Samuel's arrest. Shared past suffering ran deep between the two men, but Samuel had been so grateful for the closure they gave his wife about Sue's death that he'd offered it up like a thank you gift. Nelson had refused to confess, and Delaney chose not to pursue it. Leo would be keeping a close eye on the volatile man going forward.

Joe had provided one bit of relief from the litany of bad news. He'd run down Betty Flanagan nee Crowheart, who'd run off to marry a man she'd met in a bar, scaring her parents into filing a missing person's report. But she was safe and sound in Michigan with five kids and still hitched to the love of her life. Skeeter was a distant memory to her, one she spoke of with amusement, not fear.

An email notification appeared, from Wolverine. He read it with amusement.

Slater, 99% certain those tattoos are Bible verses for wives to submit to husbands. Details attached. Gratis. Wolverine.

Delaney had been faster than the machines, but he was glad he could trust them, too. He shot a reply with thanks for the help. Then he called Delaney next.

"Yes?" she said.

"Time to talk to Igor and his attorney. He's going to be charged this afternoon. You ready?"

"I'll meet you there."

"Uh, okay." It wasn't lost on Leo that Delaney was avoiding walking over with him. Hadn't so much as looked him in the eye since their kiss. She'd even hitched a ride down the mountain with Skeeter in one of the ambulances right after it.

* * *

He walked over to the interview room alone five minutes later. Delaney had already taken her usual seat. Igor was sitting beside a familiar attorney.

Jenn Herrington greeted him. "I'm representing Mr. Salazar."

He nodded at her. "Seems like between you and Wesley, you have the corner on the market lately. We'll be recording this interview."

She turned to her client. "Mr. Salazar, remember you don't have to answer any questions you don't want to. Anything you say, they'll try to use against you."

Igor lifted dead eyes and fixed them on Delaney. "You. You took my Ashley from me. She was meant to be my bride."

Attorney Herrington let out a long sigh.

Leo grinned. The county attorney was going to be elated. "I'll take that as a confession." This might go even better than he'd hoped. Now, if he could just get things moving in the right direction with Delaney.

But when the interview concluded, Delaney was out the door before he had a chance to speak to her alone.

SIXTY-FIVE

On Tuesday morning in the living room at the Klinkosh residence, Delaney sat in an armchair, hyper conscious of Leo beside her in another. Since they'd come down from the nightmare on the mountain, she'd managed to thwart his attempts to talk to her about what had happened. Not what had happened with Igor Salazar, but what had happened between the two of them. She hadn't been ready.

But she couldn't put him off much longer. After they finished here with Ashley and her family. Right now, they were her focus.

"Here she is!" Eliza Klinkosh beamed as she and Nevada escorted Ashley into the living room. "Freshly home from the hospital."

"We're never letting her out of our sight again." Nevada was smiling but his eyes still had a haunted look. "We almost couldn't peel her dog and her brother off her to send them to my parents for a day. We've all been knocked senseless by this."

To be powerless while your child suffers? What could be worse?

"Dad, I'm fine!" Ashley walked straight to Leo and hugged

him, then turned to Delaney and gave her an even longer embrace. "Thank you both, so much."

"I'm glad to see you looking so good," Delaney said.

"You're welcome. Freddy sends his best," Leo said.

"As do Kat and Carrie," Delaney added. "Are you feeling okay?"

"My ankles will hurt for a while. But I don't feel icky from the drugs anymore. I'm having trouble sleeping. I keep waking up from nightmares." *Like Carrie.* Ashley sat between her parents on the couch. "It kind of seems unreal now. But I know it all happened." She turned her arm over to reveal the DIY tattoo.

"We'll get that taken off," her mother said.

Ashley was staring at it. When she looked up, her eyes were too wise for her age. "How could someone know the same God as me and do all that bad stuff?"

My question exactly.

Nevada held out his hand and his daughter put hers in his. "There's madness at the extremes of almost anything. And never forget, God gave us free will."

Delaney had a sudden and surprising desire to come to one of Nevada's services.

Leo said, "We wanted you to know that Igor Salazar has been charged."

"What will happen to him?" Ashley asked.

"Hopefully he'll spend the rest of his life in prison."

She nodded emphatically. "Good."

"I heard that Ashley's teacher was also charged?" Eliza said.

Leo touched the badge on his shirt in a seemingly unconscious move. "Yes. With respect to his actions with Sue Wiley. But it turned out that Igor was selecting girls that Mr. Randolph targeted."

"That's how he picked me?" Ashley's cheeks flushed and her voice squeaked. "Because Mr. Randolph did?"

"Basically, yes. In his warped mind, he may have believed he was protecting you."

"Well, he wasn't! I could handle Mr. Randolph!"

Delaney didn't doubt it. "No other girls will have to now. He's no longer with the school."

Nevada was shaking his head. "Too many girls hurt. Our community has to do a better job keeping them from harm's way, starting with Eliza and me."

Delaney had been one of those girls. So had her daughters. "And with me."

* * *

Fifteen minutes later, Delaney and Leo headed toward their trucks parked tail to nose in front of the house. Leo's was finally back in service after its repairs.

Delaney stopped short of hers, leaned her head back, and felt the warm spring sunshine on her face. *I can do this.* "Do you have a minute?"

He turned to her, looking the kind of handsome she'd always been put off by. Yet here she was, pulled in by some kind of cosmic tractor beam. "Of course."

She leaned against her truck. "I'm sorry I've been putting you off."

"I've been waiting a year. What's another day or two?" His words were easy, but his tone was tight. Nervous.

"I needed time to think."

"Have you had enough?"

"I have. Have you?"

He gave a dry laugh. "I didn't need any."

"So, to be clear, you didn't need any because..." she rolled her hand for him to fill in the silence.

"Really? You're going to pretend you don't know how I feel?"

She shifted, laughed. "You want to pursue this. Us."

"That's one way of looking at it."

"How would you say it then?"

"That I'm crazy about you and want us to be together."

"Same thing."

He rolled his eyes, but he was smiling. "Whatever you say. Your turn now."

Her heartbeat was thundering in her ears. If she had to rank the scariest moments in her life, this one topped the list. Physical danger, risk to herself or others—those were terrifying, but she'd proven she had what it took for them. But this? Opening her heart to Leo, giving him the power to break it? The few words she could muster stuck in her throat. She swallowed. She pushed away from the truck. She put her hands in her pockets.

"You want me to say it for you?" The look he gave her was so gentle and understanding that it was almost as if he'd taken her hand and pressed his lips to it, even though they were standing two feet apart, not touching.

"Okay." She caught the inside of her bottom lip in her teeth and held it, biting down so hard it almost hurt.

"Despite how many times life and people have let you down and hurt you before, you are willing to do me the honor of giving happiness another try with me."

She pressed her hand to her mouth. Her eyes filled. *There. That's the weakness that scares me so much.* But she nodded.

"I want to pull you into my arms and hold you right now more than I've ever wanted anything in my whole life, Delaney Pace."

She nodded again.

He threw his head back and laughed. "You, Delaney, feel exactly the same way."

A tear spilled. She swiped at it. Her voice came back. "I, Delaney, feel exactly the same way." He started to come in for the hug, but she held up a hand. "But Leo... this has to be private. Just between us."

He nodded slowly. "Because?"

"You're my boss. Your campaign."

"Those are decent points. But they're not ringing true. Try again."

She threw her arms in the air. "Because I'm a commitment phobic nutjob, and I can't stand the outside pressure. Baby steps for you are giant leaps for me, Leo."

He pursed his lips. His brows furrowed. Then he relaxed and said, "I shall endeavor not to let anyone notice my feelings for you and will refrain from all mention of a relationship with you other than professional."

She held up her hand. "Pinky promise?"

They hooked pinkies. It was the warmest, sexiest little finger touch she could have ever imagined, full of the possibility of everything.

"Pinky promise," he said.

She dropped her hand. "Great. Well, I'll see you at work tomorrow."

He gave her a wide-eyed questioning look. "Really?"

She fluffed her hair and turned to her truck door with some sass in her backside. "Baby steps, Sheriff." Then she threw him a wink before she drove away, floating three inches above her seat.

SIXTY-SIX

Leo sat in his truck deleting dating apps one after another from his phone. Delaney was going to give him a chance. He still couldn't wrap his head around it. Even after the kiss, he'd thought she'd find a way to back out. But she didn't. He understood she wanted to keep it a secret for now. That made sense to him, too. For now.

He put his head back on the headrest for a minute, soaking in the moment. *Delaney. Delaney and him. The two of us together.*

His phone chimed. He grabbed it, grinning like a lovesick idiot. *Maybe it's her.*

But it wasn't.

It was Special Agent Natalie Amin, his former handler from the DEA.

They're on to you Leo. Take precautions.

They. They was the Bajeños. His joy turned to dust. His family. His job. Delaney. He had so much to lose.

But he had so much to *protect*. And he wasn't going to let those lowlifes take it from him.

He turned on his truck and drove home, fast like Delaney, his brain spinning as he started making plans. Then his phone rang again. Thinking it was related to the Bajeños, he picked up.

"Leo Palmer."

"This is Clark Applewood. I'm a special agent with the Alcohol, Tobacco and Firearms. I hear you found a stash of illegal weapons on a prisoner."

Leo felt like he had whiplash. "I'm sorry. What is this about?"

"Meet me at the jail in an hour, Sheriff."

"Why?"

"We'll talk about it then."

SIXTY-SEVEN

Delaney returned to pandemonium at the Pace homestead. Skeeter—his booted broken ankle up on a chair—had a face full of glitter and was blowing his sparkly fingernails. Delaney knew that meant Kat had painted him up to match her. While Carrie was glitter-free, she had given up the big screen to her sister and was dancing with her while Taylor Swift sang "Fearless." Kat had roped everyone in the family into highly participatory watch parties of the singer-songwriter's YouTube album playlists several times each now. Dudley was dancing too. His version was barking and nipping the air as he lunged at their heels. The dog had stayed characteristically mum, though, about how he'd gotten from Skeeter's RZR back to Skeeter's apartment. Delaney could only imagine he was making his way home but stopping everywhere he knew to look for his people along the way.

Delaney pranced into the living room belting out lyrics and flashing heart hands over her head. Kat squealed with laughter and grabbed her hand. Delaney took Carrie's in her other, winked at Skeeter, and jumped up and down in a circle.

When she was out of breath and laughing, she held up their hands. "That's all I have in me. I need to talk to Skeeter."

"No! Keep dancing!" Kat said.

Delaney broke away, shaking her head and smiling. Kat diverted her attention to Carrie, urging her sister on. Carrie kept jumping and dancing. It made Delaney's heart ache in the best possible way.

Skeeter pointed at his chest. "Me now?"

Delaney nodded. "Let's go outside."

"As long as it's not where anyone can see me in this getup."

She held open the rarely used front door. She took a seat on the porch swing. Skeeter perched at the rail looking out over the field of balsam root and lupine in full bloom, hands in his pockets.

"Don't you want to sit?" She pointed at his boot.

"Been sitting all day. I'm good."

Delaney let some easy silence pass. "You didn't have to come back to work so quickly, you know."

"The girls—" his voice broke. He cleared his throat and tried again. "You guys are the closest thing I have to a family. Delaney, I messed up. Five years ago. I made a mistake. I—"

"You've already told me this. And talked about it at length in your interviews at the station. You don't have to do it again."

He whirled, tears running down his face. "I do. I have to. I can't ever make up for what I did. It's haunted me. It's literally haunted me. Peg's suicide. And when Marilyn died..." He sank to his haunches, face buried in his hands.

Delaney scooted across the swing and put her hand on his shoulder, letting him cry it out.

He wiped his eyes. His lips were tight as he said, "I would protect you and your girls with my life."

"You have and you did. You are part of our family, too." She held out her hand.

He squeezed it, shaking his head. His lips trembled.

"And Skeeter. We're all more than the sum of our past mistakes. The sun rises each morning on our next chance. I have enough past mistakes to write a book out of. A whole series of books about. It's how we move forward that matters."

"I should have told you about Marilyn. I never dreamed it could happen to Sue and Ashley, too."

"I've seen your file. It's not like you had some secret knowledge that would have cracked the case. You were there for Ashley. You were there for me. You're here for us now. And we are here for you, too, Skeeter. I need you to remember that. You can talk to me. You can tell me anything."

"Thank you. From the bottom of my heart, thank you."

"I'd say you've already paid for it. Literally and emotionally."

"I swear, those payments I made to her dad weren't what it looked like. After Peg killed herself, he heard I'd told her Marilyn was with him. I just – well, he could have ruined me. I was scared. He asked for money to keep quiet about it, and I felt like I deserved it, somehow."

"I can't say I wouldn't have felt the same."

He nodded. He looked down, held his shirt away from his chest. "I think my glitter has run off all over my shirt."

"I'm going to be honest. It's not a good look."

He finally laughed, wiping his eyes and smearing more glitter on his arm. "I think I'll head home now. Shower. See you tomorrow night."

"One more thing before you go."

His eyes tightened and he looked worried again. "Yes?"

"I want to find my mother. I need you to help me."

"I—you mean, you want me to skip trace her?"

"I think it's going to take more than that. I have reason to believe she's alive." Liam's words haunted her. He had said, *If you kill me now, you'll never get a touching reunion with our mother.* Delaney had asked, *Is she alive?* And he'd responded, *Very much so,* before he'd fallen to his presumed death. "It's time. Together, we're going to find her, if you're in." Delaney held up her knuckles.

Skeeter sucked in a shuddering breath, then he smiled and bumped her knuckles. "Delaney's mom. We'll find her together."

"Thanks. And good night, Skeeter."

He waved and headed back around the house to his car.

Delaney rocked for a few minutes. Her hodgepodge family of half-related and unrelated souls was more battered than most. She touched her lips. Thought about that kiss with Leo. Whether it was fair to involve him in her mess. Realized she was smiling and didn't care.

The front door opened. It was getting a greater than normal workout.

Carrie stuck her head out. "What are you doing? Skeeter's gone. We're hungry."

"What did you make me for dinner?"

"Um, pizza night?"

"You made pizza?"

"Stop!" Carrie grinned. "I'll do the laundry this weekend if you'll take us to eat pizza."

"I've got news for you. You're gonna do it anyway." Delaney stood. "And, yes to pizza."

"Sweet!" Carrie did a heart hand over her head.

Delaney knew Carrie was doing it ironically, but it still worked on her. "But first, tell me about college."

Carrie sighed. "It's not for me, Delaney. At least not now. I don't want to go."

"All right. Are you planning on taking a break for a year to work and think about what comes next or what?"

"I don't know yet. I mean, I'd work."

"Is this about money? Are you trying not to spend any? Because I've got plenty. We're fine."

"No. It's not about money."

Delaney sighed. "How about this— you apply to a few colleges, just to keep that door open. A lot can change in a year. Especially after all that has happened to you this year."

"I'm not going to change my mind."

"It won't hurt anything to do the applications. It doesn't obligate you to go."

"What do I get in return?"

"What do you mean?"

"This is a negotiation, isn't it? So, if I do some dumb, waste-of-time applications, what do I get in return?"

"Besides the immeasurable value of leaving your options on the table and ensuring my sanity and happiness?"

"Obvi."

"Tell me what you want, as I can see that's where this is headed."

"Keep Gabrielle and teach me to drive her."

Delaney thought about the offer she had on the table for the rig. All that she could do for her girls with that much money. But keeping her a little longer left a door open. And through that door was an experience Carrie wanted with her adoptive mother. Delaney stuck out her hand. "Deal."

Carrie beamed as they shook on it. "I'm going to tell Kat we're getting pizza and go change."

"Me, too. Dirty deputy clothes are a no."

They went inside together. Taylor Swift had been turned off. Delaney heard a happy squeal from Kat's room. Carrie had broken the pizza news. She smiled and changed into jeans and a long-sleeve T. *Ah, what the hell.* She texted Leo and asked him to join them.

Kat ran into her room and dove onto the bed belly first. "I want horseback riding lessons if Carrie's getting driving lessons."

Delaney dove beside her and tickled her. "You're going to turn into a horse."

Kat shrieked with laughter.

"I won't."

"Fine then. Horseback riding lessons."

"Yay!"

Delaney heard a vehicle approaching through their open doors and windows. She stood, frowning.

"Are either of you expecting company?"

"Nope," Kat said.

"Not me," Carrie shouted.

Delaney went to the door. She crossed her arms and scowled. A very federal looking black vehicle had parked outside her house.

"I'll be back in a moment."

"Who is it?" Kat shouted.

But Delaney didn't answer. She didn't know for sure, but she had a bad feeling.

SIXTY-EIGHT

A man got out, brushing the wrinkles out of a black suit that was tight across his thighs. With his short haircut and black shades, he was very *Men in Black*. But the bulky body looked more like a weightlifter or former professional football player than Will Smith.

His hand was out. "Delaney Pace. I'm—"

"Someone who doesn't take a brush off well." His voice was instantly recognizable to her as the person she'd suspected it would be the second she saw the car. "Mr. Apple Pie."

Annoyance creased his forehead, but his smile didn't waver. "Close enough."

"I thought I made it clear that I'm not interested in working with the ATF?"

He looked toward her house. She followed his gaze and saw several curious faces watching them. She gestured with her head to follow her to the barn.

When they were in its shadow, he said, "This is about another matter. Information I need to share with you about a case you've been working on."

"Great. Well, let's get on with it." She rolled her hand.

"I regret to inform you that the State of Wyoming will be unable to prosecute Igor Salazar. He has been turned over to us. We'll be prosecuting him for illegal weapons charges."

At first Delaney thought there was no way she'd heard him correctly. Clouds of anger fogged her vision. She shook her head. Narrowed her eyes. Clenched and unclenched her hands. Then she exploded. "What the hell? Why?"

"I believe I just told you why. But I'll give you something as a token of goodwill, since you're someone I'd like to see working with us—Mr. Salazar is a confidential informant in an ongoing case with national security implications. It's safer for him to move to federal custody."

She stabbed her finger toward him. "Bullshit."

He put his hands up in a "don't shoot" gesture. "It's the truth."

"It's our case. Ours. And he deserves to be prosecuted for what he did, not for a few guns. We'd put him away for life. You'll give him a slap on the wrist."

"He could face thirty years to life."

"*Could* is the operative word. We never saw him in possession of them. He'll say he didn't know about them. That it was his sister. Or stashed there without either of their knowledge. We've got him dead to rights on a multitude of charges. If you don't convict him, he'll keep hurting girls. Abusing them. They'll die."

"We don't want to see that happen."

"What *do* you want to see happen, Special Agent Applewood?"

He raised his hands like he was delivering a sermon. "I am in service of the greater good."

She began to pace, gesticulating wildly as she went. It was that or punch him. "There is no greater good than protecting our children! Our girls!" *And I had the chance to take Igor*

Salazar out in self-defense and didn't do it. She was going to second guess herself on that choice for the rest of her life.

His eyebrows peaked. "That would sound good on a bumper sticker, but it's not how the world works."

"I don't buy him as a CI. A trucker hiding out and committing unspeakable crimes in one of the least populated counties in the least populated state in the nation? You've got to give me more than that. Because what you've given me so far stinks to high heaven."

"Delaney, let me be blunt since you seem to appreciate that." He rotated back and forth to maintain connection with her as she paced. "I don't have to give you anything. In fact, I didn't have to come here at all. You could have found out when you got to work tomorrow and learned that your boss signed him over to us today. I came to you because I'm willing to give you more information if you come to work for us."

Leo turned Igor over to the ATF without talking to me? The betrayal was bone deep. But it was worse than betrayal. It was heartbreak. She'd almost given the many-times-broken thing that still managed to beat inside her chest over to him. She had thought they shared a code of ethics. A common belief system.

She was wrong, apparently.

But she couldn't crumble under the weight of personal feelings right now. She had to deal with the man who'd invaded her sanctuary with this terrible news. She threw her arms in the air, but the agent didn't yield to her.

"Hear me out. You wouldn't have to give up your day job. It would just be as a consultant, on an occasional basis. With the blessing of your sheriff, of course, who has been a friend to one of our sister agencies in the past."

Was this standard manipulation by the feds? Leo's work for the DEA had practically been at gunpoint. Or was Clark telling her the truth? She'd made a leap of faith to trust Leo—and where had that gotten her? Not that she'd admit it to this man. "Eff off, Apple Pie."

He removed his sunglasses and polished them with his tie. Then he held them in one hand and locked eyes with her. "I was warned that your loyalties might be misplaced."

"Excuse me?"

"This is your chance to pick a side. Prove them wrong."

Delaney's blood boiled. She remembered how the DEA had assumed that she would side with her brother and then baited Leo to go after her. Never once had she helped Liam in any way. She'd put a bullet in him. Chased him off the side of a mountain. As far as she knew, her brother was dead. *But is he? Is that what this is about? And if he is alive, what is he doing to pique ATF's interest?*

She pushed her thoughts away and returned her ire to the agent. "Pick what side? I'm a law enforcement officer. I'm already on the right side."

"A time will come. Mark my words. A time will come where you'll remember this conversation and you'll regret it."

"Is that a threat?"

"It's a prediction."

She chuckled. "I have a prediction for you."

"What's that?"

"I predict that before you're even out of Kearny today you're going to get your ass chewed by your boss for not being able to strong-arm a Wyoming cop. A Wyoming *girl* cop at that."

He shrugged and started walking back to his gleaming car. "We'll see."

"And if this is about my brother, and he's alive and you're not telling me, remember that he put his daughter's and my life in jeopardy more than once. Kat is the most important person in my world. If he's out there, he's a threat to her. If you withhold information that gets her hurt, you'll be the one who regrets this conversation."

He stopped, his hand subtly moving to his hip as if he needed to be ready for a quickdraw western shootout. "Never smart to threaten a federal officer."

"Whoever said I was smart? I'm just a foster fail kid who drove ice-road trucks and can only get a job as a county cop." She pointed a gun with her thumb and forefinger at the sky and pulled the imaginary trigger. "Don't come back without an invitation unless you're carrying a warrant."

He opened the door of his car and got in, shaking his head.

She watched him drive away. More than ever, she felt let down by the feds. But that paled in comparison to how she felt about being let down by Leo. How close she'd come to making a huge mistake with him.

Her phone buzzed with a text. Leo.

Pizza sounds great. I have something to take care of then I'm all yours. What time?

She gritted her teeth and shoved the phone in her back pocket. No way she was including him. Thank goodness Applewood had stopped by. The news had been the worst, but at least it had come before she'd shown her feelings about Leo in front of the girls. She'd saved them from what she was feeling now.

More than ever, she realized how dangerous it was to grow up as a girl in this world. How dangerous it was for her daughters. *Well, if it comes down to it, they've got me.* She couldn't protect them all, but she could start with the two in the house. Her most important job. She drew a deep, shuddering breath, squeezed her eyes shut tight and released them, then rejoined her family.

A LETTER FROM PAMELA FAGAN HUTCHINS

Dear Reader:

You're here! At the end of *DDP4*! With all the choices for and demands on use of your time, I am honored that you spent hours of yours reading it.

If you would like to receive email alerts of all my latest releases, just sign up at the following link. Your email address will never be shared, and you can unsubscribe at any time.

www.bookouture.com/pamela-fagan-hutchins

It has been such a thrill to read your reviews of the first few books in the series and share my love for Delaney and her world with you. I can't believe I get the privilege of continuing her stories. In a crazy twist of fate, I've been writing them in Denmark, the UK, France, and California, far from my home base in Wyoming. This particular book was written in Bakersfield, California. Writing Delaney has made me both more and less homesick.

I wrote *DDP4* write after the birth of my first granddaughter. I think as a result I was really dialed in to how hard it is to "grow up girl" and to my instinct to protect all girls. Combined with the long-term travesty of how much more dangerous it is to grow up *Native* girl in North America, this book practically wrote itself. If this topic pulls at your heart, there are many great resources available online to read by searching on Missing and Murdered Indigenous Women and Girls. For a wonderful account of Native Americans in the modern West, I recommend the documentary *White Buffalo: Voices of the West*.

I hope you enjoyed *DDP4* and if you did, I would be very grateful if you could write a short review online. I'd love to hear what you thought about it, and reviews make such a difference helping new readers discover one of my books for the first time.

Writing is a solitary experience, and I am somewhat of a hermit anyway. I split my time between two rustic homes. The one in Wyoming, on the face of the Bighorn Mountains, and the other on a remote lake in Maine. No matter where we are, my companions are my husband and our sled dogs, with visits from our adult children and grandchild.

So, I *love* hearing from my readers out there in the real world. You can get in touch with me via my Facebook page where I am fairly active, through Instagram, Goodreads, or my website. I also so very greatly appreciate follows on Amazon and BookBub.

Thanks,

Pamela Fagan Hutchins

www.pamelafaganhutchins.com

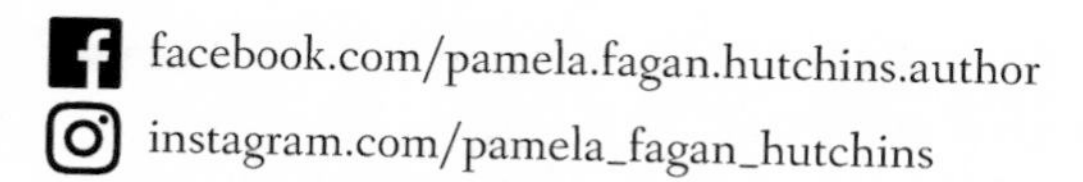

ACKNOWLEDGMENTS

My husband Eric's great-grandmother was Native American, adopted by his Caucasian great-great-grandparents. There was a history at the time of children being removed from the reservations—for schooling or adoption—that was not always with the blessing of the birth parents. Little is known about her before she joined their family. That missing chunk of her past and the possible reasons for it gnaws at her family.

Eric's maternal grandmother migrated from Hungary to the United States alone at the age of eighteen. What courage! She self-described her upbringing as Gypsy and did not return to Hungary before the death of her own parents. The family has often wondered whether she was moving *to* something or *away* from something. She always said it was because she wanted to be an American.

These women's genes would later merge into a beautiful blend across generations. They intrigue and inspire me, as do my own forebears, among them many strong women. I hope at some point Delaney will discover a Hungarian ancestor. That would be fun to write. But it is the adopted Native American girl who influenced my desire to write *Her Forgotten Shadow*.

My deepest thanks to both women. You would be very proud of the man who carries on your legacy as well as his wonderful (grown) children.

A few years ago, my husband Eric posted that we were giving away rusty, fire-damaged barbed wire. One of the takers was Daisy, who showed up with her family to claim some to use for a project. We soon learned that she'd given up oil field trucking in North Dakota—and a side gig as a reality star— for taking over the family homestead, raising her second daughter twenty years after her first, and being a service to others through philanthropy and her physical labor. She was a key player in organizing one of the largest agricultural relief efforts in the history of the United States through a huge convoy of truckers, donors, and volunteers after historic fires devastated America's Midwest. She and her family raise (and butcher) a large flock of turkeys every year to feed 300+ people at a free community Thanksgiving dinner. Daisy's the one you want as your second in a knife fight, who could have been a model or actress instead of a rodeo star and extreme trucker, and she's the friend you can knock back a cold one with or take to meet your pastor (after you've done your best to prepare them for the encounter). If by some small miracle you find her in a church, you won't see her sitting in the pews... she's the one standing in the back. She was forged in the kind of volcanic upheaval that can result in smoking rubble or beautiful Rocky Mountain ranges. Daisy, through character and force of will, is the latter. If you enjoy Delaney as much as I do, it is because of my friend Daisy. Daisy, thank you for agreeing to let me reshape you in fiction.

When it comes to creating a fictional law enforcement world, you have to start with the real thing. I am so lucky to have Police Chief Travis Koltiska of Sheridan, Wyoming, in my corner for this. A fourth generation native of Wyoming (with his kids the fifth generation like Delaney), Travis is a bit larger than life. I know him as the generous guy with the heart for his family and animals, a big laugh, and endless stories, but trust me that you would *not* want to be the perp who faces him! Which is ironic since we met him through his wife after my husband accidentally broke into a house she was listing for sale. (It's a long story that ends in years of friendship, and I swear, it was an accident!) I've included anecdotes, quotes, history, and ideas from Travis in many books. I even have a Deputy Travis who shows up from time to time in several interconnected Wyoming series. This time, he took it a step further and acted as my beta reader and coach. Any mistakes are mine alone. He improved the book immeasurably and put up with dumb questions in texts all hours of the day and night. Please email Travis some love through me as I am praying he wants to continue in this role!! Thanks, Travis, for your friendship and your help.

Huge thanks to my creative, firm, encouraging, brilliant editor Helen Jenner for patiently talking to me about these books for many, many months while waiting for her wisdom and experience with crime fiction to rub off on me and my writing for Bookouture to commence. Helen, you've pushed me through walls I didn't know I'd built to shelter deeply buried writing fears. I'm very lucky to collaborate with you on Delaney and her world. I hope there are many more to come.

Thanks also to the wonderful team at Bookouture. As a rugged individualist/indie since 2012, I didn't think there was a publisher I would ever be willing to work with. Nimble, lean, flexible, strategic, mission driven, and reader centric, Bookouture is everything I was looking for, and I appreciate them taking a chance on me. The support has been incredible, in every step of the process.

Thanks to my husband Eric for brainstorming with me, researching the perfect car for Delaney, teaching me how to adjust engine timing, encouraging me endlessly through some hard times, beta reading, and much more despite his busy work, travel, and workout schedule. Why does it seem that as soon as I started this project our life went haywire? And, most importantly, for putting up with my obsession with horses and sled/skijoring dogs!

Thanks to our five offspring. I love you guys more than

anything, and each time I write a parent/child relationship like the ones Delaney has with Kateena and Carrie, I channel you.

Finally, to each and every blessed reader: I appreciate you more than I can say. It is the readers who move mountains for authors, and you have done so for me, many times over.

PUBLISHING TEAM

Turning a manuscript into a book requires the efforts of many people. The publishing team at Bookouture would like to acknowledge everyone who contributed to this publication.

Audio
Alba Proko
Sinead O'Connor
Melissa Tran

Commercial
Lauren Morrissette
Hannah Richmond
Imogen Allport

Data and analysis
Mark Alder
Mohamed Bussuri

Editorial
Helen Jenner
Ria Clare

Copyeditor
Janette Currie

Proofreader
Liz Hurst

Marketing
Alex Crow
Melanie Price
Occy Carr
Cíara Rosney
Martyna Młynarska

Operations and distribution
Marina Valles
Stephanie Straub

Production
Hannah Snetsinger
Mandy Kullar
Jen Shannon
Ria Clare

Publicity
Kim Nash
Noelle Holten
Jess Readett
Sarah Hardy

Rights and contracts
Peta Nightingale
Richard King
Saidah Graham

Made in United States
Orlando, FL
07 October 2024